DRAGON WRITERS

AN ANTHOLOGY

Edited by Lisa Mangum

WordFire Press
Colorado Springs, Colorado

DRAGON WRITERS: AN ANTHOLOGY

Additional copyright information on page 347

ISBN: 978-1-61475-476-3

Cover painting by James A. Owen

Cover design by James A. Owen

Edited by Lisa Mangum

Kevin J. Anderson, Art Director

Book Design by RuneWright, LLC
www.RuneWright.com

Published by
WordFire Press, an imprint of
WordFire, Inc.
PO Box 1840
Monument CO 80132

Kevin J. Anderson & Rebecca Moesta, Publishers

WordFire Press Trade Paperback Edition November 2016
Printed in the USA
wordfirepress.com

Contents

INTRODUCTION: WRITING OUT THE DRAGONS

A Note from the Center about Sharing the Creative Fire and the Meaning of Tribe

We are all connected.

In 2012, I was asked by my friend Kevin J. Anderson to be a guest speaker at an annual seminar he had founded along with his wife, author Rebecca Moesta, and their writing peers David Farland, Eric Flint, and Brandon Sanderson. In contrast to the proliferation of seminars and workshops that exist to teach the craft of writing, the Superstars Writing Seminars had been created to teach writers the *business* of writing.

When the seminar was founded two years earlier, it was in part because Kevin and Company realized that when writers are starting out, we all share resources and encouragement with one another in the pursuit of our respective careers. But as best-selling authors, it becomes more difficult to commiserate and to find common ground and mutual support. So what began as a private support group soon expanded into the Superstars Writing Seminars, and during their third outing, which was held in Las Vegas, I was invited to share my own experiences and relative wisdom.

At that event, I made two contributions which have since expanded to become something more influential than any of us could have anticipated: my inspirational presentation *Drawing Out the Dragons*, which came to full maturity at the seminar and is now a core part of the annual experience, and an almost offhand comment about how, to truly become successful at anything, you simply have to focus on finding those who support you in the work you do and the choices you make. And I called that group of supporters your *Tribe*.

We are all connected.

In the years since, I was invited back first as a returning guest instructor and then as a partner, largely on the strength of the reception to and influence of *Drawing Out the Dragons*. But the concept of Tribe has also grown—something evident in the fact that a large percentage of the ever-growing Superstars attendance is alumni. It's no great surprise that participants in the seminar would bond and maintain those connections, manifesting both personally and professionally in the form of friendships and collaborations. At minimum, there was now a shared set of experiences and a large group of peers who could offer support and encouragement to one another—again, not unexpected. But Superstars has become something different. Tribe became something deeper, and much more significant and meaningful.

New attendee Ryan Richoux wrote a heartfelt post in one of our online groups about how he had attended as A/V support for our resident Canadian audio tech Stone Sanchez but soon realized that he had been drawn into something greater: Superstars was not just a professional organization. It was a family. It was *Tribe*. Everyone who attends becomes part of that Tribe, no questions asked. Everyone is accepted, embraced, and supported as if they had always been there.

We are all connected.

One definition of Tribe, in the oldest and perhaps truest sense, is "many tinders, one fire." Fuel is drawn from several sources, but everyone shares in and benefits from the flame. The same is true of the Creative Fire, and the drive we each feel to push our work, our lives, and our careers forward. A collection of experiences shared can become a seminar, but the level of support that is brought to bear by becoming Tribe is something that extends past the initial event. The Creative Fire that is brought to Superstars by each member of the Tribe is for the ongoing benefit of all.

There have been two previous anthologies as part of the Superstars Writing Seminar, both featuring unicorns, which were organized and published in order to offer scholarships to allow writers the additional resources they need to have the opportunity to attend. This year, we chose dragons as the subject, in part because the metaphor I use in my annual presentation is that dragons are the fears holding us back, and we need to draw them out and confront them in order to move forward with any decision we make in our lives.

In the midst of a both literal and figurative demonstration of this at the most recent seminar, I hesitated—and the silence was cracked by a voice from the back, a recent member of the Tribe, Emily Godhand, yelling, "You can do it, James!" That burst the dam, and the entire room shouted encouragement while I finished doing something I thought would be an Impossible Thing and which resulted in a standing ovation and a lot of joyful, inspired tears.

We are all capable of doing Impossible Things. The Superstars Writing Seminars are where we share our Creative Fire and teach one another to do them. This book is a representation of some of the best examples of writing out the dragons that our attendees can produce—and with it, another opportunity to offer the experience to more and more people. We are all connected. We are Tribe. And this is the best of what we do.

James A. Owen
Silvertown, Arizona

I Hate Dragons

Brandon Sanderson

My life has taken a turn toward my true love, writing epic fantasy, but I do miss the teaching experiences I once had. So I moonlight as a writing instructor and do my best to make time for being a professor.

One of the things that I do to maintain my teaching skills is try out various writing exercises that I might, occasionally, assign to my students. You're about to read one of those challenges to myself: to write a complete scene with multiple, distinct characters using nothing but dialogue with no tags. The idea was to get across motives, dialect and diction, and conflict, all without giving any context other than the words themselves.

It turned out very well, which is why you're reading it here. Do keep in mind, however, that though this stands all right on its own, it isn't intended to be a full story. Enjoy!

—Brandon

aster Johnston?"

"Yes, Skip?"

"I was wondering if maybe we might review my employment situation."

"What? Now? Lad, this isn't the time."

"Er, I'm sorry, sir. But I believe this is exactly the time. And, I apologize, but I don't intend to move until I've had my say."

"Fine. Fine. Be on with it then."

"Well, Master Johnston, you know how we're here to kill this dragon, sir?"

"Yes. That's our job. Dragon hunters. It says so on your bloomin' jacket, lad!"

"Well, sir, technically *you* and the other boys are the hunters."

"You're an important part, Skip. Without you, the dragon won't never come!"

"I believe you mean 'will never come,' sir. And, well, this is *about* my part. I realize it's important for you to have someone to draw the dragon."

"You can't catch nothing without bait."

"'Can't catch anything,' sir. And that is as you've said. However, I can't help noticing one factor about my role in the hunt. I am, as you said, bait."

"Yes?"

"And it seems to me that eventually, if you put bait out often enough …"

"Yes?"

"Well, sir, eventually that bait is going to end up getting eaten. Sir."

"Ah."

"You see my trouble."

"You've been doing this for a year now, and you ain't ever gotten ate."

"That sentence was deplorable, sir."

"What's math have to do wi' this?"

"You're thinking 'de*vis*able,' sir. Anyway, yes, I've survived a year. Only, I've started thinking."

"A dangerous habit, that."

"It's chronic, I'm afraid. I've started thinking about the number of near misses we've had. I've started thinking that, eventually, you and the boys aren't going to get to the dragon quickly enough. I'm thinking about how many reptilian bicuspids I've seen in recent months."

"I've cussed more than twice myself."

"So …"

"All right, lad. I can see where you're going. Two percent, and nothing more."

"A raise?"

"Sure. Two percent's good money, son. Why, when I was your age, I'd have *died* to get a two-percent raise."

"I'd rather not die because of it, sir."

"Three percent, then."

"You pay me in food, sir. I don't get paid *any* money."

"Ah. I forgot you was a smart one. All right. Four percent."

"Sir, you could double it, and it would be meaningless."

"Don't get so uppity! Double? What, you think I'm maid of coins?"

"The word is 'made,' sir."

"Huh? That's what I said. How—"

"Never mind. Sir, this isn't about money, you see."

"You want more food?"

"No. You see, er ..."

"Be on with it! That dragon ain't going to kill himself!"

"Technically, dragons—being sentient beings—likely have a suicide rate similar to other intelligent creatures. So perhaps this one *will* kill himself. It's statistically possible, anyway. That's beside the point. You see, sir, I think I'd rather change my participation in the hunts."

"In what way?"

"I'd like to be a hunter, sir. You know. Hold a harpoon? Fire a crossbow? I wouldn't mind just reloading for the other hunters until I get the hang of it."

"Don't be silly. You couldn't do that while out in the center of the field, being bait!"

"I wasn't talking about doing that *while* being bait. I'd rather do it *instead* of being bait. Sir."

"But nobody else has yer special gift, son."

"I don't think it's all that great ..."

"Why, sure it is! In all my years hunting dragons, I've *never* met someone who attracts them like you do. You've got a gift."

"The gift of smelling delicious to dragons? Sir, I never asked for this."

"Just 'cause a gift is unexpected doesn't mean it ain't a gift."

"A knife to the back can be unexpected. That doesn't make it a gift either. Sir."

"Look, son. You're special. The scent of you … it drives them mad with hunger. It'd be a shame to waste that. Do what you were created to do. Reach for the stars."

"Stars are giant balls of gas, burning far away."

"They are?"

"Yes. Reaching for them, even if it were possible, would likely burn your hand. Sir."

"Ain't that something."

"*Isn't* that something."

"That's what I said. Either way, son, you need to explore your talents."

"My talent is getting eaten by dragons, sir. It seems that's less something to *explore*, and more something to experience. Once. In a grisly, painful, and abruptly-ending sort of way."

"…"

"Well?"

"I see that yer a smart one, son."

"Thank you."

"Five percent."

"I …"

"It's here! It's circlin'! Lad, we'll have to talk about this later."

"Okay. You know what, fine. Once more. But that's it."

"Good lad. Out there you go. You remember the script?"

"Of course I remember it. Ahem. I'm so very tired! Also, I hate sunlight. So I'm not going to look upward. I'm just going to stroll along across this … er … rocky place of rocks and find a place to lay down and take a nap.

"Gosh! I'm sad that I tripped and got dust in my eyes, so I couldn't see anything for a few moments when that breeze passed me by. Just a breeze, and *not* the beating of nearby dragon wings. Not at all. Perhaps I will take my nap in this little dip in the ground. I hope no wild beasts are around to savage me."

"PSSST. Skip. Bite! The script says BITE me!"

"I'm extrapolating!"

"What's the dragon's skin have to do with this?"

"That's ex*foliate*, Master Johnston. Look, he's coming back around. Hush. Ahem. Yes, I'll just be nodding off to sleep now!"

"…"

"What's the beast doing?"

"He landed up there. I think he's suspicious. He's craning his neck down and—"

"YOU'RE A TERRIBLE ACTOR."

"Er. Really? I actually thought I was getting better. I've been practicing in front of the mirror, you see."

"TERRIBLE. I'VE SEEN PIECES OF SOAP THAT WERE BETTER ACTORS THAN YOU. YOU HAVE AN ENTIRE FLEET OF DRAGON HUNTERS WAITING, I ASSUME."

"Um. No?"

"NO, YOU DON'T HAVE THEM? OR NO I DON'T ASSUME IT? BECAUSE I REALLY DON'T THINK YOU'RE CAPABLE OF JUDGING WHAT I DO AND DON'T ASSUME. BY THE WAY, WHO WROTE THAT SCRIPT FOR YOU?"

"Master Johnston."

"HE NEEDS AN EDITOR."

"I've tried to explain that! Do you know how difficult it is to work with such awful lines?"

"THAT DOESN'T EXCUSE YOUR BAD ACTING."

"It at least gives some context, though, doesn't it?"

"NO."

"So, um, if you saw through the ploy … why are you still here? Shouldn't you have fled?"

"I … THERE'S SOMETHING ABOUT YOU, SMALL HUMAN. YES. SOMETHING … INTOXICATING. WHY DON'T YOU CLIMB UP HERE TO ME."

"Excuse me?"

"CLIMB ON UP HERE."

"You'll *eat* me."

"THAT'S THE IDEA."

"Then I think I'll decline."

"OH, COME NOW. IT WON'T BE SO BAD AS YOU THINK. THEY'RE WILL BE HARDLY ANY PAIN AT ALL."

"I don't care if there's pain or not. I'll still be dead. And you used the wrong version of 'they're.' You wanted 'there' instead."

"I DID? HOW CAN YOU TELL? THEY'RE'S NO DIFFERENCE IN THE SOUNDS THEY MAKE."

"Actually, I can hear apostrophes."

"WHAT, REALLY?"

"Yes. I can hear spelling too, actually."

"THAT'S … INTERESTING, CHILD. VERY INTERESTING. WELL, TIME TO GET THIS OVER WITH. NO USE IN DELAYING. COME ON UP AND BE EATEN."

"You don't make a very compelling argument."

"I'M A VERY BUSY DRAGON."

"Funny. I have lots of time. I could sit here all day, so long as it involves *not* being eaten."

"OH, COME NOW. DON'T BE DIFFICULT. THIS IS WHAT YOU WERE CREATED TO DO."

"What gives you that terrible idea?"

"IT'S THE CIRCLE OF LIFE, YOUNG HUMAN! THE BEAUTY OF NATURE! EACH CREATURE IN TURN IS CONSUMED BY A LARGER CREATURE, ROUND AND AROUND, UNTIL WE REACH THE APEX PREDATORS. UM … I'M ONE OF THOSE, BY THE WAY."

"I'd noticed."

"WELL, THE COWS EAT THE GRASS, THE WOLVES EAT THE COWS, THE MEN EAT THE WOLVES, THE DRAGONS EAT THE MEN. ALL VERY MAJESTIC IN ITS SIMPLICITY."

"We don't eat wolves, actually."

"YOU DON'T?"

"No. Not unless we're very hungry. Even then, they don't taste very good, so I'm told. Too stringy."

"YES, WELL, YOU'RE SUPPOSED TO. MEN NEVER DO AS THEY'RE TOLD. CASE AND POINT, THIS MOMENT, WHERE YOU HAVE THE STARTLING RUDENESS TO REFUSE BEING CONSUMED. HOW CAN I PERSUADE YOU?"

"Actually, you are persuading me."

"REALLY? THIS IS *WORKING*? ER, I MEAN … OF COURSE I AM. I'M KNOWN AS BEING A VERY COMPELLING CONVERSATIONALIST, AMONG MY PEERS."

"You didn't need that comma, and you should probably have put 'among my peers' after 'I'm known.' That's beside the point.

You see, I said you were persuading me because the definition of the word implies the act of trying to get someone to do something, whether or not you are successful. You persuade someone, then you either fail or succeed. Most people use it incorrectly. The word you wanted was *convince*. You need to *convince* me, not persuade me."

"YOU'RE NOT VERY MUCH FUN AT PARTIES, ARE YOU, SMALL HUMAN?"

"I … uh … don't get invited to parties very often."

"I CAN'T IMAGINE WHY. SO, ARE YOU GOING TO STOP WHINING AND COME GET EATEN LIKE A MAN?"

"No."

"YOU'RE MAKING MOTHER NATURE CRY."

"Good. We could use more rain. Why don't you just go eat a cow?"

"WHY DON'T YOU GO EAT SOME GRASS?"

"Um … humans can't digest grass."

"AND DRAGONS CAN'T DIGEST COWS."

"Really?"

"REALLY. HUMANS WERE DESIGNED AND BUILT TO BE EATEN BY DRAGONS. IT'S THE NATURE OF THINGS."

"I find that rather unfair. Who eats you?"

"THE WORMS, ONCE WE'RE DEAD. IT'S ALL VERY METAPHYSICAL."

"But you *have* to eat humans?"

"IF WE DON'T, WE DIE."

"How are there any humans left?"

"WE DON'T NEED TO EAT VERY OFTEN, LITTLE HUMAN. ONCE EVERY FEW MONTHS. THERE'S A MORE THAN LARGE ENOUGH POPULATION OF YOU TO SUSTAIN US. YOU DON'T RUN OUT OF … WHAT IS IT YOU EAT, AGAIN?"

"Cows. Pigs. Carrots. Very few wolves."

"YES, WELL, THIS IS MUCH LIKE YOU EATING THOSE THINGS."

"Except for the part about me dying."

"THINK OF THE GOOD YOU'LL BE DOING."

"Good? By keeping a dragon alive to continue terrorizing?"

"NO, BY SACRIFICING YOURSELF FOR ANOTHER. IF I DON'T EAT YOU, I'LL JUST END UP GOING OFF AND FINDING SOMEONE ELSE. PROBABLY A FAIR YOUNG VIRGIN. POOR CHILD. IF YOU THINK ABOUT IT, GETTING EATEN RIGHT NOW WOULD BE A VERY BRAVE THING OF YOU. NOBLE, HEROIC."

"Well, when you put it that way ..."

"THAT'S IT, COME CLOSER."

"... maybe I'll come right up to the base of that ledge ..."

"MY ... THE SCENT OF YOU ... I ... WHY ARE YOU STOPPING ...? COME CLOSER! I CAN'T ... I CAN'T ... RAAAAAWR!"

"Have at 'im, lads!"

"Aaah!"

"RAWR!"

"HURK!"

"My arm!"

"Keep stabbin'!"

"FOOLISH LITTLE MEN! GAR! GR ... BLURK!"

"Is he down!"

"You know what I say, lads. There's always room for more stabbin'! Keep at it. And you, you did well. Even if you did ruinate the script."

"Ruinate? *Really?* Did you just say that?"

"Well, you're always using those big words and all. So I thought ..."

"Never mind. I'm going to go wash off this dragon blood. Can't believe that I put up with this ..."

"He doesn't look happy, Master Johnston."

"Oh, don't worry about Skip. He'll be fine."

"I don't know. He looks really mad this time."

"Don't worry. I've got a secret weapon."

"Really?"

"Sure. Tonight, after we're all fed and happy ..."

"Yeah?"

"I'm going to give him a *six*-percent raise."

O O O

Brandon Sanderson has published numerous novels with Tor—*Elantris*, the Mistborn books, *Warbreaker*, *The Way of Kings*, *Words of Radiance*, and the young adult fantasy *The Rithmatist*. Five books in the middle-grade *Alcatraz Versus the Evil Librarians* series are being released by *Starscape*. He was chosen to complete Robert Jordan's Wheel of Time series; the final book, *A Memory of Light*, was released in 2013. His newest YA novel, *Calamity*, was released by Delacorte in February 2016. Currently living in Utah with his wife and children, Brandon teaches creative writing at Brigham Young University.

MUSE

Jody Lynn Nye

The tattooed human female glared up at Ulm Drak and took her hands off the flat, silver machine in her lap.

"See here, Mr. Scalyface, you've been blabbing on since I got here, and you haven't really said anything noteworthy yet. I'm being paid by the job, not the hour."

The huge red dragon snaked his serpentine neck downward until his amethyst-purple eye was level with the young woman's head. She did not look like any of the maidens in the fields or villages of old, with her cropped black-and-cobalt hair and the silver rings that pierced her nose, ears, and eyebrow. In the black leather trews and jerkin, she looked more like a blacksmith's boy. The sharp ruby scales on the back of his neck stood on end in pure irritation.

"That is not my name! Show me respect, Jamie Blandisssssssh!"

"Earn it," Jamie replied in a level tone, her eyes steady. "Show me why Castle Rise Books is clamoring for your autobiography. So far, all you've told me is you've slain many knights. What are the details? When was the last time? What were their names? Or can't you remember?"

Ulm Drak recoiled, offended. This new world was strange to him. Encountering humans who did not fear him was unprecedented in his life. He had not ventured far from his green Welsh valley for a long time. Was this how things were now, outside the circle of his reduced hunting grounds?

"I … No one has ever asked for their names. They were my enemies. They tried to kill me."

Jamie started tapping at the tiny squares again.

"I've been researching in online archives for multiple deaths in the surrounding parishes," she said. "The most recent here in Wales seems to have been the year 1630. Does that sound right to you?"

Ulm Drak snorted, and a small gout of flame shot out of his nostrils.

"I do not keep track of your human calendars," he said. He hesitated. "What year is it now?"

Jamie laughed. "Nearly four hundred years later. Let's explore current events, then. If the calendar is a bust, what else was going on then? A plague? A fire? An invasion? Cold winters?"

"Cold," Ulm Drak said, recalling scale-rattling winds that blew into the mouth of his cavern. How glad he had been to find warmer environs. "Deep snow. The wild creatures had gone to ground. I needed food. The villagers thought to deny me their sheep and cattle."

"Huh," Jamie grunted. She bent her head over the device. Under her fingertips, it emitted soft thudding noises like the footfalls of a rabbit. "What kind of cattle?"

The dragon settled back on his clanking hoard and emitted a sigh of pleasure. His long purple tongue snaked out of his mouth and licked his chops.

"Tasty ones."

"You're not one for details, are you? Horned cattle? Black pelts? Long pelts?"

Ulm Drak remembered spitting out mouthfuls of red fur. "Hairy."

She lifted the machine from her lap and turned the small glass square toward him so he could see.

"Like these?"

He peered at the box. Small cattle with long horns and stringy mops of hair moved upon its surface.

"Yes, those," he said. "Very flavorful. I see few of those in the fields now. Now they are all the same hue as castle stone or black and white. What a marvel your small box is! Almost as if I am watching through a window!"

"It's a computer. Um, a scribe in a box," Jamie said. "This is the screen."

"Truly a wonder," Ulm Drak said, curling his long body in a different direction so he could see the screen change from one picture to another. When it turned into a white square with black lines on it, he lost interest. "How have you come to master this piece of magic?"

"It's not magic. It's technology. It's always been in my home and my school," Jamie said, offhandedly. "I started when I was little, and I think I've become rather good. I've taken tutorials to learn how to operate the programs."

"What do you do with these *programs*?" Ulm Drak tasted the word.

"Well, I study things I want to know," Jamie said with a loud exhalation of breath. "I'm into traditional gardening, like my grandda, so I've been looking up plants that would have grown in our cottage garden centuries back, like when you were marauding over the country. I read up on school topics. I completely got into Shakespeare. Brilliant writer. He absolutely inspires me. I think of him as my muse."

"And you learned to manipulate this *computer* so well," Ulm Drak said with admiration. "You are a wizard, and this is your scrying mirror. Why are you here, instead of elsewhere working wonders?"

She put her leather-clad elbow down on the rack of buttons with a wry glare. "I'm here, instead of being back at home in my sad little flat in London writing books on my pet topics, because I need enough money to fix my motorbike. So tell me stories about you. What's it like being a dragon?"

"What is it like to be human?" Ulm Drak countered, shrugging his mighty wings. Despite having accepted the contract, he felt awkward discussing himself. "I suppose it feels the same to you."

"Focus!" Jamie commanded him as fiercely as his own mother would have. She aimed a tiny finger adorned with a sharp silver claw toward his nose. "No riddles! We're not talking about me; we're talking about you. Isn't it amazing and splendid to be a dragon?"

The dragon hesitated, peering toward the stone ceiling of his cavern.

"I never thought about it. I just *was*. Am."

"What about flying? Doesn't *that* feel amazing?"

"Yes," Ulm Drak admitted. It was so much a part of him that he couldn't think of it as something separate to be admired or analyzed. "I like flying." He stretched his wings. Before they were fully extended, the tips touched the stone walls. He retracted them in irritation. "I don't often leave here. It frightens the humans in the building above. Tourissssts," he added with scorn. "They call the noisy knights in blue jerkins. They try to enter my stronghold, but I do not permit it."

"Don't you want to?" Jamie asked, wrinkling her brow with an incredulous expression. "Flying on actual, real wings seems to be a lot like zooming out on the road on my Harley. If I were a dragon, I would be flying all the time!"

Ulm Drak settled down on his hoard, nudging the piles of gold this way and that to make a more comfortable nest. Jamie winced at the loud, seductive clattering of coins and *objets d'art* as they tumbled into one another. This female was indeed different than any he had met before. Apart from exclaiming "Brilliant!" at the sight when she had arrived, she showed little to no interest in his treasure.

In a way, he was hurt by her indifference. Did he not possess the riches of not one but seven Spanish treasure ships? Did he not have the crowns of nine kings for a pillow? She was refreshingly free of avarice—or was too subtle to show her interest. He intended to keep an eye on her all the same. The most innocent of visitors had tried to rob him in the past. Their bones were long ago digested, and the gold that they had sought had lain undisturbed long enough to acquire a honeyed patina.

"Why don't you crave my treasure, Jamie Blandisssh?" he asked. "Why aren't you afraid of me? You are a mere mortal. I am fearsome and powerful! I could eat you in a bite. I could burn you to a cinder."

She glared at him, her lip curled up to show a gap where one square front tooth was missing. "That's not my job. You should have hired a Damsel in Distress. I'm a Damsel Who Causes

Distress. Don't try to fit me into a mold, Scaly. No one messes with me. My gang at the King's Head pub know better than to cross me."

"Gang?"

"We ride out together. We're all gearheads, and we like the freedom of the open road."

Gearheads was another strange term, but *gang* sounded like knights of old who had lived during his youth. "And you lead them?"

"I've got what you call a 'take-charge' personality. My girlfriend and my boyfriend both know I'm the leader of our household."

"Ah," Ulm Drak said, pensively crossing one foreleg over the other. "I had a mate once. Just the one."

"What happened to her? Him? It? Did you have a fight to the death?" Jamie's eyes widened avidly.

"Her," Ulm Drak said, slightly taken aback at her reaction. "No. We simply grew apart. Each of us wanted our own hoards. What do you fear, if not dragons?"

She waved the question away. "I was never really afraid of them. Until you turned up, dragons were only theoretical dangers. There are things all around that will *really* mess you up."

"Like what?"

She raised one thin black eyebrow high on her forehead. "If you tell me stories, then I'll tell you stories. Fair's fair, eh? You first. How did you end up here in the mountains?"

Ulm Drak sighed, expelling a long plume of steam. "It all seems so long in the past."

"Talk!" Jamie shrieked, battering the computer's keyboard. "And why aren't you living in a cave a thousand kilometers from everyone else? You're practically in the middle of a major population center. And why are you living under a pensioners' residence when you could still be kicking ass and taking treasure?"

"It is not a pensioner's residence," Ulm Drak protested, hissing all his *S*'s peevishly. "It is the castle of Prince Gwydr—a mighty warrior, but no match for me. I took it from him as spoils of war. I burned the village. The people I didn't kill ran away. This town grew up around *me*. I did not live here among humans on purpose. I could have moved, but I might have lost some of my treasure. I allowed the old ones above to take shelter during the war a few years ago because they showed me respect. Some of the people remember me in my heyday—well, no. Those have died. But the castle is good protection for my hoard. I don't really feel like moving it all. I don't have to justify my actions to you!" He wrapped himself in a tight ball and flicked his tongue at her. She made him so uncomfortable!

Jamie shook her head in scorn. "You got rich too soon. You have these amazing wings. If I had those, I'd be soaring through the clouds every day, scaring jet pilots."

"The NATC clearance troubles are not worth my time," Ulm Drak grumbled. He wished she would go away and leave him to count his coins. "Free flight brings the ones in blue. Sometimes they pelt me with small stones and little bursts of flame that sting. It is a nuisance."

"Why do you care what they say or do? You're a dragon! You could *eat* them. I'd walk tall with my dragon pride and kick out whenever I felt like it. You've become too civilized, Mr. Scalyface. You're hardly real any more. It's going to be difficult to write your memoirs when you sound about as dangerous as my granny."

Ulm Drak glared. "How dare you! Set down my story as I have told it to you!"

"I'll try to write this up," Jamie said, shaking her head. "But you'd best not go on the talk shows. Your story's such a yawn, the audience will laugh. It's a shame. People ought to realize that they live among miracles. I know a family of ghosts who haunt an amusement park outside of Chester. I wrote a magazine article about them. People get a scare; the ghosts get company. Everybody's happy."

Ulm Drak considered the flitting spirits that sometimes coursed through his stone halls. Humans craved being frightened by those pathetic visions? He sat up on his nest of treasure, his head nearly reaching to the ceiling. Why, he could terrify people into running so far away that they would never come back to the isle! His wings opened on his back and stretched outward, until they hit the stone walls and retracted again. He settled back, clutching piles of coins to his red-scaled chest.

"I am glad for them," he said, feeling the soothing coolness of gold sliding through his talons. He lifted fistfuls and let them drop, studying each one. He recalled the source of every coin, every amulet, every piece of jewelry. "It's too much trouble to cow humans, particularly for their amusement. I fought for my life. I strove to earn my place, and I hold it. I hunt to eat. I crave gold, so I protect it from those who attempt to steal from me. That is enough. No. That is why I want my book out, so people know how I was back then, when thousands feared me."

"You could still be fierce," Jamie said, sitting up with dawning delight on her face. "I saw it in your eyes, just for a moment. It was exciting!"

Ulm Drak had felt the moment too, but it was past. "No, no, I can't. Those days are over."

The delight turned to disgust. "You're complacent. Ooh, what a waste! You're not a dragon anymore, you're a newt!"

Again, the easy courage of the young human aroused Ulm Drak's curiosity. She felt free to insult him, never fearing the flames that were a breath away from burning her to death.

"What does frighten you?" he asked. "If not ghosts or dragons, what haunts your nightmares?"

Her eyes grew dark, and she sank back into the small wooden chair.

"There are humans who don't care about anyone's life, not even their own," she said. "They commit cruelties for fun. I've seen them torture animals and beat up anyone who tried to stop them. If they'd been rabid dogs instead of rabid people, they'd have been put down for the good of the state. The King's Head has been invaded by them. We welcomed them at first, but they started shit. The punters are terrified of them. *We're* terrified of them. You don't know what they're going to do, if they're going to go mental on you. They take anything they take a fancy to and cut you if you try to take it back."

Humans who preyed on their own kind. He nodded. He had seen many like them over the centuries. Thieving cowards who stole and picked on the populace and tried to rob him.

"But *I* steal treasure from humans," Ulm Drak said. "How are these different from me?"

Jamie tilted her head to one side. "I'd call you lawful evil, like in *Dungeons and Dragons.*"

"There are dragons? Other dragons?"

"Only on paper—like you were, up until recently. These bangers are chaotic evil."

"And that frightens you," Ulm Drak said, summing her up with a thoughtful gaze. "I'm glad to see that you fear something. What do you intend to do about it, Damsel Who Causes Distress?"

"Nothing I *can* do. Enough about me," Jamie said impatiently. "It makes me mental to think about them. I have to deal with them too often." She contemplated the gold sifting through his claw and gave him a curious look. "So, what's your favorite piece of treasure? People like that kind of thing. It gives interesting detail to your biography."

He chuckled and snaked his head around the cascades of glinting metal in pleased anticipation. Those were memories he liked to recall. The spikes of a golden circlet, bronzed by time, caught his eye. He plucked it out of the sifting mass with a careful claw.

"Let me see. The crown of Queen Myfanwy? No, it's just a handsome piece with many rubies. No special tale there." He picked through a pile of armor, seeking the brilliant silver sheen he had enjoyed contemplating on many a long, cold winter's night. It had never lost its glow. "This breastplate was worn by a young Welsh princeling. I never knew his name, and I regret that. How brave he was, facing me, but it was all for naught. The armor's breastplate did not save him. It was only fireproof, not immune to a fall. I dropped him from a cliff. The breastplate, as you see, is unscathed. I have his sword, too. Spoils of war."

Jamie made a face. "A little too grim for the book blurbs."

Ulm Drak laughed, spouting puffs of smoke into the damp air. He shouldered aside a mound of darkening gold ingots and king's necklaces until he found the piece he sought. Delicately, he set the plain, slim, silver rod, nearly black with time, down on the floor before her. The single moonstone at its end, the size of a human fist, glowed with its own pale blue light.

"How about this? The staff of the enchantress Lilith. She threw it at me in a fit of pique but said I could keep it afterwards. Ah, we were good friends, Lilith and I."

"That's perfect," Jamie said. She raced back to her computer and clattered away like a woodpecker on a tree. Her fingers leaped up high and came down one final time, like a fox pouncing on a vole. "All right, then, I'm off. Back tomorrow. See you."

She stuffed the computer into a black shoulder bag and headed toward the gate. The heavy latch, formerly attached to a cathedral door, was on the inside to keep out intruders, but it was easy to lift. She could show herself out. Ulm Drak was already prepared to forget her presence.

Something about Jamie's hasty footsteps attracted his attention. They seemed different than when she had arrived, more unbalanced. As she was his first visitor in a long while, Ulm Drak had studied her closely. He looked around. The mound of treasure beside her chair looked as though it had been disturbed. He leaned closer to sniff, then shot out of his nest. He beat her to the heavy door and peered into her face, which was the size of one of his eyeballs.

"Back off, Mr. Scalyface," she snapped.

"No," he hissed. He darted his tongue in and out of his mouth, tasting the air. "Return the gold! Return it! I should have known that no human could resist my precious hoard. Give it back now!"

She opened her black leather jacket. From an inner pocket, she took a heavy, square-linked chain that had belonged to a minister of King Alfred the Great. She opened her hand and let it slither to the floor. Ulm Drak seized it and looked it over to make certain it hadn't been damaged.

Jamie laughed at him. "I wondered if you'd get up off your scaly arse."

A test? She dared *test* him?

"I should kill you!" he snarled, holding himself back with difficulty. "I should burn you where you stand!"

"But you didn't," she said sadly. She shouldered her bag and went out the door into the last embers of twilight.

Ulm Drak watched her go. Both of them had failed the other. She was not the honest human he thought she'd be. He was not the fearsome beast she had hoped to find. Ah, but which was the greater failure?

He slunk back to his nest to sort out the thoughts that tumbled and ricocheted through his mind. When had he ceased to be a dragon? When had he lost his reality and become a mere wurm? How ashamed his ancestors would have been!

He toyed with his treasures, realizing for the first time how the gleam had gone from them. Jamie Blandish had forced him to consider memories that had become almost as tarnished as most of his hoard. In centuries past, he had carried out raids, stealing treasure, and slaying his enemies without a backward glance. He held his territory by being willing to fight to the death—but he had won. *Then.* Could he still? Would he? Why did he seldom go forth into the world? Had he become too complacent, as Jamie had complained?

How he hated her! Her scornful eyes cut him more deeply than a knight's lance. He was no coward! He should have killed her! He *would* kill her when she returned. Yes, he would!

Ulm Drak's belly grumbled with hunger, but he was in too bad a mood to go outside to snatch a sheep from one of the nearby farms. Instead, he piled all his treasure in one gigantic heap in the center of the empty cavern and burrowed into it. If he was going to live like a wurm, he might as well sleep like one.

His dreams were as uneasy as his thoughts.

* * *

"Shh!"

The hissing was not like an avalanche of treasure, but a noise from a living animal. Ulm Drak poked one tall red ear up through the mound of gold until the cup caught another wisp of sound. The old ones who lived above him in the restored shell of the castle rarely stirred this late. His snout winkled its way forward until it was clear of the sharp aroma of gold. By the musky smells of hunting animals and the cool spring dewfall, it was still night outside.

His favorite prey, the white-tailed deer, was miles off. New odors reached his sensitive nose. Humans lurked closer than they usually did after dark. These also bore the flavor of petrol, leather, and oil, not unlike Jamie Blandish. He sniffed harder. In fact, the writer's odor was among them. On top of her cool aroma, which was flavored with the sneeze-inducing scent of floral soap, he smelled sharp, acrid bile.

As silently as he could, he slithered out of the treasure pile and crept toward the door. A creak came from the church door, the unmistakable sound of the latch being lifted very, very slowly. He sat beside the widening gap to watch.

Humans could not see in the dark. These, eleven in number, had faint pinpoints of light that they shone at the rough stone floor.

"Are we going to see it?" whispered a male with a long, narrow face. "Dragon actually lives here?" The cadence of his voice was unlike either the old ones or Jamie.

"Yes, he does," she hissed back. "But you won't see him unless you be quiet!"

The white pinpoints crept along the floor until they reached the mountain of gold, then leaped and danced about on it like fairies in the twilight. Ulm Drak was curious, but not worried. So many had come over the centuries to see his treasure. He had even let a few of them peep in before scaring them off.

"God in His heaven!" one of them breathed. "Go get it. Take what you can. Hurry!"

Ulm Drak's ire rose in his belly. "Take?" he snarled. "Take *my* gold?"

As one, the pinpoints turned to play upon his face. He showed all his teeth and breathed a gout of flame into the darkness. That ought to have set them running.

To his surprise, the thick-voiced one barked an order.

"Kill it!"

The people in leather aimed rectangular weapons at him. Red flashes in the darkness heralded painful stabs, a dozen at a time. Ulm Drak bellowed in pain. He struck at them with his claws. They answered his attack with their own claws, long curved blades with short handles. Those cut deeply into his fingers and forearms.

While he battled, three of them broke away and ran toward his hoard, pulling black bin bags from their pockets. He heard the clank and jingle as they gathered his beloved possessions. The guns spoke again, stitching him with pain. Ulm Drak pounced on the first shooter, tearing the weapon out of his hands and throwing it away into the darkness.

"You have betrayed me, Jamie Blandish!" he bellowed. "All of you, leave and never return! I will tell Castle Rise Books to send someone else!"

He knocked two of the men flying, but the others redoubled their onslaught. One of the machetes cut into his cheek from the left, then sliced down upon his shoulder. They were trying to take his head. They meant to kill him!

For the first time in more than a century, Ulm Drak was besieged. The attackers behaved like rabid dogs, raking him with gunfire or chopping at him with their swords. They did not fear him or for their own safety. The thin veneer of courtesy that he had acquired to deal with the occasional visitor was torn asunder. Hah! They had guns and knives, but he had faced wizards and *real* heroes. None of them would live.

He leaped into the air and pounced, again and again, biting, clawing, and burning. The humans screamed in fury. The red flower peppered him with more bullets, but he ignored the pain. He bore in upon the gun wielders, tearing each one limb from limb. From the pool of blood and body parts, he bellowed his triumph. The ones taking his belongings attempted to escape, firing at him as they ran. It was so easy to beat them to the door. In the backwash of their pathetic fairy lights, he saw the grim set of their jaws.

"Surrender," he growled. But they would not. He opened his mouth and lit the room with his breath. Soon, no living enemy stood against him.

Thin, bitter laughter came from a place near the wall. One of them was not dead. Ulm Drak glided over, raising his claw for the final blow.

"You have betrayed me, Jamie Blandisssh," he snarled.

Jamie lay on the floor, looking up at him. Even in the dark, he could see the big, dark mark on the side of her face. Her arms were bound to her body and her wrists to one another with thick, stinking tape. Ulm Drak blinked. She had been their prisoner.

"I must have had too many pints," she said. "I talked about your treasure. They wanted it. They made me lead them here."

"You are unharmed?"

"They beat the stuffings out of me," Jamie said. "Broke another tooth. Maybe my arm, too. But God, it was worth it to watch you!"

Ulm Drak recoiled, nearly forgetting all his own wounds.

"You did that on purpose! I killed those people—"

"Those *people* were scum," she said. "They killed a man in another town last night, and they were laughing about it. They've been terrorizing *my* people. My gang was prepared to risk their lives to get rid of them. You performed a public service, and you absolutely kicked arse. It was wonderful! You ought always to be that alive."

"You … You're as bloodthirsty as a dragon!" Ulm Drak shouted.

Jamie gave him a lopsided grin. "Thanks."

"More bloodthirsty!" the dragon insisted. But he slid a wingtip under her back to help her to sit up, and rent her bonds with his teeth. The tape tasted terrible. She rubbed her wrists.

"I was. But I was desperate. Yeah, I did tell them about the hoard on purpose. I knew you'd come through. The country is a lot cleaner tonight. They have ceased to exist, and I know I will breathe more easily."

Her tone of finality alarmed Ulm Drak. He studied her. "You don't really care that you drew people to certain death, do you?"

"I do care! I'm not a dragon, but I'm not sorry they're gone." She put both hands on his foreleg. "They were *animals*. They were the bubonic plague. There are people who shouldn't be in society. They *terrified* me."

Ulm Drak's head reared back. His chest flooded with outrage. "And I don't?"

Jamie smiled. "You do, but I respect you. The only respect for them I had was the fear they made me feel."

"I've never been terrified," Ulm Drak said, tasting the word. "What is it like?"

"Oh, no," Jamie said, sitting down cross-legged on the floor. Her movements were uneasy, probably because of the battering she had taken, but her insouciance was undamaged. "You tell *me* stories, not the other way around."

As if the tarnish had been cleaned off his memory, the stories started coming back, of deeds he had performed long, long ago. Ulm Drak found he could not talk fast enough.

"I had forgotten all about the young dragon who wanted to steal my entire hoard! Eight hundred years ago, I believe it was," he said, licking the wounds on his shoulder and belly. They would heal swiftly, probably more quickly than Jamie Blandish's bruises. "And all of south Wales was once invaded by a swarm of acid-spitting snakes. How that stung! But I eradicated them, every one!"

Jamie laughed delightedly. "More!" she said. "This will make Castle Rise Books drool!"

The two of them talked until Ulm Drak noticed the first red rays of sunlight peering over the mountains through the open gate.

"Come with me, Jamie Blandish," he said, rising to his feet. "We shall fly."

"Don't you care if the neighbors complain?" she asked, jumping up to follow.

"Not a whit," he said, ignoring the mess on the floor. He would clean it up later. "I reclaim my life, and it's thanks to you."

Jamie stood on his back, balancing with her arms out, her hair whipping behind her as he climbed high into the fresh spring morning. The blue-clad men were summoned in their black-and-white checked vehicles, but he did not care. They were no more than ants far below them on the ground. To take the air again felt wonderful!

"Yahoooooo!" Jamie screamed.

"As good as riding your motorbike?" he boomed over the rush of the wind.

"Almost," she said, climbing up to cling to his shoulder. His crest drooped in disappointment. She punched him in the side of the neck. "Better, you nutter! This is the real thing, what we puny humans reach for when we make machines that soar. *You've* got reality. Don't lose it again."

"I won't," Ulm Drak promised, turning his snout so the air rushed over it. "Never again."

After every interview session that followed, he took Jamie Blandish flying. In her pleasure, he rediscovered the joy he had known as a young dragon. At first the people in the town were terrified. He didn't care. They lived in *his* land, not the other way around.

In time, they gathered in massive crowds to watch him. He let his wings, widespread for the first time in eons, cup the cool air and float over the crest of the mountains. No, never again would he retreat to a hole and pull it in after him. Never.

* * *

Even after Jamie Blandish returned to London to write the book, Ulm Drak went flying whenever it pleased him to take to the air. He spent the times in between polishing his hoard to the gleam it always should have worn. It seemed that he had not felt so well in ages. A very small part of him regretted having to dispose of the "animals," but their deaths had had purpose. His life had been refreshed. He added their guns and swords to his hoard. Spoils of war.

His sallies forth became so well-known that on the eve of his book's publication, Castle Rise Books arranged for the "Meet the Author" event to be held in Cardiff Motorpoint Arena, far to the southwest, to satisfy the masses who wanted to attend.

It was farther than he had flown in centuries, but with every mile his confidence grew. He reclaimed the skies as his birthright. Jets vectored miles out of his way. He laughed at them.

He sailed in over the amphitheater, casting a shadow on the thousands of people awaiting him, and was gratified by their shrieks of surprise and terror.

When he came to a landing in the roped enclosure at one end of the field, the publicist, a middle-aged man with thinning hair like a monk's tonsure, ran to meet him. Ulm Drak had met him before, when he had accompanied the publisher's representative to his cavern.

"You must understand, Lord Drak, that people are delighted," said the man, "but they are also a *wee* bit terrified to discover that they have been living practically on top of the den of a living dragon! The size of the venue is to protect you as well as to handle the crowd. And it is quite a large crowd, as you can see."

"I am a dragon. Is this not why they are here?" Ulm Drak inquired, fixing a baleful eye on the stout man.

"Uh, why, yes! It's fine if they're frightened, but not that frightened." Swallowing his own nervousness, the man bustled him toward the roped-off area. In it, a broad table was piled high with neat stacks of books. Behind it lay a massive hoard of glinting golden items. "We brought you a big lot of treasure. You'll sit in here for the event."

Ulm Drak took one sniff and kicked the clattering mess with a scornful foot.

"Those are all fake!" the dragon roared. "Plate! Plastic! They have been painted gold!"

"Er, we did the best we could, Lord Drak," the man said. He was trembling. "Please, it's only for a short time. It will look so good in the newspaper photographs—a big red dragon on golden treasure. The image should sell a massive number of books. It's good publicity. Please."

Although Ulm Drak was disappointed, he understood that to gain more genuine treasure for his hoard they had to make a glut of sales. Reluctantly, he made a nest in the midst of the mass of gilded dishes, chains, and furniture. The smell of the gold spray paint made him sneeze. He could not get comfortable. It was undignified.

The crowd had lost its fear of him and was straining at the ropes, trying to get a better look. Nearly all of them held up small boxes in his direction, and flashes came from camera operators lurking on both sides. Ulm Drak snarled. He might as well have stayed in his cavern. His reality was seeping away from him, like oil into sand. He sighed, making the pile of rubbish in which he was ensconced creak.

"Would you ... would you like to see your book?" the publicist asked. "I must say, it's been very exciting, reading the memoirs of a monster whom we heretofore thought was mythological. The critics have been more than kind."

At extreme arm's length, he extended a gold-edged, hard-backed volume to Ulm Drak. The dragon snatched it between his claws and examined the cover.

"Ahh."

"First time holding it?" the publicist asked, with a little smile.

"Yessss," Ulm Drak breathed. He examined the tome as though it was a piece of fine sculpture, flicking through the pages, catching a phrase here and there. His history, set down in writing for the very first time. His adventures, told as he wanted them told and handed down for future generations. This was more precious than any other item in his hoard.

The book was a beautiful thing, beginning with the cover illumination. Artists had become so much more sophisticated since his youth. The last time he had been portrayed, he'd looked like an elongated blob of blood with golden eyes. This was like looking into a smooth pool of water. The image did not hold a spark of life, but it was more than satisfactory.

His name had been embossed across the top in gloriously ornate gilded letters. Below it, much smaller and in black print, was Jamie Blandish's. He growled low under his breath. Her name should have been larger, nearly as large as his.

As if in answer, a loud growl erupted, increasing in volume until it was nearly the equal of the dragon's displeasure. A thick-tired cycle burst from the nearest archway and hurtled toward him. It wheeled to a halt, and the rider leaped from the saddle to rush toward him. It removed its helmet, revealing Jamie's gap-toothed grin.

"Nice, eh?" she said, pointing to the volume in Ulm Drak's claws.

"It is," Ulm Drak said. His tail flicked peevishly. "You have not been to visit me in many days."

She tossed her head. "On another assignment, Mr. Scalyface. I have to make a living."

The publicist gasped at the audacious name, but Ulm Drak began to laugh.

"This is your means of flying, then?" he asked, peering at the two-wheeled device. The black-and-silver machine was huge compared to her small frame, but she had tamed him, and he was far bigger.

"Yes! Fixed, thank you very much." Jamie said. She glanced toward the waiting crowd. "I only came to see you, to congratulate you on the publication, and to say thank you very much for the opportunity. It was brilliant, all of it. Now everyone will know what a fantastic dragon you are and have always been. I'm privileged because I got to see you in action."

Suddenly, all the things that had felt fake dimmed into unimportance. The one true treasure in the entire arena stood before him. He snaked out his long neck and curled it around her.

"Stay, Jamie Blandissssh," Ulm Drak said.

"No, I can't," Jamie said, peering over his shoulder toward the reporters and photographers. "I'm not supposed to be here. I'm just your ghostwriter. I was lucky to get my name on the cover."

"I am Ulm Drak! I do not take no for an answer. I kill those who try to thwart me." He picked her up by the collar of her black leather jacket and set her down on a gold-sprayed wooden throne in the midst of the heaps of false riches. "I want those mere mortals to meet my inspiration. Without you, I would not be the dragon in our book."

Jamie laughed, and he heard the rush of wind in her voice, reminding him of the glory of flight and the return of his freedom.

Ulm Drak turned defiantly toward the crowd of humans and peered dangerously at them. "Now, who is first?"

O O O

Jody Lynn Nye lists her main career activity as "spoiling cats," but she has had plenty of experience with dragons. She lives northwest of Chicago with one of the above (cat, not dragon) and her husband, author and packager Bill Fawcett. She has written over forty books, including *The Dragonlover's Guide to Pern* with Anne McCaffrey, eight books with Robert Asprin, most of them in his *Myth-Adventures* series (Gleep!), a humorous anthology about mothers, *Don't Forget Your Spacesuit, Dear!*, and more than 150 short stories. Her latest books are *Rhythm of the Imperium* (Baen Books), *Wishing On a Star* (Arc Manor Publishing), and *Myth-Fits* (Ace Books). Jody also reviews fiction for *Galaxy's Edge* magazine and teaches the intensive writers' workshop at DragonCon.

A Pretentious Sonnet I Wrote Because I Had Only a Few Hours to Learn Iambic Pentameter

Adric Mayall

Dedicated to Quincy J. Allen,
for exactly the reasons you'd expect.

I fly through skies, soar bright and wild and free.
My grace is all one knows, but honor, too.
A tale of feats, told under cypress tree,
Doth make hearts sing, all joy; my gift for you.
Raise up, my friend, see skies above. So pure.
All love and wing and scale and flame, my form.
Gone into myth and legend, I endure.
Of dreams I make, of thoughts so very warm.
Now see my magic, hear my roar, know me!
But know in heart, I will be feared by all.
In truth, you should, with great celerity
Take heed and tremble, lest your death I call.
Can you tell why my rage doth shall outshine?
Have ye spied all first letters in each line?

O O O

A.J. Mayall currently lives in Northern California with his husband. By day he is a vetter for the e-book publisher Smashwords. He's also the author of *The Art of Madness*, the first in a new urban fantasy series. He has worked in the video game industry and wrote event content for City of Heroes and Eden Eternal. The rumors that he is a menagerie of hive-minded sentient spiders wearing a human suit are sheer fallacy and should be ignored.

The Dragon Went Down to Dyfi

Frog Jones

Jonathan strode to the center of the amphitheater without hesitation. Soft dirt scratched beneath his doeskin boots. His bright blue tabard hung over a flawlessly clean linen tunic. His wide-brimmed hat shone with bright plumage that whispered quietly in the soft breeze coming off the Dyfi River.

The Eisteddfod, the great competition of bards, had been a mere formality for several years. Jonathan felt no anxiety entering the competition. He knew his victory to be a foregone conclusion. The purple-robed Prifardd, the head of the Bardic Guild, looked on with mild interest. His high-backed wooden chair was carved with the image of Y Ddraig Goch, the Red Dragon, the heraldry of the kingdom of Gwynedd, and the words eisteddfod aberdyfi. It was a chair that, by all rights, should have belonged to Jonathan.

The Prifardd stood slowly, then announced the only performance that mattered. "Our final act is Jonathan Evans," he said in a tepid tone.

Despite his lack of enthusiasm, the crowd erupted in applause, stomping and hooting. The only silent ones wore the blue tabard; the other bards who'd performed in the amphitheater before him.

Everyone knew they'd been competing for *second* place.

Jonathan took his seat on the old, wooden stump, worn smooth by years of bards sitting in this very place. He brought his harp to his lap and began to play.

The tune that flowed forth was, technically, perfect. His hands followed the strings, but his eyes remained fixed on the Prifardd's. Jonathan should have held that honorable title, but the Prifardd refused to join the competition. Thus, Jonathan could enter the Eisteddfod every year, demonstrating to one and all that no bard could match his playing. But he could not sit in the chair.

His hands, calloused from practice, flew over the strings with a will of their own, leaving his mind free to dwell on the greatest crowd the Aberdyfi Eisteddfod had ever drawn. They'd come to watch *him.* He may not wear the purple robe or sit on the bardic chair, but no other harper commanded the price of Jonathan Evans in the inns of Gwynedd.

Jonathan did not listen to himself. Music, as a finished product, lacked significance; the note he had just produced was nowhere near as important as the string he had yet to pluck. His hands wove complicated melodies on the right, while his left danced along the big bass strings further away. His flawless performance concluded, and the crowd erupted in applause.

The Prifardd stood, shaking his head, and declared Jonathan the greatest competitor of the day.

"I challenge the Prifardd!" Jonathan said in a formal cadence. This, too, was tradition. The Prifardd could choose to defend his title or to decline.

The bard began to shake his head.

"Coward!" shouted Jonathan. This was distinctly *not* tradition. He leaped to his feet, swinging his harp by its shoulder with his right hand, pointing at the Prifardd with his left. "Every year for four years I stand before these people, and every year for four years you declare me the victor. Aberdyfi knows, Gwynedd knows—*you* know—that I should sit in that chair. You dishonor your robes by hiding. I say you are a coward."

The crowd grew silent.

The old bard simply tossed the victory pouch in the dirt of the amphitheater floor, turned his back on Jonathan, and left the auditorium. The crowd, hushed, followed him.

Jonathan Evans, four-time champion of the Aberdyfi Eisteddfod, stood alone in the amphitheater, holding his harp.

* * *

Not even the fastest harp in Gwynedd could defeat the Bardic Guild. No crowd he could draw was worth being placed on the guild's blacklist, and so no innkeeper would let him through the door. For a full year, Jonathan played for pennies near the fisherman's wharf.

He kept his harp tuned, and his fingers still knew their path across the strings, but his eyes were dim and his head sagged low. His bright-plumed hat and elaborate hose were replaced by simple, rustic clothes. The gray wool of his tattered pants and shirt clashed with the fine polished carving on his harp. He made his home on a pallet under the wharf. The rank smell of dead fish and rotting seaweed filled his nostrils, and the cold air off the sea chilled his joints into a constant, stiff ache.

He still drew a crowd, but they no longer cheered for him. Instead, they gathered to see the "Beggar Bard." A rough clay bowl sat in front of him to catch the occasional penny from the crowd, a pitiful homage to the complex melodies and harmonies his fingers plucked.

Once again, the people gathered for the Eisteddfod, but Jonathan, the once-great champion, could no longer enter the amphitheater.

A small, blond-haired boy, towed by his mother, stopped in front of him. "Mama, look!" said the boy. "It's Evans the Harp! He's playing outside this year."

The mother shot a distasteful glance at Jonathan, then moved her son to the other side. "Never you mind him. We're here to see the *real* bards."

"But Mama!" said the boy. "He *is* a real bard. He wins *all the time*!"

Jonathan smiled at the boy, then favored the woman with a nod.

"Your mother's got the right of it, boyo. I'm just a harper on the street. Go in and listen; mayhap you'll get to hear the Prifardd himself take the stage. He hasn't done that in five years, you know. Me, all I ask is a coin these days."

The woman frowned, but she placed a penny into his bowl. "Your coin, sir. Now come along, Bran. They're about to begin."

Bran kept his eyes on Jonathan as his mother pulled him into the amphitheater.

After the first round of applause, Jonathan's fingers stilled, and he placed his harp into its well-oiled leather case. He closed his eyes to listen.

To hear the "acceptable" bards, the ones approved by the Guild, grated on him like broken glass. The soft breeze off the Dyfi carried their tunes to him, and he picked their flaws from the air and wallowed in them.

Too slow. Missed the fingering. Bad accent. Jonathan's knuckles turned white as he clutched his harp case and listened to the grand display of mediocrity.

Eventually, his senses bruised to the point of assault, he shook his head, picked up his harp, and walked off. There would be no more pennies today; the Beggar Bard had earned his last. And so, while all the people of Aberdyfi gathered to hear the bards of the Eisteddfod, it was Jonathan Evans who first saw the dragon.

* * *

Y Ddraig Goch. The Red Dragon.

There were songs about the dragon. No bard in living memory had seen it, but all the old lays agreed that it slept in a rocky cave high atop Cadair Idris. Some songs lauded Y Ddraig Goch as the defender of Gwynedd. Even High King Cadwalader had placed the Red Dragon on his banner, claiming the great beast's patronage.

But other tales were not so kindly.

The Red Dragon took all the sheep from a village and left the people to starve. The Red Dragon enslaved the people of a town and demanded tribute. The Red Dragon unleashed his fiery breath upon a castle, destroying it simply because it could.

Yet all the stories agreed that Y Ddraig Goch was a being of immense power.

And now it flew in the skies above Cadair Idris. It circled the mountain, coiling upward into the air with its long, serpentine body and great red wings.

Then, Y Ddraig Goch spread his wings wide and began to soar—straight at the village of Aberdyfi.

Jonathan could only stare as the great beast approached. He heard the lackluster performances of the Eisteddfod stop and the cries of the villagers begin, but he was mesmerized by the great beauty of the dragon. Its horns swept back and away from its head, fading from a deep red to a pinkish-white. Its snout sharpened almost to a beak, and the scaly plates about the dragon's face added to its avian appearance.

The neck and body, however, were pure reptile. Four scaled legs curled back against its body in flight, and the leathery-red coating of its wings was shot through with deep scarlet veins and thick bones. The sun glinted off the dragon's scales, reflecting as from a shattered, bloodstained mirror.

Jonathan heard screams erupting behind him. Y Ddraig Goch circled the town, then flapped its wings and landed in the amphitheater, its red body disappearing into the sunken stadium.

Jonathan heard screams erupting, and the townspeople of Aberdyfi boiled over the lip of the amphitheater in panicked flight away from the terrible, awesome creature.

"Stop." The command was issued in a pitch so low it could not be—and most certainly wasn't—human.

Jonathan savored the rich, bass timbre of Y Ddraig Goch's voice as it rumbled through his entire body.

"Be seated."

The people, feeling the same force, stopped in their tracks and turned back toward the amphitheater. Jonathan could not resist either. The Beggar Bard had little of a life left to preserve.

Jonathan looked over the lip of the amphitheater. The dragon's right front claw rested on the bardic stump where Jonathan had so often sat. The beast craned its neck to bring himself face-to-face with the Prifardd.

"Tell me, Prifardd, who here shall champion Aberdyfi in the Eisteddfod?"

The Prifardd's eyebrows rose, and he shrank back into his seat, under the carving of the very beast who addressed him. "Champion?" he asked, his voice high and shaking.

"Champion. I desire to place a challenge to this village. None in Gwynedd can claim superiority to me. In Degannwy, they bragged once of their impregnable castle, which I broke upon their heads. In Aberffaw, they claimed their woolen sheep as the greatest in the land, so I did feast upon them. Here, you claim the prowess of your string-pluckers. I shall not have my people thinking that I may be bested in anything. For I am Y Ddraig Goch—the true Lord of Gwynedd and all Wales. And I shall not be outdone."

The Prifardd swallowed hard. To his credit, though, he stood tall before the dragon. "If you wish to enter the Eisteddfod, then by all means, I shall permit—"

"Permit? You permit nothing, mortal. I am here to place a challenge before the greatest harper in the land, not to stand in line. Come, Prifardd. Name your champion. I shall even set stakes. In the unlikely event that your champion best me with his song, he shall have my harp."

At this, the dragon raised its front leg from the stump and wove intricate patterns in the air. A great, golden harp appeared, perfectly fitted for the sheer mass of the dragon. Its strings were separated enough to allow gargantuan claws to pluck with ease, making the grade of the sound box shallower than usual. This lengthened the harp to a proportion that made Jonathan blink with the strangeness of it.

The strings themselves glinted steely gray, and Jonathan wondered what material could take a pluck from those claws and sound true instead of snap. Whatever it was, when combined with the gold framework of the harp itself, and given the immense size of the instrument, Jonathan could only begin to guess at its value. He stared at the dragon's harp longingly, then looked down at his oiled-leather case.

"Of course, in the event of a loss, I shall burn your village and seize your champion. He shall be chained in Cadair Idris, eating only of my scraps and playing songs of my glory whenever I wish it. If you have no champion, then I shall simply burn the village for its arrogance and leave it at that. Come—who among you thinks yourself the greatest of the string-pluckers? Who shall test me in this contest of art?"

Silence fell over the auditorium. All the bards gathered in line for the Eisteddfod looked at each other, then at the dragon. None of them moved to volunteer. The Prifardd stood stock-still, staring at the dragon as though the power of his gaze alone could protect Aberdyfi from this terror.

Jonathan strode down the aisle.

"Y Ddraig Goch! My name is Jonathan Evans!" he shouted, his voice piercing the silence. The crowd turned to stare at the Beggar Bard as he worked his way down to the amphitheater floor. "I am banned from competition in the Eisteddfod, and therefore engaging with you may be tantamount to sacrilege. Nevertheless, I accept your wager. I believe you shall come to rue this day, for I am the greatest harper the world has ever seen."

"Faugh! This beggar is the best you can send, Prifardd? Is he truly your choice of Champion? Or do you mean to doom a madman rather than risk one of your own?"

The Prifardd turned to the dragon and said, "You are mistaken, Sir Ddraig. He who stands before you is Evans the Harp, the Beggar Bard, and the most skilled harper Gwynedd has ever seen. If you seek a challenger, he is our choice. Only I beg you to allow for a single day before the competition so that he may be once again inducted into the guild. Otherwise, as he says, his participation in the Eisteddfod would be sacrilege. Not even the great Y Ddraig Goch would choose to offend the Gods, I believe?"

The dragon snorted, and a cloud of acrid smoke engulfed the Prifardd.

"A single day. At nightfall tomorrow, we shall test the harp of the Beggar Bard against the harp of Y Ddraig Goch. And the world will see that no human shall ever be the equal of me."

Y Ddraig Goch unfurled its red wings, poised itself, then sprung into the air and away from the amphitheater, leaving Jonathan standing in the aisle, harp already halfway out of its satchel, staring at the Prifardd.

"What need have you of a day? The last time I joined the Bard's Guild, it was but a simple ceremony."

The old man strode toward Jonathan. When close, he bent his head and whispered. "Hush, man. Do you want that drake to hear you and circle back? Take a day; tomorrow is the hardest competition you're ever like to have. Come to the Three Princes Inn. Let me buy you a supper and an ale, that your fingers will not tremble. You should be prepared." The Prifardd glanced pointedly around at the crowd of villagers still in the amphitheater. "We should *all* be prepared."

Jonathan understood. "And let the villagers clear out?"

"Those who can. You are a great harper, Jonathan, though you lack somewhat. But let us bet with the lives of as few as possible."

Jonathan nodded, conceding the point. As much as he wanted to hear what the dragon could do with that titanic harp, he did not want the deaths of the villagers on his head.

"The Three Princes, then."

* * *

The Three Princes drew the best-paying crowds in Aberdyfi. The inn was built out of hewn lumber, the same as most of the town, its furniture simple and rough. However, the innkeeper insisted on a maniacal fastidiousness from his employees.

Thus, when the Beggar Bard entered the inn, the patrons all turned to stare at him. Wearing his ragged clothing and smelling very much as though he belonged in one of the town's lesser establishments, Jonathan tried to keep his head high. The innkeeper met Jonathan's eyes, then jerked his head up the steps.

Jonathan nodded his thanks and proceeded upstairs.

The Prifardd had left the door to a room open; he sat inside next to a small, wooden desk. Two candles flickered their meager light in the dark, windowless room. On the bed lay a set of fresh clothes, and next to the bed a steaming tub of water had been drawn.

Jonathan eyed the tub with longing.

"Go ahead," said the Prifardd. "You should look—and smell—your best to play in the Eisteddfod tomorrow."

A year ago, Jonathan would have turned up his nose at such charity. To strip down in front of a man he held in contempt would have humiliated him into rage. But the Beggar Bard's desire to slough off a year's worth of filth and rejoin the ranks of humanity overrode any lingering sense of pride. He quickly pulled off his reeking rags and lowered himself into the steaming water.

"So," said the Prifardd, "do you truly believe you can best Y Ddraig Goch?"

Jonathan stared at the Prifardd for a long minute before answering. "You feared to play against me in the amphitheater. Do you now doubt that I am the best hope for the village?"

The last time Jonathan had accused the Prifardd of cowardice, it had shattered his life. He braced himself, waiting for rage, rejection, or exasperation. When the Prifardd instead cracked a half smile and shook his head, Jonathan found himself breathing in relief.

"Best hope? Yes, you are that. But just because a rat is grander than a mouse does not mean he has good odds against the cat."

Jonathan leaned his head back into the tub and let his eyes follow the flickering candlelight as it danced on the exposed wooden rafters. "Aye, that's true. But a life in chains in a dragon's lair, living off scraps, can't be much worse than the life of the Beggar Bard."

"And knowing the rest of the village burned?"

"I didn't hear anyone else volunteer. Those who can flee are on their way away from here. At least I bought them some time."

The Prifardd shook his head. "You didn't do this for the village. You've never cared about the village. The only thing Jonathan Evans has ever cared about is his own pride. So why volunteer? Tell me the truth."

"Because I am the best," said Jonathan. "I'm the best harper to walk the streets of Aberdyfi, and if any harp is fit to challenge Y Ddraig Goch, it's mine. I did it for my pride."

"And that is why you will lose," said the Prifardd.

Jonathan shook his head. "A bard's pride is what holds him together. Without pride, your hands twitch and tremble on the strings. Without pride, your voice shakes with the trepidation of the performance. Pride is the lifeblood of a bard, and you call it my weakness?"

"No," said the Prifardd. "Your weakness is not your pride; it is your reluctance to feel anything *other* than pride."

"How else can I play against a beast as mighty as Y Ddraig Goch?"

"Your music has always been the music of arrogance. Fast, perfect, splendid. You play the harp in a grand style, a style that makes you seem larger than life, that makes the audience feel your pride as though it were their own. When your fingers dance the strings, you convey the only emotion you have ever wanted to convey."

"And I do it well. So speak your problem."

"My problem is this: not even the pride of the great Evans the Harp, four-time champion of the Eisteddfod, can match the pride of Y Ddraig Goch. You are pitting yourself against a beast whose pride has lasted for eons, whose every interaction with man seems to be bent on ensuring that man keep his place beneath the wings of the dragon. You are up against a being whose pride you simply cannot surpass. If you try to impress the audience—what few remain—with your pride tomorrow, then you will be remembered only as the foolish slave who challenged the Red Dragon."

"So what would you have me do, old man? Weep for the crowd? Fear the dragon and the doom it brings? I am who I am, Prifardd. And if you truly believe your way superior, you would have met my challenge in the amphitheater."

"And I would have lost. Oh, I admit it. Had I accepted your challenge, you would wear the purple robes and sit in the wooden seat, and I would simply have gone back to being Davies the Song. But our art would have lost all depth in the process, and the guild would have suffered for it. You are brilliant, but you are only brilliant at conveying one thing."

"So let me *do* what I am brilliant at," Jonathan said, sliding his upper torso out of the tub and locking eyes with the Prifardd.

"You are the moon before the sun. Make this a competition of beauty, not brightness." With that, the Prifardd rose from his seat. At the doorway, he turned his head and said over his shoulder, "At least think on the last year, and whether remaining a beggar or a slave is truly your desire."

Jonathan scoffed and lowered himself back down into the warm, soothing water. If this was to be his last free night, he would certainly make sure to enjoy it.

* * *

Y Ddraig Goch's teeth shone bright white against his crimson-scaled face as Jonathan entered the sparsely-populated amphitheater. Jonathan kept his gaze fixed on the dragon's, not flinching from the great beast.

The Prifardd, seated on his wooden chair, broke the silence. "Y Ddraig Goch challenges, and shall therefore perform first. Evans, step to the wings. Sir Ddraig, begin at your leisure."

The great dragon stretched its wings over those few for whom witnessing this competition was worth the risk of the dragon's rage. It brought its claws up for its spell-weaving, adding those deep, guttural tones. This time, when the harp appeared, it was joined by a number of others. There were lap-harps, such as Jonathan's, great floor harps, and wire clairseach lining the floor of the amphitheater.

"Very well, Prifardd. I shall present my challenge. Let all here witness that no human bard can compete with me, for I am Y Ddraig Goch, the greatest being in Wales."

The floor harps started playing on their own, their low tones creating a powerful bass line. The sound resonated among the stone seats of the amphitheater, bouncing back and forth and combining with the deep sound boxes. The lap harps and the clairseach began weaving a counterpoint to the bass.

Then Y Ddraig Goch set talon to string, and began to play its great golden instrument.

Power.

The power of the dragon shone in its music, filling the auditorium with a sense of awe and wonder. The dragon played with head high, and the music it made struck hard, fast, and true. It was a song of glory in battle, in competition. A song of dragons, not men.

Jonathan could hear the weakness in his own species, in humanity, thrumming through his body as Y Ddraig Goch channeled all its draconic arrogance into a rhythm of climbing, rising, self-glorifying crescendo. The final notes, a stately challenge to all, left Jonathan breathless, with one thought firmly in his mind:

I cannot win.

He stared down at his lone harp. The tool of one man, and a traveling man at that, could weave no such interdependent harmony as Y Ddraig Goch had put forth. His harp could not compete on the same stage as the Red Dragon. As the dragon backed away, ceding him the amphitheater with a sneer, Jonathan trembled.

How can I follow this act?

"You are the moon before the sun. Make this a competition of beauty, not brightness."

And what was beauty? Jonathan pondered that question on his slow walk to the player's stump, now rough from the claws of the dragon. How did one make something beautiful without brightness? He sat on the stump. What could he possibly put into his music that Y Ddraig Goch could not?

He looked out over the crowd and caught the eyes of the small child Bran. His mother, head bowed low, did not meet his eyes. Why had she stayed? Why had she allowed Bran to stay? Their doom had been sealed by his arrogance, as had the doom of all those who surrounded him, waiting for his feeble response to the wall of sound that still seemed to reverberate in the very stones of the amphitheater.

Jonathan took a breath, then reached forward his left hand and plucked a single, low string. It rang true, the old sound box of polished wood giving warmth to the single note. He had exactly one performance left in his life, and he knew it. He could not waste it.

He plucked again, moving a step and a half higher. His right hand ran a pentatonic scale, more out of habit than desire. He moved slowly, in a bittersweet haze, savoring each note as it rang. Each pitch sounded clear, true, and simple, and a tear made its way down Jonathan's cheek as he began his final performance for any human ear.

And there, in the wetness the tear left atop his harp's shoulder, lay his answer. His left hand hit a minor chord, and he began a slow, mournful melody.

He could not match arrogance with arrogance, but the dragon was a being who had never known sorrow. He grasped at his pain in desperation, the pain of his potential loss, and then, as his confidence began to grow, the pain of his year spent on the streets. He let all of it flow onto his strings, and his hands danced a pattern they'd never traced before, shifting in and out of minor keys in a slow dirge.

And then hope. It had a different flavor from the bombastic flair of his previous performances. His arrogant strut that came from technical perfection had been replaced by a soaring rise, moving out of the minor key. His left hand traced a rapid bass line while his right kept to the pentatonic scale, playing a clean, simple melody over the pounding bass as he channeled the ability to overcome imperfection into the music.

And it was this the dragon lacked. Jonathan's music did not boast of perfection, but rather of tenacity. He played the song of hope, not pride, and as he locked eyes with Y Ddraig Goch, he let his music tell the dragon that humankind's beauty lay not in being without flaw, but rather in overcoming. In triumph. His final coda sang with the joy of it, a bouncing reel that washed away any wall between audience and performer, and he saw that even one of the dragon's mighty talons had begun to tap along with the music.

When he finished, he simply bowed to the dragon. Y Ddraig Goch lowered his head and craned his long, serpentine neck out to Jonathan.

They froze in a tableau. The giant, perfect drake and the smiling, imperfect human, gazes locked. The only sounds were the rustle of the cold breeze off the Dyfi and the rumbling breath of the dragon.

After a long minute, the Red Dragon pulled its head back, then slowly pushed the great, golden harp in front of Jonathan. Wordlessly, Y Ddraig Goch spread its wings to take to the air once more.

"Dragon!" shouted Jonathan.

The great beast stopped, mid-flap, to turn its gaze back to Jonathan.

"Thank you for your challenge. It was an honor to Aberdyfi. If you choose to join us for the Eisteddfod next year, I would be happy to join you once again on the floor of the amphitheater to test our songs against one another. Perhaps next time no wager of harp against town will be necessary."

Y Ddraig Goch snorted, a gout of smoke billowing from its nostrils. It made no verbal response, but rather beat its wings, launching into the air. However, instead of flying back directly, the great Red Dragon circled the village, dipping his wings as he did.

Next year's Eisteddfod was sure to draw the biggest crowd yet.

O O O

Frog Jones writes with his wife, Esther. Together, they are the coauthors of the Gift of Grace series, published by Sky Warrior Books. He also appears on the 3 Unwise Men podcast, as well as in a number of other anthologies. He can be found among the mist of the Olympic Mountains because all fantasy authors should play in a rain forest from time to time.

THE FINAL FOLD

Josh Vogt

The yellow police tape matches my scarf, which whips about in the nipping wind. I tug it down to keep my vision clear as I survey the scene, searching for what I know must be there. I scan past the police officers, the gawkers, the body lying under a black sheet until I spot it.

There, just off to the side, already marked by a tiny flag with the number six on it: a violet origami panther. A streak of blood ends a few inches away, a crimson arrow pointing to the paper animal. Yet despite the gore splattering the area, the parchment is spotless. I know if I got my hands on the piece, the paper would be creamy to the touch, warm, almost pulsing.

I wait, a mere observer, as people snap photos and murmur with muted excitement. I'm not the only one to spot the calling card of the Origami Killer. The serial killer's namesake has appeared at each site where he's struck. Nine deaths now in a matter of months. Nine lives burdening my soul. This is my fault, after all.

I taught him so well.

I glare at the panther, folded cunningly so crinkles form illusionary eyes on the creased forehead. They're aimed at the body, but I can sense the creature glancing sidewise at me, mocking.

Too late, sister, that look says. *You've always been the slower one.*

A quivering part of me wants to point and shriek, "There he is! He's right there!" I want to lunge across the tape and snatch up the origami, tear it into confetti.

I've tried before. Gotten locked up for it, even, spending a horrendous night in a cell. Saw myself on the news the next day, a flash of a manic-eyed girl, sickly thin with a heart-shaped face, clothed in the same torn jacket and jeans I wear tonight. I looked like a junkie, clawing as the cops took me to the pavement. My right shoulder still pops if I move my arm too fast.

This time, though, I've a plan, albeit a desperate one. Yet desperation has empowered many unexpected triumphs throughout history, and I cling to the frail hope that this might prove true for me as well. After all, our kind exists to protect the weak and ignorant. To use our gifts to uplift and inspire—not indulge in senseless butchery.

I stride into the nearest building, an abandoned apartment complex, and take the stairs to the roof. A peek over one ledge assures me I'm on the right side of the building. Below, the people cluster, unaware.

Shivering, I strip. My clothes make a sad heap on the gravel rooftop. So bared, the wind slashes me like frozen razors.

No time to let it cut too deep. Breathing out, I sprint for the ledge. Sharp pebbles bite into my soles. I plant a foot and leap.

As I inhale, I let my emotions swirl up and engulf my mind, mingling with the sensations of this transcendent moment—the weightlessness … the freedom … the terror of the inevitable plummet. A spark flickers in the core of myself. The energy of this precious instant ripples through me, and I transform.

My body folds in on itself. Limbs thin. My skin pales to ivory, bony arms and legs becoming even more angular. My field of vision narrows as my nose stretches into a sharp beak. The world enlarges around me as my form shrinks to the size of a fist.

Now an origami crane, I flap paper wings and drift down. Gusts buffet me, threatening to slam me into the brick or cast me far across the city. Yet I maneuver with a lifetime of practice, tucking and twitching here and there until I settle upright a few feet from the corpse. Nobody notices my arrival for almost ten minutes. Then …

"Hey, we missed something here. Who's the idiot cataloguing all this?"

I hold still while they poke and prod me. I'm a source of intense scrutiny, considering the Origami Killer has never left two works of art behind before. What could it mean? A warning of even more deaths? A mistake they could exploit?

Eventually, latex-gloved hands gingerly pick me up and deposit me in a small plastic bin—not the same as my brother's, but I know they've done the same to him. The bin blocks out everything but the sense of being shifted around. Conversations rumble like distant thunder. The world sways as if in an earthquake. I am set down on a hard surface. One more piece of evidence, packed for transportation to the station.

I wait until the vehicle I'm in thrums to life and heads down the street. Then I let the frantic need—Escape! Move! No delays!—of the moment whirl through me once more. My parchment form shifts in response.

This time, I fold into a monkey, strong and agile. After pushing the lid off, I flip out of the container and onto a metal shelf bolted to the side of a van. Bags and bins and buckets line the rest of the shelving; my brother already waits for me on the rack opposite. He is in the form of a rhinoceros. His receptacle lies overturned behind him. Brute force is his preferred method, making the world conform to his twisted version of reality.

For a moment, we simply stare at one another. It's been more than a year since our last confrontation. When we do speak, it's in rustles, crackles and snaps, flaps and crinkles. A language papyrophiliacs might hear in their deepest dreams.

Have you missed me so much, sister, he asks, *that you come just to watch me escape? Or have you finally decided to join me in crafting a never-ending tableau of flesh?*

Neither, I reply, shuddering with fury. The power responds, folding me into a cat, back arched, mouth open in a silent hiss.

He laughs with the sound of pages scattered on a breeze. He folds into a lion, paper claws extended. A languid stretch reveals his pleasure in the situation.

Ah, this game. I will delight in playing with you one last time.

Never a game, I say. *A craft. A gift. One you've defiled.*

His feline form yawns. *You always told me to follow my passion, wherever it guided me. To let raw inspiration guide my foldings. Why judge me now just because my vision doesn't align with yours? Isn't that a bit hypocritical?*

I lash my tail. *We are meant to uplift. To show humanity how the simplest act of creation can bring about beauty and joy. Not death and despair.*

He chuckles. *Oh, but that is what I do. With every life I take, I help others feel the joy of being alive more keenly. With each soul struck down, I give others the chance to shine all the brighter. Not my fault if they ignore the opportunity.*

You pervert our purpose to sate your own appetites, I say. *There's still time to stop. You don't have to keep killing.*

If you refuse to see this as the artistry it is, perhaps you're the one who's lost perspective. He folds into a bear on hind legs and peers down at me, no doubt inspired by thoughts of unassailable superiority. *So many words, sister. Why not simply see which of our creations overcomes the other first? Could it be you're frightened of losing?*

I barely keep a shiver from shuffling my form. Oh, yes, I am afraid. But he cannot see it.

He unfolds into a flat sheet, which flutters as if caught in a breeze.

Here, he says. *I'll make the first move.*

He folds into a hawk and wings across to my shelf, talons reaching. Ever the predator. Yet I refuse to be easy prey.

I fold into a butterfly and clap my wings as hard as possible, knocking him aside with a blast of air. He smacks the metal wall with the sound of wadded pages tossed into a wastebasket. As he falls, he folds into an alligator and scurries for me again. I become an elephant and stamp toward him. He shifts into a jackal and leaps.

I fold into an octopus and grasp him tight in my tentacles. For a heartbeat, I could tear him in half. I could end this. Yet my desire to preserve life makes me waver. Despite the horrors he's committed, I still want to protect him, even if it's from himself.

The moment passes. He twines into a cobra and slithers free.

Too slow, he says, coiling up, hood flared. *Or too soft? True creation requires sacrifice. You taught me that. And so every life I've ended is laid on the altar of my virtuosity.*

You can only demand that sacrifice of yourself, I say. *Stealing it from others is obscene.*

He folds into a scorpion and scuttles closer. I become a frog and shoot a craftily pleated tongue. It sticks to a claw and yanks him off-balance. As he wavers, I fold into a whale and roll, trying to pin him. He becomes a locust and buzzes into the air. Shifting into a mosquito, he dives at me with a needlelike proboscis—and as a horse, I rear and strike him out of the air with my hooves.

We fold faster, forming a menagerie of origami creatures. Each of his incarnations is powered by his craving to tear and shred and rend, while I, with waning strength, fight to subdue and defend and uphold.

Claw meets fang meets paw meets coils meets flipper …

Then he folds into a shark and gouges a chunk out of my side.

Ragged pieces of me flutter to the floor of the van as I stagger. I become a turtle, yet the tear remains in my shell. Should I return to my human form now, the wound would gush blood. Perhaps expose bone.

Now a tiger, he prowls about. *You can't win, sister. You never understood that creation requires destruction to have any meaning. You've never embraced our full potential.* He stalks closer. *In the end, know that I am grateful. You taught me all the forms so well.*

I gaze at him mournfully. *I didn't teach you all of them.*

He pauses, claw poised to rake me to scrap. *What are you talking about?*

Breathing in, I surrender to the moment—my sorrow … my despair … my love for the brother who became a monster. My heart and mind merge, and the spark of power within me flares into a bonfire.

I make my final fold.

He crinkles into a spider. *What have you become?*

An end. I flap paper wings and flex powerful limbs.

He trembles ever so slightly. *You never taught me that form!*

Heat builds within me, impossible embers already consuming me. Smoke wafts from the hole in my side. *It's a technique you were never ready to learn. It requires … sacrifice.*

I lunge and drive him down. He folds multiple times, trying to escape, but my claws spear him like thumbtacks into a corkboard. My brother screams.

Sister, please! I know you. You can't destroy me.

This is creation, I say. *I make a gift of hope to all those you'll never have the chance to hurt. And for ourselves, I offer a measure of peace neither of us could've imagined or accomplished alone.*

I open my mouth with a dragon's screech. Flames gush forth, and both our worlds end in a masterpiece of ash.

O O O

The works of author and editor Josh Vogt cover fantasy, science fiction, horror, humor, pulp, and more. His tie-in fantasy novel, *Pathfinder Tales: Forge of Ashes*, was published alongside the launch of his urban fantasy series The Cleaners, with *Enter the Janitor* and *The Maids of Wrath*. He's an editor at Paizo, a Scribe Award and Compton Crook Award finalist, and a member of SFWA and the International Association of Media Tie-In Writers. Find him at JRVogt.com or on Twitter @JRVogt.

Li Na and the Dragon

Scott R. Parkin

Li Na felt her body break in the fourth hour of her labor as she squatted down and curled tightly around her swollen belly, screaming for her reluctant seventh child to come quickly.

Not the sharp pang and long sting of skin tearing to make way for the baby, but a sudden snap and release deep within her body, as if jabbed in the spine between her hips with a blunt pole. Almost before the dull thud registered came a sudden heat spreading outward and taking her strength as it moved into her chest and face, arms and legs, ears and fingers and toes.

She fell backward against her rest chair but was too weak to catch hold of its shallow arms. She slid sideways and flopped to the floor as the midwife reached out with fingers that flailed at empty air. Hands tugged her away from the plain wooden chair and laid her flat on the lacquered floor, pressed down on her belly, and tugged at the baby as it emerged.

Li Na heard voices, but words fled behind an insistent ringing, like the thin, metallic voice of Huanglong, the yellow dragon whose shrine she served.

"Let the child be a boy," she whispered, her leaden lips fighting to form each word. "Great Huanglong, guardian of rivers and master of words, give my husband a son to carry on his name. Bless my long service to your shrine with this one comfort. Please."

But as she watched the bright red stain spread slowly across pale yellow floorboards, she knew it would not be. This was the curse of her family—that the women of her house would bear only daughters. Penance for the sin of a long-forgotten ancestor who had angered Huanglong's master and doomed the family name to extinction.

She should have told her husband, Li Zhou, of the curse in the very beginning so he could release her and find a wife able to fulfill that most basic duty. But they had been so much in love, and the idea of parting seemed so much deeper a pain …

The midwife brought the baby to her, and Li Na saw that she was right; her seventh and last child was indeed a girl. She tried to lift her hand to caress her beloved daughter, but her arm would not obey. Li Na tried to whisper a blessing of comfort to this child who would suffer both the burden of her own curse and the blame for her death, but her lips would no longer move.

So Li Na gazed at her daughter as she stole rapid, shallow breaths until first whiteness, then darkness, took even this simple joy from her.

She wept silently that the only gift she could bestow on this, her last child, was a memory of sorrow.

* * *

Li Na awoke to the soft tickle of her daughter's breath on her neck, the baby's reassuring weight pressing against her breast. She lay quietly, eyes closed, and enjoyed the moment.

She had not died after all. Still, she would bear no more children. It was for the best.

Though her face still felt flushed, her hands were icy, even beneath the thick blanket that covered her. A dull ache pulsed deep inside, an insistent throb that flared with each breath. Her mouth was sticky-dry and tasted of the bitter herbs Li Na recognized as lei gong teng, laced with a powerful narcotic meant to keep her still and asleep so she could heal.

She heard the rustling of slippered feet and felt hands tug at her blankets and adjust her headrest. She caught the sharp scent of cinnamon and ginger and cloves—her husband. He had left the care of his warehouse to others so he could watch over her. Of course.

Li Na felt light pressure on her chest and probing fingers checking her daughter's wrap. When he began to lift the infant away, Li Na reached up to stop him and gasped as sharp pain sliced through her core. Her eyes snapped open, and Li Zhou knelt over her, his own eyes wide in surprise.

"Let me hold her," Li Na croaked from a dry throat.

"You should be asleep," Li Zhou said and gently touched her cheek. He reached above her head and brought back a dark green wu lou gourd. He tipped its long neck toward her mouth so that thick, bitter potion spilled onto her lips. She swallowed three sips before she let the potion pool and run off her lips, and he took the medicine away.

"Water," she said.

He lifted a yellow, dust-colored gourd, and Li Na let cool water soothe her dry mouth and parched throat. She emptied two gourds and still wanted more. It was no surprise, considering how much she had bled.

"Hui-Ying, bring more water!" Li Zhou hissed over his shoulder.

A moment later, light, hurried footsteps announced her oldest child's arrival, and cool water again touched her lips. The narcotic potion had begun to take effect and dulled her pain enough so she could turn her head and see her tall, slightly built, eleven-year-old daughter kneeling at her father's elbow, the young girl's eyes wide and her lips tightly pressed.

Li Na finished the third gourd and smiled at Hui-Ying as Li Zhou pressed the dark green bottle on her and bitter potion again washed her lips. She dutifully swallowed three more times and saw her daughter's expression soften. Hui-Ying studied the healing arts and was quite adept even at such a young age. She had most certainly created this unfamiliar potion as the fruits of her own study and talents and was clearly relieved to see it work.

Li Zhou reached out again and snatched the baby from her chest, handing her off to Hui-Ying. "Take that away and change the wrapping; it's soaking wet."

Li Na wanted to protest, but the potion had taken what feeble strength remained and she could only watch as Hui-Ying hurried away.

"Sleep, dearest," Li Zhou whispered, and she struggled to focus on his face. Though his eyes were now tender and his manner gentle, she had seen the hard look on his face and felt the harsh tug when he snatched the baby away.

As forced sleep took her, Li Na wondered how it was possible that her husband could love her in the same moment that he clearly despised her precious daughter. Were they not the same flesh, each created in her own time from love and hope?

* * *

The baby's cries from the next room woke Li Na. Not the simple fuss of wetness or the long wails of hunger, but the sharp, strangled shrieks of pain or abandonment. Why was her daughter in the dragon temple? That was Li Na's personal stewardship; no one entered except in her company.

She struggled to sit, then stand as she heard the angry rumble of Li Zhou's voice beneath the cries of her daughter. Pain pulsed in her center, but it was still dulled by the bitter potion, and she was able to tolerate it, though it stole her breath away.

Li Na staggered to the small room's single door. It was deep night, and only the light of a single, small lamp wavered on the low teak table at the end of the short hallway to her left. She stumbled forward, gripping the door frame, then lurching to the side and leaning heavily on the small table. There was wetness on her thigh; she had begun to bleed again.

" … ignored her pleas and let this mistake happen." Li Zhou's voice was hard, his words clipped and spat out as though hurling stones at an enemy. "You have stolen her time and devotion from me, yet given nothing in return."

She leaned against the wall beside the narrow doorway and gasped against the lightness in her head, the weakness in her legs, and the rising pain deep in both body and soul. She gazed through the curtain of amber beads that separated the bright light of the great yellow dragon's temple from the darkness of her husband's house.

Li Zhou knelt before the simple cedar and river stone shrine, his hands raised as if in prayer, but his fingers were clenched into tight fists. Her newborn daughter lay naked on the shrine's offering board, tiny arms and legs shivering in the chill of the late-night breeze from off the great Huang He River. Her skin was mottled purple and white from cold and distress as she shrieked without cease.

Her husband stood suddenly, and she saw the long, white linen wrap that should be protecting her daughter wadded in a heap on the floor.

"If you will not grant her wish, then hear my demand." He snatched up the linen and shook it at the brass statue of Huanglong that stood atop the small shrine. "I have no use for a living daughter, a dying wife, or a dragon shrine that wastes my resources to no benefit."

She heard a high, rich metallic sound like the pure ring of a bell and recognized it as the voice of Huanglong. The great yellow dragon was growling, a sound she had heard only once in her life—years ago, when Huanglong had used the word of its power to vanish a mischievous tortoise after it had damaged the dragon shrine.

Her husband seemed unaware of the sound.

"This is my bargain and my oath," Li Zhou spat through clenched teeth. "Change that mewling thing into a son or else take it away and use it to restore my wife's health. If you fail to do one of these things by sundown tomorrow, I will tear this temple from off my house and cast its parts into the great river."

He flung the wad of linen at the small brass dragon statue and stalked through the temple's open front gate and out into the cold night.

Li Na gathered the remains of her paltry strength and stepped forward, despite the growing pain. Huanglong's ringing metal growl never abated, and she stumbled through the curtain of amber beads. Her heavy feet knocked into each other, and she sprawled forward toward the dragon shrine where she lay still, her face flat to the worn wooden floor. Though her daughter shivered and shrieked only two arm's-length away, Li Na knew Li Zhou was in greater danger.

"Great Huanglong," she whispered, "guardian of rivers and master of words, please forget the foolish words of my husband."

"It is unforgivable!" the tiny metallic voice cried. The ringing growl grew louder and more resonant. "To deny the worth of creation in which he had part—"

"He is afraid," Li Na said, her voice thin. "His one great hope lies unfulfilled on your offering board; his one great comfort lies broken before you. It has made him desperate."

"It has made him stupid!" Huanglong shouted and sailed down off the top of the cedar shrine, its small brass body moving with fluid grace. It plucked the linen wrap from its tiny horns and draped it over the shrieking baby, then gazed down on Li Na.

"If he is stupid, great Huanglong, it is because I have lied to him these fifteen years. He knows nothing of the curse that your master rightly breathed out against my ancestor, and so does not understand that what he asks is impossible."

The ringing growl suddenly stopped and heavy silence filled the small temple, broken only by the distant rush of the mighty Yellow River—the Huang He—and the soft susurrus of night wind. Even her daughter's shrieks ceased for a moment.

"He wishes your daughter dead and has named her a mistake," the yellow dragon said as the infant's cries rang out again. "To imagine that a dragon would seek the life of an infant in exchange for *anything* ... How can I forgive such disrespect?"

Li Na gathered her arms under her and pushed up. Sharp pain arced through her hips and gut and brought bile to her throat, but she faced Huanglong.

"I don't ... I can't ..." Tears streamed from her eyes. "His dying hopes have driven him mad in this moment of frustration. I know Li Zhou to be loving and kind and generous."

"And yet."

"No," she said, her voice stronger. "No. He wishes for my health, not her death. If he has spoken vainly, it only proves the depth of his fear."

Huanglong gazed down at Li Na, and she gazed back, unfazed. "He feels nothing at all for her," the dragon said, though its mouth did not move. "That much is true."

"Can you protect her?" she asked, then quirked the barest hint of a smile that faded instantly. Words had power and meaning, especially to the great Huanglong who had taught the secret of writing to Humanity. "*Will* you protect her?"

"If your daughter asks, I will answer. Whether she hears is hers to choose."

No promise of protection, then. No detail as to *how* the great dragon would answer—whether by direct word or by indirect symbol. Li Na bowed her head. It was the best she could hope for. It was not in the nature of a dragon to give a specific answer when an indistinct one was possible.

"And Li Zhou?" she asked.

"I will grant neither of his demands."

Will not rather than *cannot.* It was still possible, then.

Li Na took a deep breath and gathered her feet under her. Pain screamed throughout her body and made spots dance before her eyes. Blood flowed freely; it streaked her simple gray shift and slicked both her thighs and ankles. Her life would end here this night—that much was clear—but there were still tasks to perform.

She clasped her hands above her and bowed low until her head touched the floor. "Great Huanglong, guardian of rivers and master of words, please forgive the vain words spoken by my husband, Li Zhou, who is in anguish."

The baby shrieked louder and kicked at the thin linen covering her.

"Your daughter needs you," the dragon said.

"Great Huanglong, guardian of rivers and master of wor—" She gasped again, and her arms began to shake. The potion had failed, and she felt the slow tear of her own flesh deep inside her body. "Master of words, please forgive … both me and my husband." Her voice was the barest whisper.

Li Na waited for the dragon to speak, but the only sound she heard was her daughter's abandonment crying into the chill night. She made to repeat her prayer a third time, but her strength had fled and all she could do was wait. As she listened for the sound of the dragon's high, tinny voice, her daughter's cries began to fade.

Yet even as her sorrow welled up at the dragon's silence, she could not blame Huanglong either for her lies or for the terrible oath Li Zhou had made. Her husband's misunderstanding was her own fault; in her reverence of the dragon, she had kept too many things to herself.

Her breath came slower now, and the pain began to ebb, first to a dull ache and then vanishing altogether. So this was the sensation of dying; not unpleasant. Li Na felt a touch on her head and was surprised that she had the strength to sit back.

Huanglong stood before her, its golden body no longer a tiny brass statue, but fully twice the length of a man and made of iridescent flesh that pulsed with life. Where the statue was smooth and vague, the true shape of Huanglong clearly revealed each tawny hair on its long, camel's face with its scant beard and branching, golden stag's horns. Each of the glistening amber carp's scales on its wingless, serpentine body spoke of perfect balance between necessary opposites—yin and yang, discipline and compassion, thought and deed. Even down to the five-hand-length eagle's talons that protruded from each of its soft lion's paws.

It was the first time Li Na had seen the dragon's true form, and it quietly spoke of so much more power than even she had ever imagined.

Though its body curled back and around the small cedar shrine, its head was level with her own, and it looked her straight in the eye with its piercing amber gaze. In its upturned right paw rested her daughter, quiet now and snugly wrapped in linen. Li Na took the child from the dragon and hugged her tightly to her breast.

"I cannot undo your injury, but I can ease your pain," the dragon said in the same high, tinny voice she had always known. "I have heard your words, and they are true. So by the word of *my* power, I declare the oath of Li Na's husband forgotten."

She bowed low. "Thank you, great Huanglong."

When she raised her head, the dragon spoke again. "While I can forgive your husband his words, I cannot change his heart. He has called this child a 'mewling thing' and a mistake; he sees her only as a failed promise."

If only she had more time. But the dragon could not undo her injuries, so she could not explain to Li Zhou that no promise had ever been made to her.

She nodded her understanding. "Is it possible at least to remove my family's curse from this child? She will bear enough burdens without this additional weight."

The yellow dragon closed its eyes. "I did not speak those words; I cannot rescind them."

Li Na wept, and a wave of fatigue washed over her. Her time had come. She reached down and gently kissed her last child on the forehead. "I'm sorry, little one. Find peace as you can."

She lay down carefully on her side and pressed the child to her face. As her eyes fluttered closed, she heard a voice. Not the high, tinny voice of Huanglong, but a deep, rich voice that echoed in every part of her being. Not loud, but penetrating.

"The curse declared against the line of Pang Ji is ended," the voice said.

Li Na opened her eyes but saw only Huanglong, who now bowed its head and crouched low to the ground. She tried to sit up so she, too, could give honor to this unseen dragon to whom even the mighty Huanglong bowed, but her body refused to obey.

"Can you give my daughter peace, great dragon?" she asked, her voice barely a whisper.

"I can watch over her," the encompassing voice said. "If that is your wish."

"What must I do to earn this great blessing?" she asked. "I have little left to offer."

"Any bargain is between you and me alone; not even your husband may know of it."

"But he is my love and my strength, and he has already suffered so much for my secrets. Is there no other way?" Silence. No, then. "Then I will hear the costs, great dragon."

"This child will live in loneliness until the last days of her life. She will be buffeted by forces and powers she can neither see nor imagine. Her destiny is to be utterly forgotten in this world."

"Must you heap such misery upon her?" Li Na asked.

"I do nothing; such are the natural consequences of choices already made," the penetrating voice said, and she knew it to be true. The nature of dragons was to aid, not interfere; to give counsel, not direct; to buoy up, not crush down.

Though she felt no pain, her strength had gone. There was no more time.

"But you will watch over her," Li Na said, "if I consent?"

"Yes."

Footsteps sounded on the sandy ground outside the front gate, and Li Na struggled to keep her eyes open. Li Zhou stepped into the temple holding a bowl of rice and a cinnamon stick—the same offering she made every day in this temple. He stopped when he saw her lying on the ground before the shrine, clutching their daughter, her dress streaked with her own blood. He dropped the bowl and rushed to her.

Li Na saw that Huanglong had returned to its perch as a brass dragon atop the simple shrine and smiled. She wondered if her husband could even have seen a dragon in its natural form. He clearly could not hear their voices. Of course, he did not serve them and so did not earn their blessing; she was their messenger at this time and in this place.

"Choose her name," the penetrating voice said.

Li Zhou knelt by her side, oblivious to the great dragon's powerful voice. "Forgive me," he said. "I've made a terrible mistake."

She wanted to pull him close, to whisper comforts into his ear. She wanted to ease his pain and soften his heart. But it was too late. All she could do now was answer the dragon and believe in both the dragon's power and her husband's good heart.

"My child shall be called Kai," Li Na said, and she let her eyes droop closed.

"Don't leave me," her husband cried, and bent over her, clutching her close. "I need you."

The great dragon's voice echoed throughout her being:

"You act with compassion and wisdom. Serve me here, and I will not only watch over Li Kai, the last child of Li Na, but I will ensure that she chooses her own fate—though destiny must still have its due. Yours is the power of creation; ours is the magic of inspiration. By this pact, Li Kai shall know and wield both."

And while she knew her husband would misunderstand her words as speaking to his bargain and not her own—that he would be injured by them every day until his heart grew cold and hard—it was a necessary thing. She had chosen her daughter's name carefully, knowing the words of Li Zhou's vain oath.

"The bargain is accepted," Li Na said with her last breath as her husband wailed out his grief.

He had demanded that either Li Na live or the child be made into a boy. Though such was impossible in this life, she nonetheless chose a man's name for her daughter—at first to give her husband peace, but later to give her daughter hope.

This last creation of her flesh would be called Kai, which meant *victory*. She would choose her own fate by the power of her own soul and with the aid of dragons, who alone among creation were honorable in all things.

There could be no other choice.

O O O

Scott R. Parkin is an award-winning author, critic, and essayist with more than thirty short story sales in SF, fantasy, and literary fiction. A recent prizewinner in the L. Ron Hubbard Writers of the Future Contest, his fiction has appeared in a wide variety of venues, including *Marion Zimmer Bradley's Fantasy Magazine* and the *Fiction River: Valor* anthology of military SF stories.

WAYNE AND THE GATOR

A Modern Retelling of Sir Gawain and the Dragon

Kristin Luna

Wayne steered *White Falcon*, his fifty-inch-bottom GT with a D50A Suzuki motor, next to the dock on the north edge of Lost Lake, Louisiana. "Wayne's Gators" was painted on both sides of his boat, and Wayne had made sure it looked as brand-new as possible for his first solo alligator wrangling job.

After tying up his boat, Wayne took off his hat and slicked back his sun-bleached hair. He took note of the ancient flatboat already docked, its chipping paint and the rusted motor. Moss grew up the sides, and it looked like it hadn't been taken out in a couple of decades. Humidity choked the swamp and made everything, including the boat, smell like a lagoon of molding alligator poop.

"You can tell a man's character by the state of his boat." Wayne muttered his former boss's words. He chastised himself and put his hat back on. The long, three-hour ride from his house in Cocodrie to the bayou swampland around Lost Lake had made him irritable. "C'mon, Wayne, mind your manners. You need this job; get your head on."

He steadied himself on the rickety dock and then made his way to the house on the shore. The house matched the flatbed boat—rusted metal siding made up the walls, and crude cutouts, probably formed with a welding torch, formed its windows.

"You Wayne's Gators?" A deep voice bellowed next to him.

Wayne whipped his head to the tree line on his left. An enormous man emerged, tall and as thick as a cypress trunk, barefoot and in overalls. He stared at Wayne with deep-set eyes.

"Oh," Wayne exclaimed. "Not sure how I missed ya there, sir. You Witcher?"

The big man nodded.

Wayne's gaze traveled down to Witcher's mitt-like hands, which held a fraying rope. Attached to the other end of the rope was a fifteen-foot alligator lying in the grass.

Wayne stumbled back, putting lots of space between himself and the creature.

"You're awful squirrelly for a gator grabber. And sure young and pretty for one, too," Witcher croaked. He looked down to the alligator, which sat still as a statue with its mouth open. "This here's Princess."

Wayne swallowed. "Well, it looks like you already took care of the gator problem you called me in for."

"What? Princess? Naw, she ain't the problem. Had her since she was a cuss of a runt. Caught 'er when I was a boy. She's just an old lady now. You don't have to worry 'bout her none. The problem is somethin's been comin' after her at night. Lookie here." The big man motioned Wayne over.

Wayne approached cautiously.

"Look 'em scratches. Deep," Witcher said. He smelled like vanilla-flavored tobacco.

Wayne studied the marks striping the massive alligator's back. "Could've been done by a male. They can get aggressive during mating season."

"Thought you'd say that." Witcher reached into an overall pocket and fished out six-inch-long claw. "This look gator to you?"

Wayne took the bonelike claw in his rough fingers. He tested the tip on the callous of his pointer finger. Just the soft touch drew blood.

"Holy Moses," he muttered.

"Look, *boug*," Witcher said, putting his hand on his hip. Wayne clenched his jaw at the brute calling him "boy" in Cajun French.

"You look mighty young for a job like this. Truth is, you were the only one available. Called Bobby over at Alligator Hunter, then Manuel at Gator Alley. Neither could come 'til next week. But my Princess might be dead in a week or two, know what I mean?"

Wayne wiped the sweat from his brow and shifted his weight.

"Mr. Witcher, I'm grateful you called me. I know I look young. I'm twenty-six years old, but I've been wrangling and catching gators since I was fifteen. I know where they sleep, what they like to do during the day. Hell, I even know what kind of smells they like." Wayne looked down at the claw and rolled it in his hand, debating if he should tell Witcher everything. When he looked back up at Witcher's skeptical face, he decided to say it. "Bobby, who owns Alligator Hunter, trained me, actually. I helped him build Alligator Hunter into the business it is today. I was his apprentice for seven years."

"Ah, okay," Witcher said, rubbing his belly. "Now we're gettin' somewhere. He's the best bayou gator grabber for two hundred miles. Why'd you leave 'em? Could'a had a good clutch of money by now."

Wayne sucked at his teeth and looked down at Princess. "Difference of opinion," he said curtly.

"Well, I ain't gonna dig in that snake hole. But if you think you're up to it, then you got my business." Witcher pointed out over the swamp. "I saw somethin' the other night. Was slitherin' up that bayou there. Long-ass tail. My guess is you're dealin' with one helluva male … or somethin' else entirely."

Wayne licked his chapped lips and nodded. "Well, I best be on, then. Should be back by sundown, gator or no."

"All right, then. Good luck." Witcher smiled, revealing a number of missing teeth.

Wayne took one last look at Princess, who hadn't moved an inch, and turned to the dock.

Back on *White Falcon*, Wayne pulled out a map of the bayous surrounding Lost Lake. He traced the twisted bayou Witcher had mentioned, noting that it feathered out into a network of smaller rivers. He sighed, looking at his watch. Ten o'clock in the morning. He decided to stay on the bigger bayou for the rest of the day. He'd set a few traps if he found any gator activity along the banks.

Wayne started up the motor and started out onto the river. The water was thick and muddy thanks to a heavy thunderstorm the day before. But as Wayne looked up at the sky, there was nothing but clear blue.

He studied the banks as he sped along Lost Lake, then continued up a channel that sprouted to the north. He passed an alligator snapping turtle that bobbed lazily in the water. The croaking of frogs overpowered the sound of his purring motor, along with the mating calls of crickets and grasshoppers and the occasional high-pitched squeak of a pelican. The heavy, musty smell of still, tepid water permeated all others.

About one nautical mile in, the bayou forked. Carencro Lake to the right, and to the left, the unknown.

Wayne turned left.

He followed the winding river east, taking note of a few alligators lazily resting near the banks, just their noses breaking the surface of the water.

The sun beat down overhead, and with the humidity, he had already sweated through his shirt. If he upped his speed, the wind would cool him off, but at the cost of possibly missing telltale signs of a large alligator.

Wayne checked the map again, noting he was halfway between Carencro and Fourleague Bay. He sighed, checking his watch. Eleven thirty. He looked out to the riverbank, scanning for any slithery imprints in the mud. Nothing.

He carried on for three more hours, carefully watching the banks.

When he came to a heavily wooded part of the channel, Wayne paused, then killed the motor. Not only were there no signs of alligators, there were no birds singing, no frogs croaking. All around him, there was nothing stirring in the air or the water. Wayne rubbed his tanned hands together, feeling his excitement mounting. He started up the motor again, but this time on a lower speed. He steered closer to the left bank and went downriver almost a half a mile, searching for tracks. When he found none, he steered to the right bank and went back the way he'd come.

About two hundred yards in, along the right side, Wayne spotted a series of thin, broken branches and smothered grass and weeds pressed firmly in the mud. Bald cypress trees framed the way into the forest where indentations in the mud continued as far as his eyes could see.

Wayne steered *White Falcon* to the trees. He strapped on his rubbery fisherman overalls and hopped out, his thick boots splashing water up the side of his boat. He tied White Falcon to the trunk of a young cypress using a buntline hitch knot that Bobby had taught him when he was just starting out. He stared at the knot for a moment, fear seizing him.

You'll never make it on your own, he remembered Bobby say with a sneer the day he quit. *Come on back when you fail. I'll be waitin'.*

Wayne took a deep breath. He reminded himself in a quiet whisper, "You need this job. You need the money to keep the business going. You can do this. You gotta do this, or you'll have to go back to Bobby with your tail between your legs. And he'll make you do things you don't wanna do."

He clenched his teeth, picked up his tranquilizer gun, and headed into the forest, following the smooth pathway made by the tail of a large alligator.

Mosquitos bit at his sweaty, exposed skin. Wayne swatted a few away and ignored the rest. If he gave away just a fraction of his focus to the bugs, then he could miss a sign of the alligator, and all of his training and experience couldn't save him then.

Not far into the marsh, Wayne spotted a heaping den of broken branches.

"What the—?" Wayne whispered. He squatted low, observing the formation. It had a similar shape as a cave, but it was made from brambles and twigs, like a nest.

Wayne took off his hat and wiped his brow. He took a deep breath and fitted his hat back on.

"Moment of truth," he whispered. He looked down and patted his gun. "Do no harm, but do right by me, ol' girl."

As he neared the nest, Wayne realized it appeared to be more like a cave than he first thought. He hesitated at the entrance. He had known some folk who preferred to live deep in the swamps. Antisocial, but they meant no harm to anybody. He toyed with the idea that a vagrant lived in the stick cave, but he looked down at the ground, and sure enough, an alligator's tracks led in.

Wayne turned on the flashlight attachment to his tranquilizer gun and stepped inside.

He took careful, measured steps. He swallowed as he shined his flashlight on the tubular alligator poop littering the ground, which contained with what looked like bone fragments. Wayne shivered and continued into the cave.

He came to a bend and stopped. He listened, but there was only silence. Wayne slowly turned the corner, tranquilizer gun pointed and ready.

The flashlight washed over the left side of the cave. Nothing. He slowly dragged the light to the right until something caught in the glow.

Wayne blinked. Then blinked again.

The strangest-looking alligator Wayne had ever seen basked in the light. Its nictitating membrane covered its eyeball, signaling to Wayne that the creature slept. The animal wasn't an inch longer than ten feet, but it looked thicker than most alligators. Its long, needlelike teeth glittered in the light.

Wayne took a careful step back, and a twig snapped underfoot.

The creature hissed, the membrane snapping away to reveal its gleaming emerald eyes. Wayne cursed as he took two more quick steps back.

The alligator emitted a gravelly purr, then lifted its back. The simple movement displayed its wide, dark green wings.

"Holy Moses," Wayne whispered.

The alligator tilted its head to the side with its mouth open, then brought down its leathery wings.

"What the hell are you?" Wayne looked down the barrel of his gun.

The alligator tilted its head further to the side until it rested on the ground. Then it promptly flipped over onto its back, mouth agape, its unusually long tongue flopping out the side.

Wayne flared his nostrils and furrowed his brow. He took his eye from the gunsight and studied the thing in front of him. The alligator started wagging its thick, ridged tail.

"You remind me of somebody," Wayne said, slowly lowering himself to the ground. He picked up a stubby piece of branch. "Somebody who loved to play fetch." He threw the branch to the side of the cave near the winged alligator.

The creature flipped back onto its feet. It playfully spread out its wings and slithered over to the branch. It picked up the wood in its teeth, then bounded toward Wayne.

Wayne put his gun back up, finger on the trigger.

As if it knew Wayne's intention, the alligator stopped five feet away and dropped the branch. What Wayne could only describe as gleefully, the alligator scuttled back to where it had been and turned back toward Wayne, its heavy tail pounding the dirt with anticipation.

The alligator wrangler scratched at his sweaty scalp through his hat. "You're about the craziest thing I've ever seen," he said.

The gator continued to wag its tail, thumping it on the ground.

"You're just like a big dog, aren't you? Like a big alligator dragon dog … thing."

Wayne remembered the claw in his pocket and pulled it out. "Couldn't have been you, terrorizin' that enormous alligator Princess, could it?" He held up the claw in the light, then pointed the flashlight at the gator's feet. While the gator's talons on the right foot were intact, it was clearly missing one talon on the front left.

"Holy Moses and the commandments," Wayne said. He pocketed the talon and took off his hat. "Look here, little guy—er … girl. Yeah, you're a female, aren't you? Not quite big enough to be a male. I'm gonna come to you real slow-like, all right? You can munch on this hat if you want to, but I'm bettin' you're not gonna." Wayne moved closer to the alligator, gun raised and waving his hat in front of him.

Just as he suspected, the alligator didn't attack. She raised her wings slightly, then made a humorous attempt to jump up and catch the hat. Wayne stood a foot away, dangling the hat above the alligator, whose only interest was in catching her new toy.

Wayne felt affection bloom in his chest. "Bobby would've killed you right off, soon as he saw you." He swallowed, remembering the day he quit. Bobby had asked him to kill an old alligator that wasn't doing any harm. When Wayne refused, Bobby gave him an ultimatum: either he shot the alligator in the head right then or he could quit. Wayne didn't wait a heartbeat. He quit.

Wayne brought his focus back to the alligator. "He would've shot you, but you're as intimidating as an old lab dog, ain't ya?" He lowered the hat closer to the alligator, and the creature grabbed it, proudly displaying her catch in her mouth.

"Lord knows I'm not a smart man, and this will surely prove it," Wayne said. He took a deep breath and put his hand out in front of the alligator's snout. He clenched his teeth, ready for the odd alligator with wings to snap his hand off.

Instead, Wayne felt the cold sliminess of the reptile's snout as she rubbed against his hand affectionately.

For the next hour, the alligator wrangler took his time getting closer to the creature, as much as his fear would allow. He rubbed the alligator's chin, which she seemed to prefer, and felt along the ridges of her back to the tips of her membraned wings. He examined her talons and tail, talking to her all the while until he realized his fear had completely disappeared. How quickly and easily the creature had trusted him touched Wayne.

"I don't know how this is possible," Wayne said, coming back around to the alligator's snout, "but let's not say no to a gift horse."

The dragon rubbed her chin against Wayne's shin. He bent down and scratched the scales while the creature thumped her tail.

"I think I know what you were doing with Princess. You just wanted a friend to play with. But you can't try to play with Princess anymore. If you do, I'm sure Witcher'll come out and look for you himself with that ancient flatboat of his. He'll look for you night and day, and when he finds you, he'll blow your head off himself. Don't worry, I think I got a plan. But you gotta do this one thing for me."

Wayne coaxed the winged alligator into his boat in just five minutes' time. By late afternoon, they had wound down the river and back to the shore of Lost Lake.

As White Falcon pulled up to Witcher's dock, Wayne saw the burly man sitting in one of his rusting white lawn chairs with Princess spread out next to him in the tall grass. Wayne killed the motor and hopped out to tie up the boat, throwing an extra rope onto the dock.

"Any luck?" Witcher bellowed, approaching.

Wayne knotted the rope and straightened. He took off his hat and wiped down his sweaty brow. "Might've found where it sleeps. See that?" Wayne gestured to the front of his boat. Long, deep gashes decorated the boat's otherwise spotless hull just above the waterline.

"Coo-wee!" Witcher's eyes widened. "Think it did that?"

Wayne leaned toward Witcher. "I *know* it did that."

"Did you see it?" Witcher licked his lips with excitement.

"Do you ever feel like something's watching you, Mr. Witcher? Like you look out into the swamp, and you just know that something just beyond is looking right back at you?"

Witcher nodded. "All the time."

"Well, that's how I felt the whole time out there today. And then I heard an awful, high-pitched sound coming from the hull. Like nails on a chalkboard. I hightailed it back here to see the damage," Wayne said, then fished his phone out of his pocket. "Do me favor, will ya? I need to submit video evidence to my insurance. Can you just hit that button there? Yeah. Just like that. Now just keep that on me while I point out the scratches and say what happened."

Witcher positioned the phone between his thick fingers, then took a few steps back on the dock to get a wider angle. "Okay, I got ya."

"Great," Wayne said, crouching near the bow's hull. He put his hand near the scratches, then discreetly knocked on the side of the boat.

Exploding from the water, the alligator heaved herself onto the dock. She kept her wings close to her sides, though her glowing green eyes looked especially vicious next to her razor-sharp teeth and white talons.

At the sight of her, Princess slithered to the back of the house, and fast.

Wayne jumped on the ten-footer, wrapping his arms around the alligator, making sure to keep her wings clamped to her sides. He made a show of his efforts, grunting with gusto.

"*Coo-wee!*" Witcher yelled again, still holding the camera.

"You gettin' this?" Wayne yelled.

"Hell yeah, *boug*, get you some!" The enormous man hooted.

Wayne positioned his head close to the alligator. "Okay, girl, I'm just going to tie you up here, just sit tight."

The alligator croaked in return, putting up little fight.

Wayne grabbed the extra rope he'd thrown to the dock and made quick work of tying it around the alligator's snout.

Witcher hooted and hollered, keeping the camera focused on the action.

Wayne made a show of making sure the rope was tight, although it wasn't at all snug around the snout. He covertly scratched the alligator's belly in thanks, but when the girl's wings started to come up, Wayne quickly pinned them back to her sides by wrapping his arms around her. Then he sat up, straddling the beast.

"Can you believe this?" Witcher turned the camera on himself. "That there's Wranglin' Wayne of Wayne's Gators!"

Wayne took the beast by the tail and dragged her onto White Falcon. He hoped Witcher hadn't seen how the alligator pushed off the dock, helping Wayne maneuver her weight with ease.

"Wait right there, I've got my shotgun," Witcher offered.

"No, no," Wayne said, putting up a hand. "I'm a strictly no-kill business. I catch 'em, then I release 'em out in protected swampland where they belong. This big girl won't bother you anymore."

"Suit yourself," Witcher said, walking up the dock to bring Wayne his phone. "No wonder business is so hard on ya. You're the only no-kill gator grabber I've ever met. Bobby sure ain't no no-kill business."

"No," Wayne's face sobered. "He sure isn't. But I'm looking to do things the right way, Mr. Witcher."

"Well, *merci beaucoup*, son. I didn't know if you could do it, just a young blood like you. Sure surprised me! You can be sure I'll be givin' you a call from now on."

"Thank you, Mr. Witcher, for taking a chance on me." Wayne smiled, then looked down at his phone.

"You should post that video. People'll eat that up."

Wayne squinted at the burly man. "You wouldn't happen to have Wi-Fi out here—"

Witcher grunted. "Well, sure I do, son. Hell, this *is* 'Merica."

Wayne's smile grew. He uploaded the video while Witcher gawked over the alligator in the boat.

"If I ain't seen a stranger gator," Witcher said.

Wayne came over to the side of the boat and leaned on it. He pulled out the talon Witcher had given him earlier that day and handed it back.

The man took it in his hairy, weathered hands, then held the claw arm's-length from the alligator's foot. "Well, I'll be. That's her alright. I just can't believe this little girl was the one spookin' my Princess." Witcher looked up and surveyed his yard. "Wherever she is."

Wayne clapped his shoulder. "You won't have to worry about that anymore. Princess'll be safe from now on."

Witcher reached into his overall pocket and pulled out two one-hundred-dollar bills. "You earned it, kid."

The men said farewell, and Wayne boarded *White Falcon* and headed east.

Once they were out of view, Wayne slowed and untied the alligator's snout. He rubbed the beast's sides, and she thumped her tail with pleasure.

It took them three hours to get to Wayne's stilt house in Cocodrie. He drove the boat into his boathouse, tied it up, then led the alligator out of the boat.

"This is your new home, girl," he said, rubbing her chin. "And I bet you're hungry. I'll feed you, and I'll let you stay here, but no more terrorizing, you hear? No trying to make friends with the neighbors' dogs."

Wayne went inside and grabbed a raw steak from the refrigerator for the alligator and a beer for himself.

The sun set in gradient oranges and blues while the alligator tore the steak to shreds and Wayne sipped his beer.

Wayne fished his phone out of his pocket. He looked at the screen and rubbed his eyes. Seven missed calls. Seven new voice mails.

As he listened to each message, all asking after his wrangling services, Wayne rubbed the alligator's ridged back.

"Well, girl, looks like we were bound to turn each other's luck around."

The alligator extended her wings, mouth open, looking full and satisfied.

Wayne looked to his boat, his treasured possession, and eyed the deep gashes. "Maybe it don't mean much about a man at all," he murmured, taking another swig of his beer with one hand and patting his alligator with the other.

O O O

Kristin Luna has been making up stories and getting in trouble for them since elementary school. She especially loves young adult literature, fantasy, Nic Cage, literary fiction, and wouldn't even be opposed to reading yeti erotica. She has written book reviews for *Urban Fantasy Magazine*, writes for the blog *The Fictorians*, and her short stories have appeared on Pseudopod and in other anthologies published by WordFire Press. She lives in San Diego with her husband, Nic, and eats way too much Taco Bell.

Lullaby

John D. Payne

As plaintive cries from the nursery chamber intruded on my unconscious bliss of slumber, I curled up in a ball, wrapped my wings more tightly around myself, and squeezed my eyes shut. "Go back to sleep," I whispered to myself. And to the children.

No good. Their voices kept rising, both in pitch and in volume, until the shrieks stabbed their way into my skull and banished sleep completely. Maybe permanently. With a heavy sigh, I gathered the strength to heave myself up and out of bed.

"Sweetheart," Sam asked, "why do you do this to yourself?" He had the uncanny ability to jump from deep sleep to coherent conversation in an instant. It was perhaps the second-worst thing about him.

"Unngggh," I replied. *Well put. You truly are a gifted communicator. A real wordsmith.*

"Just let them cry," Sam said. In the darkness, I could hear him shifting his weight to prop himself up, accompanied by the ringing, watery tinkle of precious metals and jewels being displaced by his movements. At the sound, the cries from the children grew louder. More heart-wrenching. More insistent.

"I'm coming, I'm coming," I grumbled. I regretted the words as soon as they were out of my mouth. Poor things. They didn't mean to wake me. They didn't know, couldn't know. They were so small, so helpless.

"It won't kill them to wait," Sam said.

I could sense him lying close to me in the darkness. His recumbent form was the one source of warmth in the otherwise frigid sleeping chamber.

"It might kill me." It ought to get easier to ignore their crying when I was so tired. But if anything, exhaustion made it worse. At this point, as sleep deprived as I was, it was a special kind of torture. It must have been, or I never would have considered getting out of my warm bed and onto the cold floor.

Our chambers should have been warm since they were built into the side of a fire mount that still had a few active lava tubes. But we had given the warmest room to the children. It was the right decision, but it meant that my floors were always cold. Which annoyed me.

I stoked this spark of annoyance until the flames in my belly grew bright and hot. Then I opened my mouth and uncorked a spray of fire on the floor until the stones gave off a dull, red glow. There. Much better. I got out of bed and put my feet down, enjoying the warmth.

Sam shook his head. "We've talked about this. Every time we get up—"

"Every time *I* get up."

"Hey, now. You know that's not fair."

My head whipped around, and in an instant I was facing him on all fours, wings spread and tail lashing from side to side. In the faint but growing glow, the light tinged an angry red by its journey outward through my flesh and my scales, I could see him lift his forelimbs in surrender.

"Fine." He rolled his eyes. "Every time *you* get up—"

"Thank you," I murmured, my belly fires slowly cooling.

"—it reinforces the pattern. Behavior rewarded is behavior repeated." He took a deep breath. "I'm sorry, sweetheart, but there's only one way out of this cycle, and at some point we're going to have to grit our teeth and do it."

I considered that for a moment, but renewed cries from the next chamber interrupted my train of thought.

"At some point, fine. But not now."

"If that's your decision," he said, "then I'll go. It's my turn." He heaved himself upright, which set off a new cascade of gems and precious metals.

I reached over and gave him a pat. "No, I will."

He hesitated.

"Stay," I said. "I mean it. Go back to sleep."

"Well, that's hardly fair to you."

"If you go, I'll lie awake anyway. One of us might as well get some rest."

He chewed on that for a moment, then said, "Okay. But I take the next shift." Then he rolled over and was instantly asleep.

Which is the very, very worst thing about him.

I checked the larder but found nothing that would soothe the brood. So instead of going straight to the nursery, I popped outside to scoop up a few morsels. All the while, I cursed the past version of myself from the last time they'd woken up.

"You could have set something aside for next time," I muttered, feeling more than a little hungry myself. "But no, you wanted to go back to bed. Lazy cow. Think of someone else for a change." My future self nodded in approval, taking my side. But my past self didn't even bother to respond. She just slept.

Flying through the nearby valleys as quickly as possible, I tried to focus on the task at hand and not get distracted by the scenery. The children were still hungry and crying, after all. But I couldn't help noticing that our pest problem was back.

Humans, it looked like. Or maybe elves. Either way, it was quite a big colony from the look of things. It seemed like Sam had just cleared out the dratted things, but of course you never really got rid of them permanently. Like a persistent rash or a chronic cough, the infestation just kept recurring.

I made a mental note to mention it to Sam when I went back to bed. He would handle it; he always did. And came back covered with scratches and bites all over, every time. Poor dear. He was so cute when he complained about his little wounds. Thinking of him brought an involuntary smile to my face and a warmth to my belly.

He really was very sweet, I thought, turning a dreamy and languorous spiral in the air. A good provider, a doting father, a fierce protector. A fine mate. And nearly my size. Well, at least three-quarters my size. Very respectable, for a male.

The warm summer breeze felt good in my wings, and I felt lighter and lither than I had in ages. Part of me yearned to climb and soar and ride the winds until I became one with them, floating like a cinder in the smoke.

But the children needed feeding. So I swooped back home, limbs and jaws laden with delectable nibblets.

Sam was absent from our sleeping chamber, but I found him in the nursery. From the look of things, he had tried in vain to appease the children with the meager scraps he had scrounged from the larder and now was attempting to pull rank on them, silly thing.

"I am Shamel-Shesha, the Enduring One," he cried, sounding more desperate than commanding, "I rule all things from the molten core beneath to the empty void above. Please stop biting me!"

Suppressing a smile, I rushed to Sam's aid. Murmuring to the children in my most soothing tone, I pulled each of the little dears off their father, which in most cases elicited a shriek from both parties.

The babies were, by and large, easy to mollify. They didn't have long memories. Pop something sweet in their mouths, and they would latch right on and forget why they had been crying in the first place.

Sam was somewhat more difficult to appease. Instead of going back to bed, he stood there rubbing his wounds and heaving pained sighs. The faint light coming up from the lava tubes left much of his face in shadow, but it wasn't hard to see that he was upset.

I wanted to go to him, to take him in my arms—or at least run my claws along his dorsal spines the way he liked. But I was lying on the floor of the nursery, encircling the brood with my body and tail and cuddling them close with one wing. They had stopped crying, but if I put them down, we'd be right back where we'd started in a heartbeat.

So I gave Sam what I hoped was a sympathetic smile. "I'm sorry, dear. They really got you good this time, didn't they?"

"Yeah." He sucked in his breath as he craned his neck to examine a particularly nasty-looking bite under his left forelimb. "Those little teeth. So very sharp."

"Well, they're at a curious age," I said. "Maybe they just want to know what Daddy tastes like."

With my attention on Sam, one of the little ones decided to make a break for it and attempted to wriggle free. I quickly swept her back with my free wing, which she bit.

"Mommy, too, apparently," he said.

"Apparently." I pried the scamp loose and plugged her little mouth with half a cow's head that one of the others had dropped. Soon, she was happily—and noisily—enjoying her treat and seemed to have no more interest in escaping. "It's a phase. They're less than a century old. They'll grow out of it."

"Yeah."

For a while the only sound was the slurping and smacking and crunching of the children feeding. Very messy, of course, but also very cute.

I looked up to see Sam still standing there, watching me.

"I ..." He hesitated, then threw his forelimbs up in the air. "I thought you were going to feed them."

With my free wing, I gestured expansively at myself and the children, a mute answer to his accusation.

"Yeah, now you are. But I thought you were going to feed them right then. And instead, you went I don't even know where, while they just got hungrier and madder and louder. So there I am, lying there, listening to this and wondering what in the name of Alala is going on because you told me to go back to sleep because you were going to handle it. If you wanted me to take a turn, you could have just said so. I offered, if you remember."

He shot me an accusing glare.

I glared back. "We didn't have anything to feed them. I stepped out for literally less than two weeks to grab them something to eat."

"Two weeks is a really long time for them. And they don't like waiting."

"What should I have done instead?"

"You could have said something. Let me know. I would have been happy to go in and entertain them while you were out."

"Evidently not, since that's what you did and you aren't happy."

He flexed his claws in frustration and exhaled a stream of bright orange flame.

I shook my head, searching for the words that would help Sam see how ridiculous he was being. But before I could unleash the stinging rebuke I was carefully constructing, I noticed the children had grown noisy again.

Looking down, I realized that in my irritation I had unconsciously let my belly fires grow hot, and it was making the brood restless. Some of them were trying to climb out of the protective ring I had made with my body, others cried plaintively, and one seemed intent on chewing my wing to shreds. The whole point of coming in here was to soothe them, and instead we were stirring them up with our argument.

"Sweetheart," Sam began, sounding very, very tired.

"One moment, please," I said.

With some effort, I tried to calm myself and cool my temper down from a boil to a simmer. As the scales on my abdomen grew less scalding, the children once again let me draw them in close. Feeling them wriggling happily in my limbs, snuggling up tight, it was easy to let go of the anger.

Sam stepped closer, his neck and head hanging low and his wings dragging on the rough stone floor of the chamber in mute apology. Looking abashed, he leaned down and placed a kiss on my forehead.

"Forget I said anything," he said. "Stupid of me to pick a fight."

I lifted my head to rub the dorsal spines slowly against the sensitive skin under his chin, eliciting an involuntary shudder of pleasure and a low rumble of satisfaction. "Don't give it another thought," I said. "We're both exhausted. That always has us at each other's throats."

"True." After a pause, he nipped at my neck playfully.

I smiled. "Go back to bed, dear. I'll get the children to sleep."

He hesitated, looking as if he were about to say something, then nodded and left.

"All right," I said to the children. "Who's still hungry?"

They all were, of course. I did my best to distribute the livestock equally so that everyone got a nice, full tummy, but some of the brood were more aggressive and got more than their share.

In scarcely more than a few days, all the food was gone. Most of the brood were stuffed up nice and plump, their eyes heavy and their limbs limp and languid. They hardly stirred as I lowered them back down into an inactive lava tube to sleep. They curled up in a heap, one on top of one another, sharing their warmth as their bodies struggled to digest the massive feast.

Soon, there was just one left, the littlest. Having fed poorly, she fussed and cried and would not be contented.

"Now, now," I said, stroking her as she writhed in my limbs. "You're just fine. No need to cry. Everything will be just fine."

A pang of guilt struck me as I uttered the words because in truth, I was worried about her. We both were. Sam had said she wouldn't last long enough to get her wings. I hadn't said as much out loud, but I couldn't help but share his opinion.

That's why I had already given her a name. Belinda. Bright One. She was less than half the size of her brothers and sisters, but her eyes were sharp and attentive. More than any of the others, she made me wonder how much she understood.

"I know you want more," I said, lifting her up to my face, "but there is nothing left for you."

She stopped crying for a moment and leveled a gaze at me that was nothing short of an unspoken accusation.

"I'm sorry. Next time I'll bring more. And I'll make sure you get your share."

Screwing up her little face, Belinda wailed in a voice that was louder than I could have believed from such a tiny creature. I held her close and jiggled her up and down lest her cries wake Sam or the rest of the brood.

"Hush now. Hush."

After what seemed like years but was certainly no more than a week, Belinda finally quieted down. But she wasn't sleeping peacefully in my arms, her face wore a look of such terrible betrayal that it absolutely broke my heart.

"All right, all right. We'll go grab something."

Holding tiny Belinda close to my heart, I went outside to see about something to eat. I couldn't see anything right away, which was irritating because all I really wanted to do was get this little one fed so I could go back to sleep. Nursing my irritation into a flame, I burned back the vegetation creeping up the sides of our mountain and immediately spotted a crispy herd of blackened deer.

"Mmm!" I murmured to the bundle of wiggles in my forelimbs. "Roasty-toasty treats. Let's give them a try, shall we?"

Belinda tried the deer and loved them. But despite her evident pleasure and my own impatient coaxing, she seemed determined to take her sweet time eating them. Not wanting to waste the time, I looked around to see if there was anything else that needed doing while I was outside.

My gaze was drawn once again to one of the pest colonies, just outside the circle of burned-back vegetation and apparently completely unscathed. Annoying, but easy to fix.

I blew an experimental jet of flame at the nest, but it was made of stone and didn't combust well, so all I really did was stir things up. A whole host of the nasty critters came boiling out of every crack and crevice, many of them headed straight for me.

"Oh, no, you don't." I put my foot down and squashed several of the ugly things flat. "No itchy bites or scratches for me, thank you."

It made little impression on them, so after a few more desultory stomps, I decided to let Sam handle it once he was up. Suppressing a yawn, I scooped up Belinda along with the rest of the charred herd of deer and headed back inside.

She was asleep before we got back to the nursery. Asleep and adorable. A delicate little baby snore whispered out of her slightly parted mouth. Her long tail drooped, the tip occasionally twitching. And somehow the most adorable thing of all was her grotesquely swollen belly—her skin stretched, her scales straining to contain a meal that probably doubled her mass.

"Aw. You finally got a good meal, didn't you?" I stroked her little nose, and the ghost of a smile flitted across her face. "That's all you needed. Just a tummy full of yummy food, and now we can all have a good rest."

I stooped to lay her down amid her siblings, and she instantly awoke, crying lustily.

Of course.

I sank down to the floor of the nursery chamber. Maybe it was the sleep deprivation, but I felt like having a bit of a cry myself. I'd been up for weeks now—maybe months. It had been nearly a century since I'd had a decent sleep. Why had I sent Sam back to bed?

"All right," I told Belinda, jiggling her up and down. "You're as tired as I am. So why are you still awake? What's wrong? You're not sick. Do you want something? It can't be food. We already took care of that."

She slapped petulantly at me and hissed.

"What are you mad at me for? I'm trying to help here. If I knew what you wanted, I'd give it to you. Believe me. There's nothing I'd like more. If I only knew what was going on in that little head of yours."

She whined and struggled, shaking her head rapidly back and forth like she had a sheep in her mouth and was trying to break its neck.

I laughed. "Or is there nothing going on at all? I mean, you're not even a century old yet. There are humans that live that long, I think, and they're certainly not intelligent." I sighed. "Maybe you're so young you can't really comprehend your own self. You don't know if you're hungry or thirsty or sleepy or hurt. You're just unhappy, so you cry. That's all there is to it."

As if on cue, she started crying again. I got up and walked around with her, which seemed to help.

"Here I am, one who has ascended beyond the realm of the clouds to touch the Boundless and hear the music of the stars, and what defeats me? An unhappy child."

Wait.

The music of the stars?

"Do you want to hear a song?"

Instantly she quieted, her bright eyes wide and looking right at me.

"I guess you do."

And so I sang.

At first it was wordless. But at some point, I'm not even sure when, words came. I sang about a little baby named Belinda, and her mother and father who loved her. I sang about brothers and sisters, sleeping cozy and warm all together. I sang about the safety and strength of the mountain all around us.

And then I sang about the humans. I don't know why. It was stupid. They were pests. I probably still had some of them stuck to the bottom of my feet. But holding this little one, this youngling, I couldn't help but think about other tiny creatures, whose lives were measured by the spastic flickering of day and night instead of the graceful, steady cycles of sunspots.

I sang about a baby human, and the mother who held her and rocked her in their own little home of stone. I sang about the baby being tucked in with all the other children, resting warm and safe and quiet.

For whatever reason, it did the trick. She stopped fussing, closed her eyes, and slept. She never stirred, even when I put her down in the lava tube with her siblings and one of them rolled right on top of her.

Thank goodness for small miracles.

I made my way back to bed. It felt indescribably wonderful to be off my feet and lying down. There was a pleasant clinking as the piles of precious stones and metals shifted to accommodate me. Sam stirred.

"How'd it go?"

"They're down, all of them. Hopefully that's the last disturbance."

He grunted. "Well, whether they sleep a long time or not, I've got next."

"All yours."

He leaned over and kissed me.

"Is there something for them to eat?"

"Yes." I yawned. "Nearly a whole herd of deer."

"Good. Anything else I should know about?"

"No, nothing." I turned over, wrapping my wings around myself. "Oh, except for … Have you seen the human colonies out there?"

"Humans? Looked like elves to me."

"Whichever."

"Already on my list. I'll get rid of them first thing."

"Actually, I was thinking maybe we could leave them there. Just for a while."

"You want me to—?" He cut himself off and blew out a long breath. Then he shrugged. "Whatever you say, dear. Sweet dreams."

"Sweet dreams."

He, of course, was snoring almost instantly. It really was unfair. Especially since I was wide awake, despite the peace and quiet that reigned in our chambers once more.

My mind kept going back to our pest infestation. What would it really be like to live a life so brief? To feel yourself dying from the very moment you were born? Even if they were intelligent, how could they possibly care about each other, about their young, the way we did? Such a creature simply didn't have the time to invest in the raising of a child, especially given how fragile they were.

Yet I couldn't help but think of that human mother from my song, rocking her own little babe to sleep. The image haunted me, no matter how I told myself that it was only a lullaby made up on the spot to calm a restless child.

Now it was my turn to be restless, my poor, exhausted mind seizing upon disturbing impossibilities. I rolled over and thought about waking Sam for a moment, but then told myself not to be silly.

"Settle down. Go to sleep."

I closed my eyes and listened to Sam's slow and steady breathing. After an increasingly fuzzy eternity, I felt myself drifting off at last. As sweet slumber came to claim me, two last thoughts crept in behind my dreams.

If humans really could sing songs to their young, what would they sound like? And if they could tell tales, what would they say—about us?

O O O

John D. Payne lives under several feet of water in the flooded-out ruin once known as Houston, Texas. He is currently undergoing nanobot-assisted gene therapy to develop gills so he can keep up with his alluring mermaid wife and their two soggy little boys. His hobbies include swimming, sailing, diving for treasure, and fending off pirates.

John's debut novel, *The Crown and the Dragon*, was published by WordFire Press in 2013. His stories can also be found in magazines and anthologies, including *Leading Edge, Tides of Impossibility: A Fantasy Anthology from the Houston Writers Guild,* and *A Game of Horns: A Red Unicorn Anthology*.

For news and updates, follow John D. Payne on Twitter (@jdp_writes) or read his blog at johndpayne.com.

Eat Your Heart Out

Joy Dawn Johnson

It had been three months, seven days, two hours, and thirty-one minutes since the last time Aria had killed. She was ravenous.

And, oh, Conner had never tasted as good as he did tonight. Aria licked her lips from their kiss. "I could just eat you right up."

Conner chuckled. "If you're hungry, I can make breakfast. I know you love to eat."

He had no idea.

Well, maybe he did. She'd spent enough time raiding his fridge. Any normal girl would have been embarrassed. He'd never said a word to her about the dinner-for-four she wolfed down six times a day. If anything, he encouraged her to eat more. Clothes that had fit her curves when they'd met now hung from her bones. Eating regular food had dulled her hunger for a time, but it wasn't working anymore.

Some people ate in bed. Aria ate whomever she bedded. What else was a half-succubus to do?

Apparently, starve—thanks to a little thing called love.

A hunger pain shot through her stomach, and she winced as she grabbed her coat. "I've gotta go." She managed a smile for him.

No man had brought out her human side before, but Conner made her care about killing, and worst of all, care about him. Now he was withering away in front of her eyes, and there wasn't a damn thing she could do about it except leave him, which was the last thing she wanted to do.

Conner used to have a spark in his eye, a great belly laugh, all the good stuff. His broad shoulders and nice bum had drawn her to him in the first place. Then he went and ruined it all by being the first male she'd spent more than two hours with and didn't want to bite his head off. Not that that was how she fed. Her way was much more … bed-rocking pleasurable.

"Sure you have to leave?" he asked. His voice was so hoarse it pained her.

Her stomach growled. Not a dainty sound, but a mighty rumble loud enough to disturb Conner's geriatric neighbors.

Conner tucked a strand of hair behind her ear. "Stay for breakfast."

This was the third time she'd been with him all night without doing anything more than talk. They both wanted more; she just didn't know which part of her was hungrier.

Aria hugged him, feeling him slump against her from exhaustion. Every time they kissed, she took a little more of his essence. He didn't know what was happening, neither did his doctors. It's not like she could tell him, "Don't worry, I'm only sucking out your life force, but I'm doing my best not to kill you—really."

She should just get it over with and finish him off. She needed to do something soon, or he'd be dead anyway. Her stomach rumbled again, reminding her that if she didn't feed, she may as well dig two graves.

"You have to take care of yourself," he said, looking at her with hollow eyes.

Here he was wasting away, and yet he was more worried about her. At times like these, Aria thought he might truly love her, but she was sure that the only way someone like him would be into someone like her was because of her succubus half. The part of her that killed anyone she bedded. To save everyone time, she'd always made it a point to be the easiest girl on the block. It wasn't nice to play with your food.

Conner turned from her, and she took a step forward, ready to take him, to end his pain, though everything inside screamed for her to stop.

"I have something for you," he said as he picked up a box from the table. Carved across the top was a field of marigolds. "It took me a few weeks to finish the details."

She knew it was because his hands shook.

Aria balled her fists, looking at the handmade chest, knowing he suffered because of her.

He opened it to reveal an inlaid mirror in the lid and a small pile of dried flowers. "I picked these from the spot we first met."

"Why do you have to go and be so sweet? Now there's no way I can kill you."

"Kill me?"

Well, crap. "Look into my eyes." He could never resist the succubus half of her. "I said, 'Now I want to kiss you.'"

"Kiss. Yes. I want to …" He cupped her cheek.

She took his hand. She couldn't keep hurting him, and being a succubus, she would do just that. Aria took a step back, then another. "I can't." He already looked so weak.

The look of rejection on his face was almost more than she could take.

"I'm sorry."

"Don't do this again." He reached for her.

She thought about the other times she'd tried to push him away—or eat him, depending on the night.

"I know you feel for me. If you don't like the gift—"

"It's wonderful. You're wonderful." Even a few more days with her could kill him. "You're mine."

"I'm yours."

"I have to figure something out." She released him from her power. He slumped over, and she caught his shoulders just in time to keep his drained body from collapsing to the floor.

As she walked down the front steps, Aria opened the lid of Connor's gift and looked into the mirror. Being a succubus, every time she saw her reflection, it appeared different. So goes the phrase, "Beauty is in the eye of the beholder."

She'd liked who she was for centuries, but being what she was, she'd lose her love.

Aria had to go see the matchmaker.

* * *

Naga's shop had a flavor of the month. Right now it seemed to go for the cheap, tchotchke vendor vibe. Aria looked around the shop and rolled her eyes at a pair of booty shorts that said "Broom Rider." Her stomach growled again. She had to think of something, or fueled by her desire to feed, men would begin to stream into this shop, and between the extendable flyswatters to the "Bite Me" shark collectible frames, the store was already overcrowded.

Aria ducked under the blow-up zombies wearing cheap, glitter-tastic sunglasses and leaned over the counter to find a new clerk—of delicious linebacker proportions—on hands and knees, head deep inside a box, pulling out fuzzy coffee mugs. Aria groaned. She was tired of giving Naga the "stop eating the help" speech.

"I'm here to see the matchmaker," Aria said in her most soothing voice. No sense playing around. Just a few words to any male, and they were hers.

The clerk extended a hand and pointed in what seemed to be a random direction. "Matches are over there."

Aria peered over the counter and frowned. The clerk had spoken in a higher voice than she'd expected, given the stocky build.

"Not matches. I'm here to see Lady Naga."

"No dragons here." The girl popped her head out. "Thank you, come again."

Aria leaned in to read "Julie" scripted in a nearly unreadable font on her lapel. A female behind the counter was about as helpful to Aria as a fruit basket to a vampire.

"How do you know Naga's part dragon?"

"Damn."

Classy. "Trust me, if anyone's stepping through that door, it'll be to see Naga."

"She's going to kill me," Julie said as she pointed at the rear door.

Aria wasn't going to tell her how right she probably was.

The back room had been decorated Naga-style.

Matchmaking meme posters covered the walls with sayings like, "SEX: If it doesn't look like a demon is being exorcised, you're doing it wrong." Tiki torches set the mood, and a plastic red-and-white tablecloth draped across her favorite seventeenth-century oak table. Leave it to a thousand-year-old half-dragon to miss this decade's—this *century's*—fashion sense.

Naga sat in an oversized, leopard-print beanbag chair, buffing her claws. She always wore a cutoff shirt that exposed abs that any girl would kill for—metaphorically, of course. Today's crop-top said "Eat Your Heart Out" with a picture of a real heart replacing the word. Naga's toned abs changed into green and yellow scales in the way a skilled graffiti artist got the blending just right. Though her eyes and hair looked nearly black in the flickering light, her scales still held their usual iridescent shine. She'd coined the phrase, "Business up top, party animal on the bottom," but it got mixed up in translation through the years. She and Aria had hit it off right away, both being half woman, half supernatural killer and all. Bonding over body counts.

The dragon raised a finely tweezed eyebrow at Aria. "Just can't get good help these days."

"What's the deal with the shark frames? Last time I checked, there's never been sharks in Minnesota."

"I'd originally asked for rubber dragons because *you know.*" She glanced at her tail moving restlessly around the bag, as though it had a mind of its own. "The sharks were five for one. How could I resist? I'd be losing money if I didn't get them."

"Tell me again why you opened your store in the largest mall this side of the world when you don't actually sell anything anyone wants to buy."

"No one makes a cinnamon bun like this food court. Two for one on Fridays. Who doesn't like a good pair of buns?"

Aria's stomach cramped at the thought of food. She sat on the open beanbag and told Naga the situation. "I can't keep being who I am and be with him."

"I've known you for over five hundred years," said Naga. "You've always loved who you are. Why now?"

"I have all these *feelings.*"

Naga shuddered.

"I know, right? But I feel so much for him." Even saying it made her warm, so different from anything she'd ever known.

"Let me get this straight. You love his man buns, and you're considering turning away from your sexy dark side for some mortal?" Naga burped a fireball, then cleared her throat. "Pardon me. Had a Mexican for breakfast."

"From the food court? Didn't know they served breakfast." Then the stench of charred flesh hit her nose.

"Speaking of meals, have you tried using ranch on your mortal? It goes with everything."

"What kind of matchmaker encourages eating mates?"

The dragon flicked her tail. "The smart kind."

Aria's stomach growled, as though to compete with Naga's indigestion.

"So what, you want me to make you forget him? Make him fall in love with someone else?"

"No. I want to become full human or a full succubus. You can make it happen."

Naga stopped filing her nails and busted out with a flaming belly cackle that left the tablecloth smoking. "Oh." She blinked. "You're serious."

"I love him." He made her laugh every time he told a corny joke. She giggled just thinking about it. *Giggled!* Humans giggled. Elves giggled. Succubi *ate* gigglers.

"You have to love yourself before you can truly love another."

"I do love who I am."

"And yet you want to change for him." She set down the nail file. "Love's tricky. Especially for you. Being part succubus and all, he's probably completely under your spell. If that's the case and I fully brought out your human half, you'd lose him anyway."

A heavy weight pressed in Aria's chest. She tried to take in a breath, reminding herself that this was the only way. She'd tried before to leave Conner. "You didn't answer my question. Can you destroy half of who I am?"

"No."

Aria felt like she was sinking and any moment, she'd be swallowed by the beanbag chair. Right about now, that would be welcomed.

Naga leaned over and pulled a single sheet of paper from her matchmaking kit. She curled her dragon's tail across the table so Aria couldn't see, then began writing. "I don't work that kind of magic." Naga folded the paper and handed it to Aria. "Only positive magic. I can't destroy a part of you without destroying all of who you are. But I can create a new version."

"I wouldn't be me anymore?"

"You would be, in a way. How much are you willing to give up for a mortal? It is your choice. Choose him, and your everlasting youth and supernatural allure would be gone. Choose your supernatural nature and become the strongest living succubus."

With her eyes, Aria followed the red-and-white check of the tablecloth until it ended in scorch marks. "If I stay with him any longer, I'll kill him." *Or starve.*

Naga studied her for a long moment. "Question is, will you like the 'you' that you become?"

* * *

Aria may as well have been in line for Hell itself. Standing there made her wish succubi were known for wearing cloaks so she could hide her face. Just the smell of the place lowered her sex drive, something she'd thought impossible.

"So what will it be?"

Aria groaned and said, "Two orders of your original."

"So, like, do you mean two buns or four? Two for one."

Aria snarled. "Four cinnamon buns."

The clerk was lucky Aria only went for men or else she'd be putting this one out of her misery. The blonde was much too old to be using the word "like." The woman whirled on her heel to get the order started. If Aria chose human, she'd be the one sporting crow's feet in a few years. All without the perk of bending half the population to her will.

The clerk unhooked the metal tongs. "So I was talking to my boyfriend, and he was like, 'You're great and all, but you're trying to change me.' So he bolted."

Aria was about to ask if she was talking to her when another perky, middle-aged woman popped up from behind the counter holding several stacks of cups. "Were you?"

Did these people multiply or something?

"I mean, I did ask him to not eat his steak like a corn dog," the first clerk said as she pulled out the second bun, making Aria wish she'd only ordered two for Naga.

The dragon had sent her on this delightful errand to give her time to prep for the ceremony and decide what she wanted. Though the folded paper Naga had given her was small, it weighed at her hip. Aria wanted to know what it said, but Naga warned her to not read it until she was ready.

As she watched the women, she knew she should keep her mouth zipped, but that wasn't happening. Before Conner, humans had been little more than sexy blood bags, but now, she actually gave a damn. "Love is a good reason to compromise. Would you be willing to change yourself for him?"

The clerk shrugged. "Like, I don't know."

"What do you mean you don't know? You want him to change but you're not willing to change?"

"Like, what do I need to change?"

"Are you kidding me? You're forty years old, and you talk like there's a Malibu Barbie stuck up your butt. Now you listen to me. Love is a two-way street. We all shave parts of ourselves off in order to make relationships work. It only becomes an issue when you forget who you really are." Aria stopped, panting. She looked around. Everyone stared at her as if she'd gone crazy.

The clerk finished bagging her cinnamon rolls. "This isn't, like, really about me and my ex anymore, is it?"

"No." Aria slumped, suddenly exhausted. Here she was giving relationship advice when she was trying to choose between killing her boyfriend or part of herself.

Aria pictured Conner making that face when she lost her succubi hold on him. She tried to push the image from her mind. How much was she willing to give up for something that wasn't even guaranteed?

Aria's stomach growled, and both women gave her a "Did that seriously come from you?" sort of look.

"You sure you don't want another helping?" the second clerk asked.

Aria was about to snarl at her when she realized the question had been innocent. Not something she ever would have noticed before meeting Conner. It wasn't like she could tell the girl that all she needed was sex, aka kill the lucky guy. As the queen of one-night stands—considering no one lived until morning—the concept of cheating had never exactly crossed her mind before.

Aria left with buns in her hand and paper in her pocket. She detoured down the long hallway where the restrooms were—because apparently everyone needed to walk an extra half mile when they needed to go—and stopped at the drinking fountain. Cool water wet her tongue but did nothing for her thirst.

The men's restroom door swung open, and she doubled over. She tried to keep her hunger suppressed but knew she'd failed when she heard the moan.

She turned to face an absolutely delectable twenty-something-year-old. He had the kind of build that would have made any girl swoon, not just the wham-bam-kill-'em-ma'am kind.

He slapped a hand against the wall. "You smell good." He jerked his arm away and shook his head. "I'm so sorry. I don't know what came over me."

For a moment, she leaned in to take the guy. She'd be doing him for Conner, really.

"What the hell?" He gasped as his arm went around her waist.

Aria stepped away, feeling his reluctance, tired of being little more than a predator.

Tears streamed down his cheeks. "I don't know what's happening. I just got married."

"It's called pheromones, and I can't seem to turn them off right now." She tried to pull away but couldn't in her weakened state. Changing tactics, she switched to her most soothing voice. "You don't want to do this."

"You're right," he said, still pulling her to him. "I don't want to do this."

Another man walked out from the restroom. The moment he saw the struggle, he said "Is he bothering—" but his words slurred as he focused on her.

"Oh, hell." She dodged the first guy's kiss and slapped the bag of buns over his head, propelling him right into the second guy. She took off down the hallway, praying she'd be fast enough in her condition.

Knowing she couldn't keep living like this, Aria was ready to read the paper. She pulled it from her pocket, rolled her eyes, and headed back to the dragon.

* * *

"What happened to Julie?" Aria asked.

"I needed some protein with my cinnamon buns," Naga said.

"Too bad. I kind of liked her."

"Me too." The dragon's scales rustled along her tail as she picked her teeth with the point of her tail. "She wasn't too salty."

"Your buns." She handed them over. They'd been smashed.

"Ran into trouble?"

"Nothing I couldn't handle."

"This is the biggest change in your life, and yet these buns are still warm."

"Meaning?"

"You didn't even think it over long enough for them to go cold." The dragon held up a finger, coughed, then burped out Julie's name tag. "Wondered where that had gone. Don't know why I bother printing them out anymore."

Aria studied the tag and thought about all the nameless, faceless men she'd killed. There was only one she wanted in her life. Existing without him wasn't an option, but it was more than that.

"I need to change." She held her stomach, which was tearing itself apart.

Naga pulled off the half-burnt tablecloth. "If you're changing because *you* want to change instead of changing for someone else, then let's make this happen."

Aria unfolded the paper. "Exactly what am I supposed to do with this?"

The dragon had written two words, "Him" in purple and "Me" in red. Interesting since Naga had used a black pen.

"Circle which you choose."

"What is this, grade school?" Aria picked up the pen, about to make her choice, and stopped. Both choices could have several interpretations. "Are you trying to trick me?"

Naga smiled. "Of course."

* * *

Aria woke with a splitting headache. Like half a dozen club-wielding giants had used her head for target practice. Was this what it felt like to be, well, whatever she'd become?

Eh, she'd had worse. Eating a trio of drunk sailors would do that to you.

But that was all behind her.

She was still hungry, but was that thanks to wanting man buns or the cinnamon kind?

She'd made her choice. It was Conner. It had always been him.

But dragon writers were tricky.

Her heart raced as she held up the box Conner had crafted. His skilled hands had etched every groove just for her. Unsure of what she had become or if she'd like what she saw, she held the edge with her thumb, but it was like the box had been glued shut.

He'd be there any moment. Would she kiss him or kill him?

One deep breath. The hinges made a small creaking noise as the top lifted.

"Oh, good God." Her fingers shook, and she nearly dropped the precious box. "I'm *me*."

For the first time, she wanted to meet him for breakfast, not have him for it. Relief flooded through her but turned icy at the knock at the door. She loved herself, but that didn't mean Conner would feel the same.

Hand on the knob, she realized that after opening the box, a door didn't seem as hard.

She put on her best smile and swung it open. "Hey, you."

O O O

Joy Dawn Johnson has a BFA, an MBA, and ghostwrites for a *USA Today* bestselling author. She is a member of the Society of Children's Book Writers and Illustrators and was the 2015 recipient of the Superstars Writing scholarship funded by the *One Horn to Rule Them All* anthology.

Visit Joy at joydawnjohnson.com.

WHICH WAY TO THE DRAGON?

Michael Angel

Schnitzengruben, Bavaria

AD 635
Tuesday

The herd of sheep grazing in the pasture didn't stand a chance. Quietly, the dragon approached from upwind, the better to hide her stink of sulfur and brimstone. Her outstretched wingtips brushed the edges of the twin peaks that overlooked the valley. She descended with the breeze, silent as a ghost-feathered owl. It was only when the sheep heard the final beat of her wings that they bleated in terror, scattering in all directions like a spilled pile of soap flakes.

The dragon drove her talons downward in a scooping motion. She caught a single fat ewe by its woolly haunches and carried the animal off. She headed for the cleft between the peaks to consume her lunch at leisure. Now, had anyone of an appreciative mind been watching, they'd have declared the dragon a singularly beautiful animal. Long and sinuous like a great golden-red snake, spiked at the ends with claws and teeth.

Unfortunately, no appreciative mind was available as a witness.

The shepherds angrily waved their crooks at her from far below as the dragon sped off, disappearing into the glare of the midday sunshine.

"Damn you, you sheep-poaching lizard!" one of the shepherds cried. "A thousand curses on you!"

The sound of cantering hooves cut him off. A gray stallion crested the hill, and his rider reined him in. The rider was a big man, as it was reckoned in that part of Europe. Gray eyes glinted beneath a shaggy mane of straw-colored hair. He jingled as he rode, and the glint of chain mail was visible beneath his black, fur-trimmed coat. The handle of a long bastard sword, sheathed in a worn, scaly scabbard, projected up from between his shoulder blades.

"Ho, shepherd," the man said, holding up his palm in a gesture of friendship. "Which way to the dragon?"

The shepherd, who looked at the newcomer peculiarly, simply pointed in the general direction of the peaks.

"Up there?" the rider asked.

"Ja," the shepherd said. "She feeds up there."

"All the better."

"Better for what?"

"For doing my job," the rider said as if explaining the concept to a small and not particularly bright child. With a dramatic flourish, he pulled his sword from its sheath with a mighty ringing sound. "Behold, I am Rothgar, son of Wulfgar, and I am a slayer of dragons!"

The shepherd considered. "You work for the church?"

"No," Rothgar said, puzzled. "I work for myself."

"Ah," the shepherd said, nodding. He pointed to the cluster of natty houses below. "A solicitor, then. You'd best be off down there. The town council will speak with you."

"My thanks, shepherd."

"Neh, don't thank me. I wouldn't expect too much."

Rothgar scratched his head as the shepherd walked away, but he nudged his mount forward and down into the valley.

The town was tidy and thrifty looking, with neat cobblestone streets and buildings coated with fresh paint. Rothgar was surprised, therefore, when he saw that the town council was having a noisy meeting in what was undoubtedly the local tavern.

"We must move forward with this resolution!" an old man stated with authority. The other men gathered at the tables banged their beer steins against the table in agreement. "We are resolved that we shall try to rid ourselves of the dragon!"

"Try?" Rothgar snorted, and the room went silent except for the sounds of creaking chairs and swiveling necks. "You need not try, for it shall be done. I am Rothgar, son of—"

"Ratgar?" someone asked.

"*Rothgar,*" Rothgar repeated, more loudly. "Son of Wulfgar, slayer of dragons."

"Really?" the speaker said. "Ja, then I am Jalk the Giant Killer."

"Jalk and his beanstalk is a fable," Rothgar said. "Your dragon is not. Hire me, and you shall be free of it."

"Why should we hire a foreigner?" someone else asked.

"I am not a foreigner," Rothgar said. "I was born in the north, near to the eaves of the Teutoburg Forest."

"Well, you talk funny, so it's really the same thing."

"Do you want this dragon slain or not?" Rothgar said, his temper slipping a notch.

"Oh, very well," the speaker said. "We were about to put the whole thing to a vote, but go ahead, let's hear your proposal."

"Fine," Rothgar said, settling down a bit. Now things were going according to the script. "Tell me about the dragon."

"Speaker Erbrechen! Speaker Erbrechen!" came the clamor.

The old man waved tolerantly, cleared his throat, and addressed Rothgar.

"She came upon us nigh ten days ago," said Erbrechen. "She swoops down upon us, taking our cattle and sheep. If we shoot arrows at her, she burns our barns and shops."

"How big is she?"

"Forty feet long!" someone interjected.

"Forty-two!" someone else said.

"Neh, it's fifty if it were a day."

"Are you counting her tail?"

"Look," Rothgar interrupted, "she's big. I get the picture."

"Big enough," Erbrechen agreed.

"Long teeth?"

"Like swords!"

"Tail?"

"Bladed."

"Breathes fire?"

"Oh, lots."

"Hmm." Rothgar counted on his fingers, then said, "Counting time and materials, I will do the deed for fifteen hundred gold crowns."

There was a stunned silence. Then the crowd burst out laughing. The townspeople started speaking all at once.

"Fifteen hundred?"

"Feh, we could bribe the dragon away with that kind of money."

"Ridiculous! What does he think we are?"

"Mister Rothgar," Erbrechen said as he tried to still his shaking belly, "thank you for your offer, but we've come up with some cheaper alternatives." He turned to the crowd. "Vote?"

The villagers raised their left hands, fists clenched, and shouted, "*Stimmen sie zu!*"

The meeting broke up rather quickly after that. Rothgar stood in the middle of the empty floor, flabbergasted. He slumped in the nearest seat, dejected, until the barkeeper came up and tapped him on the shoulder.

"Hey, you. Buy a drink or get out."

Wednesday

Rothgar sat on the tavern's back porch, chin in hands. He took a sip from his stein—a small one, as he wanted to sit for a while.

The townspeople gathered on the open field to the east. "Okay!" one of them said. "Here she comes!"

The dragon flew across the lake by the town, a fat cow clutched in her talons. The townspeople dove under the tarpaulin of red and yellow fabric they had set out before dawn. On cue, they stood up and marched forward.

The person at the front held up the frame of timber and straw fashioned to look like a dragon's head, complete with working jaw and blinking eyes. The other members of the team swayed their parts of the dragon's body back and forth in a sinuous motion, banging on drums and bells and creating an incredible din.

The dragon stopped in midair and dropped her cargo. The bovine gave a plaintive "Moo!" as it plunged into the icy water and began cow-paddling to shore. The dragon swooped low, nose to the ground, and with a great snort, sent a sheet of fire over the false dragon on the ground.

The townspeople, their hair and eyebrows smoldering, quickly dropped the cloth and either rolled in the wet grass or jumped in the lake. The dragon circled the town once before it left. It let out a deep, throaty laugh like thunder.

Rothgar smiled. He downed the rest of his beer in one gulp and strode over to Erbrechen, who was brushing ashes off his tunic.

"Whose bright idea was that?" Rothgar asked sardonically.

"The snake handler's." Erbrechen pointed to a young boy with a snake draped over his bony shoulders.

"Well, dragons are like snakes," the boy said. "And snakes don't like loud noises or challengers, ja?"

"Try a stupid stunt like that again, and you'll all be so much roasted meat," Rothgar said.

Erbrechen and the boy exchanged a look. "What did you have in mind?" Erbrechen asked.

Rothgar flexed his biceps and smiled. "I have, in my mercy, reconsidered my offer. Fourteen hundred crowns, not a *pfennig* less."

A look of consideration passed over Erbrechen's face. "Care to discuss it over a cup of herb tea?"

"No! Take it or leave it, old man!"

"Okay," Erbrechen shrugged, turning away from him. He raised his voice to the townspeople. "Let's go; time's wasting if we want to try the next plan!"

Rothgar swore and stomped off. That night he drank enough beer to float a longship.

Thursday

The dragon landed atop the bull's carcass that had been staked out in the middle of a clearing just outside of town. She began tearing off chunks of meat with gusto.

"What do you think?" one ratty-looking peasant said to Erbrechen.

Erbrechen, Werner, and Rothgar had hidden in the deep underbrush, out of the dragon's sight. "She looks pretty occupied, Werner," Erbrechen replied. "Your boys going to do anything soon?"

"Ja, don't you worry," said Werner. He pointed to the nearby cottages. "They're all the village's best timber jacks. They made our homes from these trees. They know what to do."

With a *crack*, the largest tree behind the dragon toppled forward.

Rothgar stood, eyes locked on the large pine as it curved forward towards the dragon's back.

The dragon snapped her head around as fast as a whip. She caught the falling timber in her massive jaws and swung her burden around. With a careless flick, she tossed the tree away. The mass of timber whirled end over end and crashed on top of a row of the cottages.

"*Scheisse!* My house!" Werner wailed.

The dragon turned in their direction. She blew a ring of smoke in derision, then flew off, unconcerned.

Rothgar coughed into his hand. "Erbrechen, I've been thinking. How about we settle up for twelve hundred gold crowns?"

"Twelve hundred? Are you joking?"

"Eleven!" Rothgar said, his palms out in supplication.

"Sounds like you need the work. Care to discuss it over some herb tea?"

"Damn it, I don't want any tea, I want the job! Why won't your lord pay me for my services?"

"Lord? Who said we had a lord?"

"Well, I just assumed—"

"Ja, you assumed," Erbrechen said wryly. "You like bridge tolls?"

"Well, no."

"Highway tolls?"

"No, not really. What does this have to do with anything?"

"How do you think a lord 'pays' you for your services? Taxes, that's how! Well, this town doesn't like taxes, so we broke away and set up independently."

"But you're the town speaker."

"So? Feh, you think I would hold meetings in the tavern if I had money to build a town hall? It's expensive to meet in the tavern. You can't even sit down there unless—"

"—you buy a drink," Rothgar groaned, rubbing his eyes. "I know, I know."

Friday

This time they had ten sheep carcasses staked to the ground in a clearing across the valley.

"You people are just stupid if you think she's going to fall for that again," Rothgar grumbled.

The dragon made a neat banking turn on her left wingtip and settled in the clearing for her meal. She picked delicately at the warm mutton, pausing every now and then to burp up a stringy ball of wool.

Erbrechen looked at Rothgar.

"Shut up," Rothgar growled. Erbrechen and the snake-handler boy were in the thicket with him. Rothgar tapped the boy on the shoulder.

"Tell me one thing," he said. "How do you know the dragon's a female?"

"Oh, that's simple," the boy said. He plucked the snake from its perch around his shoulder and held the wriggling animal upside down. "See? This one's a girl too."

"There's the flag!" Erbrechen said, pointing at the green piece of cloth waving from the top of a nearby hillock. Behind the summit, the townspeople's huge catapult twanged as it loosed the five-ton boulder from its hide platform.

The rock whistled over the hillock and came down silently from almost straight above. The dragon gave a squawk, and as she spread her wings, the boulder smashed down with a horrid, crunching sound. Black dragon blood flew through the air in a fine mist, sizzling as it hit leaves and grass. The outstretched wings, which stuck out from under the rock, quivered once and were still.

A raucous cheer went up from the townspeople. They whooped and tossed their hats in the air, rejoicing. They had almost settled back down when, with a mighty shudder, the rock tipped back on its edge and rolled off.

Rothgar stepped forward, drawing his sword.

The dragon raised her head shakily. With an angry shriek, she beat her wings and rose above the clearing. She roared, making the waters of the lake quiver, and she spat forth a jet of flame that set the woods to the west afire.

Erbrechen hurriedly ordered all the village's men to fight the blaze before it reached the town.

The dragon flew off unsteadily.

Rothgar was waiting at the tavern, stein in hand, when Erbrechen returned. He motioned Erbrechen to take a chair, sized the man up, and spoke.

"Nine hundred. Don't tell the dragon slayer's guild or I'm in trouble."

Erbrechen considered. "Care to discuss it—"

"Over a cup of herb tea?" Rothgar nodded fiercely. "Fine, whatever the hell you want, let's deal!"

"Hermann, let's have the special over here," Erbrechen said. The tea was laid out, steaming hot, and Erbrechen carefully poured two cups. He picked up his cup, inhaling the aromas and savoring the scent. Rothgar tossed his back and pounded the table with his fist.

"I've satisfied your stinking custom, old man. Now, do I get the job or not?"

"After all we've done, only to fail? You've got it."

"About time! Now, the dragon's lair—can you show me how to get to it?"

"Ja, I'll draw you a map."

Erbrechen pulled out a sheet of parchment and drew in lines and noted landmarks in a flowing script. He laid it out on the table.

Rothgar studied the parchment shrewdly. It was hard to make out some of the smaller words. He lay his head on the table, got a good look at the lettering, then let out a great snore.

Saturday

Rothgar awoke with a moan, sick to his stomach. He lay on his back, and he could make out the sides of an open wagon around him. He tried moving his arms and legs, and it came as a bad shock when he discovered he was bound. Erbrechen and a second old man leaned over him.

"What the devil are you doing?" Rothgar demanded. "Untie me at once, or I'll cut your hearts out with my sword!"

"Can't do that, son of Wulfgar," Erbrechen replied. "You see, you took the job, so you have to finish it."

"You drugged me!"

"We had little choice." Erbrechen shrugged. "That dragon, she's intelligent for her kind. She speaks some human tongue."

"Ja, and apparently, we were successful in our efforts to drive her off," the second old man agreed.

"Sort of," Erbrechen said. "She flew down while we were fighting the fire after you left. She said we were becoming mighty fine pests after we clobbered her with that rock."

"Liar!" Rothgar snarled. "She would have eaten you all!"

"Oh, neh," Erbrechen said. "She's smart. Why work for your food when you can pick up a fat cow or sheep whenever you like? If she killed us, she'd be depriving herself of her meals. But she promised us that she'd leave for other parts so long as we promised her two things."

Rothgar didn't like the way the conversation was going.

"First," Erbrechen said, "she wanted us to give her a dozen sheep carcasses, for rations when she sets out. Second, she wanted us to sacrifice to her our most beautiful maiden."

"What?"

"Well, it's just good form. If word got out that a dragon had gone soft, well, nobody would take her seriously! This way, both she and our town save face. It's a win-win situation. Very economical."

"I'm hardly a maiden, old man," Rothgar said through clenched teeth.

"Well, we're in luck. Dragons can't see too well." Erbrechen reached down, lifted Rothgar's head by the hair so the dragon slayer could see. "You should be flattered. We were able to lengthen my daughter's blue gown before we slipped you into it." He held up part of Rothgar's locks. "And the young girls at the school braided these lovely mountain daisies into your hair—"

"You bastards!" Rothgar shouted, straining mightily to free himself from the ropes. His muscles bulged under the robin's- egg blue dress, but they failed to part the bonds. "I swear, I've slain entire families for less than this!"

They came to the end of the road, right below the cleft of the peaks. They carried the struggling Rothgar from the wagon and lashed him to a nearby tree.

Erbrechen pulled out a small box and opened it. "Lipstick or rouge?"

Rothgar told him where to stick both items.

"If you don't decide, I'll use both," threatened Erbrechen. "And I'll pick shades that don't match."

Rothgar seethed. "Lipstick."

Erbrechen finished his work and climbed into the wagon with the others. They started their creaky ride back down the mountainside.

"You have my word that we'll do our best to make sure your next of kin gets the six hundred crowns!"

"Nine hundred!" Rothgar called back.

He cursed them floridly as they dwindled in the mist. In due time, he ran out of breath. Later that day, all was silent except for the beat of approaching leathery wings.

* * *

Medieval accounts about dragons incorrectly liken them to simple animals. Dragons were quite intelligent, thoughtful creatures at heart. And once their word was given, they always kept it.

Schnitzengruben, with its easy-handed government and light taxes, soon became a major trading spot known throughout Europe. People would remark about the calm waters of the lake, the high, dark forest, the charming houses, and the clean streets. The people themselves were also highly regarded. Their services were sought throughout Germany as blacksmiths, carpenters, and bankers.

However, they *never* produced so much as a single dragon slayer.

O O O

Michael Angel's worlds of fiction range from the unicorn-ruled realm of the Morning Land to the gritty "Fringe Space" of the western Galactic Frontier. Author of the bestselling *Centaur of the Crime*—where C.S. Lewis meets CSI—his books populate shelves in languages from Russian to Portuguese.

He currently resides in Southern California. Alas, despite keeping a keen eye out for griffins, centaurs, or pegasi, none have yet put in an appearance on Hollywood Boulevard. Michael Angel's welcome mat is out at his website, so feel free to visit: michaelangelwriter.com.

MANIFEST

Brandon M. Lindsay

On the workbench, the tiny yellow dragon stood with its wings spread, curving them around a wet, shapeless lump of clay. As if flecked with topaz dust in sunlight, the dragon's wings began to shimmer. The clay twitched, though nothing touched it. It twitched again, and then a thumb-sized nub sprouted from the side of the clay.

Torra sat at the workbench on his unpadded stool, hands in his lap, doing his best to ignore the spectacle of the dragon's magic. He leaned forward, instead focusing his attention on the clay. Or rather, what the clay *ought* to be.

It wasn't difficult. Torra's ability to visualize his intended creation in exact detail was his claim to fame. Even among the dragon artisans he was well-renowned. His craftsmanship was considered the best within two hundred leagues.

A hole sprang into being in the clay, and the nub morphed into a small handle, big enough for a single finger. The rest of the clay flattened out. Then the outer edge folded up, twisting as it did. Torra liked to give his creations a unique signature, and the subtle twist was something even the other dragon artisans had difficulty duplicating—and many had tried.

Steadily, the clay began to take on the shape in Torra's mind, that of a delicate teacup. One fit for a lord, which was the point. It was to be the final piece of a set for Lord Hail, and in minutes it would be identical to the other fifteen cups Torra and his little dragon had already made.

A crow flew past the window, squawking loudly and startling them both. The dragon jerked its head up at the noise and launched out the open window with a cry of its own, task forgotten.

"Melly!" Torra half-stood. "Melly!" He slumped down onto his stool, shaking his head with a wistful smile hidden in his beard. "Incorrigible beast."

Carefully, Torra picked up the cup with his club-like hands, turning it as he inspected it. The coloration was all wrong. The white-with-blue-trim glaze ended abruptly halfway up the cup, leaving the rest of it looking like plain fired clay. It was still a beautiful piece, but flawed, and one that he and Melly couldn't complete without breaking. He would have to sell it to some wealthy merchant with a taste for oddities at a tenth of the original price.

Torra sighed and stood, wincing at the pain in his back. He would worry about completing the set later. He had been cooped up too long and wanted to go outside. Besides, at this time of day, his old friend Roke was probably waiting for him, and who knew when Melly would return.

He picked up his cane—specially made, with Melly's help, to fit his deformed hand—from its spot next to his bench. He didn't need it to walk, but it did make the process more bearable, no thanks to his back. Torra made his way out of the tiny workroom and through the storefront. It was small, too, since he spent most of his time on commissions and didn't have much to show. However, the pieces he did show, ranging from crystal vases to elegant-yet-sturdy goblets, were among his finest.

Torra flipped up the wide latch—again, specially made for him—and shouldered open the door. The western horizon was edged with twilight. People rushed on foot up and down the thoroughfare to finish the last of the day's business before all the shops closed up. Only a few oxcarts trundled up the cobbles away from the farmers' market, laden with wares. The driver of one cart, a mustachioed man with a wide-brimmed hat and even wider shoulders, smiled and waved.

Rather than waving in response, Torra bowed his head deeply, as he always did.

Once the cart was parked in front of the shop, Roke slipped down from the driver's seat. "Fine day for a footrace!"

"Of course." Torra gestured towards Roke's ox with his cane. "As long as I can use *their* feet to carry me."

Roke shrugged as his grin widened. "No matter. I'd still win."

Torra chuckled. "How's the market today?"

"Been better." Roke grimaced but immediately brightened. "Say, where's that little troublemaker of yours?"

"You answered your own question. She got distracted and flew out the window in the middle of a commission."

"Not surprising." Roke leaned an elbow against the rear wheel of his oxcart. "It'd be nice if you didn't have to depend on her."

Torra felt a stab in his heart as he looked down at his disfigured hands. "Wouldn't it?"

Roke blanched when he realized what he had said. "I'm sorry. I didn't mean it like that. I thought, maybe if you had a different dragon—"

"No," Torra said, forcing a smile. "It's my fault for pining for things that cannot be. It was *my* momentary weakness, not yours. And yes, Melly may be unreliable, but I'm lucky to have her. Many aren't so lucky."

Torra had lost his hands in a fire long, long ago. Or at least, that's what he believed. It unnerved him that he could recall none of the details. And for some reason, when he thought of his hands, he recalled the morning eight months ago when Roke had found him just outside of town, cold and ill and disoriented, with his fingers fused together, his hands useless. He was haunted by the mystery and often found himself wishing he could remember a time when his hands hadn't been ruined.

"Well," Roke said, sweeping his hat off his head and clutching it to his chest as if in mourning, "I should get this back to the warehouse."

"And I should get back to work myself." Torra glanced down the street towards the center of town. He smiled. "Ah! There's Melly now. Still chasing that crow, I see."

Torra caught a glimpse of shimmering topaz, diving and circling around the crow. The crow winged into the crowd of people bustling through the street as they rushed to finish their daily business and get home to their families. Melly didn't hesitate to follow. Torra didn't like braving the streets at this time of day. Not two weeks past, a man had gotten his foot crushed under a wagon wheel during the evening rush.

The crow burst up out of the crowd. Melly didn't.

Torra watched and waited, but still she didn't appear. He felt his stomach sink. "Something happened."

"I can go look for her."

"No, no." Torra forced a smile. "I'm sure she just … found something shiny to chew on." He kept his eyes fixed on the last place he saw her, hoping she would fly up out of the throngs unharmed. The crowds looked impossibly thick, and with every passing moment, his dread increased.

Roke looked at him, eyes filled with concern. "If you like, I'll wait here with you until she comes home."

Torra considered the offer. "Actually, I would like that." He watched the street a moment longer before going into the shop with Roke.

* * *

It was well past midnight when Melly returned, coming through the same window she had left through. She flopped heavily to the workbench and moved no more.

Her body was a wreck. It was a miracle she had flown at all. Torra stood up from his stool, gathered up her limp form as gently as he could, and simply held her close.

Roke laid a hand on his shoulder. "I'm sorry, friend."

Torra laid her back down on the bench with a deep, rattling breath.

At dawn the next day, they buried Melly behind Torra's workshop, close to the place where he and his dragon had created so much together, in the shade of a short pitaya tree. Torra didn't know why he chose that spot, only that it seemed right. As Roke dug the hole, he found another set of bones, small and brittle, like those of a bird or even another tiny dragon. Torra didn't know what had been buried there before, but at least Melly would have some company as she was laid to rest.

The task done, Roke laid a hand on Torra's shoulder. "Not to disrespect your loss," he said, "but when is the commission due?"

Torra understood his concern. Lord Hail was not a forgiving man. "Three days."

Roke let out a low whistle. "What will you do?"

"Lose my shop, I imagine. Get thrown out in the street. Starve." He lifted his mangled hands. "I can't even feed myself, Roke. There's no way I will finish in time."

"You could," Roke said, "if you had another dragon. I know of a way."

Torra glanced down at the freshly churned dirt of Melly's grave. It seemed cruel to think of replacing her so soon, but adding to his own suffering would solve nothing. "Tell me."

"Well, I can't say I know too much, but there's a woman who lives just past the Skywood …"

* * *

By the third hour, Torra's cane was doing more to support his weight than either of his legs as he shouldered his way through the Skywood. It wasn't a true wood, however. Instead of trees, there were huge plants as wide around as a tree but with soft, pale flesh growing straight up like reeds. The branchless stalks tapered, always leaving some patch of sky visible as they rocked back and forth in the breeze.

Now the sky was filled with clouds. Torra had wasted no time because he had none to spare, stopping only occasionally to rub his aching back. The going was hard; the hollow stalks of the Skywood were tightly packed with barely enough room for a foot between them. More than once, his cane had gotten tangled in their roots.

Torra was leaning heavily on his cane when he came to the looming cliffside abutting the edge of the Skywood. A narrow crack, barely wide enough to allow him to enter, split the cliffside. From within, a warm light glowed and wavered.

Torra went in.

The crack widened into a sandy-floored chamber. In the middle burned a low fire, smoke drifting up to gather in a haze under the rough stone ceiling. On a wicker chair behind the fire sat the woman.

If she could be called that. Torra had expected a wizened old witch, not this black-haired girl young enough to be his granddaughter.

With dark, sharp eyes in her narrow face, she glanced up. "You again," she said, gesturing to the log opposite her.

Frowning, Torra sat on the log. He glanced around the cave. It was clear the girl lived here. A thin, worn bedroll was tucked in the corner amid some thick roots. Low shelves, also made of wicker, huddled around the edges of the cave. Some were packed with books; others were filled with trinkets. He was surprised to see a number of his own works there: a crystal decanter, a pair of strongwine thimbles, a bread plate.

Torra wondered how she had gotten ahold of them. Judging by her worn, gray dress—and the fact that she lived in a cave—she was of very meager means and couldn't possibly have been able to afford even his failures, much less these finer works. And though her face was strangely familiar, he knew she had never given him a commission.

Torra cocked his head in puzzlement. "Have we met before?"

The girl stood and, sighing, walked around the fire to face him. "I tire of this conversation, Torra," she said. "So let's get on with it, shall we? I assume you've come for another dragon."

"Y—yes." She knew his name. *Had* he met her before? He searched his memory, and the recollection seemed to be there, but stubbornly out of reach.

She watched his eyes with interest and smiled at his expression. "Ah, so you remember *something*."

Torra glanced away from her piercing, intent gaze. "Not really. It's more of a sense that I should."

She nodded and sat down next to him on the log, pushing her thick black hair over her shoulders. "How long did you have your last dragon?"

"Well, I guess I've always had her."

The girl stared at him. "You've had an infant dragon. For sixty …"

"Sixty-two."

"Sixty-two years," she finished, then cocked her head. "At what age do dragons mature, I wonder? Perhaps your friends know the exact day you got her." She shrugged. "Or perhaps not." It was clear by her tone that she *didn't* wonder but was trying to push Torra to think about it.

Gently, she covered his disfigured hands with her own small yet perfectly formed ones. He couldn't help but stare at such capable hands with yearning. Her voice snapped him out of his thoughts. "When did this happen?" She asked the question as if she already knew.

Torra withdrew his hands from under hers and stood. "Enough with the games," he said. "Enough with the riddles. Tell me whatever it is you have to say."

The girl stared at him, saying nothing, and he felt sweat dampen his back.

"Are you telling me that Melly and this"—he raised his hands—"are related?"

The girl returned to her wicker chair, resting her hands on the chair back as she stood behind it. "The power of dragons isn't free. There is a cost. Of mind and body."

"You mean you alter my memories and those of my friends." Torra lifted his hands. "And you cripple me."

She nodded. "I took your left hand eight months ago, and with it, your memories of how you got your dragon—Melly, as you called her. And the magic doesn't only affect you but everyone affected by you. As far as anyone is concerned, you have always had that same dragon, and you have always been crippled."

"My *left* hand? What of my right?"

"This isn't the first dragon you've replaced," she said.

Torra closed his eyes as he remembered the bones he had found beneath the pitaya tree. They had doubtless belonged to his first dragon. Which he had also let die.

He felt a surge of emotions—sadness, confusion, anger—directed at himself, this girl, this cruel world.

When he opened his eyes, he saw that the girl had backed up a step and was eyeing him warily. "Remember that everything that has happened here, *you* have chosen. I'm not responsible for the things I must take. I don't set the cost. The magic does." She gestured vaguely towards the cave entrance. "But if you've found a better offer, by all means, take it."

Torra did consider leaving. But his only other choice was losing his livelihood. Perhaps he could live for a short while off the pieces he'd already made, but what kind of life would that be? A life where he was unable to create anything? He had always looked at the world differently from other people—not as full of deficiencies, but *opportunities*. Not as full of gaping holes, but merely empty places to fill with new, better things.

Yet to see those empty places and not be able to fill them ... Torra could imagine no worse fate.

Exhaling, he let his anger subside, unfair as it was, and in a low voice said, "What will you take this time?"

She crossed to him and picked up his cane to inspect it. "This," she said. "To start."

* * *

Roke found Torra naked and crawling out of the Skywood the next day.

"Heavens, man!" Roke rushed to help him up and cover him with a cloak. "What are you doing out here like this?"

Torra wrapped his arm around Roke's shoulders. "I could ask you the same thing."

"Well, you weren't at home, so ..." He frowned. "Anyway, here you are."

Torra grunted. "I'm afraid I lost my cane somehow. You'll have to help me." Torra's right foot had been run over by a wagon some time ago. At least, that's what he thought. It happened so long ago that he had forgotten any details about the incident; he merely knew that it had happened. Now, however, his foot ached as fiercely as if it had been injured only yesterday.

"Of course, of course," Roke said. They began to make their way back to town.

Something small and bright red flitted overhead with a squawk. Roke took off his hat and waved it at the tiny dragon in mock outrage. "And where were you, you little troublemaker! Letting your master wander into the Skywood alone."

Torra grinned as Roke half-carried him. "Don't give her too much trouble, Roke. Without Melly, I'd be lost for sure."

* * *

Torra sat on his stool staring at his workbench, hands in his lap. The bench was bare, save for tiny Melly, whose red head was cocked, looking up at him.

Clay. He would need clay to finish the final cup for Lord Hail's commission. It would be a simple matter of finishing it. Then he could get on with his life.

The life of a crippled dragon artisan.

But did it have to be that way?

Deep within his beard, a smile slowly formed. Instead of clay, he set his broken hands upon the workbench. "Let's get to work, Melly." As the ruby glow from her wings enveloped them, Torra visualized healthy, capable, perfect hands. The hands of a craftsman.

Hands as they ought to be.

O O O

Brandon M. Lindsay grew up on a steady diet of science fiction novels until he discovered his true literary love, epic fantasy. Born and raised in Seattle, he now lives in Tokyo, Japan, where he is working on his novel series.

Heart of the Dragon

L.J. Hachmeister

Good morning, Jenni."

Jenni barely heard the elderly voice above the cacophony of industrial rock blasting through her earbuds as she trudged up the steps from the basement apartment. Lifting her head just enough to see the speaker sitting in the pink plastic chair by the front door, Jenni offered her upstairs neighbor the obligatory nod before resecuring her messenger bag higher on her shoulder and hurrying off toward school.

"Be well, dear!"

That was Mrs. Bloom, always cheery and bright, even in the city slums full of unwanted people and bad memories.

"Ridiculous woman," Jenni mumbled to herself. As she turned up the volume on her cell phone, she saw a text from her mom.

Working late, be home at 11. Make yourself dinner, then do your homework.

"Yeah, yeah—"

Another text followed.

And be nice to Mrs. Bloom. Love you!

She jammed her cell phone back in the front pocket of her leather jacket and quickened her pace. Any annoyance with her mother faded to the back of her mind as she came up on 41st Street. Already late, she didn't have the option of taking the long way around.

With every step, her heart crept farther and farther up her throat. Bullies were one thing—

Keep your eyes down, don't look, go faster.

—ex-employers were another.

It's early, she told herself, scanning the empty street as the sun crept over the gray, sagging buildings to the east. Without thinking, she removed her earbuds and thumbed the dragon pendant around her neck. *No dealer is going to be up at six a.m. looking for me.*

"Jenni Li ..."

Cold fear shot down her spine, but she didn't look up.

"Where do you think you're going?"

She stopped dead in her tracks.

Out of the corner of her eye, she saw someone with black boots and torn jeans emerge from the alleyway between Chung's Liquors and a junk shop. She didn't need to see his face to know who it was.

"Thought you ran off," he said. The stink of his cologne carried over the sour garbage smells from the alley. She didn't know which was more sickening.

"No," she muttered.

"Let me guess—you quit the delivery biz and are back in school. You a repeat senior?"

Shrugging, she tried to count her breaths, to calm herself, but with every step Chen took toward her, she felt herself unraveling.

I won't work for him again, I can't—

"You into dragons?" he said, reaching for her necklace. She faded back a step, but he caught her by the arm and yanked her forward. With a smirk, he inspected the imitation gold pendant. "Not real fitting for a mousy girl like you."

Shame, then anger, heated her cheeks.

"Look," he said, lifting up her chin with his index finger.

She avoided his gaze, not wanting to see his pocked face or the cold violence darkening his eyes.

"Got a client in Little China."

"Can't," she said, stepping back to free herself from his touch.

Expecting retribution, she cringed, waiting for the blow.

Instead he chuckled, producing a small box wrapped in yellowed newspaper from the pocket of his desecrated US Army jacket.

"I'm not asking. I need this delivered, and you owe me for dropping the last package."

"But I paid you back," she said, voice trembling.

"Money won't buy me back my reputation."

She didn't know how to respond. Why would Chen want her running an important delivery after she bailed on him months ago?

"I need someone invisible. Someone who wouldn't get noticed around all those other chinks," he explained.

A million different retorts ran through her head, but she did nothing except stand there, shoulders slumped and eyes cast downward.

Do something, say something, she told herself. *Tell that jerk where to shove it—*

"Take this to the apothecary on Thirteenth."

Mrs. Wu's place? Remembering her last venture inside the dank shop, Jenni curled her toes in her boots and scrunched the ends of her jacket sleeves in her hands. Mrs. Wu's severe face, and the bite of her hand as she slapped her across the cheek for knocking over a stack of books, made her wish for any other assignment.

"Do this, and we're even. Fail, and I'll pay your sweet mama a visit just like I did Ahjee."

Ahjee, her gentle but dopey cousin who'd messed up one too many drops. A closed-casket funeral didn't hide what Chen's cronies did to him or mask the cries of her heartbroken aunt.

Jenni took a quick, sharp breath. *Just this one job*, she thought, nausea licking the back of her throat. She glanced side to side, checking the vacant streets before taking the package from his outstretched hand. It felt heavy for its size.

"Good girl," he said with a wink. "See you tomorrow."

Securing her hoodie a little tighter around her head, she took off, the dragon pendant bouncing against her chest, a reminder of all that she wasn't.

* * *

Roach and his usual band of followers found her two blocks away from school. In her mind, she could drop off the package in Little China, then double-back to school and make it in time for homeroom. Roach, one of her fellow delinquents from Saturday detentions, had other plans.

"Hey, chink," he said from across the street, flicking away his cigarette and jumping off the hood of a junked-out car. A few other kids, milling around the abandoned bowling alley parking lot, followed him as he ran over to her. "You ain't supposed to be around here."

Picking up her pace didn't help. Neither did ignoring his demands to stop.

"I said, turn around!"

Hands grabbed her hoodie and yanked her back. The force of the movement snapped her neck forward, making her arms flail, feet stumble. Before she could orient herself, a blur of fists and kicks connected with her face, back, and legs. She tasted copper in her mouth, felt something warm wet her face.

"Back off, Roach, man. She's had enough," she heard someone say.

"Check her," he said. "She must be making deliveries again—only reason a loser like her would be out here."

Gritting her teeth and trying to guard her wares, Jenni endured the rough, searching hands as they ripped her jacket off and dumped the contents of her messenger bag onto the street. Eventually, Roach found the small box wrapped in yellowed newspaper among the pile of her ruined papers, notebooks, and collection of art supplies.

"What's this?" he said, ripping open the package.

She tried to turn over, but he stomped down on her hip, pinning her to the asphalt. From her limited vantage point, she saw the newspaper bits fall to the ground and soak up the residual motorcar oils.

Do something!

"Ink? Oh, is this for your 'art'?"

Confused, she craned her neck, spying the glass bottle full of black ink he held in his hand.

Roach grabbed one of her notebooks and thumbed through the pages, laughing at the numerous sketches and doodles she'd made around her class notes. "Dragons, more dragons. God, I didn't think you could be a bigger loser."

With a snort, he tossed the notebook back on the pile. After hocking up something from his throat, he spat in her face. "Stay out of here, chink, or I won't be as nice next time."

As Roach and his cronies walked away, already laughing about something else, the adrenaline wore off, and the pain of her injuries came to the forefront of her attention. With shaking hands, she collected her things, stuffing papers and notebooks haphazardly back into her messenger bag. Only after she rounded the street corner did she wipe the mixture of spit and blood from her face.

Tears came easily, but anger rushed in before they had a chance to turn into more than frustration and fright. *If only I could make them pay.*

She leaned against a building, her breath hitching in her chest. *Stupid. Stupid, stupid, stupid.*

She slammed her fist into the bricks, not caring about the sting. Her face and ribs throbbed, but she let the pain come over her, allowing it to fuel the impotent rage that had been simmering inside her for as long as she could remember.

The package—

Had she picked it up? Furiously, she dug through her things until she found the inkwell at the bottom of her bag.

With a sigh, she stuffed it back in and hurried toward the apothecary.

This is the last time, she promised herself. *No more Roach, no more Chen. Graduate, then get the hell out of here. Somewhere better, anywhere …*

As she hustled toward Thirteenth, winding between street vendors and low-hanging paper lanterns that marked the border into Little China, she kept her head low, avoiding the gazes of the residents who might recognize her. Her mother, once a prominent member of the Chinese Cultural Center, couldn't show her face in even the lowliest junk shop. Not after two out-of-wedlock children, the mysterious death of her ex-boyfriend, and her eldest daughter running away with her girlfriend.

At least Mae got out.

Mrs. Wu's place stood out from the rest of the shops. No golden Buddhas, fake swords, or bamboo trees in the windows. Instead, she kept the curtains drawn and the signage to a minimum, with only the Chinese word for "apothecary" written on the front door.

Using the back of her sleeve, Jenni wiped away the rest of the blood from her nose as she stared at the doorknob. *Get in, give it to her, go. Don't let that old hag scare you.*

Trembling, she pushed open the door and tiptoed inside.

The smell hit her first. Spices and dust mingled in the air, tickling her nose and throat. Memories, mostly impressions, of better times touched her mind, back when her mother used to let her tag along for her morning errands. But the stacks of old books, dried leaves, and grasses hanging from the ceiling and the gloomy light of the single bulb over the counter made her remember where she was and who she had to deal with.

Eyes darting back and forth, she made her way down the aisle congested with bags of crushed seeds and plants until she came to the counter. No sign of Mrs. Wu, not even a hint of her sour odor.

I could just leave the package here—

As soon as she set the inkwell on the counter, a chill ran up her spine.

"Jenni Li."

A vein-riddled hand smacked down on her shoulder. Jenni wheeled around to find Mrs. Wu in her face.

"What are you doing?"

Too afraid to scream, Jenni stood there shaking, eyes downcast, away from the stare of the white-haired witch.

"Just going to drop and run?"

Run—she commanded her legs. No chance. They felt like blocks of wood, completely cut off from her control.

"What happened to your face?" Mrs. Wu said. A scraggly finger lifted her chin, but Jenni shifted her gaze, not wanting to look into the black eyes of the witch. Still, she saw the stained teeth, the chin full of curly gray hairs. "Having trouble again? What is it this time—other gangs, nasty school kids? Debt collectors for your mother?"

Jenni's stomach twisted with every breath she took, taking in Mrs. Wu's moldy smell.

"Yes, trouble. And much anger, just boiling beneath the surface." The yellow-toothed smile broadened.

I don't like the way she looks at me, Jenni thought, shifting back and forth, wishing she could just jump out of her skin.

"You like dragons," the old woman said, tapping the pendant around Jenni's neck. "Not quite fitting for a girl of your nature. Still, you wish for their spirit, don't you? Especially now, when you should stand up to thugs like Chen."

Surprisingly, she found her voice. "Yes."

"Yes?"

No more than a whisper, she continued, "I could do so much more if …"

"If?"

"If I had their strength," she finished.

"Child, dragons are so much more," Mrs. Wu said, her deep voice belying her lithe figure. "They are creatures of legend, mystical beings. But this is how you see them—for their strength?"

Jenni chanced a look at Mrs. Wu. Sharp eyes gazed back, reading her every move. "Yes."

The old woman grunted. "And so shall it be, then."

"What?"

Cackling, she curved a finger at her. "Follow me."

With her shoulders hunched forward, Jenni followed, terrified and curious as the old woman led her past the curtain to the back room. *What am I doing? I need to get out—*

Oddities from all over the world adorned the walls and shelves, including figurines of deities and spirits forgotten in modern history books. Burnt and dusty books, feathers and skins from animals long since extinct, seduced her with their unusual textures and colors. She had all but convinced herself to keep going until she saw the jars of miscellaneous body parts.

"Not leaving yet, are you?" Mrs. Wu said, catching her by the sleeve as she turned to run.

Too terrified to answer, Jenni shook her head, wishing for the power to do something, anything.

"I'm not going to hurt you," Mrs. Wu said, turning her back to Jenni as she rummaged along one of the antique shelves against the far wall. "In fact, your mother came to me for help when her nasty ex-boyfriend wouldn't leave her alone."

Wait—did the witch give him that heart attack?

Mrs. Wu must have caught her look of disbelief. "Not all answers come from the gods they tell you about at school."

The old woman cleared off the clutter from a table pressed up against a boarded-up window, and then dropped her prize—a gigantic leather-bound book—in the middle. Loose leaves poked out of the sides, and a big strap tied it together. Hands clasped behind her back, Mrs. Wu waited for Jenni to open it herself.

More curious than fearful, Jenni undid the strap and opened up the book. Light and sound, concentrated in a singular blast, toppled her over. As she collected herself off the floor, Jenni saw the old witch thumbing through the pages and muttering to herself.

"Ah, here we go. Dragons."

Holding on to the edge of the table, Jenni leaned forward and dared a look. Dragons of all colors, shapes, and sizes moved across the pages in an intricate dance of wings and tails.

"Impossible …"

"No, child; there is still magic left in this world."

Jenni moved to touch the page, drawn to the dazzling colors and energy radiating off the parchment.

Mrs. Wu caught her arm with surprising speed. "All power comes at a cost."

"W-what?"

"The writings and images in this book are made from a very special ink."

Jenni had already made the connection. *Like the ink I brought her.*

"The stains of unfulfilled dreams, ashes from unkept promises, the dark matter of desire. Know what you want and who you are before you draw from these images."

Anger from deep within shattered her daze. Jenni wrenched herself free of the woman's bony grip. "You're a crazy old coot."

"Just like your mother," Mrs. Wu screeched as Jenni ran out of the back room. "Afraid to embrace all that can be!"

Jenni jumped over the counter, then paused. The ink lay out for the taking.

Don't be stupid.

Remembering the beauty, the magic of the dragons dancing across the pages—an impossibility in the only reality she knew—she grabbed the ink and stuffed it in her jacket pocket.

As she ran out of the store, she thought she heard Mrs. Wu's cackle carrying in the winds.

* * *

Jenni heard the second period bells chiming from across the schoolyard block.

Either way I'm screwed, she reasoned, imagining Mr. Welton's lecture if she dared show up tardy.

But she couldn't go home. Bigmouthed Mrs. Bloom would be on the front porch, ready to call her mom and tattle that her delinquent daughter had skipped school yet again.

With a sigh, she hiked up her messenger bag and headed for the used bookstore around the block. Angie, the girl who worked behind the counter, immediately lit up the second Jenni set foot in the store.

"Jenni Li! Where have you been? Do you have the day off school?"

She spoke so fast that Jenni didn't have a chance to get in a word before the dark-skinned woman ran out to give her hug. As soon as Angie's arms wrapped around her, she stiffened, discomfited by the affection.

"Hey, what happened to your face?"

"Nothing."

"It doesn't look like 'nothing.'"

Jenni blushed, then turned away.

"Hey, no stress. You can hang out here for a while, okay? Come on, I saved a few books for you, and your favorite reading place is open."

Angie was about ten years her senior, but she was old friends with Jenni's sister, Mae. Since she had no ties to Little China and didn't seem to care about the Li family's cultural shaming, she kept up contact with Jenni and her mom, bringing Jenni books about dragons whenever a new one was donated.

"Thanks," Jenni mumbled, avoiding Angie's gaze as she wedged herself in the far corner of the bookstore, out of sight from customers and staff.

"You know you can talk to me, okay?" Angie asked, setting down a few books next to her.

Jenni kept her head bowed, too angry at herself to answer.

"All right, I'll be up front. I'll check on you in a bit."

As soon as she heard Angie humming to herself at the counter, Jenni sighed in relief. She waited another minute before taking out her algebra notebook and art supplies from her messenger bag and opening to a blank page.

Carefully, she removed Mrs. Wu's delivery from her pocket. The black ink in the antique glass looked darker than a starless night. After selecting her smallest brush, she paused.

"All power comes at a cost."

Mrs. Wu's statement rang over and over in her head. But any sense of caution evaporated as she thought of the magic at her fingertips.

She dipped the tip of the brush in the ink, then touched it to the paper. Electricity coursed up her arm and warmed her center. With every stroke, she felt more alive, more attuned than she had ever been as she sketched out her fiercest design.

When she finished, the winged beast laid out perfectly before her, she set down the brush and waited.

Nothing happened.

Frustrated, she checked the inkwell, turning it over in her hands.

Stupid old hag. Probably tricked me, slipped me some hallucinogenic herb or—

Something moved on the page. She looked down, her jaw dropping as her dragon unfolded in three dimensions, colors burgeoning from its new depths. Without thinking, she reached out, wanting to take in its yellow eyes, feel the sharpness of its green scales and dark horns.

So beautiful—powerful—

A question rose in her mind from an unknown source.

What do you want?

She thought of Chen and Roach and all the other bullies and thugs dominating her life.

Loneliness and anger answered: *I don't want to be afraid anymore.*

The dragon circled on the page, its brilliant wings shimmering in the low light.

I want the strength of a dragon.

She touched her finger to the paper—and screamed. Black fire coursed up her arm, branching out into her chest, stomach, and legs. Smoke filled her lungs, and her back arched as the weight of some unseen beast burst out of her skin.

"You okay?"

The words jarred her back to her surroundings. Still dazed, Jenni looked around, remembering the bookstore and recognizing Angie's confused face.

"Umm, I heard you scream. What's going on?"

Jenni looked down, expecting to see her arms burned to a crisp, her body in pieces. Instead, her hand, perfectly intact, hovered above the ink dragon.

"Sorry," she mumbled. "Thought I heard something."

Angie lifted an eyebrow. "You sure you're okay?"

She nodded, unsure if she could trust her own voice to convey any certainty.

After Angie went back to the counter, Jenni turned her attention to the drawing. The picture appeared flat and unremarkable.

I'm going crazy, she concluded, tearing it out of her notebook. But as she scrunched it up and prepared to throw it away, she stopped. She felt something different, a heat inside her building from her stomach and rising to her mouth. Curious, she let go of the angry breath inside her. Fire belched from her lips, curling toward a shelf stuffed with old books.

"Oh, God—"

The fire caught, spreading fast.

Quickly, Jenni stuffed her belongings—and the torn-out page—back into her messenger bag and ran out of the bookstore. Fire trucks and police cars sped past her as she tore down the street, spurred by thrills and excitement she had never dreamed of.

She grinned, square white teeth sharpening into points.

* * *

As the afternoon sun slid lazily across the cloudless sky, she made her way back home, none too careful about her route. This time, when she came upon Chung's Liquors, she kept her head bowed and smiled.

"Why are you here, Li?" Chen stopped his conversation with a vendor, his hands already in fists as he turned to Jenni. "Did you deliver the package?"

"Shove it, Chen."

"You want me to skin you alive right here?"

Out of the corner of her eye, Jenni watched vendors close up their displays and pedestrians quicken their pace. With a casual shrug of her shoulder, she turned down the alleyway between buildings, drawing Chen into the shadows.

"You little—"

His hand slapped down on her shoulder, but she angled away and took shelter behind a Dumpster. She didn't want any witnesses.

"That's the last time you'll ever smile," Chen said, producing a hunting knife from his belt.

She didn't hide her delight. "This is for Ahjee," she whispered. She took a deep breath, drawing from the new, hot place inside her. Spewing orange and red flames, she didn't let up as Chen screamed and fell backward.

Shouts and commotion from the street. Someone must have seen the fire. She took off, running as fast as she could down the alley, Chen's cries following her all the way home.

* * *

Jenni waited across the street in the dying evening light, crouched behind a bush until Mrs. Bloom went inside for the night. As soon as Jenni was safely inside her apartment, she locked herself in her bedroom. Posters of rock stars regarded her with their usual drab indifference as she threw her messenger bag and jacket on the bed.

What just happened? Oh my God—

Thoughts bombarded her as she paced her room.

Did I really breathe fire?

(Did I kill Chen?)

I just wanted to scare him so he'd leave me alone!

She regarded herself in the stand-up mirror. The new cuts and bruises, and the usual boring features stared back at her, except for—

What happened to my eyes?

She didn't recognize the yellow hint to them, nor the diamond shape to her pupils.

Frightened, she backed up into her bed. She watched the stranger reflected back at her do the same.

This can't be real. Magic? The strength of a dragon?

Furious, she threw her jacket at the mirror and stomped into the bathroom. Hoping a shower would clear her head, she disrobed, stepped inside the stall, and turned on the water.

It's a stupid kid's dream.

The water felt cold against her skin. She cranked it up, all the way to the hottest setting. Still, she couldn't stop shivering, even as her skin turned pink, then red.

Can't get warm—She rubbed her arms, and balls of skin formed underneath her palms. When she looked down, she saw something green and shiny where she had abraded her skin.

Not real—

Scales. Beautiful and slick, they felt as real to her touch as the remainder of skin on her arms did. Under the scalding hot water, she rubbed away at her stomach, revealing even more of the bony plates.

She turned off the water and ran to her bed, diving underneath the covers.

Not real!

A voice, too deep to have originated from her small body, jangled her from within. *This is what you wanted.*

A rap on her front door. Then three more knocks, each more urgent sounding than the last. She pulled on her hoodie and a pair of pants, trembling as she crept to the door and looked through the spy hole.

Roach, and at least five of his thugs, stood outside.

"I heard you screwed up Chen. Sounds like you ain't playin' nice these days, little girl."

She gritted her teeth as an ancient rage filled her mind with visions of terrifying things. Entire cities laid to waste in a single, fiery breath. Wings tearing through the skies. Teeth biting through armor as knights begged for mercy.

"I don't want to be afraid anymore," she whispered.

Before she could think twice, she unlocked the front door and leaped forward, snatching Roach and bolting up the stairs. As he screamed and fought her iron grip on his throat, his cronies scrambled to regroup.

"Let me go, please," Roach cried, clawing at her face as she pulled him behind an abandoned building across the street, out of sight.

"Stay away from me." The severe bass of her own voice shocked both of them.

"Who are you?" Roach said, squinting in the low light.

He doesn't recognize me—

"Monster!" he cried, rearing back and clambering away from her.

She waited in the shadows as Roach ran down the street, screaming, his cronies yelling for him to slow down.

After she slunk back into her apartment, she closed the front door and slid down to the floor. As tears formed in her eyes, she heard her cell phone ring.

On hands and knees, she crawled to her bedroom and picked up her phone.

Mother.

She didn't dare answer.

Still, something inside her, untouched by whatever beast had taken residence inside her skin, made her pick up.

"Jenni? Sweetheart, are you there?"

She tried to make her voice high, but it still came out as a deep rumble. "Yes."

"Who is this?"

Terrified, she hung up. She texted her mom the best lie she could think of: *Bad connection. I'm alright. Doing homework.*

I'll send Mrs. Bloom by to make sure everything is okay.

Jenni looked up at the mirror. Bright yellow eyes stared back. When she gasped, she saw her new set of razor teeth.

No—I'm fine, she texted, tears sliding down her face.

Do something, she told herself, too afraid to look in the mirror again.

She dialed the apothecary number. It rang for what seemed like ages before she heard the old witch croak at the other end: "Yes?"

"What did you do to me?" she demanded, the low pitch of her voice shaking the walls.

The old woman paused, then answered in a delighted tone. "You, the thief, ask me what *I've* done?"

"Change me back!"

"Your mother begged me, too, when she didn't like the results of her magic. You have made your choice; these are the consequences."

A click followed, then a dial tone.

Enraged, she pulled up the sheets of her bed, tearing them apart. Steam rose from her skin, and her back hunched forward as a terrible ache coursed through her spine. She cried out and thrashed as spikes grew from her vertebrae, and a tail ruptured through her lower back.

"Stop, please," she sobbed, searching the floor on her hands and knees. She found the crumpled up paper and unfolded it with black-clawed fingers.

"I don't want a dragon's strength …" She pulled the ink and her brush from her bag. With shaking hands, she dipped back into the dark liquid. "I want … I want …"

A few trembling strokes around the dragon, two desperate lines to join it all together.

Thinking of her mother, of Angie's bright smile and warm embrace, of Mrs. Bloom's eternal cheeriness, Jenni reached out and touched the image.

* * *

"Dear, you look different today," Mrs. Bloom said as Jenni stepped out of her front door. "What is it—a new haircut?"

Jenni walked up the stairs with a smile as the sun woke up the morning skies.

"No, but thanks," she said, offering her neighbor a hug.

"Where are you off to on a Saturday morning?"

"Gotta return something I borrowed," she said, tapping her messenger bag. Even buried in the sea of notebooks and art supplies, she felt the dark ink swirl in its glass housing.

"See you for lunch, then?"

"Not today. I'm helping with repairs at the used bookstore, and righting some other things."

Mrs. Bloom nodded and sat back in her pink chair. "Be well, dear."

Before she made it down the block, her mom caught up to her, duster still in hand.

"Sweetheart, I found this under your bed while cleaning."

"It's just another dragon drawing," she said, taking the wrinkled piece of paper from her mom.

"So beautiful," her mother said, her eyes going back and forth between the paper and Jenni.

"Thanks," Jenni said, tracing the heart shape encompassing the dragon.

"No," her mom whispered, her eyes growing wide. Years of fatigue and misery, once etched into her brow, seemed to melt away. "Not the drawing. You."

"Aww, Mom."

Her mother touched the pendant around Jenni's neck. "Not a dragon, but the heart of one. That's what I see in you."

Jenni kissed her mother's cheek. "Love you."

Her mother beamed. "Love you, too."

O O O

Author L.J. Hachmeister writes and fights—though she tries to avoid doing them at the same time. The WEKAF world champion stick-fighter is best known in the literary world for her epic science fiction series *Triorion*—and her even more epic love of sweets. Connect with her at www.triorion.com.

Salvation, on Painted Wings

Kevin Ikenberry

Huck stared at his satcom radio in shock. "Come again?"

Overhead, the four sleek Dulcet exofighters joined up with parade precision and shot northeast towards orbit. "Hammer Two Five, this is Angel Lead. Keep the faith. Orbital gun platforms are out of range for twenty-six minutes, and we're out of ordnance. We're BINGO fuel, but we'll be back with reinforcements. Out," the pilot said, apology lacing his words.

The only aircraft supporting Huck's sector were low on fuel and unable to remain. He and Fleer were alone in their emergency pickup zone atop one of Honalee's ugly mountains in the middle of a failed invasion.

"They expect us to hold out that long?" Fleer grunted through blood and snot, lying in the mud at Huck's feet. Together they'd held off the buzzers for six waves, until one of the insectoid bastards had gouged Fleer's stomach with a stinger.

Huck hadn't seen the things flank up behind them on the rocky mountainside until it was almost too late. He'd thrown a ring bomb, letting the circular pulse of plasma run down the slope to neutralize another wave. The Dulcets hadn't made any real progress against the buzzers. Truth be told, flyboys couldn't be trusted to find their ass with both hands and a map. The sleek exospheric interceptors were no match for the pissed off wasp-things.

"Ain't got much choice, man." After Fleer had been hit, they'd retreated to the center point of the platoon's hasty fighting position. The radio was the only thing still making noise in the shattered headquarters. Bodies surrounded them on all sides. For a while, someone had been groaning, but before Huck and Fleer could figure out who, another buzzer wave attacked and the groaning fell silent. "Got two ring bombs left. They'll either give the Dulcets time to come back and get us outta here, or …" He looked at Fleer and shook his head. *He ain't gonna make it.*

"They'll come back in time," Fleer said, and coughed again. The wet smacking noise in his chest sounded worse with every tortured intake of breath.

"Special Forces get priority evacs." Huck's lips curled in disgust. All Special Forces ever did was mock the rest of the armed services and take the best gear. The generals always protected them first, often leaving the rest of the forces to fend for themselves, or worse, DIP—die in place. Honalee was yet another failed invasion that would be spun to the folks back home as a marginal success. "Only ones coming back for us are the grave diggers."

Fleer coughed again and began to choke. Huck knelt and pulled him into as much of a sitting position as the deep gouge in his stomach allowed. Thumping his fist on Fleer's back, Huck chanted softly, "Relax, buddy. Just breathe. You'll get it; just relax. Breathe slow." After a minute or so, Fleer's breathing returned to a strained rattle. "There you go. There you go."

"Thanks, bro," Fleer said as Huck laid him back down in the dirt. He grabbed Huck's sleeve with a bloody hand, his smile never faltering.

Huck laughed and shrugged it off. "Don't mention—"

Fleer's hand came up, palm out. His hearing had always been better than Huck's. After another ten seconds, Huck heard the buzzers coming back to life from down the mountain. The ring bombs scared the things, rendering them catatonic for twenty to thirty minutes, according to the old Earth Corps training circulars. It was really only ten minutes, maybe twelve. Once the buzzers—two-meter-tall, wasp-mantis hybrids—started humming, it meant an attack was only minutes away.

"Damn it," Huck spat again. "Can't catch a damned break, man."

"The Dulcets will be back," Fleer whispered. His eyes were far off, staring up into the high, wispy clouds across the cobalt sky. "Have faith, Huck."

"I'm pretty much done with faith, buddy. We ain't got enough rounds for faith to have a chance."

The futility of it rose up fiercely, but Huck swallowed it down. Quitting was not an option. He reached for his pulse rifle and thumbed the battery switch from safe to fire. Withdrawing the projectile magazine, he gently tapped it against his helmet to better seat the rounds inside the flimsy metal box. The drill sergeants all said it was bullshit, but they did it too. It hadn't made a damn bit of difference since the old Army started using weapons made by the lowest bidder. Old habits from Earth died hard beyond the Belt, especially on buzzer-held planets like Honalee.

The droning grew louder. Lieutenant Boyce had said the hill was the best defensible position on the whole damned planet and the perfect place for an evacuation if the invasion faltered. Orbital bombing, he'd said, wouldn't be enough to hold off the swarming insects. Transports would need a good, defended position on top of key terrain to have a prayer of getting the infantry out alive.

Sixteen hours of fighting later, theirs was the last manned outpost in the sector still fighting. Boyce had been right. Too bad he'd taken a stinger to the head in the first wave.

Get a leader worth a damn, and they always die, Huck thought with disgust.

"Have faith," Fleer grunted again. "I mean it."

"I heard you, buddy." Huck patted Fleer's shoulder. "You rest."

Fleer shook his head. "Prop me up. I can cover your six one more time."

Huck studied his friend's gray face and saw fear behind his intense blue eyes. The kind of fear he had seen in almost every man's eyes during his six months on planet. They got that look when they realized that Earth and everyone who might care for them was six hundred light-years away. The look when they realized that not going home alive was inevitable. Fleer believed he wasn't gonna make it, and he wanted to die with some last vestige of honor.

Huck grinned with gallows humor, channeling one of their drill sergeants. "Fine, you ape. Gimme your hand."

With a grunt, Fleer got to his knees, assuming the hasty fighting position they'd shored up over the last few hours. Huck passed him a pulse rifle with a full magazine and a spare to sit at his knees, and then laid out the same arrangement for himself.

"We let 'em get up as high as they can before I set off the ring." Huck knelt with his back to Fleer and shouldered his rifle. "We buy us some time for evac."

Fleer grunted. "You sound like you believe me about them coming back for us."

Huck laughed. "No, just trying to make you think I do."

The buzzing increased, echoing from nearby hills. The attack had begun. Huck heard Fleer cough again and felt his hand squeeze the upper part of his boot. He reached back and squeezed Fleer's boot in response. In training, back on Earth, it meant, "I'm ready and I have your back."

Countless buzzers skittered toward them in the gathering darkness, and Fleer had simply said good-bye in the only way he'd been able to muster. They were going to die here, but they would die together. They'd been together since basic training on Ganymede four years earlier. Huck snorted, wiping away sudden tears, and yanked down his targeting visor. The shadows coming across the hill snapped into bright focus. In the distance, the first sets of antennae surged over the crest of the hill and danced as they sought a target.

Huck and Fleer remained still. Rifles at their shoulders, fingers beside their triggers, they waited for the buzzers to move. The first ones came from Huck's right, skittering across the hilltop.

Two quick bursts from Fleer's rifle put them down, the heat from the expended shells wafting over Huck's face and neck as more of the creatures approached from the left. Huck centered his rifle on the first, its six forelegs flailing grotesquely as it reared on thick hind legs. Snipping pincers glinted in the fading light, but Huck didn't see them. He found center mass, exhaled as he'd been taught, and dispatched four of them with five shots.

The familiar chuffing of Fleer's rifle gave Huck the focus he needed to immerse himself in the moment. Center, exhale, squeeze.

Center, exhale, squeeze. Working right to left and left to right, he went through the first two hundred rounds in less than a minute. Buzzers fell with each shot, littering the ground with their yellow-and-red bodies and making their followers easier targets as they clambered over their fallen comrades.

A group of four buzzers vaulted up the steepest part of the hill, stingers flying. Huck felt one pass between him and Fleer, but his friend's rifle poured rounds into the attacking bugs. Adrenaline surged.

"We're gonna make it!" Huck screamed over his shoulder. He raised his rifle again and mowed down the marauders. An incoherent scream came from his chest. Rage moved his body, standing tall in an onslaught of stingers that fell like rain around their position, though none struck him.

His rifle clicked on an empty cylinder, and Huck slapped in a new magazine. In that split second, he realized Fleer's rifle had fallen silent. He turned and saw Fleer face-forward in the dirt, at least twenty buzzers rearing up to hurl their stingers.

Huck's knees quivered as his shaking arms brought the rifle up to fire.

The buzzers, their carapaces shimmering gold in the sunset's light, hummed so loud he felt it through his body armor. He squeezed the trigger once and brought down one of the bastards. He moved to the second—

WHAM!

The soil around him rose up in a giant curtain as the concussion wave knocked him across Fleer's motionless form. Dirt rained down for several heartbeats. Huck came up, ready to fire, and stopped. The buzzing was muted, scared, but still close by. Reaching to his load-bearing vest, he pulled a ring bomb, removed the safety clip, and let the spring-loaded arming lever fly off. He tossed it high into the air and flung himself over Fleer, pressing them both into the dirt.

The weapon detonated, and ice-blue plasma rings raced down the mountain in expanding, concentric circles.

The buzzing stopped.

Huck wiped his face, pressed a finger against a nostril, and fired a mucus-laden dirt clod onto his buddy's boots. "Damn you," he muttered. He reached down to his vest again. There were no more rifle magazines in his pockets and only a single ring bomb.

I'll be dead before the sun goes down.

At his feet, the radio clicked to life. "Hammer Two Five? Hammer Two Five, this is Puff Zero Alpha on station. Do you read? Over?"

Huck blinked as the realization came. They were calling him. They'd come back after all. He leaned forward to grab the radio as it squawked again.

"Hammer Two Five, saw your plasma ring. Please respond. Over."

Huck licked his lips and pressed the transmit switch. "Zero Alpha, this is Hammer Two Five. Over."

"Good job, Two Five. We've got a bit of cleanup to do, so you boys keep your heads down for a couple of minutes." The voice drawled like a character from a movie Huck had seen during his last liberty. Something from way back in the twentieth century with men riding horses and bugle calls. "You holding up okay, son?"

Huck felt a smile touch the corners of his mouth. "Roger, Zero Alpha. Will keep my head down."

"Any other survivors?"

Huck startled. He hadn't bothered to check Fleer. He reached back and felt for a pulse. It was there, but weak as hell. "Roger, Zero Alpha. My buddy's in bad shape. We need immediate evac. Over."

"I'm gonna get on that, son. Got a few thousand customers to take care of for now. Keep your head down—that's an order. Puff Zero Alpha preparing to fire. Out."

Huck pulled Fleer toward the center of the fighting position and knelt by his side, ready to lie across his unconscious friend if necessary. Through the high clouds, Huck spotted four wide contrails moving quickly through the atmosphere on a course toward him. At the center of the four white lines was a massive, twin-tailed aircraft. One which Huck had only seen in aircraft recognition training manuals. With long, drooping wings full of bombs and missiles, the EB-77 Dragon was the sexiest thing he'd ever seen in the sky.

He chuckled. "Holy shit, Fleer. You ain't gonna believe this!"

It was the mightiest bomber in Earth's fleet. There were only a handful in existence, but in the hands of a capable pilot and crew, it carried enough conventional munitions to lay waste to a good-sized island, if necessary.

Huck waited until he could almost make out the sleek, pointed, supersonic nose cone before he flung himself across Fleer. A series of mighty explosions hit the base of the mountain to the west and worked around one hundred and eighty degrees. The Dragon screamed overhead and streaked east into a tight, high-G turn before arcing back toward the other side of the mountain.

Huck looked up and watched it approach. "Yeah! Give it to those bastards!" He fell back over Fleer's body, laughing and pounding his hands into the dirt. Hope surged. With the Dragon on station, the Dulcets could streak in to clear the path for rescue operations, and the gyrocopters wouldn't be far behind. "We're gonna make it, Fleer!"

Again the mountaintop shook from impacts far below. Above the last explosions, Huck could hear the buzzers screaming, no longer droning.

"You still with me, Two Five?" The pilot's voice crackled from the radio.

"Hell yeah, I am! Hit those guys again!"

"Negative, Two Five. The next part is up to you," the pilot radioed. "They're preparing to swarm. These things are gonna charge up that mountain in about thirty seconds—all of 'em. Every last one of them left alive is coming for you with everything they have. You've got to let them come, Two Five. They've got to get all the way there before you go coma."

"I got another ring bomb, Zero Alpha."

"Won't work this time, son. You have to trust me on this."

Huck flinched. "They're about to kill me and Fleer both, and you want me to coma?" In their field kit, infantry troops carried a syringe designed to shut down the bodily functions to a fraction of activity to allow easy extraction from the battlefield. "I'm not supposed to do anything?"

"Affirmative, Two Five. We can keep scaring 'em with bombs or we can kill 'em once and for all. That requires you being out cold. Trust me, son. We'll get you out. But I have to drop on your position. Over."

Huck nodded to no one as realization dawned. Standing orders applied, so he'd have to call in the strike on his and Fleer's position. For some kind of weapon he'd never heard of. Their only chance to survive. He looked at Fleer.

Screw it.

"Puff Zero Alpha, this is Hammer Two Five. You're cleared to drop on my position. Over."

"Acknowledged, Two Five. Turning inbound now."

From below, the screaming buzz intensified into an awful crescendo, shaking the ground.

He rolled Fleer face up, retrieved his friend's syringe, jabbed it into his thigh, and pushed the fluid in. He tapped his friend's chest and smirked. "Yer out, buddy."

"Here they come, Two Five. Twenty seconds." The Dragon's engines roared in the distance, and their thunder rumbled across the narrow, mountain valley.

"One down, Zero Alpha."

Huck fumbled out his own syringe from his first-aid packet and readied the shot. The first buzzers appeared over the edge of the rocks and reared into the air. More came from every direction. Huck saw the Dragon racing toward him, high in the western sky, against the setting sun. Flashes glimmered along the leading edge of her heavy wings. Thousands of projectiles streaked toward him and the buzzer swarm.

"What are you firing, Zero Alpha?"

"Just a little Dragon breath, Two Five. Nothing to worry about. Now go coma, son."

Huck looked down as the buzzers fell toward him, their pincers slashing the air wildly. He plunged the syringe into his thigh between armored plates and pushed the plunger. Vision swimming, Huck crumpled to the dirt.

"Give 'em hell, Puff," he said as consciousness faded away.

The darkness did not come. Instead, Huck found himself in a cool blue dream. Afterimages danced across his retinas like strobe-lit phantoms. Numb and detached, like his body was not his own, he felt every hair on his body stand on end. The air turned cold and sharp as a kitchen knife before crackling with a smell he knew was ozone. His consciousness ebbed and flowed until he heard the beating sounds of an approaching gyrocopter.

The medicos threw him onto a litter, slipped an IV into his arm, which instantly woke him up, and ran him toward the waiting gyrocopter. They shouted questions at him, but he wasn't listening.

Above the smoke swirling like autumn mist, he saw a dark shape with gilded wings painted gold by the sunset. He watched it punch through high clouds. The Dragon circled slowly, as if waiting for trouble.

With a glance to his left, he saw Fleer's color had returned. The medicos loaded him into a stasis tube for transport back to orbit. The medical display was green. Fleer was going to make it. This time, Huck let the tears fall.

He laid his head back against the litter and shivered as adrenaline left his system. Exhaustion took over. His every limb rubbery and heavy, Huck closed his eyes.

For a moment, over the beating gyros, he heard the Dragon scream through the atmosphere. Huck held on to the sound until it was long gone, knowing that he would again see his home world and live to tell his children and grandchildren about a Dragon named Puff who had saved his life.

O O O

Kevin Ikenberry is a retired Army officer and the author of the novels *Sleeper Protocol* and *Runs in the Family*. As an adult, he managed the world-renowned U.S. Space Camp program and served as an executive with two Challenger Learning Centers. He lives in Colorado with his family and continues to work with space every day.

The Essence

Frank Morin

Rawiya stood in the shadows, watching the raucous crowd of merchants, and decided that time was a fickle thing. How else could three months have passed in the blink of an eye, and yet leave her feeling as if she had aged half a century?

She blamed the dragon.

Three months had been enough time to transform a ragged band of starving street urchins into a newly-formed guild. Rawiya carried the official certificate, still stiff and starched, fresh from the archivist's writing desk. She allowed a smile.

One hour would be enough to shake the city.

That hour started now, and it would end with the gavel that closed the reverse auction for overstocked dragon essences.

Right on cue, Asim crept to her side and crouched on his haunches. At fourteen, he was a year older than she and far stronger, but smart enough to know she served better as guild leader.

"All the merchants are here," he confirmed. Most of the twoscore men didn't really matter. Only the five, those who had risen through the ranks to rule the dragon essence market, mattered.

"And the gandayak position?" she asked.

Asim beckoned, and Ghulam slipped through the nearby shadows to join them. At his side bounded the tabby kitten he had named Tab.

Ghulam was eight, and her best spy. "We have a problem. They're trying to hold out some of the big ones."

"You're sure?" she asked.

He nodded emphatically. "Tab overheard the whole thing."

He gestured at the marvelous tube collar Rawiya had acquired from the sylph. The kitten could slip into tight places that not even Ghulam could enter and, with one end of the collar fastened to Tab's throat, he could listen to the other end of the tube and hear everything.

The children thought it magic, and Ghulam and Tab worked so well as a team, their bond seemed almost mystic. Rawiya was content to let the children believe the theory, although the sylph insisted the concept was simple science, mingled with a tiny bit of dragon inner ear essence they'd acquired.

Today that invention had proven its value and secured their everlasting position in her new guild. As long as the next hour went according to plan.

Rawiya frowned. "They just can't let go. I bet they'll try setting up a rival secondhand market."

"It'll ruin everything," Asim warned.

Rawiya considered the problem for a moment, grateful the shadows along the wall concealed them from the merchants' gazes. She could not succeed if the gandayaks split the market.

"I'll have to use the conditions," she decided.

"We agreed they'd never go for it," Asim cautioned.

"They'll have to," she said, rising. "I'll have to push them harder."

She patted Tab. "Ghulam, you did well. Give Tab a little milk when you get back."

Grinning at the extravagant gift, Ghulam scooped up Tab and slipped away.

Taking a deep breath, Rawiya stepped out of the shadows. The auction yard was bathed in soft, multicolored light cast by cloth canopies draped in crisscrossing layers high above the stone-walled court.

A few merchants glanced in her direction, then looked again. Female merchants were rare, and they never ventured into the gandayak-controlled essence market. The merchants had never seen one so young.

Rawiya was just blossoming into womanhood, but to their eyes she probably looked barely eleven. She'd fought hard to conceal any evidence of her gender under layers of filth and shapeless rags. Until that fateful day she'd dared the unthinkable and ventured into the lair of the Vermilion Dragon, concealment had been her only safety.

Now she knew knowledge was far more powerful.

Her skin, for once scrubbed clean, seemed to glow in the muted light. She had been thrilled to learn that her hair, barely long enough to tickle her shoulders, was actually a rich auburn color.

Three months ago, Rawiya would have fled from the penetrating gazes of the merchants, never daring to approach, never dreaming she might be washed and wearing an actual dress. Her short green cape added a splash of color and confidence to her attire as well as concealing the damaged back of the bodice. The seamstress who had discarded it had considered it unsalvageable.

That made it perfect for a beggar stepping into a new life.

She just had to beat the five most successful merchants in the essence market at their own game. She reminded herself that she held the advantage. If she played her hand right, they'd cheer her on even as she stole the prize right out of their fingers.

The merchants disliked the gandayaks that much. One of the sly creatures stood at the auction podium, looking increasingly frantic. Gandayaks had always made Rawiya nervous. They were shaped like small humans with sickly green skin and exceptionally large yellow eyes that rarely blinked. Their nimble hands sported extra thumbs and seven fingers.

She touched the precious dragon quill concealed in her pocket. As usual, it granted her insights into everyone's stories.

Even the gandayaks' stories. The one at the podium was named Satomi. The leader of the clan, he was devilishly clever—and relentlessly mean to the children who crossed his path. For the first time, she saw beyond the physical aspects of his race.

Rawiya discerned his story, one of brilliance overshadowed by greed and turned septic by selfishness. The dragons were waking, and they would exact retribution for the mismanagement of their essences.

In a way, the gandayaks had saved Rawiya's life. The Vermilion Dragon had chosen to help her instead of eat her, in part so she could deliver the first round of punishment to the gandayaks.

For five long years, Satomi had brokered the sale of the prized dragon essences to the various races. But he had not filled the dragon hoards as he had promised, and he had focused so much on the most lucrative essences that he'd left many others unsold when he could have easily found buyers at lower prices.

Satomi was having a bad day.

Rawiya understood bad days.

At times, she had considered bad days the story of her life.

As soon as Satomi noticed her joining the crowd, he seized upon the potential distraction she offered. "You, girl. This auction is only for the authorized." The diminutive creature's guttural accent made him sound fiercer.

The merchants turned to stare. Rawiya withstood their scrutiny, scanning the crowd she knew well, reading their stories. They were all successful, most were selfish, and a handful were vicious. Three she considered downright dangerous.

Rawiya smiled. "I am new, but I meet the requirements."

"Who are you?" demanded Satomi, his yellow eyes glittering with satisfaction that he'd broken the downward spiral of the auction.

He'd need more than a moment's distraction, though. The merchants were worked into a gold frenzy, and Rawiya needed to push them even further. As a beggar, Rawiya had long been invisible, scurrying through the shadows of the essence market, silently witnessing most of the sales by those merchants. She knew them all—and exactly what essences they had sold from which dragons.

To her, each sale was a story, and stories lived in her heart.

She doubted any of the merchants commanded the breadth of knowledge she did. Her intelligence was augmented daily by every one of the children she struggled to keep alive day to day, who brought her information with the help of their eavesdropping little kittens.

"I am Rawiya," she declared loudly into the near silence, "Leader of the Crimson Urchins."

That triggered a round of loud laughter, led by Satomi, his eyes darting across the crowd, gauging the mood. Rawiya let them laugh.

"There's no such guild," declared a stocky merchant in a rich velvet coat and a ridiculous hat. His name was Melville, one of the five she needed to defeat.

His story was easy to read. Hard-won skill layered over sly craftiness that rivaled the gandayaks', buttressed by avarice. He specialized in the coveted Adventuring Hero package. It included essence of dragon heart for bravery, essence of dragon blood for healing potions, and essence of dragon scales that could transform a hero's armor into a nearly invincible fighting suit. He feared only the loss of his prestige and property.

She could work with that.

"Any who dispute my claim to the Crimson Urchin guild can take it up with the bureau of guild registration. They usually respond within a fortnight, with a sufficient bribe," Rawiya said calmly.

That elicited more laughter, and Melville advanced, eyeing her closely. "I know you, girl. You're that beggar always bothering my clients."

"Yes, the one with all the little orphans," a lesser merchant piped in.

To that man she said, "And I thank you, as always, for your generosity."

She didn't bother thanking Melville. He was more apt to kick a child than feed them.

A tall sylph slipped through the crowd to her side. She was grateful to see him, one of her secret allies. Enitan was not a merchant. Few of his race were. Most were healers or scholars, and he was one of the most brilliant. He topped seven feet like a willowy cloud. She could almost see the thoughts flashing through his amazing brain. Literally.

The sylph were a mostly transparent race with no distinguishable genitalia. They rarely bothered with clothing other than thick-soled socks. Their homeland on the Misting Isles in the Bitter Ocean lacked the sharp rocks found in the human realms, and they hated the restriction of shoes.

Enitan preferred bright pink socks. He said they reminded him of sunrise in the mists. Tab loved pouncing on them.

The lure of the dragon essences had drawn the sylph from their far-off homeland to offer their services to study dragon essences and research new uses. Despite the potential for future revenue, the greedy gandayaks had rejected the offer. Rawiya had recruited Enitan to help her after reading his story in his clear eyes.

"The girl makes a valid point," Enitan suggested.

"Why doesn't this surprise me?" Melville snorted. "One beggar standing up for another."

"You seem unusually flustered," Rawiya said. "Do you really fear my little guild so much?"

Melville's face flushed as merchants roared with laughter that secured her place in the crowd. He waved her away. "We've wasted enough time on you." He turned back to the gandayak at the podium. "Satomi, resume the bidding."

Rawiya was quickly forgotten as merchants resumed their bids. Most of them spent more time browbeating the gandayak for his business practices than actually bidding, though.

"We could have all increased profits by twenty percent across the board," shouted a thickset master merchant named Oswald, spraying spittle over the fancy hats of his neighbors, "if you hadn't limited quantities!"

He specialized in the Mighty Elements package. Wizards across the fourteen realms loved the essence of fire and wind from dragon breath. Oswald's second-best package was the Winged Fury, which used the dragon wing essences to imbue flight.

"And I can't sell a single breath of dragon steam at the prices you demand," exclaimed Zeph, a florid-faced, beefy fellow who breathed as loud as a fully-stoked bellows.

That was one essence Rawiya was thrilled to know the wily merchants had undervalued. She and the sylph had plans for that steam. Zeph made a wonderful living catering to ladies seeking the Princess Package, with essences that enhanced beauty and grace. The Love Me Tender package was his second-best revenue maker, prompting nervous lords to demand counter-essences, which he happily provided.

"Gentlemen," Satomi called to the hostile crowd in what he clearly hoped was a friendly tone but which came across more as condescending, "we've had our differences, but the market has never been better, no?"

No. The market was ripe for revolution.

* * *

Dragon essence had been the key to the gandayak rise, and it would do the same for Rawiya.

For dragons to reach higher planes of magic, might, and pure awesome glory, they needed three things: years of undisturbed slumber, piles of fresh gold and jewels, and, most important for the other races, to shed their old essences.

Most lesser reptiles, even the deadly serpentlike jaculi, shed their skin. Dragons shed far more, peeling away the outer shell of their entire being, like giant onions.

The essences that made up that shell were barely-tangible pieces of every aspect of a dragon, from the deepest innards to the mighty scales. Those essences could be ingested to produce amazing enhancements.

Only a couple dozen dragons remained in the world, and the other races had become adept at hunting them for their essences. But no one wanted the supply to run out, either.

So the gandayaks procured the most profitable treaty in the history of the world. They gained exclusive access to all of the dragon essences. The dragons got to slumber without worry of sneaky heroes disturbing their rest. The world gained access to dragon essences, and their gold fed the hoards that in turn fed the dragons' souls and ensured the cycle would continue forever.

That was the promise, anyway.

"You've saddled us with goods we cannot sell while holding back the essences we really want," Melville declared, eliciting a round of shouted agreement. "Today is the reckoning. Don't act so surprised!"

Bundling essences into packages had helped focus demand and drive prices to astronomical levels. The gandayaks had raked in gold that rivaled the dragon hoards. That was part of the problem. They touted the benefits of their top packages so much, no one wanted to buy the essences left over. No one even bothered researching most of them.

Worse, essences only lasted up to five years. Essences that hadn't sold within the first three years suddenly became less desirable. Who wanted to be a short-term hero? Warehouses full of overstocked or unwanted essences did not make money for the dragons, who expected gold.

Still, the market had worked wonderfully for the first few years. The war against the jaculi made unrivaled progress. Essence-fueled heroes even drove the giant nuckelavee and their troll pets from the northern borders.

Those days were about to change.

The dragons were waking up. The Vermilion Dragon, known for her wisdom, her command of history, and her stories, was the first. Even though her scales, breath, and wings were as mighty as any other, they hadn't sold. They had seemed somehow inferior.

That meant less gold for her—and less essence regrowth.

That meant a grumpy dragon.

Rawiya and the dragon had seen mutual benefit and made their plans. She'd left the dragon cave, endowed with wisdom and learning and the rare dragon quill.

"Everything is a story," the dragon had breathed to her. "The power of the quill is mightier than any of the lesser races can comprehend. Use it well."

Three months had passed like a dream. So much had changed.

So much remained to be done.

"My friends," Satomi said, his green skin looking more sickly than normal, "I am afraid you misunderstand the purpose of today's auction."

"We know exactly what we're doing," shouted the merchant Zeph.

Wringing his hands, Satomi whined, "But this is a reverse auction."

"Today *you* pay *us* for once," shouted a tall merchant named Fletcher. He specialized in the Castle Bash military siege equipment packages that used the essence of dragon claws and foreheads.

"Yes, we will pay." Satomi sighed. "Yes, there is a regrettable supply of unsalable essences. By contract, we must rid ourselves of that supply."

Melville snorted. "The world knows about the overstocked supply. They are clamoring for the secondhand essence market."

Satomi cringed. "These lesser essences will never compete for the sales we all enjoy," he insisted. "There may be a way to discharge them, perhaps to the sylph and other academics, but we all know no heroes or rich lords will pay for essences on the verge of expiration."

"We'll deal with that market," Zeph shouted. "You deal with paying us to get rid of them."

"Hence the dilemma." Satomi eagerly switched gears. "By your own words, you admit that you expect financial gain from these essences. Thus we award the contract to the one who offers the lowest transfer fee."

"That's what you hope," shouted a short merchant named Baldric, who was almost as wide as he was tall. Rawiya always thought of him as Bald-Width. "My bid will cost you six thousand gold up front, and one thousand gold per month thereafter before I'll take that mismanaged dragon weight off your hands."

He was a celebrity in the gourmet foods market. His Feasting Royals packages leveraged the unique tastes of dragon fat essences.

Bidding resumed with a vengeance, driving the prices higher as merchants vied to demonstrate their frustration at the gandayaks.

Then Melville made his move.

Every story needed a villain, and Rawiya had expected he might assume the role.

Bidding had continued to escalate, despite Satomi's pleas. It stalled around seven thousand gold for the initial transfer fee. Satomi looked desperate. Melville's voice cut through the clamor like a butcher knife.

"One thousand gold for the initial transfer, and five hundred per month thereafter!"

Shocked silence crashed over the merchants who had been jubilant just seconds prior. They rounded on Melville like a pack of angry hounds.

Satomi looked like he had been given a royal pardon.

"You can't," Baldric exclaimed. "Traitor!"

Rawiya almost felt bad for Bald-Width. She was secretly looking forward to the new line of discount gourmet food packages he was planning to launch with secondhand essences.

"Yes, yes," Melville waved their objections aside. "We're all angry, and you lot would have carried on for hours, but one of us has to show some sense. It appears I'm the only one who will."

As the other merchants shouted curses at Melville, Satomi cried, "You will take all the essences we deem unsalable at that price?"

His seven-fingered hand raised the gavel, poised to strike and seal the bargain and the double-cross Tab had uncovered.

"And as part of the deal, I will require a twenty percent discount in your brokerage fee on all of my future mainstream essence package sales."

Satomi's hand slowly sank. He looked disgusted that he wasn't the only one with a secret agenda. The other merchants grasped the significance of that requirement in a single, horrified heartbeat.

"You scoundrel," shouted Fletcher, looking ready to reach for a sword. "Owning the entire secondhand essence market is not enough? You would drive us all out on the street and own the entire mainstream market too?"

"We can't compete with a twenty percent spread," Baldric exclaimed, looking ready to pass out.

"Compete as you can," Melville said with a condescending smile. "Perhaps I can find work for you."

Before the assembled merchants regained their wits and began clamoring for their own desperate deals that would play right into the gandayaks' greedy little hands, Rawiya spoke loudly.

"I bid a one hundred gold initial transfer fee, with ten gold per month. Along with some minor provisions."

Every merchant gasped. Satomi looked like he wanted to vault the crowd and kiss her, while Melville's face darkened with rage.

"You dare speak amid your betters?" he thundered. "You worthless little nobody!"

"We've already established that I have the right to be here," Rawiya responded calmly, fingering the quill in her pocket. "Yelling about it now won't change that."

Melville approached, his rage building. She watched, judging how far to push.

"You know nothing of these matters," he shouted in her face, trying to terrify her into submission, a tactic that should have worked on a street urchin.

She softly coughed behind one raised hand. "You should choose your foods more carefully before breathing into a lady's face."

Just the nudge he needed.

Melville cuffed her on the side of the head. With her years of experience on the street, such blows were expected, and she could have easily avoided it. Instead, she let it land, but rolled with it, exaggerating its impact and tumbling to the stones with a cry of pain.

Melville stood over her, fist raised to strike again. "We aren't playing games here, girl. Get back to your shadows, or you're going to get hurt."

Rawiya rose to face him, wincing as she probed her smarting cheek. "Am I mistaken, or is there not a rule of conduct enforced within the league of merchants that prescribes a penalty to one who attempts the use of force and threat of injury to interrupt or subvert the pending sale of a competing merchant?"

Of course there was. She'd just quoted it verbatim.

Fletcher pushed Melville back, his expression satisfied. "There is indeed … lady."

He had hesitated, but he'd actually used her title. It felt good.

"You can't be serious," Melville exclaimed.

He had angered the other merchants enough that they scrambled to defend Rawiya's honor. Even Satomi. The incredible deal she'd offered was the bait she needed to lure him in. And Melville had set up the situation perfectly for her.

"We are all witnesses," Satomi proclaimed. "Violence was done with intent to intimidate and to destroy a pending sale. Melville is guilty."

"She's a street urchin!" Melville protested as merchants pressed in upon him, hands grasping.

"One with every right to be here," her friend Enitan reminded him. The sylph leaned close to Rawiya. "Are you all right, my dear?"

"I'm fine."

Better than fine. It was like a dream come true, watching the angry merchants strip Melville of shoes, purse, and coat. Fletcher presented the tokens to her. The purse held more coin than she had seen in her lifetime; it would feed the children of her guild for years.

She ignored the shoes but swept the huge, luxurious coat around her shoulders. It was far too large, but she didn't care. It was the finest piece of cloth she had ever touched. With a flourish, she transferred her precious dragon quill from her little dress pocket into the deep pocket of the new coat.

Melville noticed.

"Deceiver!" he howled, shoving a hand into her pocket. "Thief and villain!"

He hefted the quill and rounded on Fletcher. "See, proof, you fools! I own the only dragon quill, and it's worth five thousand gold if it's worth a penny. She stole it from me, just as she's trying to steal these essences from all of us!"

They didn't want to believe him, but merchants hated thieves more than any other type of criminal.

"You lie," Rawiya said. "Return my property."

"Enough!" Melville thundered, striking at her face with the quill.

Exactly what she needed him to do.

Rawiya did not wait for the blow to land. Instead, she slipped to one side and grabbed his hand.

A thunderclap and explosion of crimson light burst from the quill, tumbling Melville through the air. He shattered the podium and crashed with Satomi off the far side of the platform. The blast knocked most of the other merchants off their feet.

Rawiya stood alone in a clear circle, holding the dragon quill. It pulsed with a bright vermilion light. Glowing tendrils like crimson lightning crept up her arms and settled into her hair. The air smelled of cinnamon.

"This quill is mine." She waved it. "Clearly. Gifted to me by the Vermilion Dragon herself barely three months ago."

"Three months?" Satomi breathed as he climbed off the groaning form of Melville and returned to the platform.

Rawiya faced him, hands on hips. Time for the final push.

"She's not very happy that you haven't sold her essences—I'll tell you that for free. I expect she'll be visiting soon."

Satomi's color drained until he looked almost human. "She's coming here?"

"Probably. She said she might wait for the Obsidian Dragon to awaken first."

Satomi cringed, and his huge yellow eyes blinked closed for several seconds, as if he was fighting not to cry.

"So I suggest we complete our business," Rawiya added.

"Yes, of course," Satomi exclaimed. "You can tell her how we worked everything out."

"I will," Rawiya agreed. As Satomi scrambled to find the gavel to formally accept the deal, she added, "But first, three points."

Satomi sighed, rubbing his eyes. "Please make them quick."

She extracted from her dress pocket a rolled parchment. "I have here the conditions of the transfer." She added softly, fighting to look casual, "Would you like to inspect them?"

"I'm sure they're fine," he said, his desperation driving him exactly where she needed him.

No gandayak had ever accepted a deal without knowing the fine print, and the other merchants looked stunned.

"The second item," Rawiya said, "is for my esteemed colleagues. I lack the facilities to process all of the essences. I will establish the secondhand essence market, but I'm going to need all of your help to sell the essences."

As she had hoped, they began clamoring for specifics instead of resuming the original bidding process.

She raised her hands for silence. "I will grant licensing to each of you to produce packages of your choice. You will pay the dragon hoard percentage directly, and you will pay me twenty percent of the sale price. The rest is yours."

They grinned, already envisioning profits. They had to know she would profit enormously with all of them paying a share to her, but a moment ago, they had been staring zero percent in its ugly face.

Melville staggered to his feet, and he barked an ugly laugh. "What a load of rubbish! You've forgotten one critical element, girl."

"Indeed I have not," she replied, cutting him off. "The third item to complete our business today is resolution for your crime of attempted theft of my quill."

"How was I supposed to know it was yours?" Melville exclaimed.

"You could have asked," she said. "But no, you had to try stealing it."

"I did not," he protested, but for the first time, his confidence cracked.

"Oh, yes, you did," Fletcher gloated. "With violence."

Enitan said, "Per my understanding of league rules, such a crime must be compensated by a payment of ten times the value of the property stolen."

Melville sank to the edge of the platform, his face ashen. "Ten times?"

"That's fifty thousand gold by your own reckoning," Baldric chortled. "At least."

"I don't have that much coin," Melville muttered, looking like he was trying to awaken from a nightmare.

Satomi rose with gavel in hand. "Then your property is forfeit. Your home, your shop, your merchandise, and the contents of your vaults all transferred to ownership by the Vermilion Lady."

Vermilion Lady. Rawiya liked that.

"So we have a deal?" she asked.

Satomi pounded the gavel again. "Deal. Secondhand essences sold, per our agreement and your written terms."

"Thank you," Rawiya said.

He actually smiled in victory, not realizing what he had done.

* * *

Rawiya sat in an overstuffed chair in her new mansion, reveling in the unique sensation of victory. The plan had worked better than she'd dreamed.

Enitan and a dozen sylph had already moved into the huge mansion with her and the children of the Crimson Urchin guild. There was more than enough room for all, even though the sylph were already complaining about the kittens pouncing on their socks.

It was a small price to pay for unfettered access to study dragon essences. Rawiya's children and their kittens had eaten their fill for the first time ever, and were sprawled, semi-comatose, across the plush living room at her feet. Some of the kittens slept while floating above the couches. Someone had slipped a bit of dragon wing essence into their dinner, and they hadn't yet learned how to land.

More children would join her guild. Word was spreading like wildfire. Merchants were clamoring to secure contracts for essences, and more sylph were scrambling to inventory everything. Workers were lining up to help build her secondhand essence market.

She planned for a lot more than that, including housing for all of the orphans until she could find the right estate in the country where they could move to. She dreamed of a swimming hole, green pastures full of ponies, and thousands of socks for the kittens to play with.

Satomi had nearly fainted when he read the full terms of the agreement. Rawiya gained immediate control of all of the essences not included in existing packages, even when arriving fresh from newly slumbering dragons. In addition, all essences from the gandayak packages not sold after three years would become her property.

In a single day, the secondhand essence market dwarfed the gandayaks' holdings. She didn't care how much they charged. She didn't plan to compete for the business of mighty heroes or silly ladies.

Production of new inventions would start immediately.

The first was a new form of heat, fueled by the vast quantities of dragon steam essence. It would offer relief to thousands who would otherwise suffer the bitter cold of the onrushing winter with no remedy.

The second invention would change the world. Enitan had discovered that essence of dragon intestine, mixed in a secret solution he had devised, could dissolve human waste into pure water with a scent of spring flowers.

She couldn't wait for the entire city to stop reeking of sewage.

"Tell us a story," begged four-year-old Jamila, hopping to pluck her slumbering black-and-white kitten out of the air.

"All right," Rawiya said as other children took up the call and kittens started swooping overhead. She grinned. "I will tell you about the Vermilion Dragon. Because tomorrow, she is coming for a visit."

O O O

Frank Morin loves good stories in every form. When not writing or trying to keep up with his active family, he's often found hiking, camping, scuba diving, or enjoying other outdoor activities. For updates on his sci-fi time travel Facetaker novels, his popular Petralist YA fantasy novels, or other upcoming book releases, check his website: www.frankmorin.org.

Reconciling with the Dragon

Melissa Koons

To: The Doctor with the Glasses

It's been four weeks since I left your camp. When I stumbled my way out of the darkness that night, I had no idea what you had done to me. What months of being closed up in your camp was intended to do to a person. It took a period of adjustment, and I know you are out there, looking for me, but I'm reconciling myself and you'll never find us. Not yet. In the meantime, until I see you again, you will be glad to know that I have taken to many coffee shops and public gatherings to learn more about my reconciliation that you introduced me to. It's strange being in these places; there is so much light.

This reconciliation isn't what I expected. Hell, I had no idea what to expect, but I didn't expect this. I knew there was a Dragon in me: angry, volatile, greedy. You brought that Dragon out. Your devices, as horrible as they were, succeeded. I saw its glowing scales as its golden eyes flared ominously into mine. When I stared into those hateful eyes, I couldn't bear to be in the same room as it. I didn't want it.

It has the power to destroy, and that is all it wanted to do. That is all it had been allowed to do.

I was afraid that it would kill me: open its jaw and swallow me whole until there was no trace of me left. What had existed of me, I feared, would disappear without a trace, without memorial, without even a whisper on the wind. I would simply vanish, and all that would remain was the Dragon.

So I did what any clinically sane person should do.

I ran.

I heard the search party you sent after me. I saw the bouncing light from the torches you carried. But it was still there, that Dragon. It was breathing down my neck at every turn. I couldn't escape those flaming eyes or those teeth.

It was only when I accepted that there was no running from it that I could begin the reconciliation process. That's why I like frequenting these coffee shops. I had never noticed before—never been driven to sit and actually look at the world and the people surrounding me—but coffee shops really are the perfect place to see things as they truly are. Every one of these people here has a Dragon. I have yet to see one as angry as mine, but then again, those Dragons don't typically like coffee; they need something much stronger to quell them. I haven't returned to those places I know, although my Dragon wants to.

The woman by the door has a blue one. She sits at the same table every Saturday afternoon with a book and a pen, sipping on hot tea because coffee is too bitter. Her Dragon is docile, resting its head on her shoulder while she reads. Before you pulled my Dragon out of me, I never would have noticed the air of loneliness about her. Her Dragon sucks the heat from the air and makes the woman shiver in her self-inflicted isolation.

I don't have the expertise or training that you do, Doctor, so I have no answers for her. I can only wonder what made her want to keep the world at arm's length while her heart continues to yearn for connection. It's sad, really. She's only in her late twenties or early thirties. She still has so many possibilities available to her, but her Dragon keeps her tethered to her emptiness.

The boy with the red hair at the booth by the counter—he has a black one. He is talking to a girl around his age; they both look like they are right out of high school. Her Dragon is pink and frightened of the boy with the red hair, but she talks to him anyway.

I've never seen him here before, but I can see why the young girl's Dragon fears him. She fidgets in her seat, shifting her weight and shuffling her feet. She toys with a locket around her neck, twisting it this way and that on the silver chain. Her Dragon urges her to leave—pokes at her, makes her itch—but the desperation the girl feels for a false reality that was promised to her makes her silence the Dragon.

If you were here, I know you'd help the poor girl. You'd see the way the boy's black Dragon looks at her, and it would make you squirm. You'd know just what to say, Doctor. You'd smile politely and pull the girl away while making everyone around you think the world was a perfect place. As I watch the young couple's interactions, I am torn. The heat from my Dragon's breath burns my neck, and I know what course of action it wants to take. Before I can decide whether or not it would be wise to unleash the destructive force within me, they leave.

I'm pretty sure I won't see that girl again.

Talk to you soon, Doctor.

Me

* * *

To: The Doctor with the Glasses

I passed a man on the way to the subway today. He seemed average enough, nothing special about him that caught my eye, but something in his scent called out my Dragon and made it snarl. You should have seen the terror in the man's eyes as he stared at my Dragon. His legs quivered, and my Dragon engulfed him in flames. I felt powerless as I watched the exchange. I wanted to stop the Dragon, to pull it back, but there was nothing I could do. I still fear it will turn on me one of these days and devour me if I'm not careful.

Maintaining this reconciliation with my Dragon is not as easy as I had hoped. Then again, you never promised me easy. I wonder, from time to time, if I had stayed at the camp with you, would it still be this difficult? The man from the subway ran away from me. I can't blame him. I ran away from the Dragon, too.

I felt horrible after the exchange with the man. The whole ride on the train to my stop, I pondered why the Dragon felt it necessary to attack him. What drew the Dragon out? I thought I had gotten a handle on it, had learned to keep the Dragon in check, but obviously I was wrong.

It seems I am not entirely in control—the Dragon will not follow my commands blindly—but I am not at its complete disposal, either. Ever since you brought it out, my usual process for coping with it no longer works. Now there is a strange kind of power struggle between my Dragon and me, but we are learning. It was so accustomed to devastation and I to repression, but our status quo has been upset, and neither of us know where to go from here.

When I got to my coffee shop, I took my usual seat against the wall and nodded a hello to the woman with the blue Dragon. I sat there maybe an hour, watching people come and go before I had puzzled out an answer about the man in the subway. He was nothing special: he wore an untailored suit that came off the rack; he held a coffee in one hand and a briefcase in the other. The only thing slightly remarkable about him was his hair: a bright red that seemed far too familiar.

It's been two weeks since I've seen the boy with the red hair and the girl with the silver locket. I had had an uneasy feeling from the start, so when I saw her face on the news, I wished I had let my Dragon out to do with the boy whatever it had wanted to do that day. She's been missing for three days now, which I suppose is better than some alternatives. If only she had listened to her Dragon, if only she had acknowledged its existence, maybe then she'd be safe.

I look around at all the people who come and go, and it astounds me how many of us live our whole lives in denial of that single presence. We were taught as children to believe in magic, to play pretend and create entire worlds of fantasy. Somewhere along the line, that was beaten out of us. It was as if imagination was only encouraged, nurtured, and accepted until the age of ten. Then we were beaten constantly—steadily—with heavy tools to make us better, wiser. We were beaten with logic and reason, responsibility and obligation, expectation and convention, until we no longer believed that Dragons were ever real.

If it wasn't for you, Doctor, my Dragon would have consumed me long ago without my ever knowing it was there. I repressed it with toxins, ignoring its presence, until it would have devoured me. My fears of vanishing would have come true, and, unlike the girl with the silver locket, no one would have ever known I was gone.

Now I know. Dragons are very real, and they live within us all whether we acknowledge them or not. Not all Dragons are as angry and bent on annihilation as mine is. I'm observing that the person affects their Dragon as much as it affects them.

The new barista behind the counter has a red Dragon. Her Dragon has feathers and a long, snakelike body with large eyes and a strange beard. It has a kind smile, just like her, and it whispers words of comfort and wisdom to all the patrons.

When she first started working, I thought she could see Dragons like I can, but I was wrong. It is only now, in her retirement, that she seems to have let her Dragon out. I can tell by the eagerness with which it greets the customers; she kept it locked in a cage for far too long, and its desperation for interaction shows it.

I think that's what made mine so angry: keeping it buried and denied for so long. The barista's Dragon became desperate to share her knowledge and character; mine became vengeful.

I look over to the girl with the blue Dragon and I hope, for her sake, it doesn't take her until her retirement to let her Dragon free from the cage they both have locked themselves into. Otherwise, her sad Dragon might fill with resentment, and she will find that neither tea nor bitter coffee can appease it—only something stronger, found in dark places, could placate it then.

I don't know what to do, Doctor. I'm not ready to find you yet; I want to figure this out on my own. I am learning about my Dragon more and more, and the relationship between man and Dragon is not what I had thought. I thought one of us had to be in control—one of us had to be dominant. That is the understanding of the world that was beaten into me.

Perhaps, like with everything else I'm learning, that too was wrong. Is it possible that, together, we can build something new?

That doesn't seem right. I don't think my Dragon is capable of building since its first reaction is to destroy—like with that man. The fear I caused in his eyes would have been shameful to you.

Talk to you soon, Doctor.

Me

* * *

To: The Doctor with the Glasses

I stopped going to the other coffee shops and public spaces I had been frequenting. It's been a week now since the girl with the silver locket went missing, and I can't stop this burning feeling filling me. I thought maybe I'd find the boy with the red hair at another shop. My Dragon led me from place to place, but he was nowhere to be found. My Dragon is growing anxious—I can feel it breathing down my neck with its hot, angry puffs.

It's incredible, Doctor, this secret I have learned. It was the one you were trying to guide me towards, but I couldn't hear it then. I wasn't ready that day in your office when I came face-to-face with my Dragon for the first time. It's so simple, though. I can't believe I didn't see it before.

I can only hope the boy with the red hair doesn't know this secret. If he does, the girl with the silver locket really will be gone forever.

Knowing the secret of the Dragon allows you to create anything—build anything. There are no walls or limits. There are no sticks of reason or logic to beat us with. Now I know why you wanted us to reconcile so badly. It is only through the reconciliation of the Dragon and the self that we can enter this space where we are unencumbered by the external and can return to that world we once knew together as a child. The world where we can begin to build, to create.

I return to my coffee shop every day. I sit in the same spot, my back against the wall, watching the people as they come in and out of the door.

The woman with the blue Dragon has started coming in more frequently as well. She used to come only on Saturdays, but now she and her sad Dragon come a couple times during the week in the evening, too. She stays for long hours until the sun goes down, her nose pressed in a book or a notepad. I only get a nod when she walks in, an acknowledgment of another regular.

She seems so weary, Doctor. I wish you were here to help her. Whatever is on her mind, it makes her Dragon build a higher wall around her to keep anyone from ever getting close.

There is nothing I can do for her. The only thing I can do is sit here and wait, letting the creation of a plan build between me and my Dragon.

Talk to you soon, Doctor.

Me

* * *

To: The Doctor with the Glasses

I saw him today. The boy with the red hair finally returned to the coffee shop. I've waited for him for weeks now, knowing that one day he would return.

Still no sign of the girl with the silver locket. I've been keeping up with the news just for her. They've searched the county high and low, but I know she's not here.

The boy's black Dragon flirts with the barista confidently, wrapping the older woman in a similar net of charm and deceit that had captured the young girl.

No, this boy took her far away from here.

My Dragon blows smoke out of its nostrils at the sight of the boy with the red hair, but I calm it down. I don't want it to unleash its anger prematurely and ruin the plan we have created. Our reconciliation is still delicate, but without it we will never be able to bring our creation to fruition.

The woman with the blue Dragon looks up at me, her eyes studying me for the first time. Her Dragon had slowly started to take notice of other people around her instead of just reading over the woman's shoulder. This is, however, the first time she really looks at me. She'd grown accustomed to me—she's seen my hair, my eyes, my face. She's gotten comfortable with me; she'd smile and give a nod in greeting. Now, as my eyes follow the boy with the red hair, I see her face lift and her eyes fix on me in a way they never have before. Out of my peripheral vision, I notice her finally see my Dragon.

She is shocked, as most people are, I imagine. Not only is it a golden Dragon, glowing with raw power and energy, but, as I said before, Doctor, my kind of Dragon doesn't frequent coffee shops.

She is scared, perhaps, and I am sorry for that. I like her enough, though we have never spoken, but I can't take the time right now to reassure her—the boy with the red hair is walking away. I stand up, leaving my almost-full cup of coffee on the table, and follow him out the door.

The woman with the blue Dragon watches me the whole time, and I can feel her unspoken questions pelting me like bullets. All I can offer her when I pass by is a sad half smile, but I am unable to hide the fire in my eyes. Maybe that will answer something.

The boy walks with arrogance. His step is assured, and he reeks of so much hubris it takes all the control we have to keep my Dragon at bay just a little longer. The boy doesn't seem to know we're following him—that, or he doesn't care. His Dragon whispers to him that he is untouchable—and he believes it. He half listens to his Dragon and believes that he is in complete control.

His Dragon and I know better.

When he gets in his truck, I let my Dragon out.

"Let's go for a ride," my Dragon says, crawling into the front seat beside him.

The boy looks scared, and his Dragon steps in and tries to compensate for it by mouthing off. But my Dragon is older, more experienced, and more practiced than his. My Dragon is angrier, crueler, and more resourceful than his. Most importantly, though, my Dragon knows a secret that his doesn't: it is even more powerful now that we have reconciled and neither of us have to fight for power or control over the other.

The black Dragon wants to fight, but the boy with the red hair is too frightened.

My Dragon wins.

We go for a ride. It's not a long ride, only an hour or two, but long enough to get out of town. My Dragon is patient and steady, not blowing fire or devouring the boy until it has what it wants. I wait quietly for my time to step in. It is not my turn yet.

The boy takes me to a house and parks in front. He keeps his hands on the wheel and his eyes trained forward, but the shaking of his knees tell me that he is scared. His Dragon doesn't know what to do. Does it fight? Does it run? Does it go down in flames and take me with it? Luckily for me, the boy allows his fear to repress his Dragon and thus has no solution.

I get out of the truck and follow my Dragon into the house. These are the dark places where it used to find absolution. It is familiar with the dim lighting and the unkempt floors. This is what my Dragon used to call home.

It's a good thing you're not here after all, Doctor. You wouldn't be able to handle the stench.

The girl with the silver locket isn't hard to find. She's the only one in the house. I find her crumpled body, clothed in dirty garments and her own vomit. Her pink Dragon is frightened, grown weak after days of trying to get the girl to leave. I recognize the familiar resignation in the pink Dragon's eyes.

My Dragon steps aside and lets me take the needle out of the girl's arm. I scoop her up gently. She moans a little, and her eyes flutter open and then close again. She is too high to maintain consciousness, but her Dragon follows us as I carry her out of the house, her head lolling from side to side with each step I take.

I'm not prepared for the flashing lights when I step out. I'm not prepared for the onslaught of officers or seeing the boy with the red hair pressed against a cop car with his hands behind his back.

I had been prepared to steal the truck after my Dragon did with the boy whatever it wanted to do to him. I was going to teach the boy my secret: when you join with your Dragon and take it into you, there is nothing on this planet that can stop you. Nothing you cannot create; nothing you cannot bring into manifestation with words, tools, or will.

Paramedics are taking the girl to the hospital. I'm going in for questioning.

Talk to you soon, Doctor.

Me

* * *

To: The Doctor with the Glasses

It was the woman with the blue Dragon. I hadn't expected it to be her. I never would have guessed, but you probably would have. The moment she sat across from me in the interrogation room, it all kind of clicked. She is an investigator for the police department, and when she saw my Dragon come out and follow the boy with the red hair, she grew suspicious.

"I watched you leave, and the fire in your eyes told me that you knew something horrible was about to happen. I watched you follow the boy, and when you climbed into his truck, I knew something was terribly wrong. I called for backup and had them follow you. When you went into the house, the officer questioned the boy, and he confessed everything," she told me.

Apparently, the boy with the red hair had coerced the young girl with the silver locket to go with him. She had agreed—at first—to see the fantastical world he promised her. When she told him she wanted to go home, well, the black Dragon wasn't okay with that.

I won't give you the details—you don't need them—but he manipulated her and made her stay. He showed her those toxins so familiar to me, which prevented her from listening to her pink Dragon. His black Dragon had kept her drugged so she couldn't leave.

The hospital says she'll be fine. They'll probably send her to your camp when she's ready to be released. You can help her; I know you can.

"How did you know it was him?" The woman with the blue Dragon asked me. Her Dragon stood behind her, protecting her from everyone and everything that came through that precinct. I finally understood why she kept the world at arm's length. I would, too, if I had her job.

I wanted to answer her question, but I couldn't. I didn't know how. Nothing about how I was able to find and save the girl with the silver locket was traditional. I didn't use logic the way it had been beaten into us all. Nothing about my methods were conventional or responsible or obligated.

I listened to my Dragon. I melded with him instead of keeping him separate, and we found a solution together that I never could have seen on my own. I ignored what had been beaten into me and embraced what had been beaten out of me. I let the magic of imagination, intuition, and ingenuity guide me. I combined reason and logic with this magic and let it create something new.

How do you explain that to someone who couldn't possibly comprehend this secret? Who hasn't reconciled like we have? So I shrugged in answer because I had no words to say.

The woman with the blue Dragon tilted her head and studied me for the second time. "I can't condone your methods, but you saved that girl's life, and I thank you for it. Her family thanks you for it. You found her just in time to prevent her from getting lost in that world of addiction."

I stayed silent and stared at her, my eyes flicking over to her Dragon every now and then to ensure that it was still the docile beast I had come to know and recognize. It still had that cold sadness around her, but there was also a steady strength within that self-inflicted isolation that I hadn't seen before. I looked back to the woman with the blue Dragon and smiled. She was going to be fine.

One day, her Dragon might tear down all those walls and let that strength carry all the weight of her world instead.

She pursed her lips and leaned back in her chair. "Just answer me this: How did you manage to do what none of the officers here could?"

I smiled at her and shared with her the secret of the Dragon—that together you have unlimited creation.

Once I was done, she stayed silent. She tapped her fingers on the table, and I feared she would condemn me as crazy like the judge did five months ago. That's when I first met you, Doctor. My, how time flies. Then, the woman with the blue Dragon stood up to leave. Her eyes twinkled at me. Perhaps maybe, just maybe, she did know the secret after all.

"I think it's time we got you back to the rehabilitation center you're missing from, Kevin." She patted my shoulder, her Dragon grinned at me, and then they left. I should have known she'd figured me out.

See you soon, Doctor.

K

* * *

To: The Doctor with the Glasses

So, Doctor, I am here at the police station, sitting with my Dragon in the front room. I know you've been searching for me, and I'm ready for you to find us now. I have learned how to maintain this reconciliation, and it's not as hard as I thought it was.

Allowing the Dragon to rule only leads to destruction. I know that better than anyone. Being back in that dark place, holding the girl with the silver locket in my arms, I knew what I had escaped, and I never want to go back.

And it is not about repressing the Dragon, either. That only leads to emptiness.

It is a balance between the two; a balance between logic and magic, reason and fantasy. It's about creating a partnership. In order to create the impossible, one must embrace the magic within us. It's always been there—though we have been conditioned to ignore it.

I'm waiting for you, Doctor. Once you get here, I want to learn all your secrets. Now that I've reconciled myself with the Dragon within me and it is destructive no more, I know that there is so much more we can create. Is it possible to make all the fantasies I dreamed of as a child real? I know you have the answers, Doctor. Come find me so we can get started.

Kevin

O O O

Melissa Koons is the author of "Orion's Honor" and loves to write character-driven stories and novels focusing on the question of identity. She has a BA in English and secondary education. Melissa currently works as a freelance writer, a novelist, a tutor, and as a testing specialist at a local community college. Visit her at authormelissakoons.wordpress.com.

His Greatest Creation

Jace Killan

Captain Thomas Drysdale would never meet her. He'd never touch her face or kiss her good night. He'd never teach her how to play ball or cheer for her at a game or a concert. If only he could've found out before entering hyper-sleep. He could've delayed going under for a couple weeks and imparted so much wisdom to his daughter-to-be.

Even if it were only for a couple of seconds, he could've said, "I love you." But he had missed his chance. She'd live her life wondering. He'd be long dead by the time she and the others arrived at the earthlike planet T2-6GMA.

Would he have stayed had he known?

After nearly three decades of hyper-sleep, Tom awoke to discover he had a daughter. She had made dozens of videos that had been transmitted before his ship entered the wormhole.

Each video tugged at Tom's heart, forming an undeniable connection through time and space back to Earth, galaxies away. He had watched them all, most more than once.

His favorite had been taken after Emma's fifth birthday. She held a stuffed purple unicorn in one hand and a fluffy pink dragon in the other. Her blonde hair had darkened to light brown since her last video, and her face had brightened with freckles. Emma had named the unicorn Missy and the dragon Stinky. Apparently it was a boy dragon and liked to tease Missy the unicorn, but that was to be expected with a name like Stinky.

Tom fought back tears from the memory. He sat in the ship's lab, peering through zettabytes of research, most of it prepared by him and his team prior to launch.

On the large display in the center of the lab, Tom placed the schematics of the *Genus Phrynosoma*, or the Arizona Horny Toad. He could easily alter the creature's size, but professional ethics would caution otherwise. A large change in mass would affect the animal's nutrition, which could alter T2-6GMA's ecosystem.

The lab's software, Algorithm Rendered Creation System, or ARCS, could analyze the potential impact to T2-6GMA, but Tom would doubt the system's algorithms until they landed and synchronized with the earthlike planet. And he couldn't wait until then. He owed this to Emma. It was the one thing he could do for her, the one legacy he could leave her.

Tom used salmon scales to replace some of the lizard's exterior. ARCS recommended sweat glands to keep the scales moistened and pliable. It also made more sense to convert the lizard to warm-blooded.

He and his team had tried converting a warm-blooded animal to cold-blooded with eventual success. They had proposed to integrate their hybrid, cold-blooded raccoons into the jungles of South America. The native raccoons had fled or died when the temperate zones hit sixty degrees Celsius. But he had been accused of playing God, and the program ended, as did that breed of raccoon, the Coatimundi.

He never meant to play God, and he would argue with those who accused him of doing so. He only replicated and reorganized God's unfathomable handiwork—he couldn't *create* it.

The pre-rendering showed the horned lizard head, like a battle helmet, perfect for protection, along with a sleek pink body. Tom quadrupled its size to about that of a basketball. The wider body would be able to plump up due to the lizard's innate defense mechanism, though he nixed its ability to shoot blood from its eyes.

Tom added enhanced sensory nerves to the scales and a modified larynx with laryngeal muscles and a neural oscillator to facilitate purring like a kitten.

This dragon would like to cuddle.

The pre-rendering lacked something. Tom returned to the video of his five-year-old daughter for reference. Through his tears, he saw it. Wings.

Bats were the obvious choice, but ARCS wouldn't accept the addition no matter how they were altered. And feathers were impossible to create. If he went that direction, he'd best scrap the project and start over. But what about dinosaurs? They had evolved into birds. Perhaps he could evolve a bird's flight system back to that of a dinosaur. Tom programmed ARCS to perform the analysis.

To kill time while he waited for the results, Tom headed to the garden, the largest, innermost chamber of the ship.

Tom's hyper-sleep ended over three years earlier so he, as the ship's only passenger, could activate and watch over the garden and greenhouse. The animals and plants needed to develop maintainable levels by the time the ship landed on T2-6GMA.

Lined inside the garden were rows upon rows of insulated white terminals of varying sizes. Tom ran his hand over the smooth plastic capsules as he passed them, reading their displays and noting each life-form to be delivered to the planet.

Over nine centuries ago, a meteor had struck T2-6GMA, bringing on an interglacial period similar to the one Earth had experienced over the past couple million years. Tom's mission consisted of repopulating the planet and preparing it for occupation some sixty Earth years from now, when the colony ships would arrive.

Earth, before Tom had left, had made significant recovery from the centuries of abuse it had endured from its careless inhabitants. With a population of thirty billion, Earth wouldn't continue to heal unless population controls were enacted or alternative habitations were identified.

Society chose the latter.

Tom volunteered for the noble expedition—but that was before he had met Emma's mother. Not that he would have stayed for her, but had he known she was pregnant, maybe. It was too late for regrets. The ships were on their way, hopefully with his kin.

Tom walked through his usual routine of checking the systems and vitals. He ventured into the greenhouse next, enjoying the earthy smell and humid air, a contrast to the ship's dry, sanitary conditions. With all systems normal, he returned to his experiment in process.

ARCS had found and pre-rendered wings suitable for the reptile, though Tom could hardly call it that now with its warm-blooded circulatory system.

ARCS recommended a more complex capillary system for increased circulation and a dietary tract requiring moderate acids and significant sugars to produce the requisite energy to fly. The dragon would live off stone-fruit trees like peaches and plums, harvested from the very saplings now growing in the greenhouse. Once ARCS verified that T2-6GMA would provide a conducive atmosphere for the plants, the greenhouse would open to the elements, promoting growth and expansion under natural light.

Vegetation already existed on T2-6GMA, though the land consisted mostly of tundra. Around the equator, however, the temperate zones would maintain a steady twenty-five degrees Celsius. Life had probably found a way, and Tom was excited to see what awaited him upon his arrival. Surely there grew a variety of vegetation and other life: amoebas, bacteria, insects, maybe even a horned toad. Still, Tom would bring millions of years of evolution to the young planet.

ARCS accepted the completed design once Tom corrected a few lingering errors. He instructed ARCS to render the final critter, then returned to his cabin. He wanted to see Emma again.

On the screen stood a beautiful, college-aged woman, eyes bright with life and love and passion. He vaguely remembered a similar look in her mother's eyes.

"It's been awhile. For me, at least. For you, maybe only a few minutes since you watched my last video. Hopefully you're watching this and didn't get bored of me during my teenage years."

Emma smiled and bit her lip. She was nervous. Tom hadn't noticed that before.

"You know," she said, "I've wondered a lot about you. I wonder if you know me. If you're proud of me." She paused, clearing her throat. "I wonder if you would've stayed if you'd found out about me before you left."

Tom knew what she was going to say, and still he wept as he had the first time he had seen this final video. He couldn't possibly have stayed. Even if he had known her mom was pregnant. It had taken him nearly a decade to prepare for the expedition. They'd spent billions of taxpayer funds. Prudence would have suggested he avoid the fling with Emma's mother. But how could he think such things now, staring at the only thing he had ever actually created, his beautiful daughter?

Why should it matter? Even if he had stayed, it might not have worked out with her mom, as kind as she was, and obviously a good mom to raise such a wonderful daughter all by herself. Had he been around, he would've had to work a lot anyways, assuming he still would have had a career. He might have hardly seen Emma. There were millions of deadbeat dads who never even knew they had kids. Why should it bother him so much that he wasn't there for her?

Truth was, he would've been a great dad. He would have loved her as he did now, only she would have known it too.

Emma wiped a tear from her eye. "I'm told that you are nearing the wormhole and will be out of transmission range soon, so this is probably my final video. I want you to know that I am proud of you, Daddy. Many people here consider you a hero for sacrificing most of your life to your mission. I don't begrudge you. I admire and respect you. You were here with me, even though we've never met. You've been here with me my whole life."

Something off camera caught her eye and she smiled big. "Daddy, there's someone I want you to meet."

A man in a marine uniform entered the video. "Hi, Tom."

"This is Spencer Hill." Emma giggled. "And we're expecting."

Emma withdrew her halocard. It activated, showing a rendering of the fetus.

"It's a boy, sir," Spencer said.

"We're going to name him Thomas," Emma added.

Spencer left, and Emma told him to wait at the side for a moment.

"Our kids and their kids will know about you. I'll make sure they know about the sacrifices you've made for us. You'll be Grandpa Drysdale the Pioneer."

She blinked, prompting tears to spill down her face.

Tom reached toward the screen, imagining touching her cheek.

"I love you," she continued. "I hope you land safely, and I hope your video feed works or all these years were a waste of time." She stopped, shaking her head. "No. This has been wonderful for me, and I've got to have faith that you were able to meet me—"

"And me!" Spencer reappeared. Emma pushed him aside and giggled through the tears.

"Maybe there's some way I can know you got these messages. Mom says you're a genius. She told me that you gave her a flower before you left and asked her to decode its DNA. She did. It said, 'You're pretty, like this flower.'" Emma rolled her eyes. "Really, Dad? I never told you, but that was kind of lame." She shrugged. "And kind of cool. And really geeky. And it made me think that maybe you could bioengineer something and encode a message on its DNA. I thought about a flower, but I don't want to go around in my old age decoding every flower I see. So I wondered if you could—"

That was all. That was the entire message. As Emma had predicted, no further videos followed. Tom spent months agonizing about what to do, how to leave her a message from his grave. Then, yesterday, when he'd rewatched his favorite video, it hit him. He'd make Stinky the dragon.

He used the same console to make a video of himself. "Emma," he said, "I'm glad you found this. I've been so very proud of you. You've brought so much joy to my life." Tom spoke about his childhood and his parents, shared anecdotes and experiences that he had experienced throughout his life. He talked of his research and studies. He spoke of philosophy and religion, imparting all he had. Hours later, Tom fell asleep, spent.

When he awoke, he transferred all of the video feeds—his and Emma's—to ARCS. He transferred his personal journals and ship logs and all his personal files, photos, videos, old social accounts, any and all data involving his life. Then Tom returned to his experiment. The dragon had finished rendering into an organic likeness of the stuffed toy. Tom uploaded the video feeds and processed them for encoding. He synthesized the data, integrating it into the rendering's DNA.

As a final touch, before sending the dragon for male and female production, Tom wrote words into its DNA sequence. "For Emma. I love you. I am proud of you. I thought about making you a purple unicorn, but that'd just be silly. A fruit-eating, purring dragon is much more enjoyable. And hey, you can tell your grandkids that your old man made you Stinky. Love, Dad."

Imagining the smile that would light Emma's lips when she discovered his note, he paused a moment, wanting to offer her something more.

He keyed in a final thought: "P.S. I would have stayed."

O O O

Jace Killan lives in Arizona with his wife, five kids, and two dogs. He works as a CFO for a biotech company. He volunteers with the Boy Scouts and enjoys everything outdoors. He also composes music and is a novice photographer.

Shattered Pieces Swept Away

Gregory D. Little

Draconis was impossible to miss, for it was very large and the world had grown tragically small.

Holed up in the wide boughs of an easily climbed tree, Hursk popped his head above the forest's tattered canopy. The rushing hiss of the ocean behind him was an affront to his ears, foreign as it was—or had been—to this place. The sea now lay south, once the direction of Hursk's homeland. Only a shattered crescent of land still poked above the waves, the barest fraction of all the peoples and cultures that had been lost.

Ahead, Draconis stamped and chuffed fiery mucous from its strangely webbed mouth. Four-legged with a short neck and a long tail, flame utterly wreathed the beast. It *was* flame, flesh of molten rock grafted to a metal armature of a skeleton. He could feel the heat from here, miles away.

Draconis's huge, lamplike eyes seemed unfocused to Hursk, sweeping the lands around it but not truly seeing anything. Unlikely he and the boy sitting in the tree with him would be spotted so far away. The forest separating them from the dragon was already alight with fires from its passing.

Any motion from the behemoth shook the ground beneath the trees, sending ripples hissing through the canopy of leaves. The southern tip of the mountains stood as its backdrop, yet it seemed of a size with them, as though a hand of the same scale had forged each.

Hursk wasn't sure if the gods, may they rot forever in their prison, had made the mountains, but he knew they were to blame for Draconis.

"Do you see it?" Whispering up from the branch below, Marnium was the lone, young soldier offered up by the fledgling central government as a replacement after Juriel's and Parnata's deaths. And Yalla's. The last name was sharp in Hursk's mind, a dagger without a hilt.

No one left who wants to fight, and the so-called leaders don't care.

"I see it."

"And?" Hursk could hear the boy's restraint creak, trying to hold in all that eager energy. "Has it gotten bigger?"

"No." It was hard to say, in truth. Past a certain point, degrees of immensity became absurd to try to gauge. But it appeared the rumors were true. The gods' imprisonment and the resulting end of the war had stripped the great beasts of their more frightful abilities along with the will that had driven their actions. In a way, it almost disappointed Hursk. The idea that they no longer faced the creatures at their best insulted the memory of those who had fallen so recently.

Crocodilius had been a fight worthy of story and song. Or it would surely seem so to someone else. The weight of the last smiter in Hursk's pack called up the bitter memory of that battle. Forged to look like downward-flowing winds hardening into a wide, hammerhead base, the wrighting was the only remaining weapon capable of felling a great beast. Its twin had been the tool that actually felled the colossal crocodile. Hursk tried to think around that part because of what the victory had cost. A smiter could be used only once. And against Draconis, last and largest of the great beasts, even that wouldn't be enough.

Not on its own.

Hursk climbed down from the tree, motioning Marnium to follow. His joints squealed in protest, though gray had only partially invaded his wiry black hair and the beard fanning down toward his chest.

Old before my time.

He sometimes looked at Marnium and felt as though the boy was a different species entirely. He and all the pups his age couldn't even remember when the war had begun. Hursk and his team had fought through every blood-soaked minute of it.

"So what do we do next?" Marnium's eagerness retained its edge, it seemed.

Ahead, the dragon swished its head back and forth, chuffing as though scenting the air. It had caught whiffs of them, even this far away. All the great beasts had that powerful sense of smell—designed, as they were, to extinguish humanity.

"We lay our trap," Hursk said, descending as fast as his creaking joints allowed.

The imprisonment of the gods was how most people marked the end of the war. That half of the gods' gargantuan beasts had survived an additional year barely seemed to register with the war's survivors unless it was their city being stomped flat. That now only one beast remained—even if it was the largest and most dangerous—probably didn't even rate a corner crier.

But whether the rest of the battered human race cared or not, Hursk and Marnium had work to be about.

* * *

"Another," Hursk said, pointing. The tree was different from its neighbors, its bark gray and flinty, with a faint sheen. In a world without the gods and their tools, such a tree would have been impossible. Now, perhaps, it would be again. But destined for extinction or not, it served Hursk's intentions well enough.

It would not burn.

Marnium approached at Hursk's gesture, a set of two plate-shaped wrightings in one hand. The first resembled a rounded grid like a cage, while the second possessed scalloped edges and a rippling back. Each soul-powered tool had been forged for a different purpose, and each was useless to them without its fellow. Parts one and two of the trap.

This had been Yalla's area of expertise, with Parnata as her backup. Hursk had trusted them to handle it, not needing to understand the workings himself. He had taught himself eventually, but only after his beloved Yalla lay smashed beneath Crocodilius and Parnata similarly crushed by the dying Viperid.

Too late, in other words.

These particular wrightings were frightful things, a destructive power that didn't belong in the world any longer. Hursk was the last soul that carried the knowledge of them.

The boy hammered the wrightings into the trunk of the tree, the heavy iron content of the bark making the task a brutal one. Marnium was eager but useless except for his strong young back.

As the boy worked, Hursk pulled chalk from an oilskin bag in his pack and marked the tree with a wide, white band at eye level so it would be easy to see from a distance. He inspected the boy's work and found it satisfactory, the third such in a row.

Hursk handed the boy the map, pointing out the curving line they must trace.

Marnium frowned. "I don't understand. Why are we cutting way over toward the mountains? Don't we have more of the cordon to set up here?"

Hursk almost batted the question away as a waste of breath. The boy didn't need to understand, however much he wanted to. This beast was the last of them. Marnium was here as a witness to the end of a world, not a student of how to repeat it. Yet Hursk found himself talking.

"It's scented us. It will head this way. We need to keep it in the cordon we're building, and that means zigzagging back and forth, leading it along so that it never gets too close to the boundary."

So they did, darting across the landscape. Steering clear of the searching, stomping beast was both easy and difficult. They always knew where it was, but that did not mean they could move faster. And its nose was acute for something so massive and with fire for flesh.

As the sun set, the pair of them, footsore and weary, made camp in a small clearing near running water. Hursk buried the required wrightings in the loamy earth while Marnium pitched the tent. But when the boy went to bundle into his cold-weather gear for sleep, Hursk stopped him.

"You stink," he said, wrinkling his nose for effect. "Go bathe in the stream. We don't want it coming upon us in the night."

"The camp will be frigid when I get back," he whined. "I'd be better off sleeping in the stream. Why do we even need those cold wrightings?"

"Cold fights fire," Hursk said simply. He knew he was being maddeningly cryptic, and he didn't care. *He doesn't need to learn how to do it. He doesn't* get *to learn.* The boy wasn't part of his team. He was a mule, strong and somewhat useful despite a stubborn streak.

"Why aren't *you* bathing?"

"I'll go when it's my turn to watch." The words were absolutely true but also pregnant with a promise of later untruth.

Marnium stomped off in what could only be termed a huff, returning nearly an hour later when Hursk was feeding a steady stream of fuel into the fire, which struggled against the cold wrightings buried beneath the camp. The boy made a point of shivering as he bundled up.

"Senet?" Hursk asked when the boy approached to collect his cup of stew. A peace offering. Marnium obviously wanted to stay angry, but he had taken to the game, a crude simulation of war, like a leech to flesh. As they set the board, the anger on Marnium's face melted away. Hursk had known it would, and was glad of it.

He wanted to destroy something, if only symbolically.

* * *

The next day was so similar it disoriented. They moved quickly across the cordon area, filling in more of their fence with the necessary wrightings, sometimes less than a mile from Draconis as it lumbered in the opposite direction, tracking their scent. When they were so close to the beast, it was all they could do to stay upright each time it planted its feet. The overpowering heat carried a sulfurous stench that stung the nostrils. With the creature's every pass, the forest became less and less complete. There was no way to check that all their cordon trees were intact.

They simply had to hope. The boy fretted openly over it; Hursk didn't.

They returned to camp as dusk fell. Hursk again ordered Marnium to bathe, promising to do the same later, which was still true. The Senet board again came out with dinner, but this time the game dragged as the boy insisted on conversation.

One last job to do. Then it won't matter. Though the thought was always with him, Hursk was careful never to voice it aloud.

"What did you do before you hunted great beasts?"

"Fought the gods," Hursk said around a mouthful of stale bread that tasted like wood pulp. Left unsaid was, "like any person worth their salt."

The last time he'd been near any kind of civilization, Hursk had heard talk of marking the survivors who had chosen the losing side of the war, singling them out in some way that would prevent them from blending back into human society. They would always be known as traitors to their race.

There was a certain elegant brutally to the notion Hursk could understand, but the talk hadn't stopped there. Some suggested the marking should carry down through the generations, marking not just those who had sided with the gods against humankind, but also their children, grandchildren, and great-grandchildren, forever down the line.

Though contemplating this turned Hursk's stomach sour, again, he understood. He had not asked what the boy's parents had done in the war, and he never would. Hursk knew that it shouldn't matter which side of the war a person's parents had adopted. He also knew that if the boy gave the wrong answer to that question, Hursk might murder him in his sleep.

They were nearly ready for bed, breath fogging in the deepening chill of the camp's wrightings and Marnium reeling after his fifth straight loss in Senet, when Hursk reached into his pack and pulled out a wrighting the size of his forearm. A spike with a prism decorating one end. It was the same slate gray with a dull sheen as most wrightings, but he tried to lend it great import as he handed it to the boy.

"I'm old," he said. That was true enough. "You have a young, strong back. I need you to take some of the load." A lie. "I'll tell you when I need it. Keep it where I can see it—to remind me."

Face comically awestruck, Marnium took the wrighting and threaded it through a leather loop on the side of his pack, where it fit snugly and securely.

Is this my penance for holding your death against you, Yalla? To become you in the end?

"I'll protect it with my life," the boy breathed.

"Good. Good. Now we must sleep. Tomorrow, we do it again."

* * *

Morning brought the last full day, though Hursk took pains not to let that show.

Draconis was growing impatient with its endless hunt. They found ground raked into mountain peaks and low valleys from fiery claws. Entire groves were reduced to ash and char. They had to soak rags in soiled streams and breathe through them for long stretches of their trek, the air was so foul with sulfur and grit. Gradually they strung their web, hemming in the beast with its own pathological need to hunt down and eradicate any humanity it encountered.

Night brought camp, dinner, and fresh orders to bathe.

"I'll take my turn during my shift at watch," Hursk said. This time, it was a lie, and he thought of Yalla, of looking into a mirror and seeing her beautiful brown face instead of himself. Her smile was sunny as ever, but rueful. Her dark eyes sparkled the way they always had when she'd caught him in hypocrisy.

Is it hypocrisy if you teach it to me? She gave him a long-suffering look but didn't speak. She never spoke when he imagined her. *She's more like me in death than she ever was in life.* Perhaps it was appropriate, as he was becoming more like her.

Senet brought its own revelations, as the boy put together his first victory. Hursk saw it six moves out and took only small solace that the boy did not. Sour at the thought of losing this particular game, he began to talk, a turn of events that surprised him almost as much as it did Marnium.

"Are you married?"

The boy blinked. "I … I'm supposed to be. At the autumn harvest, back home."

Hursk didn't ask where that was. It didn't matter. "Why are you here, then?"

The question touched off a war in the boy's face, one in which quarter was neither given nor expected. "Because I haven't seen anything," he said at last. "Bethin's pregnant already, and I just feel like there's so much to see—" He cut off at Hursk's muttering. "What?"

Hursk regretted even starting this conversation.

"Young fool. There's nothing left to see. The world is a ruin, a fraction of what it was."

"That's hardly my fault," Marnium said, sullen. "And I never knew that world before, so—"

"Of course you never knew that world!" Hursk bellowed. His voice shook their clearing almost as much as Draconis's approach. "Of course it's not your fault!" He scattered the Senet pieces from the board, Marnium giving a cry of frustration as they disappeared into the underbrush near the fire. "*We* ruined the world, all who once bowed to the gods! My generation and those before. Your generation will never know what it lost! Do you have any idea how I envy you?"

His breath heaved, and he forced himself to calm. Marnium stared at him, wide-eyed, and leaned back as if afraid he was about to be struck. Hursk realized his fists and teeth were both clenched.

"Do you have any idea how much I pity you?"

"What do you mean?" Marnium's words were a whisper.

"I'm haunted by what has been lost," Hursk said, his voice equally quiet. "But it will be your generation that must pick up the pieces of a ruined world and stitch them together into something functional. And you must do it without the belief that sustained us." He fixed the boy with a virulent stare. "For those we believed in, those we trusted, turned on us."

Silence claimed the clearing, yielding only to Hursk's last words as he rose.

"You were to win in six moves. Congratulations."

The boy went to bed sullen. Hursk, false to his word, did not bathe.

* * *

At a blast of heat and a whiff of sulfur, Hursk opened his eyes in surprise. He stared up at a vast, ruddy sun where no sun should be. A sun with lamplike eyes.

The crafty bastard sneaked up on us after all. And you fell asleep for it.

Draconis opened its mouth and bellowed, shaking the very foundations of the world as it stared down into the tiny clearing it dwarfed. Its mouth opened wider, a fiery glow emerging from within.

"Up!" Hursk roared. "Up!" But the boy did not need waking. Marnium sat bolt upright, vacating his bedroll and slinging on his pack with the glazed eyes of the half dead. "Run!"

They ran, and behind them, heat drove away the cold from the camp's wrightings. Sweat broke out inside Hursk's heavy winter coat where his pack jostled painfully against his back.

Then lava splashed down, and the boy flinched even as Hursk ran stoically on, risking a look behind.

Heat met arctic ground, and the molten rock hardened into a frozen splash of black stone as the cold wrightings sucked the heat away in an expanding wave. The freeze climbed up the fountain of lava, transforming the frozen splash into a growing column of jagged igneous rock, rising closer and closer to the beast's maw.

For its part, Draconis reared away from its own hardening stream of fire, as though the freeze might chase the flame all the way down its throat. The surprised recoiling gave Hursk the time he needed.

Spotting a large tree he'd already picked out for the task, he pulled the boy to a stop on the far side of it, fixing his face in a look of false horror as he let the boy's eyes follow his to the spiked wrighting tucked into the loop in Marnium's pack.

"What is that doing there?" *And so I become you, Yalla.*

Confusion and fear flitted across the boy's features. "What do you mean?" he panted around heaving breaths. "You gave it to me!"

"I told you to leave it outside the perimeter at our last stop this evening!"

"No," the boy protested. "No, you didn't! I—"

"I told you!" Hursk roared almost loud enough to drown out Draconis's screams of rage behind them. "Leave it, I said! The cordon won't function while it's inside!"

"I—I'm sorry!" Tears streaked down the boy's sooty face.

"Go now!" Hursk said, pointing the boy in the proper direction. "Leave it and come back to help! I'll lead the beast away! Follow the path of destruction!" That last part felt especially cruel, but it had to be said lest Marnium grow suspicious.

"I'm so sorry!" the boy cried again, and Hursk could not listen anymore.

So am I.

"Go!"

The boy ran.

* * *

His unwashed skin still reeking, Hursk ran back toward Draconis at an angle. The dragon had learned that simply stopping the flow of lava from its great maw defeated the cold wrightings. They could function endlessly against endless heat, but they were one-shot, dying when the source of heat did.

Draconis spent several moments smashing its own solidified tower of lava, sending chunks of rock as large as houses soaring through the air. Hursk ducked, as though he could hope to dodge such debris beyond sheer luck, and ran on.

The dragon's rage was either sated or had transcended to the next level, because it raised its head, sniffed the air twice, then turned and screamed, its lamplike eyes pointed straight at Hursk. Trees died by the score, trampled to smoldering splinters as Draconis charged. Hursk tore his eyes away and called up every iota of speed his aged body still possessed. Yet every second brought that wall of heat behind him closer.

At least it could smell only him.

Hursk fished in his pocket as he ran, extracting the trigger to the complex cordon of traps with some difficulty. Triggering the cordon too early might be as bad as not triggering it at all, but he'd not expected to be in the beast's sights so quickly. If he was reduced to slag and if the boy reached the perimeter's edge fast enough, the job would still only be half-done. But Hursk had built a very long career in taking what he could get.

Has to be done. He triggered the trap, imagining he could sense the various interlocking wrightings pounded into iron tree trunks straining to generate the fields the boy's wrighting was preventing. The rest of Hursk's team would have been appalled, had they still lived.

All but Yalla. Hursk hadn't understood until he stared her situation in the face. She would have approved. She had understood the wrightings far better than he ever could, however much he might study her notes after he'd lost her. Had he done so before, he would have realized when she pulled the same trick on him. Trying to take down two beasts at once, the team had been separated by hundreds of miles. Hursk had been forced to step in and backfill Parnata's role. Crocodilius had charged toward the edge of their perimeter, and Yalla had feigned horror at the spikelike wrighting Hursk still held in his hand.

The same one Marnium carried now.

It had been Hursk's trust in Yalla that had betrayed him in the end. His trust that he need not trouble himself to learn her business when she knew it so well. His trust that she would never willingly leave him.

His lungs burned and his legs flagged. The heat at his back was going to ignite his pack soon. The trigger wrighting in his hand quivered with strain.

Yalla had been the best of them. Just as he'd feared, Hursk, dogged but unimaginative, could not get by without her. He had failed.

He had scarcely admitted this when translucent walls of rippling blue energy leaped up fifty paces into the sky from all around, easily visible in the darkness, each glowing wall segment driving back a little of the night.

Hursk pulled up short, by necessity as much as surprise. Behind him, the crashing and rending of the earth halted too, Draconis equally spellbound.

The boy had crossed the perimeter. The nullifier in his hand no longer blocked their web of wrightings from functioning. Hursk and Draconis were locked inside a prison of energy even the dragon could not penetrate. Marnium was locked out. He would survive to make it home to his bride and baby.

* * *

The beast smacked a clawed, fiery foot against the edge of its ghostly cage, and it bounced back with a belch of flame. It roared in surprise and rage. Seldom if ever had it encountered something that prohibited its passage. Hursk smiled grimly, casually unslinging his pack and pulling out the third and final part of his plan.

Unseen by either of them, the plan's second part ought to be spooling up at that very moment.

The faintest hint of gray dawn touched the southern darkness. A hissing sound emerged. It sounded like the ocean, but certainly they were too far north, and such a sound would only make sense if they stood much closer to its crashing waves.

The dragon's head swiveled back and forth, all its senses primed for a threat as it tried to determine the source of the sound. Hursk actually felt a stab of pity. The creature looked like a dog as vast as the sky, trying to understand why its master had punished it.

The hiss became a roar, and from above the trunks of trees both splintered and whole, a dark column edged in frothing white rose up into the sky. Lit from both the frail first light of dawn and the fires of Draconis, it curved around and plummeted, sinuous as a snake and thick as a butte.

May have overdone that. Hursk moved to put more distance between himself and Draconis. More, but not too much.

Draconis had located the column too, and it stared up with something that looked to Hursk like uncomprehending horror—as near as a burning, reptilian face could come to such expression. The dragon screamed as the column of ocean Hursk's wrightings had summoned broke upon it, and the world began to shake anew.

Staying dry was impossible, the very concept ludicrous in the face of so much water. Instead, Hursk focused on not being smashed flat, dashed against tree trunks, or simply drowned. Tidal waves crashed around him, trying to sweep his feet from under him. But his old bones and sinew had learned balance long ago, and his footing held. The air became humid and brackish as steam flooded outward from the collision of fire and water. Hursk added scalding to the list of hazards.

On and on the water came, so much that Hursk feared his miscalculation would empty the entire ocean into the cordon, however impossible that seemed. When it stopped at last, leaving a foot of lukewarm water amid the ruins of the cordoned forest, Hursk took off, splashing through the shallow new sea as fast as he could. He might have only seconds.

Where Draconis had been stood a statue of black rock holding its exact shape. Hardened in place as the water robbed its molten heat, its frozen body language radiated confusion and flinching fear.

Hursk had been fighting these creatures for the better part of a decade. Whatever their outer shape, at their core, the beasts were the same. He had learned to read them over the years. Draconis was like a book. *Yalla loved to read.* At least her soul would be spared the gods' meddling. At least his own would be, too.

Draconis twitched as he approached, cracking its own flesh as its bones strained to move beneath. Its lamplike eyes, the only part of it still alight, fixed upon Hursk. It had to be now, before the dragon's uncanny abilities melted its flesh, rendering it pliable once more.

"It's all right," Hursk breathed to the creature. "I know that you are alone. I know that you do not understand."

A glow arose from the smiter in his hand as he triggered it.

Draconis shifted its stare minutely, its mouth locked in a frozen roar.

It knows.

"It's time for us to go," Hursk said, surprised to feel tears streaming down his face. "We don't belong in this world anymore." Hands steady, he threw the smiter so that it landed below the dragon's statuelike form. The smiter's glow built until it was as bright as a tiny sun.

Hursk resisted the urge to take cover. *It's time for us to go.*

When the smiter's glow winked out, the sky above struck with a force to break worlds. The air was rent by the roar of its passage, and it flowed hot like fire over Hursk, one moment lifting him into the air with the gentleness of a lover only to dash him against the wreckage of the earth in the next.

The blue glow of the cordon winked out.

He lay broken, in agony. His ears rang loud enough to hurt. He lifted his head, fighting through lances of pain in his neck. Draconis's flesh, hardened to brittle rock by the water, had shattered at the smiter's blow. Only its metal bones remained in a crumpled heap at the center of concentric rings of felled trees, all pointing away from the corpse. Its lamplike eyes had at last gone dark.

Hursk's deep sigh of relief tore something in his chest.

Dead. All dead. It was over. Now he could be with his Yalla.

* * *

A hazy time of pain passed, but instead of death, it brought the boy, a figure wading easily through the draining water. Marnium was weeping, the grief on his face so pure and bright it made Hursk want to join him in fresh tears. He and Yalla had never had children. There had been no time, and the world had not been fit for new life. Now, perhaps, that could change.

The boy would have made a fine son.

"Why? Why did you send me away?" Marnium's words were choked.

"The world is shattered, remember? It needs all the good pieces it can get. Forgive me?" In his heart, Hursk asked for himself and for Yalla both.

"For—forgive you? You did it to spare my life?" The boy's face crumpled, stricken. Then he appeared to remember his bride and child-to-be. "Of course I forgive you. I'm so sorry."

And this, Hursk knew, answered both pleas for absolution.

He spread his arms, shot through with pain, and indicated not just the ruins and the broken behemoth before them but all that remained of the crippled world beyond. "Yours now," he said. The darkness was coming for him fast. "Do better than we did."

"I will," Marnium said. "And I'll make sure they remember you."

Foolish boy, Hursk thought as the darkness broke over him like a column of ocean. *Everyone is forgotten.*

To not die alone was enough.

O O O

Rocket Scientist by day, fantasy and science fiction author by night, Gregory D. Little's short fiction can also be found in *The Colored Lens* and *A Game of Horns: A Red Unicorn Anthology*. "Shattered Pieces Swept Away" is set in the world of his ongoing fantasy series *Unwilling Souls,* for which the second volume, *Ungrateful God,* will be released in 2016. He is a member of and regular contributor to the Fictorians writing blog. He lives in Virginia with his wife and their yellow lab.

Love Notes

Nancy DiMauro

Melinda snarled as a box toppled off the stack on her rolling cart and crashed to the marble floor. Receipts spilled across the green-and-black reception area. Four years. After four years, she expected Artifactus to keep its financials in better form than this, but it looked like the company kept expecting her to fix its mess every year.

She was doubling—no, tripling—her fees.

"You gonna pick that up?" Sonya asked from the other side of the reception desk.

"Just debating if dumping out the rest would help their organizational system."

"Couldn't hurt." Sonya walked around the desk.

Melinda had worn her navy blue pantsuit to the meeting because she'd planned on picking up the records. Just not from the floor. For the fifth time. They hadn't even used new boxes, which made the stack unstable.

Tripled rates, here we come.

Melinda righted the fallen box. Kneeling, she grabbed receipts at random and crammed them in with the other papers. Sonya joined her in scooping the detritus of Artifactus's business year into the box.

"There's another one on your desk," Sonya whispered.

The sheaf of papers Melinda had been holding slid through her fingers. Her gaze drifted to the east corridor, where her office lay. The lecture she'd been preparing for Artifactus's owner flew from her thoughts. A dragon waited for her.

Over the last two months, drawings of dragons had appeared on her desk, in her briefcase, in her lunch order—hell, everywhere she turned. The intricate pen-and-ink creations took her breath away. While she'd sent the others out to be framed, the first one stayed in her messenger bag. The sight of the dragon and the maiden warmed and calmed her. It vibrated with possibility. When she finally met her secret admirer, she'd … well, she wasn't sure what she'd do, but kissing was likely. A small smile tugged at her lips.

"Did anyone see him this time?" she asked.

Sonya shook her head.

Melinda's smiled faded. Clearly, the guy was someone with mad ninja moves. Anticipation shivered down her spine at what he might have left this time.

"I have no idea why you insist on scrabbling in the dust," a masculine voice rumbled from the west side of the reception area. "You're wasted being someone's cleaning lady."

Standing taller than six feet, Simon Byrd dwarfed her. Half the staff was in lust with the man's broad shoulders and tight ass. Not that she'd noticed—much. Worse, he knew he was handsome. The office demigod stood close enough that she could beat him with one of the boxes.

Tempting. So very tempting.

Melinda fought her rising smile at the mental image of smacking the man and narrowed her gaze. "If I wanted your opinion, Byrd, I would've asked."

"Hey, Simon," Sonya said as she twirled a strand of her mousy brown hair. She was definitely Team Byrd. "Thought you were working with the boss man on the Williams accounting. Should I take the hold off your lines?"

Tax returns and financial advice were the company's lifeblood, but they'd made a name for themselves in forensic accounting. With the company almost since its founding, Byrd had pushed Renato, the owner, to expand the company's business line. Now they were regularly hired as expert witnesses in cases of corporate embezzlement or for business valuations. Byrd spent more time in courtrooms and lawyers' conference rooms than the office. The Williams case was just the latest and greatest in a string of corporate financial misdeeds analysis and related expert testimony.

When the boys were out playing celebrity accountants on a forensic file, Melinda ran the office. Her extra duties had earned her a promotion to vice president six months ago.

"We're on a break. The numbers were blurring." Heedless of future crow's-feet, Byrd pulled his wire-rimmed glasses off and scrubbed at his hazel eyes. "Want a hand?" He gestured to the boxes with his glasses.

Sonya scooped the last of the pages into the box.

"We've got it," Melinda said.

He nodded. "We could use your help. We've got the defendant moving cash through multiple accounts. We're pulling through the vendor records to trace the money."

"I'm sure you guys have it," Melinda said as she dusted off her pants. "Thanks, Sonya."

"Maybe, but you're the best we have on pattern recognition," Byrd said.

"Flattery will get you ignored. Besides"—Melinda rapped her knuckles on the battered box—"I have more than enough work to keep me busy. I don't need assignments from you. So it's a good thing you're not my supervisor. Later."

She rolled her handcart past Byrd before he had a chance to retort. After all, she had a dragon to discover.

Lights automatically flickered on as she entered her office. Her gaze fixed on the pink figure sitting on the middle of her empty desktop. She parked the boxes by her door and nearly skipped to her desk.

The little dragon fit in her palm. Its plastic felt cool and smooth. The creature wasn't really pink. Hundreds, if not thousands, of thin strings of colored plastic in grays, reds, silvers, and browns combined to give a faint pearlescent rose tint. Its eyes sparkled a deep burnished gold. Gold horns adorned its head, the ridge down its back, and its miniature claws.

She shook her head, forced her mouth closed, then sank into her visitor chair.

"Ooh, he's really upped his game," Arelis said from where she leaned on the doorframe to Melinda's office.

An odd couple, they'd been best friends since Melinda had joined the firm six years ago. Melinda preferred formal suits and heels while Arelis embraced the casual Friday vibe. Her bright purple tunic and fitted red slacks would have had Melinda running in horror if she'd seen the combination at a store, but Arelis gave the clothes a chic, modern look. Add in her bobbed blonde hair, cinnamon-colored eyes, and deeply tanned skin, and Arelis could have been a model rather than an accountant.

"Any clue who he is?" she asked.

"Not a one," Melinda said.

"Come on, let's grab lunch and wildly speculate."

Melinda blew out a breath. "Can't. I just got in."

"This is what—his sixth dragon?" Arelis toed the stack of boxes. "This mess can wait another hour."

* * *

The pearlescent dragon perched on the table amid the clutter of takeout. Melinda unfolded the lid of a Chinese food container.

Arelis drummed her chopsticks on the tabletop, something she often did when thinking. "What about Danny?"

"The new associate who has framed pictures of *Lord of the Rings* characters in his cube rather than family photos?"

"I figure he has the right level of geeky goodness to draw dragons."

Melinda cocked her head. Danny fit the socially awkward, number-cruncher stereotype of accountants. Add in the fantasy obsession, and he merited consideration. When you could get him to talk, Danny avoided eye contact, and he'd only worked for the company for three months. It made sense that her secret admirer was a shy, new employee.

"I'm not sure," Melinda finally said. "While he's got geek in spades, he doesn't strike me as the romantic type."

"It's got to be someone at the office since all your gifts have shown up here or were connected to work. If not Danny, then who?"

"You ladies are being awfully sexist," Byrd said as he walked into the office kitchen.

Melinda turned in her chair to face him.

"How so?" Arelis asked.

He pulled open the fridge and grabbed a bottle of water. Twisting off the top, he said, "Did you ever consider that Melinda's adoring fan could be a woman?"

"What?" Melinda's brow furrowed

He shrugged as he took a sip of water. Melinda watched his Adam's apple bob up and down as he swallowed. "Why assume the artist is male?"

"I, um …"

A smile brightened Byrd's face, taking him from handsome to devastating. He *liked* making her feel like a teenager whispering about her first crush.

"See?" He motioned with the half empty bottle. "Sexist. What'll you do if he's a she?"

"I'd, um … I guess I'd tell her I loved the drawings—and this little guy." She ran a finger over the ridge of its wing. "And I'd love to be friends, but I'm not gay." She glanced at Arelis. "Was that all right?"

"It was fine," Arelis said.

"Fine," Byrd snorted. "Sure. That the latest?" He picked up the dragon, the delicate creature dwarfed by his large hands. "It's a little … uninspired, don't you think?"

Standing, Melinda snatched the figurine back. "I think he's wonderful." Her tone dared him to contradict her.

"Okay, then." Hands raised in surrender, he took a step back. "Anyway, I need to get back to the conference room. Have fun playing Nancy Drew—or is it Scooby-Doo?"

"I hope your files fall on you," Melinda said.

His deep, rumbling laugh followed him out of the kitchen.

Once he vanished down the hallway, Melinda said, "Well, it isn't Byrd."

Arelis leaned forward. "Why?"

"First, he's a stuffed suit." She placed the dragon on the table. "Can you really see him making this?"

"Second?"

"We've worked together for years. The sudden interest makes no sense. Also, the fourth dragon showed up while he was at court."

"Girlfriend, you're holding out on me." Arelis pointed her chopsticks at Melinda. "What's the real reason?"

Heat flushed up Melinda's neck. She sighed. "Remember the party to celebrate Byrd's and my promotions?"

"Yeah, 'course." Arelis gripped Melinda's forearms. "Oh. My. God. You two did *not* hook up, did you?"

Her gaze went to the hallway where Byrd had vanished. "Not exactly."

Arelis crossed her arms over her chest and glared. "That's just low."

"What?"

"I'm your best friend, and you sit on *this* dirt for six months? Seriously? What happened?"

Melinda stood and walked to the counter. Leaning against it, she said, "Don't make a big deal out of this. It was just a kiss."

"Just a kiss. Right." Arelis scooted her chair closer. "Dish."

Melinda glanced at the ceiling to avoid the too-interested look of her best friend. "We'd been drinking. Well, everyone had. Byrd decided I was too drunk to get home myself."

"As if he was any less trashed."

"My point exactly. He didn't listen." She grimaced. "He never does. Anyway, we shared a ride."

The night had been cool, brushed with the first bite of winter. She'd worn a silver dress with spaghetti straps. Sometime during the ride home, Byrd's jacket had ended up wrapped around her.

* * *

The scent of patchouli and vanilla surrounded her. Closing her eyes, she inhaled deeply.

"Don't fall asleep on me," Byrd had said. "Or I'll have to carry you to bed."

The car had stopped in front of her place.

"You wouldn't," Melinda said.

"Don't tempt me."

Something sparked behind his eyes. Her mouth went dry, and heat prickled her neck.

They crawled out of the taxi and stagger-stepped toward her door.

"You don't even like me," she said.

His brow furrowed. "What makes you think that?"

The lock resisted her efforts to open it. "You know."

"No." Byrd's tone was sharp enough to pierce the fog she floated in. He grabbed the key in her hand and unlocked the door. "I do not."

Casually, she flicked on the light, dropped her bag on the side table next to the door, and staggered inside. She stumbled. Strong arms wrapped around her. Her palms flattened against abs created by an active lifestyle rather than hours at a gym.

"Byr—"

"I like you just fine." His mouth slanted down over hers.

* * *

"Oh. My. God." Arelis's fingers dug into Melinda's arm.

"Ow!"

"*He* kissed you?" Her voice pitched up an extra octave or two. "How was it? Was it amazing? I bet it was amazing."

Melinda pushed away from the counter and stalked across the room.

"Well?" Arelis asked.

"It was wonderful." Melinda sighed. "And unreal."

"Unreal?"

"It felt like … I don't know. My heart was racing. I couldn't get close enough to him. I didn't want it to end. Or more accurately, I wanted it to continue just with, you know, a lot less clothes between us." Melinda laughed softly. "I'm sure that was all the alcohol, though. When we came up for air, he gazed deep into my eyes." Melodrama dripped from her words, and she covered her heart with her hand.

"And?"

She shrugged. "And nothing." Grabbing the empty food containers, she hurled them in the trash can. "If you could've seen his expression. It was like he just realized what he was doing and was … horrified."

"I'm sure he wasn't."

"Right. That's why he turned and left without a word."

"Maybe he was just being a gentleman. Ya know, not taking advantage of your drunken self."

"That's what I told myself. But it's been six months, and he's never bought it up, never pursued whatever that was."

"Have you?"

"No." Melinda heard the defensiveness in her voice.

Arelis rolled her eyes.

"Like I wanted to revisit that humiliation. I work with the man, and these office things—"

"Hey, Danny," Arelis said.

Melinda spun to face him.

"Hey," he said, looking at the floor.

He was tall but just a bit pudgy, with skin pale from being inside too long. A thread of guilt wormed through her. He was a good kid. But with almost a decade between them, "kid" was the operative term. And he wasn't her type at all. If he was her admirer, she'd have to figure out how to let him down without hurting him or making working together too awkward.

"Well, I need to work," she said.

"Oh, okay," Danny said.

"Melinda?"

"I'm good. Catch up with you later." Melinda waved as she walked out of the kitchen.

* * *

Two hours later, Melinda stared at the scattered mass of papers on the conference room table. Byrd was right. Artifactus was getting worse with its record keeping rather than staying better organized. She traced the line of the dragon's wing. She'd accomplished very little all afternoon.

Head down, Danny ambled past the doorway.

"Danny," she said.

Blinking, he looked up, nearly made eye contact, then studied his shoes as he walked into the room. "Need something?"

"I—" Now that he was here, she didn't know what to say.

"That the new dragon?" He pointed to where it rested on top of a box.

She nodded.

"It seriously rocks. Do dragons work better than chocolates or flowers?"

"I like them a lot." She took a deep breath. "Danny, I—"

"Do you think Arelis would like something like it?" His gaze bobbed up to her eyes and back down again.

"Arelis?"

"I, um … Well, I—"

Understanding grabbed her by the throat and shook her. "Oh! Peanut brittle."

His brow furrowed in confusion. "What?"

"Arelis likes peanut brittle. Try that instead of flowers, and then ask her out for a hot chocolate."

"Oh. Okay." He shuffled toward the door. "Thanks."

Melinda's attention drifted back to the dragon as Danny left. Her short list of suspects was empty again. Maybe Renalto would know something. Before he started the accounting firm, he'd run a marketing company, and his ex-wife owned an art gallery. He'd stayed in contact with the artistic community after the divorce. If anyone here could tell her who her dragon-lover was, he could. She grabbed her messenger bag and slipped the dragon into its front pocket.

Despite being the owner of the company, Renalto's office was one of the smaller ones. He said he liked being closer to the junior accountants he supervised rather than off in a corner somewhere. His desk was actually a vintage table and always reminded her of the courtroom scene from *To Kill a Mockingbird.* A small, marble-topped coffee table with two chairs clustered in one corner. Even with a lateral file in the space, the office felt homey, not claustrophobic.

"Have a sec?" she asked.

Wooden chair legs scraped across the floor as he pushed back from his desk. "For you? Always."

Panic flickered across her thoughts. In his early fifties, he was an attractive man. His olive skin was marred only by laugh lines around his mouth and deep, chocolate-colored eyes. What if …

"How come you're looking panicked? Artifactus's files that bad?"

"No. I mean, yes, the files are worse than that. But no, that's not why I'm here."

He put on his glasses and motioned for her to take a seat in one of the side chairs. When they were settled, he asked, "What's wrong?"

"Not wrong." She tucked a loose stand of hair behind her ear. "Just—you know I've been getting mystery presents, right?"

"I'm not dead. And I tend to know what happens in my office."

"Of course. Sorry, I didn't mean to imply—"

He waved off her apology.

"It's not …"

His smile made him look much younger. "Flattering. But no, it's not me."

She slipped the first drawing out of her bag. Thousands of tiny lines made up the purple and silver dragon. He stood with his head bowed before a maiden, her hand extended as if to give or receive comfort. The image gave the sense of a gentle wind pushing her waist-length hair, far longer than Melinda's own even if it shared her same odd russet coloring, away from her face and rustling the woman's dress and the dragon's partially folded wings. A cave mouth yawned behind the woman, while the dragon rested on a dirt road as if he'd just climbed the mountain to visit. To convince her to leave her solitude and rejoin the world.

Or maybe she was projecting.

"Arelis thinks Danny's my secret admirer. But he likes Arelis." She handed the drawing to Renalto.

His eyes narrowed. "Huh. Danny definitely didn't draw this."

"What makes you so sure?"

He turned the figurine in his hands as if to study every angle. "Do you know how dealers authenticate a piece of art?" When she shook her head, he said, "Every artist has a unique voice regardless of the medium. For paintings, we're looking at brushstrokes. The same is true for pen-and-ink drawings. The way an artist draws his lines, makes choices about where to place them, are his voice. If you know how to read those lines, you can determine who the artist is even without a signature."

Melinda scooted to the edge of her seat. Anticipation tightened her gut. "You know whose work this is, don't you? He's not some sort of stalker, is he?"

"Stalker?" He gave a slight shake of this head. "Idiot? Yes."

"You know!"

Silence stretched between them.

"I've seen his work, but …"

"You have to tell me."

"He's—"

"Renalto?" Byrd's head popped into the office. "Oh, sorry, didn't know you were in a meeting."

"What can I do for you, Simon?"

A look passed between the men that Melinda couldn't identify. She slipped the drawing into her bag.

"I need you to look at the Williams information," Byrd said.

"Now?" Renalto said.

"Yes. Now." Byrd's voice had a sharp edge.

Whatever Byrd had seen in the data must have been serious to warrant such concern.

"You know," Renalto said, "if you took a more direct approach to … the data set, you might not run into such convoluted scenarios."

"Yeah, well. There was definitely something I—they—want kept quiet, I mean. Data they tried to obscure in the books. I want your thoughts on it before I go down that particular rabbit hole."

"Seems like you're well on your way down it already." Renalto turned to her. "You mind?"

She ran her fingers over her bag, its brown leather warm to her touch. She'd waited two months to solve the mystery of her dragon-loving admirer; a few more minutes wouldn't matter.

"Go ahead and look at whatever Byrd wants you to see. I still have records to organize before I head home. Why they insist on paper is beyond me."

"Great. I'll check in with you when I'm done with Simon," Renalto said.

* * *

Melinda slid out of her car. Before she realized it, the day was gone. The Artifactus files were still a mess. She'd have a junior accountant organize them on Monday and then tell Artifactus's owner that the company's carelessness wouldn't be tolerated. Then she'd track down Renalto and find out who'd been drawing her dragons.

The porch light shone on a robin's-egg blue envelope stuck to her front door. Her breath quickened. She glanced around. The usual cars sat parked in their usual driveways. If her secret admirer was watching her, his ninja skills were doing their job. Gooseflesh prickled up the back of her neck. Renalto said the guy wasn't a stalker, but that was before he'd gone to her home.

Her hand shook as she reached for the packet. Fighting the impulse to drop everything and tear open the envelope on her front stoop, she unlocked her door and darted inside. Once the door latched behind her, she dumped her bag in the hallway and strode to her office. A moment of fishing in her desk located her red lacquered letter opener. She spilled the envelope's contents on her desk.

A slip of paper no bigger than a gum wrapper fluttered out. A Chinese Ling-style dragon drawn in oranges, yellows, and blues twined across the page. Her eyes narrowed. She smoothed the paper against the desktop. A heart. It held a heart.

She pulled open the sides of the envelope. A five-by-three card peered out. She scanned the elaborate calligraphy.

"Arelis?" Melinda said before she'd realized she'd pulled out her cell phone and dialed.

"Hey, we're headed out to the Sapphire. Wanna come?"

"He left a drawing at my house." Melinda sank into her desk chair. "And a note."

"I'm on my way over. Did he say anything stalker-y?" Arelis asked.

"No." She looked at the invitation again. "He wants to meet."

Melinda held the phone away from her ear until Arelis's shriek died down.

"He left the invitation on my front door. He wants to meet at the Morrison House for dinner tomorrow."

"You going?" Arelis said.

Melinda ran a hand through her hair. "I'd have to be crazy to."

"Naw. Just romantic." A short silence filled the line. "So, you going?"

* * *

Melinda smoothed her hand down the front of her black-and-white pencil skirt. Her stomach twisted loops around itself. Every step she took in her too-high heels had her convinced her ringlets were escaping from the elaborate updo Arelis had tortured her hair into as if she was an extra for *Sense and Sensibility*. Melinda's gaze skimmed over to the bar as she walked into the upscale restaurant. Arelis gave her a thumbs-up from her perch on a stool.

The black-suited maître d' escorted her toward the back of the restaurant, away from the bar.

"Can I sit—"

On a table in a secluded corner perched a large aqua-colored dragon. Her mouth went dry and heat prickled up her neck. He was here. Somewhere. She turned, searching for a face she recognized. Nothing. Her mystery man remained hidden.

The maître d' held out a seat for her. She stepped further to the right, hoping to get at least a partial eye line to the bar. He waited with the chair extended. Suppressing a sigh, Melinda took the offered seat. She could always move once he left. He uncorked a bottle of Caymus Vineyards' 40th Anniversary Cabernet Sauvignon, one of her favorite wines, and poured her a glass.

Her fingers traced over the dragon's graceful lines. She'd asked Jean from the IT department if the smaller figurine she'd received yesterday had been made with a 3-D printer. Jean had assured her that the creature had been hand drawn with a 3-D pen. Hours of painstaking effort had gone into crafting him. This one was ten times larger. Like its cousin, multiple color strands blended together to give him a shimmering hue. He gently cupped a red heart in one clawed paw.

This was too perfect. A bit too stalker-y. And she'd lost her safety net. Nerves jangled down her legs, urging her to run. She should go. Pushing her chair back, she stood.

The scent of patchouli and vanilla wrapped around her a second before a deep voice thrummed from behind, "Hey."

"Byrd." She breathed out his name.

He took her hands in his. Her slender fingers disappeared into his larger grip. Not quite meeting her eyes, he said, "Surprised?"

"Why all this?" She gestured to the restaurant and the dragon.

"Renalto gave me until Monday to come clean." He blew out a breath. "Melinda, I made a mistake."

"What?" She pulled away from his grasp and reached out for the back of her chair. Her stomach turned. His hands guided her to her seat.

"I'm doing this wrong." He sat next to her. His thigh brushed hers. Awareness and heat flooded her. "I messed up six months ago."

"When you kissed me."

"No. When I *stopped* kissing you. Well, that night it was the right choice. We were both too drunk." He took a deep breath and let it out. "But not asking you out after was a mistake."

She shifted in her chair as she processed that *Byrd* was here. "Why dragons?"

An endearing blush darkened his cheeks. "I'd overheard you telling Arelis that I was just a dumb jock in an expensive suit."

Melinda cringed. She'd been annoyed at him for ignoring their kiss and hadn't been interested in being fair.

"I needed you to see there was more to me," Byrd said. "I was one of Renalto's artists when he ran the marketing company. I was still in school and I loved drawing, but my folks wanted me to focus on something practical. Hence the accounting degree. Anyway, I got sort of desperate when you would barely speak to me. Refused to even consider working with me on a project. Then Arelis—"

"Oh, Arelis!" She bolted up.

Byrd's fingers laced through hers. "Probably already on the way home. I thought I was dead meat when she stepped into the bar. It took some fast talking and faster drink-buying to keep her from storming out and telling on me."

"Traitor," she said with a small laugh. At the gentle tug on her hand, she sat back down.

"Arelis or me?"

Melinda thought about the question as she sipped her wine. The tastes of blackberry, licorice, and vanilla filled her senses. "Both, I think."

"I guess I deserve that." His soft hazel gaze met her green eyes. "Can we start over? Pretend the last six months didn't happen, that I didn't waste them and had been smart enough to ask you out after the party?"

Her finger traced the rim of the wine glass once before she laced her fingers through his.

His gaze settled on their joined hands, then lifted to her eyes. He leaned closer. "I want to kiss you."

"Good."

The back of his hand brushed her cheek. Then his hand slid to the back of her neck and pulled her closer.

"Do I get another chance to start over?" he asked as his lips hovered over hers.

"Yes, please," she said.

"Then you better start calling me Simon."

Rather than answer, she kissed him. His arm tightened around her waist. This time, when he lifted his mouth from hers, there was no mistaking the heat in his eyes.

O O O

Nancy is a mom, writer, speaker, and lawyer (under her alter ego name, Nancy Greene). Living on a horse farm in Virginia with her three favorite guys, i.e., her husband and two boys, and (in her husband's words) far too many animals, life is rarely boring. For updates on Nancy's writing and what she's been doing lately, please visit www.falconsfables.com and www.attorneynancygreene.

Soot and Cinder

Tristan Brand

My son, my time is nearly done.

My wings grow heavy; my flame dims. It will be dark soon, and there will be no dawn. The second sky awaits. I write this letter to spend these last moments with you, as best I can.

Wind howls through this cave. A strange thing, wind. Bringing things together that began so distant in both place and time, and each scent the winds brings is a scent from the past.

I wonder, my son, if this wind touched your wings even as it now brushes mine.

You will be one year old tomorrow. Your scales, how they must shine! Green and gold, glinting in the sun. Your wings are still weak, and though you may leap and glide about, the sky is yet unknown to you. But that does not stop you from looking up with silver eyes and yearning as I yearned—for even at this age, you are a dragon and you know your destiny lies beyond the earth. But for now, you are content flitting about the meadows of your valley, hunting rabbits and fat little voles, the mountains towering above you.

My son, soon you will be five years old. Large as a lion, but faster, stronger, for lions are limited creatures, bound to the ground, and your wings are strong now—strong enough to tear through the air after a bounding young fawn. A dragon your age feels the flame in his belly and thinks himself invincible, but your belly scales are still soft.

Your father bore the scar of a stag's horn whom he chased too young. But you will not be your father, my son, for though you have his strength, it is tempered by my wisdom, and so for now, you will wait and let the stag pass.

For now.

My son, soon you will be ten years old. Lions will flee at the sight of your shadow. Bears will cower at your roar. Your fire will burn bright as a comet in the night, and the valley will have its king. But this is only the start of your story, for like all dragons, you look forward, not back; up, not down; toward the edge of the sky and the fangs of the mountains that sink into the faraway clouds. You rise, faster, faster, seeking their summit—only to fade, for as strong as you are, the sky is still stronger.

You will try anyway. You will try and you will fail, but do not worry. I forgive you for trying, for that is what it means to be a dragon.

My son, soon you will be twenty years old, and your shadow will block out the sun. Your flame will be the heart of a volcano; your teeth and claws, swords and scythes; your scales a suit of armor a queen would sell her kingdom for—a price not nearly enough. And you will rise above the clouds, against the wind, through the high mists, beyond the snowy peaks, and there, you will see the world outside your valley.

And you will see them.

Their kingdoms, sprawling and ugly, filled with smoke from pathetic little fires, for these creatures are too weak to make their own. They spread like rats, scouring the land, leaving it broken and brittle. They think themselves rulers of this world.

You will look down at them and know different.

My son, one day you were just an egg. Pearl-white flecked with gold. The first of many I'd hoped to lay. Back when your father was still here. He was so strong, your father, so large. I can still feel his fire, the warmth stroking my back as his tail twined against mine.

I'm so sorry, my son. I did not want you to be alone.

There is a hole in this cave, where you should be sitting right now. Colder than the rest, no matter how I try to warm it. I wish you were here. I would tell you such stories! Of the time I hunted a kraken. Of your father and his father and my mother and her mother, a family line you can be proud of. Of umber skies and silver seas and an island made of ice with a spring hot enough to stoke even a dragon's flame. Of a faraway mountain where the First Dragon yet rules.

I wish you were here right now, my son, for I am drifting away, and in my weakness, I am afraid. I do not want to die alone. Even knowing you were reading these words would make it easier.

But, my son, I know you are not the one reading this letter.

A human is.

Hello, human. Your hands, do they now tremble? Try not to drop your torch. I'd hate for you to be left in the dark. I can smell your surprise, your fear, washing along the wind of time. Did you come here seeking glory? Treasure, perhaps? A fabled hoard of dragon's gold? Look as long as you like. There is naught here but a dead dragon, her scales gone dark, and this letter, etched by claw in soot and cinder.

Oh, and the bones. Did you trip over one, perhaps? Did you wonder at their fate? Others came before you, seeking my egg. Foolish little humans. They thought me stupid. They thought I wouldn't know what they'd try when they found out about the disease that stole my mate and left me bound to this cave. That I wouldn't know of their greed—as if their kingdoms did not stink of it.

They were too late, human. I made arrangements for my egg to be taken somewhere safe, somewhere far away from thieving, scavenging hands.

There must have been a hundred of them. Swarming me like rats, and, like rats, they died by the dozen.

But enough rats can kill even a lion. That was our mistake; I see it now. Letting the rats breed.

There will be a day, human, not too far away. The wind will blow clouds of ash, and you will look toward the sky and you will see a great shadow.

For though my time is nearly up, my son's has just begun.

O O O

Tristan Brand

Tristan Brand is a lifelong reader whose schoolbag always seemed to contain more epic fantasy novels than textbooks. After a brief detour in academia studying mathematics, he made his way to Silicon Valley, where he worked jobs ranging from QA to technical writing. Currently he works as a game designer and lives with his dog, Locke, and cats Edgar and Sabin.

Dragon Years

Robert J. McCarter

2000

New London, Connecticut

Henry squinted against the harsh auditorium spotlight, shielding his eyes with his hand. He could hear the collective movements of the crowd—footsteps as people found their seats, the clacking of keyboards, some low murmurs, and a few coughs—but he couldn't see much. He glanced at the screen behind him, which read, "A Brief Lecture on the Importance of Dragons in Korean Culture. Henry Winters, PhD Professor Emeritus, Connecticut College." The background was a pleasing dark blue with the familiar outline of an Asian-style dragon behind the text in white.

He licked his lips, his mouth dry. Shouldn't there be a glass of water here for him? This was his last lecture at Connecticut College, and he wanted it to be good. The bright spotlight made it hard for him to see his wife, Kyung. If he could just glimpse her, it would calm his thumping heart. They had argued right before this, and his fear of losing her clung to him, oppressed him like the humidity during Korea's rainy season. Where he had been a young man. Where he had met Kyung. Where he had learned about dragons so many years ago.

The argument had been silly. He hadn't wanted to come today, seeing all of this as a send-off for him—a kind one, but a send-off nonetheless. His retirement hadn't been easy, and he knew he had become something of a pest at the college, always hanging around. He imagined they were all greatly relieved he and Kyung were moving to Portland.

"Henry!" someone whispered from the side of the stage. Henry squinted and saw Lyle Fong, his protégé who had arranged this lecture—an act of pity, Henry was sure of it—and who now held Henry's former position as the Chair of Oriental Studies. "Everyone is waiting."

He took a deep breath and did his best to smile, his fingers tugging at his bow tie. He didn't want anyone to think him senile.

"In Korea, unlike in Europe," Henry began, his voice thin and rough, "dragons are creatures of the water, beings of creation—benevolent, not creatures of fire and violence."

He cleared his throat and looked around. "Speaking of water, I am desperately thirsty. Can I get some water?" There were chuckles from the audience, and Henry found himself relaxing.

He loved teaching, he loved lecturing—best he enjoy this last time.

2012

Portland, Oregon

Henry's hands shook as he looped the silk around in the final flourish that should result in the miracle of a real bow tie—no clip-on for him. But the smooth fabric dissolved into a flat piece of silk that bowed and then flared at the end.

He cursed in fluent Korean and picked the fabric back up.

His hands ached like glass had been sprinkled in his joints. They were bony things now and as spotted as a cheetah's coat. They looked like foreign objects to him, just like his face did in the mirror. His forehead had deep troughs, as if it was a field that had just been prepared for planting. His eyes, sunk into their sockets, were a flat blue. Long gone was the sparkle of his youth. His remaining hairs were white wisps that sprouted from his skull and refused to lie down no matter what he did.

He sighed and shook his head. Kyung had always done this for him. Her hands had remained nimble even as the years had piled up, causing her to stoop as if she carried a great burden.

"I'll be late," he said, his voice quiet and rough like the crumpling of rice paper. He took a deep breath and closed his eyes. His nose filled with Kyung's scent. The bottle of perfume he had spilled the day she died still permeated the small bedroom. The scent reminded him of her, and that was the best thing in the world—and the worst.

He rubbed at his eyes and turned from the mirror. The bed was perfectly made with a puffy blue comforter, all six pillows in their proper places. Henry had no need for frilly comforters or more than one pillow, but he kept things the same. Almost as if he hoped his beloved would return one day.

Henry closed his eyes again, his fingers caressing the silk of the bow tie. He heard the soft padding of Jag-eun Yong's feet on the carpeted floor and then felt him winding his way between his legs, rubbing up against Henry's best dress pants, his tail following behind as he did several figure eights.

Henry relaxed, a sigh escaping his lips like a soldier sneaking across enemy territory, and then he could feel Kyung, her breath warm against his ear.

"Only ten steps," Kyung whispered to him, her voice insubstantial, like a gentle wind rustling leaves. "Cross the right over the left, bring the end up through …"

With his eyes closed, Henry heard his dead wife talk him through tying his bow tie while Jag-eun Yong continued his figure eights at his feet, Henry's fingers suddenly working like they used to.

"Thank you, my love," Henry whispered after the deed was done and right before the breeze of his dead wife's voice faded away.

He opened his eyes and looked at Jag-eun Yong now sitting on his bed, staring at him. The creature was covered in dusky, dark green scales. His lizardlike body was sinuous and long. He had green fur of a sort that ran down the center of his body from between his ears all along his back and ending in a tuft at the tapered tail. This feathery fur also appeared on the tips of his ears in two long strands that sprouted on either side of his nose in something of a mustache, and in short clumps under his chin. He stood about eight inches tall at the shoulder and thirty inches long from nose to tail.

He was not a cat—certainly not a cat. And not a lizard with that feather-fur and long snout. He was a tiny Korean dragon.

"Thank you, Jag-eun Yong," Henry began. "I really—"

Henry was cut off by a sharp rapping on his front door.

Jag-eun Yong got down from the bed and slid under it with a flowing motion, like a forest stream seeking the ocean.

"Mr. Winters, are you there? It's Valery Paulson, your next-door neighbor. I have a big favor to ask of you."

Henry sighed and flexed his hands, the old ache back, and moved to open his front door.

1952

Korea

The warm, moist air made young Henry Winters's fatigues cling to his skin. He was sweating as he trotted slowly through the dense Korean forest, but it didn't cool him down. Late in the rainy season, the air was saturated. His heartbeat pounded in his temples from both exertion and adrenaline.

He stopped and squatted, hearing a faint trickle of water, and licked his lips. He was out of water, trapped behind enemy lines. They had started this mission past the 38th parallel—in communist territory—to find a downed pilot. And they had. The F-51D Mustang pilot had broken his ankle and some ribs in the crash but was otherwise fine. Henry's platoon had escorted the pilot to the extraction site only to be ambushed as the helicopter landed.

Henry had been the rear guard and had laid down suppressing fire, allowing the pilot and most of his platoon to escape—Jones and Witham hadn't made it. The helicopter had been forced to leave without him.

The meadow where the helicopter had landed was a few miles to the north. Henry was heading south as fast as he could, sticking to the dense stands of pine and hardwoods, wishing for the thousandth time that he had thought of something better to do with his life than join the Army.

He was about to rise when he heard a twig snap. He had thought his pursuers lost. Another dose of adrenaline dumped into his bloodstream, but he suppressed the desire to run and didn't move a muscle.

2012

Portland, Oregon

Ms. Paulson needs a husband, Henry thought. The woman had a twelve-year-old daughter, a demanding marketing job, and a house to tend to. Henry shook his head—it was an old-fashioned thought. Maybe Ms. Paulson needed a wife, not a husband. He shook his head again as he walked through his living room—he was a rather old-fashioned man, after all. Of all the people in their quiet little neighborhood, Ms. Paulson visited him the most, usually because she needed something.

Henry opened the door to the harried face of Valery Paulson. She was in her early forties with a round face, deep frown lines, and short black hair.

"I am so sorry to bother you, Mr. Winters, but it's Ada. The moment the bus got here, she started vomiting, none of her sitters can get here fast enough, and I have a big presentation." The words tumbled out in a rush, barely a pause between phrases.

"I am sorry for your trouble, Ms. Paulson, but I have an appointment." His fingers touched his bow tie. "I am giving a lecture today at the college."

Ms. Paulson's forehead furrowed deeply. "At the University of Portland?"

"No, Connecticut College, of course. I'm retired now, as you know, but they've invited me back one last time. Today's lecture is about dragons and Korea. Most appropriate, given that we are in a Year of the Dragon. Every culture has a legend about dragons, you know. They—"

The look on his neighbor's face cut him off, and then it hit him. He blinked rapidly, his pulse pounding loudly in his temples, his mouth sour. The room spun around him, and he put his hand on the doorjamb to steady himself.

He didn't live in New London anymore. He and Kyung had moved to Portland twelve years ago. The city had a nice little Korean community, and the moist air was good for Jag-eun Yong. He had no lecture to go to.

He cursed in Korean, just a whisper, and looked at Ms. Paulson with a smile. "Sorry. I have these vivid dreams," he lied, "and when I wake up …" He ended with a weak shrug.

Ms. Paulson's concern was written on her face, but not as clearly as her desperation. "Can you watch Ada, please? I honestly think it was something she ate, she'll be fine, and I don't think she'll be a bother, she really likes you, Mr. Winters."

Henry was going to say no when he heard Jag-eun Yong pad up behind him.

"What an unusual cat," Ms. Paulson said, looking at Jag-eun Yong and making the same mistake everyone did, seeing him the way the dragon wanted to be seen. "I didn't know you had a cat. And what unusual fur. Where is he from?"

Henry didn't answer. He looked down at Jag-eun Yong and knew that the dragon wanted Henry to watch the child. Jag-eun Yong had just given him a few precious moments with Kyung. He couldn't refuse.

1952

Korea

The air was so heavy it was hard to breathe. Henry moved slowly through the forest, crouched down, his M2 carbine in his sweaty hand. They had found him. They were stalking him. The snap of the twig had been followed by sharp whispers and the sound of movement.

Henry swallowed hard, his mouth dry and his head light. He needed shelter. He needed water. He patted his walkie-talkie, a bulky SCR-536 that hung on a strap over his shoulder, making sure the radio was still there, and hatched a desperate plan. He needed a landmark, he needed cover, but if someone was within range, it just might work.

2012

Portland, Oregon

Ada Paulson had her mother's round face but green eyes instead of brown. She was pale, her color just a tad green, and she had a thin bead of sweat on her forehead. There was a smile on her face, though. Jag-eun Yong was curled up in her lap, a gentle rumble emanating from him as the girl stroked the fur on his back.

Henry sat on his couch, staring at the two of them sitting on his living room floor in front of the bay windows, bathed in the morning light. Jag-eun Yong was not a social creature and almost always hid when people came over.

But Ada? Jag-eun Yong loved Ada. As soon as the girl had arrived, her mother bustling off, she had run to the bathroom and thrown up again. When she opened the door, Jag-eun Yong had been waiting for her. He had rubbed up against her legs, and the girl had giggled and grinned.

"Where is he—" Ada began, her sea-foam green eyes meeting Henry's. "Is he a 'he'?"

Henry nodded, liking that the girl asked the question and didn't just assume.

"Where is *he* from?"

"Korea," Henry said.

"He's not a cat, is he? I don't think cats are this different in Korea."

Henry smiled. "They are not."

"What is he? Where did you find him? What does he eat? What is his name?"

He took a deep breath and considered before answering, but seeing how relaxed Jag-eun Yong was, he opted for the truth. "A dragon. In the forests of Korea. He loves mice and crickets, but he'll eat cat food. Jag-eun Yong."

Ada's brow furrowed as she matched up Henry's answers with her questions, and then a look of wonder bloomed on her face. "A dragon? Dragons are real?" She stared at the creature in her lap, her illness forgotten.

Henry chuckled, but it didn't last long. The girl was so pale, and her cheekbones had become sharper since the last time he had seen her. Something wasn't right. "This isn't the first time you've been sick like this, is it?"

Ada's eyes widened, and she blinked several times before shaking her head and looking down at the dragon.

Jag-eun Yong opened his eyes and stared at Henry as if to say, *Finally*.

It hit Henry like a linebacker sacking a quarterback: Ada was sick from chemotherapy treatments. Ada had cancer.

1952

Korea

Henry's walkie-talkie, the volume just high enough for him to hear as he pressed it to his ear, squawked, "Package away. Impact in ten …"

The cat-and-mouse game over, he broke cover and ran through the forest, the sharp cough of rifle fire greeting him, followed by burning pains in his leg and his shoulder. He stayed on his feet and—somehow—kept running.

A shock wave hit and hurled his body forward right before the roar of the blast pummeled his eardrums. He hit the ground like a rag doll and didn't move for a long time.

2012

Portland, Oregon

Henry stood in front of his full-length mirror, fiddling with his bow tie, his mind thick with memories of the past. Of 1952, when he had been a young soldier MIA in Korea. He hadn't exactly lied to Ms. Paulson. He did have the most intense dreams, and often those dreams clung to him when he was awake.

He looked at himself—so skinny, just like Ada. Had he always been this skinny? This old? His stiff fingers fumbled with the silk of the bow tie. Was it lecture day? No, no, that had been his mistake yesterday. He lived in Portland now, not New London.

He heard a sharp crack and ducked, cowering by the bed, his old hands shaking, his knees hurting from squatting down so quickly. He rubbed at his thigh, his fingers finding the scar there, and then rubbed at his left shoulder, finding that scar too. The wounds were old. That wasn't the sound of a rifle firing, probably just that old Corvette Mr. Tanner owned roaring to life. He wasn't in Korea; he was in Portland.

It was a "bad day." Even as his mind slipped from present to past, he knew it was happening, but he was helpless to stop it. There was only one thing that would help, but only if he could remember …

He dropped all the way to the floor with a grunt, and then Jag-eun Yong was in his lap, his scales so smooth, his body flowing through his hands like water. Henry wept and said, "Thank you, my friend, thank you," as the animal soothed him. He said it over and over until he fell asleep on the floor.

1952

Korea

"Is that a cat?" Henry swayed on his feet and coughed, looking at the devastation the airstrike had caused, a high-pitched ringing all he could hear. A small creature lay at the edge of the damage near a stream surrounded by burning trees.

Blood trickled down his chest and his leg, making his fatigues stick to his skin. He continued to sway, looking at his ruined walkie-talkie and then back at the animal. "That's not a cat."

Henry shouldered his rifle, leaned down, and carefully picked up the animal; its scales were so smooth, its sparse fur soft. It didn't move, its side looking like ground beef with pieces of rib showing.

"I did this," he mumbled, referring to both the creature and the damaged land.

The animal stirred, its catlike eye slitting open just a bit. Henry trembled with relief. "We need a doctor!" he said before hobbling off to the north. He meant to go south—he needed to go south—but he was too hurt to tell the difference.

2012

Portland, Oregon

Jag-eun Yong was staring at him when Henry's sticky eyes fluttered open. He was on the hard floor of his bedroom, his hip and shoulder aching terribly. The dragon's blue irises and vertical pupil were so familiar to him and didn't look alien anymore like they once had.

Henry started to push himself up. "Yes, Jag-eun Yong, I know. The lecture. We mustn't be late for the lecture." He groaned as he levered himself into a sitting position, his hands going to his dangling, untied bow tie. "Kyung was so mad. I wish she hadn't left early without us. She could help with this damn tie!"

Jag-eun Yong turned, looking at him with one eye, and the world stuttered around Henry like someone had jiggled the reel in a film projector. He blinked several times and sighed. "These episodes are getting worse, my friend."

1952

Korea

Pain ushered Henry back to consciousness. Pain, dull and diffuse; pain, sharp and deep; pain was his world. Time passed languorously while the pain had its way with him, and he tried to open his eyes. Slowly. So slowly. A thatched roof above him, a thin mat below him. A sinuous, scaled creature curled into his side.

Henry looked, his eyes slowly focusing on the not-a-cat. Its side, just like his own shoulder and leg, was bandaged. It opened its strange blue eyes and looked at Henry. It was a brief look, but Henry knew, somehow, that this creature was his friend.

As his eyes closed, he saw a flag on the wall of the shack. A red star in a circle of white with a red band behind it and blue stripes above and below. He was north of the 38th parallel—in communist territory. He told his body to move, to get up, but he couldn't. His eyes fluttered closed as the creature nuzzled him.

2012

Portland, Oregon

Ada laughed as Jag-eun Yong lunged at the girl and then ran away, his claws digging into the carpet of Henry's living room. The little dragon ran up his scratching post—a four-foot, carpet-covered monstrosity that sat in front of the bay windows. He perched himself on top of it and hissed at Ada. The girl laughed harder and clapped.

Henry smiled. He knew the child didn't have a lot to be happy about. Her mother had come clean about Ada's illness—leukemia—and because of Jag-eun Yong's love of the girl and the good it did Ada, Henry had taken to watching her when he could. When his days weren't bad and he knew when and where he was.

Today had been a good day. He had managed his bow tie and didn't think he was late for a lecture.

As he mused, he caught Jag-eun Yong staring at him from atop his perch, a question on the magical creature's face: *Why are you remembering?*

1952

Korea

Long black hair, pulled back, dark brown eyes, a narrow nose. She was beautiful. Henry tried to sit up, but he was so weak that she pushed him back down on the mat with ease.

"Kyung," she said, pointing at herself and then pointing at Henry.

"Henry," he mumbled, his voice a croak.

She nodded. "Henree."

Henry pointed at the flag on the wall of the shack, the one that placed him in communist-controlled North Korea.

Kyung waved his concern away and pointed at the scaled creature next to him, her eyes widening. "*Imugi . . . jag-eun yong.*" Her voice was hushed—reverent, even. She then pointed at Henry and waved dismissively at the flag again. "Henree have dragon. Henree okay."

2000

New London, Connecticut

"I am sorry, my dear," Henry said after his lecture, the college auditorium mostly empty.

"There is nothing to be sorry for," Kyung said with a thin smile, patting the seat next to her. "Change is hard." The years had added wrinkles and pounds and grayed her hair, but Henry still found her beautiful.

Henry tried to smile, but it came out as a grimace. He sat and squeezed her hand. "Last lecture."

She nodded but didn't speak.

"You look tired, love," Henry said, noticing the dark circles under her eyes and her sallow complexion.

She shrugged, but Henry knew better. She had seemed fine that morning, but they had been away from Jag-eun Yong for hours, and both of them found that hard at this age. The little creature made them feel better. If she felt this badly after only a few hours away from him, then—

"You must tell me what is wrong," he said, his voice hushed.

1952

Korea

The villagers stared at him as he hobbled among the huts, his arm around Kyung as he leaned heavily on her. Or, more likely, they were staring at his scaled companion, Jag-eun Yong. The creature walked by his side, often rubbing up against his leg.

The pain as he walked was great, but his guilt was greater. Jag-eun Yong was recovering fast. His side was still an open wound, but it was smaller, the flesh growing back without even a hint of a scar.

Henry smiled at Kyung. "*Gomabseubnida*," he said, thanking her in Korean. She smiled back.

He breathed deeply of the fresh air. The shack he had been recovering in had a sour, stale scent, and he had begged Kyung to take him outside. He needed the sun, and he was hoping the clouds would clear long enough to see it.

They slowly hobbled out of the tall pine trees into an open, narrow valley. He could see rice fields in the distance, a pale green expanse, and a small stream to one side. He looked at both of his new friends, and his heart swelled.

This was all a miracle, and Henry knew it was the tiny dragon that had done it. These people had taken him in because of Jag-eun Yong. He had survived and was healing faster than he had any right to because of Jag-eun Yong. He was learning Korean, and Kyung was learning English with ease. He found himself loving the Korean culture and feeling something every time he looked into Kyung's kind brown eyes.

The cloud cover broke toward the horizon and a shaft of light lanced its way through the humid air and fell on them. Henry stopped, closed his eyes, and let the sun kiss his face.

"Look!" Kyung said.

The dragon had gone forward a few steps and had reared up on his hind legs, using his strong tail to balance. The creature sniffed and turned toward the water, its mouth opening and its thin tongue lolling out. He then trotted forward and looked back at Henry and Kyung as if to ask, *Are you coming?*

Henry hesitated. He felt the weight of the moment. This magical creature was beckoning him forth to a different life. He had joined the Army as an aimless young man after a bar brawl had put him in the hospital. He could feel the future Jag-eun Yong was offering them—creating for them—and it wasn't the kind of future he had ever imagined for himself.

"He want swim," Kyung said.

Henry nodded and grinned. "*Heeom*," he said, using the Korean word for *swim*. He gladly limped his way towards the future this creature was offering him.

2012

Portland, Oregon

Kyung had pancreatic cancer. That is what she told Henry that night after his last speech. She had died in Portland six years later. "You helped her as long as you could, didn't you?" he asked the dragon in his lap. He sat on the bed, neatly made as always, and petted his friend's fur.

That last speech, that last night, the fight they had had before he knew she was sick—it was the beginning of the end. That was why he had been skipping through time. That was why he thought he had to give a lecture every morning.

The pivot points of his life: 1952, in Korea, when he had found Jag-eun Yong and Kyung; 1964, when Henry had become a tenured professor at the University of Hawaii; 1976, when Henry and Kyung had moved to South Korea and he had taught at Seoul National University; 1988 and the move back to the United States and Connecticut College; 2000 in New London, the day he started to lose his beloved Kyung.

Each year was a dragon year on the Korean zodiac. Each change guided by the creature in his lap.

"What now?" he mumbled.

Jag-eun Yong's blue eyes found his as if to say, *You know.*

He had trouble leaving the house anymore. Away from Jag-eun Yong, his mind was cloudy like a storm-swollen river. The dragon was still creating a life for Henry—the best life he could—but how much longer could he do it?

"You have another adventure to go on, don't you?" Henry asked. The magical creature looked the same despite the years.

The tiny dragon yawned and slipped off the bed. He padded to the front door and looked back at him. *Yes.*

Henry nodded. He knew. It was time.

1952

Korea

Henry held Kyung's hand as he slowly limped out of the village that had taken him and Jag-eun Yong in, had saved their lives. It had been ninety-six days, and he was finally strong enough.

He spoke to Kyung in his halting Korean, reassuring her that they would be fine, that the tiny dragon perched on his shoulders had a beautiful future planned for them. She had tended to him, taught him Korean, and they had fallen in love. She laughed nervously, her finger brushing at the dragon. The dragon made her feel safer than Henry did.

Jag-eun Yong meant "tiny dragon" and seemed an apt name for the creature. Henry had learned much of dragons and how revered they were by the Korean people. They were creatures of water, were thought to help crops grow and heal the sick. Henry knew he owed the creature his life, and somehow he knew that Jag-eun Yong believed he owed Henry his life. He felt guilty—the airstrike had done this—but he felt lucky too. The wounds and the trauma had brought the three of them together, and now their future awaited.

2012

Portland, Oregon

The cab pulled away from Henry's quiet little neighborhood, the streets wet and the first hints of dawn lighting the horizon.

Henry directed the stout cabbie to the airport—he was going to catch a flight to Seoul, South Korea—and then silence descended, for which Henry was grateful. He stared out as the sleepy city rolled by. His heart ached for his tiny dragon, just now left behind, but he knew it was the right thing to do. Since he had made the decision, he had stopped skipping through time, his mind settling down.

Ada was delighted when he dropped Jag-eun Yong off at her house. Ms. Paulson had taken some convincing, but when it became clear how much better her daughter felt when Jag-eun Yong was around, she had agreed to adopt Henry's "very odd cat." Jag-eun Yong was now looking after Ada's future, and Henry knew it would be bright.

Henry mused on the number twelve and the Year of the Dragon as the city slid by. He was born in 1928 and Ada in 2000, both dragon years. Every major turn in his life, save Kyung's death, had happened on one of those twelve-year cycles. And Kyung had died six years after her diagnosis, square in the middle of a twelve-year cycle—a very long time to survive pancreatic cancer. Perhaps the dragon was weakest then, and his magic could no longer aid her.

Henry smiled. His tiny dragon friend had created the most beautiful of lives for them, and he was ready for whatever was next, for however many days he had left.

O O O

Robert J. McCarter lives in the mountains of Arizona with his beautiful wife and his ridiculously adorable dog, pounding away at the keyboard producing software (to make a living) and stories (to fill his soul and hopefully yours). He has written a series of first-person ghost novels (starting with *Shuffled Off: A Ghost's Memoir*) and a superhero/love story series (*Neutrinoman and Lightningirl: A Love Story*). Find out more at RobertJMcCarter.com.

DUST AND FIRE

Aaron Michael Ritchey

For Jen Greyson

In the cave, the people enjoyed the pictures the Teacher Victor drew in the dust covering the smooth stone floor. The light came from high above. The light went away. The people slept on mats beside their cooking fires. They carried water from an underground pool. They gathered food and fed their babies.

The light came. The light went. And the beast, always the beast, threatened their every minute. The beast would come like a thief in the night to block out the light, to scatter the dust and frighten the people. When the beast left, the people would weep. Why was the cave so cruel? Why did the beast visit evil upon their simple lives?

After one visit by the beast, after the Teacher Victor's pictures in the dust had been scattered, the people wept, but none more bitterly than Big Sue and Little Say. Their Ima held them and whispered that all would be good. All would be well. Even in the blackest of pits, light would still come from on high.

"Come, Big Sue," Little Say said after a time of mourning, "the Teacher Victor is going to draw a perfect circle in the dust on the floor. Everyone is going to be drawing circles. Circles are very popular this year."

Big Sue didn't move from her corner in the cave.

"What's wrong, sister?" Little Say asked.

"I am weary of the stink of cooking fires and our own flesh. I do not want to live in this cave. I want to be free of the beast." Big Sue was a dreamy girl, large and uncertain.

Little Say knew all about her dreamy ways. "Every time the beast comes, you say such things. But once you watch the Teacher Victor or once you draw in the dust, you feel better. Come, do not be strange. Let us join the others. The Teacher Victor knows how to help us in our grief."

Ima did not speak. She looked on, listening.

"Do you remember the story of the woman who dug through the wall?" Big Sue asked. "I cannot recall the whole story, but I do remember she escaped the cave and defied the beast. She was called to do more than ordinary things."

"That is just a story," Little Say said. "Stories do not mean anything."

Ima did not speak. She stood and walked to a remote part of the cave. Big Sue followed. And Little Say did as well, all the while chattering, "Sister, we shouldn't leave the people. What about the circles? What about the dust? What will the Teacher Victor say?"

The fading light from high above cast murk into the corners of the cave. However, Big Sue saw the ruins of a tunnel chipped into the rock. She felt the rough stones inside. The ceiling of the tunnel had collapsed, but someone, at some point, had dug a passage through the stone.

"Come away from there!" the Teacher Victor called. "I will show you how to draw circles in the dust."

Little Say pulled Big Sue from the tunnel and back to where the people squatted, watching the Teacher Victor draw in the dust on the floor. Many did not trust their own skill, and so they took pleasure only in the Teacher Victor's drawings and drew none of their own.

Big Sue liked to draw. She etched circles in the dust, but she kept thinking of the tunnel and the story of the hero.

The Teacher Victor came close. He was an old man, very powerful and very wise in the ways of the cave.

"Do you know the story of the woman who escaped?" Big Sue asked.

"It is foolishness," the Teacher Victor said. "It is a waste of time to tell such stories. Life is difficult. It will always be difficult. Better to live simply. We carry water. We gather food to feed the babies. That is our life. The light comes. The light goes. And on some days, the beast. Always the beast."

"Always the beast," Big Sue murmured.

"I am sorry, Teacher Victor," Little Say said quickly. "We love your drawings. We will carry water. We will gather food. We will be good."

Ima did not speak. But early the next morning, she woke Big Sue and led her back to the tunnel. Little Say followed, chattering, "But it is so early! We will be tired all day long. How will we carry water and gather food? And the Teacher Victor said he would draw triangles tonight. If I am sleepy, I will not enjoy the triangles. We should go back and sleep more."

Big Sue shushed her. "It will be okay. I remembered more of the story. The woman had to leave her home and go on a grand journey. Maybe through that tunnel. Let us try."

Big Sue removed one rock, then another, then another. Little Say did not help, only chattered. "These rocks are easy, but what if we come to a rock wall? We have nothing to dig with. What will we do then, sister?"

"I do not know. But this rock I can lift. And this one. And this one." Big Sue was amazed at her progress. Soon she had cleared enough of the tunnel that she and Little Say could fit inside. Ima stood outside, looked at them, and smiled. Then it was time to carry water, gather food, feed the babies, and watch the Teacher Victor draw in the dust.

"Clearing the tunnel should not be so very difficult," Big Sue said.

Ima did not speak.

Little Say did. "It is easy now. But it will not last. Soon we will come to a wall, and we will have to chip it away, and if the tunnel caved in once, it could cave in again. And what if the beast comes? Always the beast."

"Always the beast," Big Sue agreed. But she refused to surrender.

That night, while the others watched the Teacher Victor draw triangles, Big Sue and Little Say returned to the tunnel. As Little Say predicted, once Big Sue had cleared away the easy stones, she faced what appeared to be a solid rock wall. Perhaps the hero had been killed in the cave-in. Perhaps there was no escape from the cave or the beast.

"See?" Little Say cried. "See? The Teacher Victor called you foolish. He is right."

That night, on her thin mat, Big Sue could not sleep. She did not want to give up on her tunnel, but how could she get through the rock? She remembered more of the story. The woman, after going on the journey, would face obstacles.

Surely she had not faced such an obstacle as this: a solid rock wall, maybe miles thick. It seemed hopeless.

Big Sue tossed and turned.

Finally, Ima came to lay next to Big Sue, to soothe her. Ima did not speak, but she pushed a slender piece of iron, a chisel no thicker than a pencil, into Big Sue's hand.

"A boon," Big Sue whispered.

Early the next morning, Big Sue used the chisel to scratch at the stone at the end of the tunnel. Dust drifted down, covering her face and filling her nose with a dry smell. Rock bits sprinkled down on her hand. She found the marks of others who had scratched at the wall in the past. And what she thought was a solid rock wall was merely huge boulders that had fallen. She could get through them.

Big Sue chipped away. Little Say drew in the dust. First a circle. Then a triangle. "The Teacher Victor draws them better than I ever could. He is going to draw rectangles tonight. I am very excited."

Big Sue chipped away at the stone. She did not answer.

"Even if there is a way out, it will take you years and years to dig your way through the stone," Little Say said. "Is it not more interesting and entertaining to watch the Teacher Victor draw in the dust?"

"His pictures are lovely," Big Sue said, "but this is more important. I was given a boon, and I mean to use it to overcome this obstacle."

The light came. The light went. The beast came and took someone away, scattering the dust. The beast. Always the beast.

Big Sue wept, like she always did, next to Little Say. Ima held them both. And yet, even as Big Sue wept, the thought of the tunnel remained ever inside her.

The tunnel expanded deeper into the earth. Big Sue chiseled through rock bright with crystals, and those days were filled with wonder as the walls sparkled around her. Some days, the rock seemed softer than others. Some days, she knew at any moment she would break through to the other side and escape the cave. Other days, Little Say's voice plagued Big Sue's mind: It is hopeless. It could be miles. She was wasting her life scratching away at rock.

Finally, the people came to look at her tunnel. The Teacher Victor crawled inside and took the chisel from her. "If you insist on this foolishness, let me show you how to do it." He chipped away a piece of rock.

He handed the chisel back to Big Sue. Yes, he had skillfully removed a good chunk of stone, but she did not like the way he had done it. And he thought her tunnel all foolishness anyway. She would work in her own way.

The Teacher Victor left. Still Big Sue chiseled, though she found herself using the Teacher Victor's technique.

Others began to ridicule her.

"Look at Big Sue. She thinks she is so grand."

"If I wanted to tunnel out, I could. It is not that difficult."

"Who does she think she is to dig in such a way?"

"She has no experience. If anyone could escape the cave, it would be the Teacher Victor, and yet he stays."

"Poor Little Say. Big Sue is selfish. It seems she cares more about her tunnel than her sister."

All the talk made Little Say panic. "See, Big Sue? Now the people do not like us. They think we are strange. I do not want to be strange. I do not want you to be strange. Let us leave this tunnel. Let us enjoy the Teacher Victor's drawings before the beast comes."

"Always the beast," Big Sue said. But she kept digging. She would return to the people when necessary to carry water, gather food, and feed the babies; however cruel, the people were her family. Yet when they gathered around the Teacher Victor to watch him draw in the dust, Big Sue worked on her tunnel.

Every morning, every night, she scratched at the stone. Even when rocks shifted ominously above her. Even when the stone grew hot and the stink of sulfur assaulted her senses. Were there dragons below? Big Sue did not think so, but what if?

"You will die! The beast will come and you will die!" Little Say wailed.

At such words, Big Sue would grow afraid. What if she died in her tunnel? Worse yet, what if Ima or Little Say died in the tunnel?

The light came. The light went. The beast came, and the people wept.

The next day, Big Sue returned to her work. Ima sat next to her. Little Say chattered, but Big Sue had grown accustomed to it and to the ridicule of the people.

She remained at her task. Each day, she thought, this could be the day. This could be the day.

Then she came upon the hardest rock of all. Her chisel would not scratch through the dense stone.

At morning, at night, she worked, but the stone would not yield. She slept in one morning, then two. She watched the Teacher Victor draw pictures, one night, then two.

Big Sue knew she had wasted much of her life. There was no escape from the cave or the beast. Always the beast.

Even though she had given up on her work, the people still ridiculed her. "Remember when you tried to escape? Remember how it came to nothing?" Their barbed words were difficult to pluck from Big Sue's mind.

Ima held Big Sue close, but she did not speak. Then, one morning, Ima walked Big Sue back to the tunnel. Big Sue did not want to go, but she went. Little Say slept on.

Big Sue approached the wall she could not break through. She touched the stone. She remembered the hope and joy that had filled her. She glanced down. There on the ground, buried in stone and dust, lay a hammer.

Ima lifted the hammer and gave it to Big Sue.

The people woke up when the silence of the cave was shattered by the ringing sound of a hammer on chisel.

The hard stone gave way. Big Sue broke into a fresh chamber, and while there was no way out, she saw the chisel blows of others who had come before. They had swung the hammer. They had broken the stone. There was hope. Big Sue picked a part of the chamber that felt right and continued hammering away at the stone.

Then the beast came.

The tunnel collapsed.

A large stone fell on Ima's chest.

Coughing, spitting dust from their mouths, Big Sue and Little Say dragged Ima from the tunnel.

Ima looked into Big Sue's face. She did not speak, but she touched Big Sue's face, which touched her heart.

Ima closed her eyes.

"The beast has come!" Little Say wailed. "The beast has come and taken our Ima, and now we are lost! The beast! Always the beast!"

People raced over to the front of the tunnel. In their haste, they scattered the Teacher Victor's drawings in the dust.

The people wept.

Big Sue held Ima to her, but Ima was cold.

How could Big Sue go on? She wept.

The Teacher Victor stood over them. "You brought this darkness upon yourself. The beast came and took your Ima because of your tunnel." He was very stern and righteous. The people all agreed.

"Destroy the tunnel!" someone yelled. It might have been Little Say; Big Sue did not know.

The people roused their rage and smashed the tunnel. All the rock came down and destroyed years of Big Sue's work.

Big Sue did not care. She held the cold body of Ima to her. "This is the darkest of moments," she whispered.

"It is over," Little Say said. "Our hearts are broken. There is nothing to do but carry water, gather food, feed the babies, and draw in the dust. Will you come back to the people with me?"

Big Sue stood. Ima had showed her the tunnel. Ima had given her the chisel and then the hammer. Ima had stayed with her even when the tunnel had grown dangerous.

"Come and be with us before the beast comes again," Little Say said.

"Always the beast," the people echoed, as was their way.

Big Sue turned from the people. "Never the beast." The words felt natural to her. She picked up her slender chisel, no thicker than a pencil. She picked up the heavy hammer, fitting it into the callouses on her palm.

"Never the beast." Big Sue raised the hammer and brought it down on the chisel. A stone split in two.

She'd done this before. She knew what to do. She could not stop the beast. She could not free the people. She could not even convince Little Say to stop her chatter. But she could swing her hammer and strike her chisel.

The people left. The Teacher Victor told them not to care about Big Sue anymore. She was beyond their reach. Besides, he was going to draw swirls in the dust for them.

Big Sue broke stone by herself, and yet, when it was time, she would go carry water, gather food, and feed the babies. The babies should not go hungry because of Big Sue's work.

Morning and night, Big Sue worked clearing her tunnel. It seemed she could smell Ima in the dust. It seemed, when she grew weary, she could feel Ima beside her. In her dreams, Ima reminded her of the sparkling crystals she had seen in her tunnel. She helped Big Sue remember the stories about the heroic woman who had gone before, standing victorious in sunshine.

One day, Little Say came and leaned over Big Sue's shoulder. "Nothing will stop you. Not the death of our Ima. Not the beast. Not the people. Not me. Do you not love me?"

"I love you, sister," Big Sue said. "I will free us. We will escape the cave. We will eat flowers and fruit under the sunshine. Then you will know how much I love you."

"What is sunshine?" Little Say asked.

"I do not know for sure," Big Sue said. "But in the stories, they speak of sunshine."

The light came. The light went. The beast came. The people wept. Big Sue wept, and then she would say, "Never the beast."

Hammer fell on chisel, sparking off stone.

Big Sue spoke to her Ima, now long dead. "Maybe I shall never dig my way out of the cave, Ima. But it is a good life, my work. I am proud of my tunnel and the work I have done."

Little Say had grown quiet. She had heard Big Sue talking to their dead Ima.

Then.

One day.

The tunnel above them shifted. It was going to cave in again. Big Sue knew the ways of her tunnel after so many years.

"We are going to die!" Little Say called. "Please, sister, please. Come away! The tunnel will fall, and we will die like Ima died."

"Never the beast," Big Sue said. She was close. The stories said the closer a woman draws to her victory, the harder the journey, the darker the hour, the harder the stone.

Her chisel broke through to the other side. Light streamed in. Rocks, dust, dirt rained down. The tunnel was collapsing.

Big Sue quickly created an opening large enough for herself and for Little Say. It was easy now. She knew how each rock would react to her chisel. She knew just the right way to swing the hammer down.

"Susan." A voice called to her from outside the cave.

The light was too bright for her to see, so Big Sue had to squint, and there, standing in light more blinding than she could have ever imagined, stood her Ima. For in the sunshine, away from the cave, all things were possible.

"Sister!" Little Say wept. "Sister, the beast is coming! There is a dragon outside of the cave. He blinds us with his fire and his light. I can hardly see you. Come away. Come away before we are killed."

Big Sue slipped into the light, and it did indeed feel like fire on her skin. But it was not the beast of everyday death. Nor was it a dragon. It was sunshine.

Big Sue turned and reached her hands for Little Say. "Come, sister. Come out and escape the cave. We have done it. We have our victory!"

"I cannot!" Little Say cried out. "I do not have the courage. You are on fire. I do not want to be consumed in the dragon's flame."

"It is not flame," Big Sue cried back. "It is sunshine!"

Little Say drew back.

The tunnel collapsed and buried her.

Big Sue could do nothing but watch. Ima held her. All around them, red flowers bloomed and orange fruit hung fat from leafy trees.

Big Sue wept. Her sister was dead. She had reached the sunshine, but her sister was dead.

Ima held her and spoke. "Little Say could not follow. Would you have embraced the beast of everyday death to stay with her?"

"Never the beast," Big Sue said.

* * *

Big Sue found others who had escaped the cave. She sang with them and ate with them, carried cool, fresh water, gathered tasty, luscious food, and fed the fattening, happy babies. Big Sue's hammer and chisel were not so useful in the meadows and forests of the outside world, so she found new tools.

Mountains towered in the distance. Great purple peaks capped by blinding snow. On some nights, fire flashed in the darkness above the peaks.

"What are those lights in the sky above the mountains?" Big Sue asked.

"No one knows for sure," an old woman said, frowning. "But no one who has gone to seek them has ever come back."

"I think I shall go and see what might be making such fire in the sky," Big Sue said. "Perhaps they are dragons."

"Foolishness!" cried the old woman. "We do not leave the meadows and forests. We escaped the cave. We are safe. You should not have such strange ideas."

"I have heard others speak as you do," Big Sue said.

"Susan!" Ima called to her. She was already at the edge of the meadow. She held a single golden arrow out to Big Sue.

"You will die, Big Sue."

"I think I am Big Sue no longer. Farewell."

Susan gathered her hammer and chisel, her bow and quiver, her many tools, and took up the golden arrow to see what might be painting with fire in the skies above the mountains.

* * *

In the cave, the people enjoyed the pictures the Teacher Victor drew in the dust covering the smooth stone floor. The light came from high above. The light went away. The people slept on mats beside their cooking fires. They carried water. They gathered food. They fed their babies.

On some days, the beast came.

One day, a young man said to his brother, "Do you remember the story of the woman who dug through the wall? I think I remember. Here. Yes, here. There has been a cave-in, but there is a passage here. We can be free. This woman found a way to escape, and the stories say she overcame many obstacles to stand victorious in the sunshine."

His brother took the young man's hand. "I do not know this story. Can you tell me?"

O O O

Aaron Michael Ritchey is the author of four young adult novels, and his short fiction has appeared in various anthologies and online magazines. In 2012, his first novel, *The Never Prayer*, was a finalist in the Rocky Mountain Fiction Writers Gold Conference. In 2015, his second novel, *Long Live the Suicide King*, won the Building the Dream Award for best YA novel, and he spent the summer as the Artist in Residence at the Anythink Library. *Dandelion Iron*, the first book in his epic YA sci-fi western series, The Juniper Wars, is available now through Kevin J. Anderson's WordFire Press. Aaron lives in Colorado with his cactus flower of a wife and two stormy daughters.

Black Tide's Last Ride

Mike Jack Stoumbos

The comm above her head piped out a fierce rendition of reveille, which effectively ripped Tucker from her sleep but didn't totally bring her into the world of the waking. She muttered half a dozen curses while trying to use her tail to pull the blankets further over her head. When she realized why the attempt was futile, she nearly put her fist through the wall.

She had no tail in this body—the nerves were sending signals to nonexistent muscles in a phantom appendage, with no success or satisfaction.

The odious melody ran itself out, and she did her best to roll facedown and return to dreamland. But a human voice clicked in to replace the imitation brass.

"Maso Tucker?"

She responded with an ineloquent grunt.

"Come on, Tucker." The voice held a smirk. "We're due planetside short'f six hours now, and I'm not keen on explaining why we took out a satellite while our pilot slept."

Tucker could just imagine with what little courtesy Black Tide would barrel right through a signal orb or even the arm of a space station. It almost sounded appealing, but it would get her grounded for sure.

Not an option, she thought, or maybe said it aloud, however loud *loud* was through a significant layer of pillow.

"Tucker? I could just switch on the lights for you …" The voice trailed off, making the threat sound like a friendly offer of assistance.

"No," she tried—too quietly, probably—so again, "No, Jordan. I'm up."

"It doesn't look like that from here," Jordan snarked back.

Of course he has the camera on. Tucker threw off the covers and spilled out of bed, wanting very much to not be upright on two legs. It hardly felt natural after nearly two decades of full-time piloting. She could hear Jordan snickering in the background, either at her stumbling gait or her grumbling attitude, and thought about crawling back in bed just to spite him. But the sooner she got ready, the sooner she could get back into the driver's seat.

Tucker unceremoniously stripped off her sleepwear, letting each article fall behind her, knowing a maid would be by to pick them up. After all, pilots weren't expected to clean their own quarters. She tapped the motion sensor—though a wave would have sufficed—activated the shower, and voice-commanded the temperature settings.

Each time she washed, Tucker spent most of her time thoroughly soaping and rinsing the nineteen rings laid out symmetrically along her skin—each a long-endured, pink-to-brown bruise, each perfectly circular. Bruise the same spot too many times, and it moves a few shades past purple to an ugly muddy color. Both of her ankles boasted a patch that never fully recovered and was always tender to the touch. Still, you had to make them shine to ensure the best sensor connection.

Scrub 'em clean, make 'em shine, draggers! It was one of the first things she remembered hearing when she became a Dragon Apprentice. That was twenty-six years ago, long before she'd met BT, but she still said it to herself every morning.

She didn't wait to dry off before stepping into the suit. It went on easier while wet, and once on, it was just about the most comfortable thing you could wear. It would have been great for sleeping in, if not for the lack of insulation; the suit was featherlight and porous to the slightest breeze. It also had transparent sections that perfectly surrounded each of the bruises.

Between each transparency were lines of conductive microfilaments, a net for transmitting the body's electromagnetic signals. Of course, if there were an electrical short, the suit could also protect her from that. Tucker hardly understood the suit's science but knew the longevity of the Dragon Program had brought about fail-safes for practically everything.

Except the dragons. You couldn't fail-safe a dragon, and that was part of the fun.

As the steam of her shower receded, Tucker regarded her own wry smirk in the mirror, the thin lips that often rested in a scowl unless otherwise provoked.

She did not look particularly feminine, even by Spacer standards—certainly not by Earth standards if the fashions had held for her last eighteen-month tour. She was coated in lean muscle from head to foot, boasted a more chiseled chin and jaw than any of the men on the vessel, had hard, pale blue eyes, and cropped dusty-blonde hair with a graying pattern that favored the left side of her widow's peak.

And like all other dragon pilots, Tucker had an extreme case of forward head posture, where the neck arced forward instead of remaining vertical. It happened because *every* pilot involuntarily craned forward when they were in link. Nothing to be done about that. Attempts to chemically relax them had disrupted the connection, and methods to restrain them just resulted in sprained necks. The Allied Interstellar Dragon Association took the high road and paid to have chiropractors on staff.

Tucker's posture was worse than most, but that didn't bug her, and it certainly didn't surprise her. After all, she had the second-longest service record in the fleet—in history, for that matter—and the most hours in the drive-seat by a good percentage.

Every now and again, she'd hear a comment that she looked too old to be a dragon pilot; doubtless there had been millions of mentions that she hadn't heard, but by now, it was a compliment.

Straightening as best she should, Tucker saluted herself in the mirror. "Commander-at-Helm Sheridan Tucker, pilot of Black Tide, reporting for duty." She had said it every day for more than eighteen years.

* * *

Tucker found her tertiary apprentice standing just outside her quarters. Ensign Sonoma Keats was a bright-eyed young woman with the potential to shine the sunniest smile in eight worlds—when she wasn't standing at attention, that is.

"Maso Tucker," Keats remarked by way of greeting.

"At ease, Ensign," said Tucker, hardly breaking stride for a nod and expecting Keats to be on her heels.

Tucker turned a corner in the well-lit hallway toward the pilot's room. With each step toward the center of the vessel, the grav force decreased. The next dilating door took them out of the world of metal walls and into a corridor that looked more like tanned hide. The walls rounded into the low ceiling lined with a blue bioluminescent strip that tinted the red walls purple.

They collected the secondary pilot, Ensign Hutchinson Shaw, waiting by the final door—an out-of-place bit of tech surrounded by the otherwise living tissue. Here, the gravity was less than one-third Earth's. Shaw didn't budge from his position against the organic wall until Tucker acknowledged him.

"Maso," he barked, the remnants of a proud, nominally royal dialect coating his words.

"Hutch, how we doin'?" Tucker asked with none of the same ceremony, knowing how he bristled when she dropped the rank talk. He preferred *Mister Shaw* to the gender-neutral *Maso* anyway and would have gladly received a *Sir* from anyone who would bother to offer it. No one outside of the former UK would have.

"Maso, Captain Jordan sent the ambassador report to the Pangaurian Council on Earth."

Tucker smirked. "Uh-huh. Bet they were happy about that." She punched her private access code into the swipe-screen and then pressed her palm to a fleshy bit of wall beside it. A portion of the wall tensed, much like a throat muscle, and the door to the pilot's room dilated.

"No, Maso," Shaw answered with none of the same irony. "They are upset by the independent movements on the new Centauri colonies."

The door shut, sealed, and hazard-locked as soon as Tucker and her two ensigns were inside.

The pilot's room was even more of a blend of gadgets and guts than any of the preceding hallways. Five different screens, vast arrays of control panels, the latest reports of every single reading of the dragon's inner workings all pulsed softly in time with the well-veined pink walls. Everything faced one strange recess, just the right size for one seated human being, draped to near-concealment with long, flat tentacles, each of which had at least one perfectly round suction cup.

Sheridan Tucker parted the curtain of tentacles and took her seat amongst them, every welt on her skin literally tingling with anticipation.

Ensign Keats grabbed a belt off the wall, its pouches prestocked with a spray bottle, lotion, and wet and dry tissues, and fastened it on her way to assist Tucker. Ensign Shaw waved his hand across the motion sensors on most of the pieces of equipment, voice-commanded two of the screens to their start-up settings, and then saluted Captain Jordan when his face appeared on the central viewer.

"Captain Jordan!" Shaw announced, as if the man were physically present and about to officiate an execution.

"Tucker," Jordan called, bypassing the rigid soldier in front of him.

Tucker didn't make eye contact; she was busy following the tentacles as they made contact with her arms, legs, torso, and neck.

"Tucker, they're wanting an estimate on our touchdown time at the Interstellar Diplomat's Office. What's your guess?"

"Why? They're itchin' to send us back up with some *expert negotiator*?" Tucker teased. "Yeah, I'll have the guess to you within five minutes of full link—how's that, Cap?"

"Champin' at the bit, Tucker," Jordan reminded her, but he was still smiling. He was quite a bit older than she was, but he wore his creases and thick grey hair well. If Captain Jordan was worried about a reprimand from HQ, he didn't show it. "Should I give the zero-g alert?"

"Yeah," Tucker replied with a short gasp as the smallest of the tentacles made contact with her temples. "Within three minutes of link."

"Very good." And with a final, personal flourish, he added, "Happy landings, Tucker. Jordan out."

The screen automatically switched to the standard scrolling updates, none of which interested Tucker as not a single one was color coded for crisis. She pushed gently against the back of the pilot seat, felt the wall instinctually give. The warm suctions pressed into her lower back, her mid-thoracic vertebrae, and finally to the back of her neck, just under the base of her skull. When she next breathed in, the walls inhaled with her. She could feel the other two heartbeats and seven more appendages. The eyes were still closed, but not for long.

"Link initiated. Count 'em, Keats." Her voice sounded wispy and distant to her own human ears.

"Yes, Maso. Eight limb, and four, and four." The ensign counted by standard groupings. "Sixteen for sixteen visible"—she glanced at a nearby monitor—"and three spinal sensors, showing upwards of ninety-two percent connection. Maso Shaw?"

"All vitals in the green. Nervous and cardio systems fully engaged. Arms, wings, tail—check." He looked back at Keats and nodded.

Tucker felt Keats's hand on her shoulder, keeping her present with physical connection if only for a moment more.

Keats said, "Black Tide is ready to wake up."

Nearly fifty meters away, the giant interstellar dragon opened his eyes, and Tucker, from a throne deep in his chest, saw through them—with far more clarity and focus than she ever could with her human ones—a spinning blue-white orb set among uncountable stars.

From hardly a meter away, Keats read the statistics off the monitors, commenting on Tucker's motor control, her stretching and flexing the muscles, but it had little more relevance than a half-recalled dream to Tucker as she opened and closed her claws, flicked the ice from her tail, and roared.

The sound went nowhere in space, but it reverberated throughout the skin and organs of the Dragon down to the mechanical pods in the stomach and chest that housed most of the crew. To echo the roar, several dozen miniscule human beings happily passed along word that "Tucker's at the helm!"

From the command bridge, an inorganic station at the front of the rib cage, Captain Jordan flicked a switch on a private communicator.

The sound came out of two speakers: one beside Tucker's seat and one embedded in the dragon's skull. "Heya, Tucker. How's he flyin'?"

"Ready, ready, super steady, Cap," replied the breathy voice of the human Tucker, while Black Tide's vocal chords hummed the pitches.

She stared at the circling stars, letting her balance adjust and the vertigo subside, feeling the cold dark of open space. Tucker took a deep breath in, felt Black Tide's lungs fill with the CO_2 provided by the crew, and then breathed out the rich, high-oxygen air that would get pumped throughout the ship.

"Full link achieved," Tucker practically gasped. Though her control of the dragon was absolute, her attention to her own human body felt inconsequential by comparison. She could understand language and respond in kind, but she always sounded distracted, breathless—like someone playing a high-action, real-time, virtu-game with the speakers turned up way too loud. But virtual recreation was just pretending; when Tucker became Black Tide the interstellar dragon, every sensation was 100 percent real.

Tucker let her strong dragon arms swim through the nothingness of space, arched and twisted her back to work out any kinks. She longed to spread the wings but knew better than to do that in space; ice-coating made it difficult to refold them, and poorly folded wings seriously disrupted reentry.

Every moving part accounted for, Tucker prepared to stop the rotation, the force of which effectively created gravity within the livable areas of the ship. "Gonna level out," she said. "Call the zero-g alert."

Signal sounds, lights, and a very direct voice command echoed, telling everyone to prepare for total gravity loss. And with a combination of jets and gestures with massive appendages, she slowed Black Tide's spin until he came to a stop. Her human stomach quickly adjusted to the nausea; Black Tide didn't need to adjust at all.

One of the crewmen in the command bridge announced across the open channel, "We are at zero gravity."

"Zero-g," Tucker repeated. "Plotting course for entry." She was keen on setting her speed and angle for the navigator to analyze in less than two minutes to follow her glib, albeit sincere, estimate but was interrupted once more by Jordan.

"Hey—umm—Tucker, I got some news." He sounded less sure than usual. "Bit bad, but also congratulations. Looks like Perseids Lee, C-at-H of Red Dawn bought it a little over a year ago when we were out of the system." The Captain didn't have to fill in the blanks for her. "You've had the most years of service for the last six months. Just thought you'd want to know."

Tucker experienced only the briefest moment of pride, accompanied and overshadowed as it was by a nagging bit of dread. Now she had one less way to fight remarks that she'd been flying too long to be safe. After all, nine out of ten pilots never made it past year five, most of them due to mental breakdown and death. Only two among thousands had exceeded the fifteen-year mark. And now there was one.

"Thanks, Cap," said Tucker, trying to keep her voice even, despite her dragon connection and wavering emotion. "Hey, can I get some music up here? Something instrumental." Whether it was one of her apprentice ensigns or the communication tech who switched on the cello music, Tucker wasn't sure, but she knew that a well-accompanied swim through nothingness was the most soothing experience in eight worlds and beyond.

* * *

Tucker's heart was still pounding, her adrenaline pumping as her secondary and tertiary got her safely unhooked. They had landed perfectly in the Pacific, just off North Columbia. They were docked on a coastal airstrip and adjusting to full Earth gravity once more. Black Tide, with no human brain to control his actions, was asleep.

Beaming, Tucker thought aloud, "Do you think BT can sense where he was born? Y'know, his first assignment was here—oil cleanup in the Pacific." Of course her apprentices knew; *every* pilot knew. Prior to the space-proofing, dragons had been made for environmental cleanup. That was before Tucker's time, but she still found it fascinating and told them for the thousandth time, "That's why he's called Black Tide."

Tucker was always a little loopy after linking. After meteoring her way through the atmosphere, she looked and talked like a brand-new mother hopped up on endorphins and pain meds. She'd been telling Shaw for the last four years and Keats for the last two that breaking atmo was the best part.

Naturally, they hadn't experienced it firsthand yet, or they wouldn't still be apprentices. One of the many hitches about being a dragon pilot was that even though you kept at least two backup pilots on any vessel that would jump through more than one gate, they couldn't link until *after* the lead pilot retired. The large interstellar dragons, for whatever reason, could not relink with a previous pilot after a new pilot had achieved control.

Hutchinson Shaw had been politely waiting for Tucker to expire for longer than most ensigns, and he would probably soon find another vessel in need of a lead pilot. Tucker would miss him.

While Keats was helping Tucker towel off, Shaw interrupted, looking somewhat ill. "HQ wants to brief the senior crew immediately, in person. They specifically requested your presence, Maso Tucker."

Tucker, covered in sweat, natural and artificial lubricants, and fresh bruises, stared at him incredulously. She spat out a curse along with a good deal of saliva and mucus, not all of which was hers, and said, "All right, help me to the showers."

* * *

Sheridan Tucker loved catching fire on entry. She loved the perfect cold of the vacuum, the blinding light of a naked sun.

She hated, with just as much passion, the climate-controlled elevators of the central offices, the stifling suits she had to wear to visit HQ. She hated that she *had* to visit HQ. Four of Black Tide's crew—including captain, pilot, an ambassador, and her secretary—stood with their hands clutched behind their backs in just about the tensest "at ease" postures they could manage.

"I don't see why I had to come," Tucker said again. "Let the delegates and diplomats get blasted; let me take care of BT." The two politicians hardly reacted.

Jordan was clearly trying not to sound annoyed. "Tucker, we're not being punished. Probably just refitted and sent back. Or maybe you're gonna get offered a commendation for longest career, some photo op or something. So practice smiling, and enjoy yourself."

The elevator pinged once on floor thirty-seven, the doors slid open soundlessly, and the four were greeted by a host of painfully professional escorts. The ambassadors were taken one way, and the captain and his pilot had to go another.

On the way, they were congratulated and welcomed back by people Tucker neither recognized nor cared about. Each window they passed overlooked the incubators a hundred meters below—stadium-sized, bluish recesses in the earth where they programmed and grew pilotable organisms. Students at the nearby academy called them *hellmouths*; Tucker had just called them *spawning grounds*.

If they had been on the other side of the building, she was pretty sure she would be able to see Black Tide himself, a comatose dragon being treated after one of the longest interstellar journeys ever made in a crewed vessel. She hoped Ensigns Shaw and Keats were handling most of internal work; Tucker also hated it when the little office guppies, who'd never gone off-world, pretended to know the workings of a space dragon.

"Right this way, Maso Tucker," said a very friendly aide, who opened the door to the office of Senior Councilor Illyrius Dean.

The kidney-shaped touch-desk took up most of the room, and Dean's energy filled whatever was left. Thankfully, there were large windows to combat the oppression. He smiled a trained smile and invited them to sit down. "So," he warmed up, facing Tucker, "I understand congratulations are in order."

Jordan's eyes said, *I told you.*

"Yes," she said. "I heard."

"Longest career run. Eighteen years of dragon piloting and counting." Councilor Dean rubbed his hands together enthusiastically. "Shame about Lee, though. Were you and he close?"

Tucker gave a sideways nod. "Classmates. Friends, I guess. He was two years older than me and got his dragon a semester before I did." And before either of the men could jump in with small talk or business, Tucker blurted, "How did he die?"

Dean's happy expression didn't shift. "Brain burned out going through a gate. His second swears he was fine when they were out in the Proxi cluster, then they shifted back through the Pluto gate, and he just went limp. Total vegetable at first, then dead within the day. Dangerous work, Maso Tucker, and that's why we applaud you for it."

"And I take it you'll be sending us right back to Centauri," Jordan preempted.

The councilor hesitated. "Yes, probably. After we heard about the independent movement, we thought we'd send a crew back out. And you've maintained good contact, so …" He paused again, as if making sure not to overstep or misspeak.

"So what's the trouble?" asked Jordan, effectively taking the floor from Tucker, who stood and walked to the windows.

"It's complicated," dodged Dean without much dexterity. "That information is for the ambassadors."

"Is it just 'cause they're questioning Pangaurian control? Look, it's not like they want to go to war with you or even stop trade. They just want it to be their settlement first and part of an alliance with the Pangaurian governments second, right? And they're not the only ones."

"I know, and that's why it's such a problem. They're gathering traction, and we need to go back there with ambassadors to confront this attitude before it spreads."

Captain Jordan let slip a laugh of exasperation. He leaned across the console and said, "What's your aim here, Dean? I mean, you can't own the whole damn galaxy, can you? And Pangauria isn't an interstellar empire; it's an Earth alliance—at best, a Sol alliance—but even most of the post-belt colonies are independent. It's not like they have any weapons anyway, so what's the worry?"

Tucker listened intently for the response, but once she'd found Black Tide out the window, her eyes never left him—that oil-darkened masterpiece, a sleeping dragon more than 150 meters in length from snout to tail, winged and mounted with jets and properly sealed for space travel.

Dean matched Jordan's posture and played the buddy card—it may have even been in earnest. "Look, I'll level with you. They made pretty much the only bargain-threat combination we weren't prepared for. They said they'd stop trading entirely unless part of the deal was … we give them their own dragon program. Gene codes, blueprints, everything, so they could travel too." That was the kind of talk that could disrupt the status quo. Complete control of dragon-growing was Pangauria's primary advantage across eight worlds. "I suppose *you* think we should enable their freedom."

Tucker shrugged, not really knowing whether any eyes were on her, and heard Jordan say, "I live about a billion clicks from anyone but my crew, so yeah, I can understand the yearn for freedom."

"Not your decision," Dean informed him, "or mine. When we got the ambassador's report, we knew we'd have to refit and send you back there, try to smooth the situation, make a counteroffer."

This got Tucker to about-face. "Okay, so when do we patch out?" She was already feeling antsy about being on Earth. Or maybe she suspected what was coming next.

"Actually …" Dean trailed once more. "We—uh—the Allied Interstellar Dragon Association decided to pull you from Black Tide. The dragon is too expensive a piece of equipment for us to continue him with a pilot that's logged as many hours as you have. And you're too valuable to the Dragon Academy for us to just let you die in space."

Tucker stared at Jordan, but he looked as shocked as she felt and a hell of a lot more outraged. As she was speechless, her captain said for her, "You can't do this."

Dean almost stuttered when he said, "They already have. Ensign Shaw achieved connection and control with Black Tide while you were being shuttled here. I'm sorry."

* * *

Tucker was permitted to go back to Black Tide to collect her possessions and say good-bye to the crew. After all, there was no risk of her trying to reconnect. Without fail, every time a pilot had tried to relink with a dragon that had already imprinted with someone new, the old pilot had died of a kind of neural overload that—when later examined—looked quite a bit like electrocution.

Ensign—now *Lieutenant*—Hutchinson Shaw had been exiting Black Tide when she arrived. He opened his mouth as if to say *sorry*, then shut it again and marched past her.

In many ways, Tucker could acknowledge the logic of the situation: she had been putting her system through exceptional strain each time she linked or passed through an interstellar gate, and Shaw was a good man and a worthy apprentice who knew Black Tide better than any other replacement pilot they could have found. After the six years of academy time and four of apprenticeship, he certainly *deserved* the opportunity. Tucker just couldn't smile about it.

When she went inside, everyone wanted to shake her hand or give her a hug. The prospect of human touch was entirely repulsive from everyone but Sonoma Keats. Tucker was pretty sure she had never hugged the girl before that day but was grateful to do so.

"Tell me you'll stay on," said Tucker, and was at least mildly relieved when Keats nodded. "Take care of BT. And Hutch—he needs a good secondary."

"Yes, Maso," she said, diligently tailing Tucker to her quarters, to the lockers, and to the rec to collect anything that might have been left behind. And when Sheridan Tucker said she was going to say good-bye to the pilot's room, Ensign Keats followed without question.

Tucker entered her code and palm print, and the door opened as usual; no one had bothered to reprogram her access yet. She stepped onto the soft flesh, which gave way much more under full gravity. She took off her shoes to feel it beneath her feet again, and sighed audibly.

"Will you be alright?" Keats asked.

Tucker shrugged. "Do you know I've logged more than thirty thousand hours in that seat?" She pointed to the embedded throne, lined with tentacles that now would respond to someone else. "*Thirty thousand.* Perseids Lee, the runner-up, never even made twenty."

"It is miraculous," agreed Keats. "No one else could have done it."

Tucker tried to take a steadying breath while working backwards through the years and thinking of all the things that she had done that were considered out of the realm of possibilities. For so long, it had been like the usual "rules" of dragon piloting did not apply to her.

And if the rules really didn't apply …

"Keats, help me make one last link."

Keats didn't move. "But it'll kill you."

Tucker ran her fingers along the wall nearest her, felt her dragon breathing. "That's what they say. But that's what they've been saying for years." Tucker moved toward the door and hazard-locked it. "If this kills me, so be it—but I need to try. I need to see if I can beat the odds one more time."

Sonoma Keats's bright eyes widened in admiration and at least a touch of fear, but she said, "Okay."

* * *

When the dragon started moving, the cleaning crew reacted with shock. Those on the outside scrambled off its neck, back, and tail; a couple people had to dive through doors before they fully sealed. Alarms sounded—both the ones that said Black Tide was getting ready for space and the ones set off by the security officers.

The police force was nowhere near as fast as the dragon, and when they attempted to cut their way in, none of their gadgets could penetrate the hide. Black Tide spread his wings and launched himself from the ground amid a wide array of cheers and scolding shouts.

Inside the pilot's room, the main viewer switched itself on—the techies had managed to hack their way into the communications feed—and Councilor Dean's beet-red face appeared.

A raspy but elated voice answered him. "Maso Dean! Good to see you." Tucker kept her human eyes open. She was wearing nothing but sixteen flat tentacles.

"Come back this instant!" Dean sputtered. "That's an order!"

She shook her head as far as it would go without disrupting the sensors on her temples and neck. "I don't take orders from you anymore. I relinked! Not even a flight suit, hardly a crew, and I beat out Shaw's imprint. Try to reground me now." Once they were clear of the atmosphere, that would be nearly impossible, and Tucker knew it.

Tucker was still laughing at the speechless Senior Councilor when Keats switched off the viewer. "All systems look good, but what the hell is your plan?"

"We retrace our steps to the Centauri colony," Tucker declared, knowing that there would have to be at least a dozen skilled crew still onboard, with probably enough collective knowledge to build an incubator from scratch. "I think we have something to offer them."

O O O

Mike Jack Stoumbos is an English teacher by day, writer by nights and weekends. Between teaching classes and grading papers, he continues to plan and work on creative projects, to participate in the Seattle partner dance and theatre communities, and to compete in karaoke leagues. In recent years, he has had several of his plays produced in the Seattle area and self-published his novel, *The Baron Would Be Proud*. "Black Tide's Last Ride" is his first story to appear in an anthology.

Forging the Dragon

Peter Sartucci

"They say you make swords."

I wanted to ignore the voice, but it was a musical baritone much harder to disregard than the drone of insects or the sharp reek of burning wood and plastic that kept floating up from dead Scottsdale. Ugliness I had long practice at ignoring; beauty laid a stronger claim on my attention. I turned my head slightly and brought the speaker into view.

The man was tall, well-muscled but lithe instead of heavy with it, his tanned Anglo face an elegant symmetry of planes and curves. As handsome as the blades I make, and as dangerous. I nodded fractionally without quite taking my attention from Maria's gravestone. The last fragment of my world, gone in a fever that any doctor could once have cured when antibiotics still worked.

"I did. No more."

I let the words drop like lead weights. Unwelcome memories stirred from before my America fell with the rest of the world and left me a dazed survivor in the rubble.

The man smiled, perfect white teeth flashing beneath a waxed black moustache, and ignored the past tense. "I want to commission a sword. A very special sword, one unlike any other."

"I have always used clay molds and broken them in every casting," I answered drily, wondering if the self-assured princeling would be dissuaded. "Every blade I ever made was unique. But I'm done making them now."

The man made a sharp, dismissive gesture with one gauntleted hand. "This has to be *more* unique! I don't want just a pretty toy—I want a blade that can command loyalty from any man, a loyalty to someone greater than himself. I want a *magic* sword."

I went very still. No, I had sworn never again, no, no …

"Why do you imagine I can make such a mad thing? The world is maimed enough. If you will not make it better, at least leave it be."

The white teeth flashed again in challenge, and again he ignored what he didn't want to hear.

"I know you can. I've asked a lot of questions about you, talked to a lot of your past customers. You always delivered more than they dared hope for from mere steel. I dreamed about you too, Rumal Smith the Sword Maker—and my dreams always come true."

I tilted my head, intrigued by that last against my will. "Really? What do you do when they don't?" My dreams had rarely come true, but my nightmares did—too often.

His smile sharpened. "I *make* my dreams come true."

I raised one eyebrow, a trick I'd learned in my childhood from a TV character and could still perform long after TV had become myth. "Do you imagine you can *make* me do your will? If so, you are a fool." This might be a good day to end it all and join Maria, even if he scattered my bones over the hillside when he was done with me.

He laughed then, and I could see the charming boy he'd once been inside the hard man he was now. For a moment, I almost came close to liking him.

"No, I have something much better to offer you than stupid threats." He stepped across the small stone plaza surrounding Maria's grave, set one booted foot on the low wall, and beckoned to me.

I shouldn't have moved. I should have stayed still and out-stubborned him. I could have—men like him know too little of patience—but he had managed to intrigue me. So I got to my feet and joined him.

"Look." He waved at the Valley of the Sun, a place that had once boasted a bitterly ironic name. "Nothing but wreckage and despair as far as the eye can see."

"Phoenix has seen better days," I admitted. I could see the skeletal towers of downtown, the blowing ash of burnt-out suburbs, the fortified shopping centers of the warlords. Green fields spread from Papago Park and other oases as starving people dug out the old Hohokam irrigation ditches and put them back in service. Where once four million people had lived, a hundred thousand might remain. Why had the Gods ordained I must still be one of them?

"My work," he boasted, following my gaze to the greenery. "Farms are the foundation of any nation, the base on which to build a mighty state. If it but had a leader! One with the power to unite them, to organize the people and save them from themselves. Imagine it! 'Zona people again, together, powerful, choosing our own destiny. No longer the doormat of the Pache Raiders. No more contempt from the California Kings."

The glow in his eyes was hotter than lust.

"To do that, you'll have to break a lot of heads." I struggled against the glitter of his offering. It was so tempting. And he wouldn't be deterred by me anyway, so why not?

"From the outside or the inside," he agreed. "Bashing in skulls by force of arms produces little more than meat to feed the dogs—and Navajo mutton is cheaper. Heads opened from the inside are a lot more useful afterwards."

As farmers, soldiers, servants, and slaves. I made one last feeble try.

"My price is high." I named a sum.

He laughed, thinking he was triumphant. "Do as I ask, and you'll have that and more. I'll even mint a gold coin with your face on the back and the sword on the front." He beamed at me like a man who's just trained a new dog. "How soon?"

"Thirty days." I swallowed, envisioning what it would take. "I'll need a few things—more coal, a block of good wax, clean mineral oil for the quenching bath, a couple rubies for the eyes."

"Done. But … eyes?"

I indicated his men waiting in disciplined ranks on the road below the hill. His dragon banner rippled over their heads, an ancient symbol pressed into new life for the same old purpose: dominion.

"You want a magic sword," I told him, speaking the truth even though he couldn't understand it. "There will be eyes."

* * *

Casting is quick. Just pour liquid metal in a mold and let it cool. Carving the shape of the hilt to be cast, that takes time. I had to give it thought, too. The wooing of a spirit is not done lightly, even by me.

Meanwhile, there was the steel to heat, fold, and pound out flat again. Each time I folded it, the number of laminations doubled, two into four into eight into sixteen into thirty-two into sixty-four into a hundred twenty-eight. At fifteen folds, it contained more than thirty thousand laminations. Such a blade becomes strong and flexible in ways no other piece of steel can match.

And to wield that blade, human hands require something to grip.

Word came to me of his doings while I worked. Tales of his victories were brought by his men, sent to make sure I had all I needed—and was using it towards his goal. I ignored their questions and stared down their insolence, and they faded into hushed boasting.

Tales of the cost of those victories were brought by my neighbors, curious at my burst of activity and worried by the dragon-blazoned men who came and went. I ignored their questions too, and they, wiser, stopped asking sooner and hid themselves from his men. They brought me melons and grapes and onions from their gardens and slaughtered chickens and rabbits to keep up my strength. They guessed I would need it.

I prayed on Maria's hilltop every night, trudging up there while my forge's banked fire trickled coal smoke into the dusty sky and the latest shape of the blade cooled and dripped oil back into the quenching bath. My arms grew weary from swinging my hammer, even though I alternated one to the other. Ambidexterity is a magic all its own, and I had half a century of practice. My prayers grew weak and fumbling, confused as I fought through the net of dreams and hopes that he'd laid so expertly to trap me. Could the past be restored? But so much was broken; it was a living torment to even wonder.

Maria's remembered words finally rescued me. She'd always been my pragmatic anchor and still was now.

"Hope for rebirth, Rumal," she had advised. "Immortality would be horribly boring, but the chance to do anew, ah! That's worth praying for."

So I prayed with crystal clarity for the one thing I didn't remotely deserve but desperately wanted. By now the act of creation had become my all, and I had something to lose again.

On the twenty-seventh night, my wish was granted.

I heated the clay-covered mold and drained out the wax. Poured in the silvery metal. Set it aside to cool. Late the next day I broke the clay, extracted the shining shape so pregnant with my hopes.

It took me all of the twenty-ninth day to polish it and set the rubies. I wished I had ivory for the teeth, but metal was less prone to break. At midnight, I joined hilt to blade and was done.

He found me just after dawn, his men mustered, his cautious allies and beaten foes gathered on the old highway. All waiting to see if I had wrought what the rumors said.

"Show me," he commanded, licking his lips. His eyes were black with desire, and his captains crowded my door.

"My price?" I reminded him for formality's sake, though I knew just how little it would matter.

He surprised me by having a chest dragged in and opened. The contents were exactly as I had asked. He didn't seem to notice that I had no means to carry off such a weighty treasure.

"Now you," he commanded. "Show it to me." The light in his eyes had gone beyond mortal lust.

I bowed and lifted the wrapped shape, laid it on my cleaned workbench, and stepped back, my eyes lowered. His men crowded close, and I backed away further to allow them near, until my spine was against my forge's rear door. I didn't need my eyes to see how he carefully unwrapped it with trembling hands. The ragged cloth fell away to reveal the shining blade and its flowing script. My mortal hands had not inlaid those letters.

How his eyes kindled as he beheld the long, pure length of it! Yet he disregarded the message. Instead, he saw only the copper inlaid as a rayed sun just above the crosshilts, the dragon claws gripping sun and blade both, the scaled torso that offered a slip-resistant grip, and the toothed dragon's head with its ruby eyes that glittered where a pommel should be. Glittered and glittered even in my shadowed shop.

I saw how he raised it up. He scored one of my ceiling rafters with the razor tip, then brandished it until the air whistled. Under cover of the noise, I released the latch on my back door.

His men muttered reverently and knelt to him, pledging their fealty to the bearer of the Dragon Sword. Even his former enemies watching from the front door in distrust of him were drawn in to marvel—to kneel and bow. They all felt the blade's mastery without knowing what it was—or caring.

He gazed over their heads to me and smiled.

"Rumal Smith," he said in that voice like an angel's, "You have delivered all that I asked. But one thing more I require. This sword must forever remain unique."

The fear that had been planted in my heart the moment he told me of his desire bloomed. He would punish my success as harshly as my failure, for no other man must ever possess any blade to rival what I had made for him.

I slipped through my back door and fled up the hill.

His laughter followed. Men shouted and pursued. They were young and fit and numerous; they would catch me, given time.

But he had made his choice.

I hid in the bushes and looked down over the roof of my forge at the disciplined forces beyond. He strode out the door, the sword in hand, and vaulted onto a stone that put him a yard above the crowd. A river of men flowed up to lap at his feet. I could hear his words as he spoke.

"From this day on, I alone rule the Valley of the Sun! Let all here bow to me, and we will go forth to take this land from the peaks of the Rocky Mountains to the Pacific Ocean shore. We will conquer every village and hamlet, and even overthrow mighty

California and trample her banners under our feet. I am the bearer of the Dragon Sword, and by the might of this blade I swear it!"

He raised the sword over his head, and sunlight struck fire in the blade's script. I didn't need to see the words to repeat them in a whisper.

"I serve only the good of life and liberty."

The sword twisted in his hand and leaped free. It pivoted in a wheel of fire over his head—and plunged straight down.

Skewered from throat to groin, he tottered, turned, gazed up the hill at me hidden in the bushes. His lips tried to speak.

"Yes," I whispered. "I gave you what I promised. A magic sword."

Then I crept away as screams and shouts drew the hunting men back to the roiled army. There would be more deaths as captains and warlords and simple murderers fought over the blade. But eventually it might come into the hand of one who did not desire it, one who would use it as I intended.

Then the people of the lands between the mountains and the sea might be peacefully united, and my dead America might be reborn—if not as she was, then as something new. I could hope now.

O O O

Peter Sartucci masquerades as a real estate appraiser by day and is a writer whenever he can get away with it. He has been published in Story of the Month Club and on the SM Stirling fan-fiction website. He lives with his wife, Elizabeth, and special-needs daughter, Rachel, in Colorado, where he likes sunsets, flowers, singing, and the music of Leslie Fish, whose song "Arizona Sword" was the inspiration for this story. May the memory of the local Phoenix man who passed the old tale to Leslie lo these many decades ago be honored by my post-apocalyptic rendering of it.

On Dragon's Wings

M.J. Carlson

The first time I saw her …

It was a Tuesday, I think. In the morning. Definitely in the morning. Sometimes things get a little muddled, but that's only to be expected. I've seen a lot of Tuesdays, after all. I'm Death. I don't say this to be pompous. Nothing could be further from who I am. I merely tell you this fact to establish the validity of the story. After all, if you can't believe in Death, what are you left with—taxes?

That was a joke.

I digress. Most humans spend their entire lives denying my very existence until I arrive to carry them off to … Oops, almost gave it away. Can't let that out of the bag. Mystery and all.

Most humans think I wear a black hood and carry that silly scythe. I don't carry a scythe, nor do I dress in a black cape. What I look like to you depends entirely on how you view the end of your mortality, which is, of course, a function of how you judge your life. If, say, your life was full of missed opportunities to forgive your fellows, or devoid of love given freely, or empty of friends and family, you'll see me as something fearful.

Terrible.

If, however, your life was one of passions embraced, family and community enjoyed, and life really lived, a loved one will appear to your eyes.

Welcoming.

Peaceful.

A well-earned rest at the end of a long day.

I'm a mirror of sorts. I reflect your soul.

But this story isn't about me. It's about Molly. An altogether endearing eight-year-old with hair the color of fawn's fur in the spring and emerald eyes that cut right to the heart of the matter. Her room smelled like … antiseptic. Harsh, astringent, all alcohol and medicine. The smell of hospitals in winter only grieving parents understand. I try not to form attachments to scents or sounds, because … well …

I mostly concentrate on emotions, which is what brought me up short at Molly's bedside. She looked right up at me with laser-sharp eyes and smiled.

"Hello," she said.

"Hi."

"My mommy says you aren't real, so you can't be here."

This was a new one on me. I glanced down. I was covered in scales. They started out a deep sapphire along my spine, fading to a light sea-foam green on my underside. A glance at Molly's bedside table explained my appearance. A book with a dragon on the cover lay there.

I stretched out my leathered wings, and it felt good. I'm nothing if not flexible. I pulled my dragon's mouth into my most charming smile, teeth and all.

"I've come for you, Molly. To take you away from the pain and the fear and the tears, so if you'll just jump on my back—"

"No."

"No? You don't understand. I have a schedule. So if you'll just—"

"No."

It wasn't said in fear. I'm used to that. There was no quaver in her voice, no smell of adrenaline on the air. I dropped onto my haunches. "But you have to."

"I can't."

And here was my undoing.

Her certainty.

It stopped me. "Why?"

"Because I have too much to do." A missing front tooth lent her a lisp.

"You're a child."

"I won't be a kid forever."

"What do you mean, you have too much to do?" I'd heard this argument before. Usually from workaholic CEOs or athletes on a winning streak, their celebrations cut short by a bridge abutment or a jealous spouse, but never from an eight-year-old child.

She pulled her pale lips into a line and set her jaw at a stern angle.

"I'm going to be a writer. I'm going to tell stories and make people laugh and cry and forget how 'fraid they are of the scary things."

I folded my wings against my flanks. "But you're supposed to come with me. Now."

With her eyes never leaving mine, she reached over to her bedside table, pulled her book to her chest, and crossed her arms over it like a shield. "I tol' you, I can't. Besides, Mommy says you aren't real, so you have to go."

"But—"

"Don't be sad." She smiled at me then, and time stopped around us.

This little girl—anemic skin, hands shaking in a subtle tremor only I could see, and a sick, weak heart racing like a greyhound's after a race—was determined. Man, was she determined. But there was more.

Inside.

Steel between a hammer and an anvil—hard and sharp. And so hot it hurt to look at it.

And she was comforting me. *Me.*

I shouldn't tell you this, but I have the option to postpone the inevitable. You've heard the stories. The light, the floating, the family members, yada yada. It's interpretation. Sometimes, once in a million, give or take, I can wait. Something to do with the greater good.

Don't try it.

You can't bargain with Death. You can't cajole, or outmaneuver, or tempt me. I can't be hornswoggled or bamboozled. I can't be corrupted by guilt or shame. Whatever scheme you can think up, I've heard it, trust me. This was different. Molly believed. In a way most TV preachers would empty their accounts just to glimpse. Trust me. I know.

"You can't stay forever."

"I don't need forever."

"There'll be pain."

"I know."

"And heartache."

She nodded. Not agreement or resignation, but simple acknowledgment.

"You'll have failures. You'll have to live through the betrayal of false friends, the grief of lost loves, the pain and suffering, and in the end, I'll be back."

"I'll be ready."

"You'll be sick for a long time."

"What's wrong with me?"

It was out of my mouth before I could stop myself. "That silver liquid you found in the garage, the one you've been playing with, is poison."

"The merc'ry?"

"Yes. I should go. I have other pickups to make tonight."

"What's your name?"

"I can't tell you."

"It's a secret?"

"Yes."

"I like secrets."

"Good. Then we understand each other."

She nodded. "Life is gonna suck, and you'll come back someday."

"'Bout sums it up."

"Okay. Good night, Dragon."

I spread my wings and moved away. I'd allowed myself to get behind, and Death must be prompt.

* * *

The second time I saw her …

Different hospital. Different smells. Dimly lit room this time. Electronic machines beeped and hummed all around. Humanity's obsession with electricity escapes me. Things worked fine for a long time before all that. I know hospitals, though. I do some of my best work in them. A single sniff usually tells me where I am. Every hospital's scent is unique. It took a moment, though. Obstetrics. I hadn't spent much time on this floor, but I'd had a pickup down the hall earlier that evening. I stopped.

She was still waif-thin, probably from a diet of writing and ramen noodles. She turned her head to me when I approached. Her smile hadn't changed in eighteen years. Same pointed chin and pixie face, and the same fawn's fur-colored hair, now reaching halfway down her back. This time, though, the hair was streaked with electric blue.

Those same emerald eyes looked up at me from a young woman's face.

"Hello, Dragon."

This took me aback. People rarely see me more than once, and when they do, they almost never recall our other encounter, but Molly obviously did. I looked down and found I wore the same iridescent scales from our previous meeting and smiled.

"Hello again. I've come for you."

"No."

"No? You can't just tell me no. Now, if you'll—"

"I'm sorry, Dragon, but I can't. Not yet."

"Listen, if it's the excuse about your family or—"

She laughed. It was a full, rich laugh that rang truer than bells in a five-hundred-year-old cathedral. It seemed to take all her strength, because she closed her eyes for a moment.

"Don't be silly. They'll be fine no matter what. I've only started what I set out to do. There's so much suffering."

"Hey," I said, a little hurt. "Don't start. I'm all about easing suffering. I relieve unbearable agony. I rescue the tortured, comfort the ill, soothe the injured, and restore peace, so don't—"

"Then surely you see why it's more important I stay. We're working toward the same goals."

I confess I'm not a lover of literature or art. The odd poem, sure, and some paintings and sculptures practically glow with the emotion their creators put into them. You humans take a great deal of comfort from your art. It feeds you and sustains you in ways I don't fully comprehend. And books. Always books. You people and your words. But I digress.

"What about your pain? You've just lost a child. Most people would welcome …" There it was again, that iron-hard resolve, and I knew there was nothing for it. See, here's the thing: Death can't just grab you and rip your inner being—your soul, if you will—away. The individual has to accept on a conscious or unconscious level that they're ready. Either because their current shell is too badly broken to continue, or they've completed their assigned task, or the healing would be too long and painful, or whatever. They have to come to me.

"Dragon." She said it as if I were a petulant child with a short attention span. "There's nothing I would like more than to oblige you, but I can't right now."

I settled onto my haunches and stared at her. "You can't stay forever."

"I don't need forever."

"There'll be pain."

"I know."

"A lot."

"Yes."

"And heartache."

"I don't mean to be rude, but I believe we've had this conversation before."

I chewed my lower lip. She had me. Again. "All right. But I'll be back."

The corners of her mouth turned up. "I know."

I sighed. Some things in life you can't fight. No use trying. I turned to leave, empty-handed.

"Dragon?"

I looked over my shoulder at her.

"What's your name?"

"I can't tell you that." Where I come from, if a being with enough power knows your name, they can influence you, and I can't have that. Not in my position.

And this frail human girl had power. More than she could understand.

"It's a secret?" Her eyes twinkled.

"Yes."

It was like a private intimacy between old friends. An inside joke, I think you call it. I smiled despite myself.

She returned the gesture at our shared memory. Her adult teeth had come in, white and straight. "I still like secrets."

"Good. Then we still understand each other."

She nodded. "Life's still gonna suck, and you'll be back."

"Yep."

"Okay. Good night, Dragon. I'm sorry, but I'm really tired and if I'm to go on, I need to rest. It's nice to see you again."

I'm pretty sure no one's ever said that to me, before or since.

Molly closed her eyes and settled into her pillow. Her body barely dented the sheets where she lay, surrounded by starched white. I had other pickups to make in other places, but I hesitated a moment and watched her. Hey, it's my prerogative. Molly opened her emerald eyes, looked in my direction, and winked.

At me.

I cleared my throat and left.

* * *

The third time I saw her …

Winter is my favorite season. It suits my personality best. The crisp, sharp scent of frosted air, the calm, restful state of the world, the quiet of the snow-clad hills—I find it all very peaceful. Not like spring, with its explosion of green and growth, flowers scenting all over the place, attracting bees and hummingbirds. Too bustling for me.

Overwhelming.

Give me a quiet, frosty evening, wind-tossed ice crystals like diamonds on a window, warm fire crackling in the hearth, blankets and books and mulled wine, and I'm good.

Traditionally, winter is my busiest season, what with the freezing cold, the thin ice on ponds, the slippery, snow-covered roads, and Seasonal Affective Disorder. But winter—middle-aged men shoveling snow, the elderly who can't afford heat, the lost hikers facing down avalanches—it's always pick up and go, pick up and go. Holidays are second only to battles and plagues. Never a minute's rest.

Emergency departments are my stomping grounds in winter. I even have my own room in most of them, though you call them chapels. It's where I go and sit for a spell and wait for my next pickup. You've felt me there. I've seen it on your faces. You just didn't put the twos together and get four.

I love ERs. The drama, the excitement of a team forming a human stockade to try to block my coming, surrounding a body already as gray as granite and just as dead. The people I come for step right through your efforts and take my hand. They know when it's time, even if you don't.

One frigid January evening, I strolled through the familiar smells of fear and disinfectant into just such a scene at an ER and heard the sound of talons clicking on the polished concrete floor. I knew in an instant who the center of attention was. Molly, older now and filled out some with age and experience, sat up on the gurney and lobbed her pixie smile at me. Almost knocked me to the floor with it, actually.

"Hello, Dragon."

"Molly."

"You're looking well."

"I—" I'm never at a loss for words, yet I stood speechless.

"We really have to stop meeting like this." Her smile became a dazzling grin. Little lines fanned out from the corners of her emerald eyes. She'd grown into a beautiful middle-aged woman. The stray silver strands in her fawn-colored hair added elegance. I'm allowed to notice. There's no law against it or anything.

"If you'll step away from the table—"

"Sorry, but no."

I started to pace. I never get agitated, never grow impatient. I'm the soul of forbearance and tolerance. Perseverance personified. I can afford to be. But this was working itself under my scales, and I had to get control of the situation.

"Molly, look at yourself." I gestured with a fore claw at her shell lying on the gurney and the group working feverishly to keep her heart beating long enough to get her to surgery. "The broken bones, the internal bleeding, the—"

"It wasn't his fault. The road was icy."

"That's not the issue. It's never anyone's fault. Not really. It's time."

"I can't, my friend. Too much left to do."

That stopped me. I've been around a long time. I've met kings and queens, the philosophers and the clueless. I've picked up saints in shelters and sinners in cathedrals. I've gathered scoundrels in sheep's clothing and the pure of heart in their brothel-best, but no one's ever called me friend before. It's funny how sometimes we never know something's missing until it's pointed out to us. I brushed the thought aside. Winter's my busy season.

"Molly, please. Be reasonable."

"Why does everyone always say 'be reasonable' when what they really mean is 'see it my way'? I'd love to go with you, but my work's not quite done here."

"But Molly—"

She gripped the edge of the gurney on which she also lay and swung her legs like a little girl, one I'd seen before.

I rolled my eyes. "There'll be pain."

"You say that all the time."

"Because it's true. You're no longer young by human standards. You'll take forever to heal."

"I know."

"There's nerve damage. You may never regain full use of your left arm."

"I'll work around it."

"If you'll just step over here to me, I can make all the pain go away."

"That's so kind of you. I'm not through yet."

Sometimes you people make me want to groan. You really do. Blah-blah this and blah-blah that, and blah-blah I left my coat, or I can't have my daughter find the adult items in the bedside table. She'll be embarrassed. Or some other affectation of the living, which you no longer are. Those petty concerns all dissipate before you reach the other side, like a dream you want to remember, but you can't. This was different. Like bumping into a wall in the dark with your eyes closed. It stops you so suddenly you think it's pushed you away. That's how talking to Molly felt.

"Don't say I didn't warn you." I turned to leave once more, empty-handed as always with Molly. Her shuddering moan as she returned to agony and frustration tore at me.

People think of Death as heartless, but nothing could be further from the truth. I'm the great leveler of playing fields. Inborn talents and inabilities all come to nothing in my arms. I bring debts and fortunes back to a zero balance. And more. I remind people that their time on Earth was merely a play, each person with their part, reciting their lines, until I bring the final curtain down, and it doesn't even cost the two pennies on your eyelids.

But I feel for you. All of you. I do. That day, I heard Molly's cry and shared pain as I rarely have in my long existence. I left, wishing it was in me to share her tears.

* * *

The last time I saw her …

Let's clear up a misunderstanding. I don't come like a thief in the night. I stroll in when it's your time. I don't take anything, at least not anything that belongs to you. You all think your life is yours.

It isn't.

It's a loaner. You get to take it out and play with it, have fun, crash into things, and generally run amok. I'm the guy behind the rental counter you hand the keys back to after you entered the demolition derby.

Or not.

Some of you act like your life will last longer if you hide inside it, afraid to experience everything it can bring you. You're the ones I feel sorry for in the end, because when I come—and trust me, I will come—and I tap you on the shoulder like a ticket taker on the merry-go-round, memories are more satisfying than dreams.

Always.

I enjoy visiting humans in their homes. Hospitals are too sterile. Nursing homes are too depressing. Hotels—and the imaginative ways you choose to die in them—are preferable to either of those, and the source of some of my most amusing stories, but homes are my best visits. Sometimes I'll linger, examining the curious artifacts people attach emotion to. Bits of flotsam on the current of time. Photos of family and loved ones, treasured childhood toys, and bow-bound snippets of hair. A home reveals the heart.

When I entered that home on that day, I knew in half a heartbeat where I was. Sapphire scales covered me, my talons padded softly on the thick carpet, and I knew the story was ending.

She dozed in a comfortable chair in a corner of a tidy bedroom in a spacious home. The sunlight that filtered through the sheer curtain dappled her once-fawn-colored locks. The scent this time was a combination of sandalwood and lilac. Not at all unpleasant. Silver-framed photos of children and young men and women graced table, dresser, and a headboard made from a bookcase. Each image practically glowed with emotion.

And the books. Dozens that she'd written, the rest she'd read. And she loved each one.

She stirred at my approach and turned those familiar emerald eyes onto me.

"Hello, old Dragon.

"Hello, Molly. It's been a long time."

She let me have that pixie smile again, grown a little tired of fighting gravity but still as beautiful as the first time I saw it. "Seems like yesterday to me. Must be a trick of the mind."

"How've you been?"

"Old, and sick, and a bit tired. I only have one last thing to do, old friend."

"We're not friends. I don't—"

"If not me, then who, Dragon?"

Who indeed? I'd seen her grow from dying child to deathly ill young girl to grievously injured woman to the serene octogenarian in front of me. Our existences had brushed against each other in ways lovers only dream of. I'd seen her at her weakest moments, and each time she'd been strong enough to bend Death to her will. She stood and started in my direction, and with each sure step the years peeled back until an eight-year-old girl stood at arm's length from me. Her shell remained in the chair, a loving smile on her still-warm lips.

"I only have one last thing to do."

"Molly—"

She raised her hand and stroked her fingertips over my cheek. The gentleness of her touch was the answer. Understanding fell on me. As I said before, I've seen it all, and I can't be tricked or bargained with, but this came at me from a blind side. In all my time, in all my travels, no one has ever offered me surcease.

"You knew who I was, even then, and you offered me comfort. Each time."

"I couldn't go. You had so much pain."

"I'm Death. I don't—"

"Shh. Mommy says you don't exist, but I know better. I'm ready now, Dragon."

As I said, I carry souls away at the end. You may have a statue in a harbor, but I'm the one who takes your tired, your weak, your huddled masses yearning to be free. I'm never harsh or impatient, because in the end it's you and me, and of the two of us, I'm the one with all the time in the world. So I never jostle or grunt or shift you when I take you for that last ride.

Molly moved in close, settled herself in the cradle of my blue-scaled arms, and laid her head on my shoulder. I've never held a lighter soul and never wanted so desperately to return one to the land of the living. I've seen you cry at bedsides and never understood why. As I cuddled Molly's tiny form against my chest and folded around her, I finally understood wanting the one thing you can't have—more time, another chance. For the first time, my tears fell, raindrops on a hot summer road caught in an afternoon shower, as I prepared to fly her away on dragon's wings.

O O O

M.J. Carlson is an American science fiction author of numerous novels and short stories. He also maintains an active speaking schedule, giving workshops on writing software, story structure, and accurately writing injures from the character's point of view. He lives in Melbourne, Florida, with his Wise Reader and Muse, Sparkle, and has more computers than any sane person should have. For more information, check out mjcarlson.com.

THE DRAGON'S CHILD

Todd McCaffrey

D*rat it all*, Simon thought as the copper dragon plunged from the sky, swooped, grabbed him in its forelimbs and soared off into the midday sky in full view of the small village and the farmers in their fields. *We're going to have to move again!*

Elveth *knew* better.

Elveth was a dragon. She could shape-shift into a human, but at the cost of some very nasty migraines, the pain of which could only be soothed by immersion in a large hoard of nice, cool gold—something Elveth seemed to be abandoning as swiftly as their home.

That was the first inkling Simon had that something was *very* wrong. Dragons spent most of their days collecting gold; they were not known for abandoning it.

Simon's surprise gave way to alarm as Elveth climbed higher and higher, working with all her might to fly as fast as she could. The air thinned; Simon felt himself getting colder and colder. After a while, he realized he couldn't feel his toes … or his fingers. Not much later, he suddenly felt very warm and lost all consciousness, his last memory being the sound of wings beating in furious effort.

* * *

"Simon, Simon!" Elveth cried. "Simon, wake up! This is no time to dillydally."

Dillydally? Elveth never used that word.

"I am afraid that he needs his rest," a suave male's voice intoned slowly. "As I have told you before."

"Well, he has to wake up *now*!" Elveth said.

At her best, Elveth resolved her anger management with flames and claws. Now, halfway through her pregnancy, her temper was so far beyond control that it could only be measured in astrological proportions. In this case, Elveth's proportions exceeded both the realms of the gods of war and the gods of chaos, nearing half the sky in Simon's internal scale of measure.

"Esteemed Mother, it grieves me to see you so careworn," a young woman's voice spoke soothingly from the doorway—Erayshin, their dragon-daughter Golden's mate.

She approached Simon. He tried to move his arms to embrace her, but they seemed not to work.

Erayshin seemed to sense his movement and pushed herself away from him, leaving one tear falling on his cheek, as she said, "You must rest; you nearly died."

"He didn't," Elveth growled with all the hallmarks of a mortally frayed temper.

"Esteemed Mother, it was not criticism, merely fact," Erayshin said in a quiet voice. "Again, I must give you my deepest thanks that you came here, unbidden, on the instinct that my beloved was in grievous pain."

"Golden?" Simon cried. Something had happened to his daughter, Golden? Something Elveth had felt half a world away?

"She lives, Father," Erayshin said. He felt her small, thin hand grip his wrist comfortingly. "Her heart is broken, as is mine."

"Aleen?" Simon blurted, forcing his eyes to open. Had something happened to his grandson?

In all his years of research, Simon had discovered no other human father who had survived the birth of his dragon child, let alone his child's adolescence. And here he was, not only alive and a grandfather, but he hadn't even had to perfect his flameproof armor.

The room spun in his vision, the brilliant green eyes of Princess Erayshin, his daughter's lover, the only steady thing in the whole panorama.

Forcing himself to focus solely on the red-rimmed whites of Erayshin's eyes, Simon noted the hunger-induced pallor in her skin, saw how her brilliant cheekbones had sharpened with overlong worry and heartbreak.

"Water," Simon croaked.

Elveth was beside him a moment later with a cup of water. She somehow managed to pass it to Erayshin while at the same time moving to one side to raise Simon's torso upright.

Erayshin smiled wanly at Simon, flicked her eyes in gratitude to Elveth, and then tipped the cup against Simon's lips so that he could get a sip of the cool, clear, utterly marvelous water.

The water soothed his parched lips, wet his dry tongue, and eased his raw throat. Encouraged, Erayshin tipped the cup more and more until Simon had drained it entirely.

As Erayshin moved away with the empty cup, Simon leaned forward to grip Elveth's forearm.

"Take me to her," Simon said, ignoring the pain in his throat.

"We will have to fly," Elveth warned.

"We cannot fly too high or too long, or you will take ill again," Erayshin said.

"Take me now."

* * *

Not argument but prudence required that Simon be suitably clothed and wrapped warmly, then held tightly in Erayshin's arms as Elveth lifted them both into the night sky much later than Simon would have preferred.

Elveth flew lower than her wont, but fortunately, the distance was not great. A mere twenty minutes later, they descended toward a line of hills in the distance, veered sharply around several alarming peaks, and plunged into a clearing that only a dragon could reach. Elveth's great eyes spied a small glow in the distance that no human eye could ever see. She issued a high, piercing, trumpeting cry that echoed throughout the valley and the stars.

No cry answered, but Erayshin was not worried, insisting that before Elveth changed form, she use her dragon's flame to warm up a large flask of prepared wine, which the princess served before they moved to the glowing entranceway of the cave.

The cave's mouth was large enough to accommodate a full-grown dragon, but there were several switchbacks to be negotiated before the glow resolved itself into a large pile of charred coal glittering in the midst of a valley of gold in all forms.

In the center of the yellow valley lay Golden, her brilliant scales dimmed and muted, her eyes closed, breathing ragged.

As the three caught sight of her, they halted in shock.

"Is this any way to greet your mother?" Elveth demanded sourly, recovering first. "You will change to human form immediately and tell us what happened."

The golden dragon lifted her head, gave a pitiful whimper, and burrowed deeper into the gold.

Elveth's lungs heaved as she readied an irate roar, but Simon's hand on her arm startled her.

"Perhaps I'd best talk to her," Simon said, moving in front of his wife and climbing down into the valley of loose gold doubloons, pots, vases, scabbards, crowns, and other hard-won trinkets.

* * *

"We're here, baby, we're here," Simon said softly as he knelt down near her head. "Your mother knew something was wrong, and she just grabbed me and flew straight here—"

Coins clinked, and the ground shifted enough that Golden's eyes peered up through the mound of gold. They flicked toward him, and then there was a cascade of sound and movement as the shapely form of a golden-haired young woman emerged. She threw herself onto her father's lap, arms clutching his waist as she bawled uncontrollably.

Simon leaned forward to wrap his arms around her, patting her tenderly.

The sound of falling coins attracted his attention; he caught sight of Erayshin marching toward him with Elveth only a few paces behind.

Golden heard and raised her head from Simon's lap. Seeing her human mate, she threw herself at her, crying, "'Shin! 'Shin, I'm sorry!"

"Shush, shush now, love, it's okay," Erayshin said as she clasped her arms around her dragon lover. "We'll make it. We'll make it somehow."

Golden's hair shook as she nodded her head against Erayshin's belly.

"I came as soon as I could," Elveth said in a voice that held none of her usual temper, none of her rage, none of her terrible bluster. "Something told me—"

"Mother!" And Golden shot from her lover into her mother's waiting arms. "Mother, *please* help me!"

"Yes, dear," Elveth said, bowing to touch her chin to the crown of Golden's head, "anything, baby, anything at all."

Golden stopped mid-sob and pushed herself away from her mother, eyes wide with alarm. She glanced down to her mother's swollen belly and then up again, jaws agape until she managed, "You're pregnant?"

"Yes," Elveth said, a small glow of happiness surrounding her, "but—"

"You shouldn't have come!" Golden roared as fiercely as the fiercest of her mother's roars. She pushed Elveth toward the door. "What if something happened to the baby?"

"Then, dear, it would be my fault," Elveth said softly. She did not see the amazed looks on the faces of Simon and Erayshin. No dragon—*especially* Elveth—ever admitted to fault. In fact, Elveth had spent many years assigning blame to everyone but herself. "But I couldn't stay away when I felt that pain." She paused for a moment and raised her hands, palms up, toward Golden. "You're my daughter."

"Mother!" Golden blurted in gratitude and buried herself once more against her mother's swollen belly.

Simon and Erayshin watched, awed by the fantastic sight of a dragon mother and her dragon daughter united so closely in their love—a sight that none had ever beheld in all the history of the ages. Dragon-children killed their parents to steal their gold, as Elveth had done to her mother when she was less than half a century old.

"Tell me when you're ready," Elveth said softly to the weeping daughter who clutched at her so desperately.

Simon reached a hand toward Erayshin, who met it halfway with her own, and, together, they moved toward their dragon lovers.

Mother and daughter were enveloped between husband and wife and, slowly, Golden's sobs eased, and she began her tale.

"He's only f-f-four," Golden said. "He's always running around, tripping servants, driving everyone nuts and—"

"Shh. That's normal in a child—boy or girl, human or dragon," Elveth said with more wisdom than experience.

"But I *yelled* at him!" Golden cried miserably. She turned to face Erayshin, her lips quivering as she confessed, "He pulled my hair and I yelled at him and he ran away and …"

She buried her head against her lover and broke into tears once again.

"Don't worry, dear," Elveth said, turning a gimlet-eyed glare to Simon. "Your father will find him."

"We've looked everywhere," Erayshin said, turning her head toward Simon.

"Simon is good at thinking of novel solutions," Elveth said, her tone turning closer to her usual prickly snarl.

"And he's been a boy," Golden added, lifting her head to give her father a wan, hopeful smile. "He might be able to follow Aleen where we can't."

Simon, wisely, kept silent.

* * *

"Your place is beautiful," Simon said as Erayshin showed them around the palace thirty minutes later, after a more sedate flight a-dragonback—Simon riding Elveth and Erayshin perched on Golden's sinuous neck.

"It's expensive to keep, but the people expect it of me," Erayshin said demurely.

Golden nudged her in the side. "Don't lie, 'Shin, you love it!"

Erayshin's lips twitched, and she ducked her head in a brief admission.

"Twenty bedrooms, ten chamber rooms—not counting the ballroom or the throne room—two dungeons, a treasury, various offices—and even indoor plumbing," Golden rushed on, grabbing her princess around the waist and giving her a playful hug.

"How come *we* don't live like this?" Elveth said, casting a fuming look toward Simon.

"I'm afraid, dear, that you failed to marry a prince," Simon reminded her. He did not add that she'd never complained before, being more worried about the size of her gold hoard.

"And of course, Daddy, I think you'll *really* like this," Golden said as they paused outside a large pair of gilded doors. She waited for a nod from Erayshin and then pushed the doors open with a strength not common in small, golden-haired women—but not at all out of place in grown dragons.

"I'm sure—" Simon began as the doors opened, but he ground to a halt as he caught sight of the well-lit contents. There were windows on two sides with plenty of clear glass to illuminate the room, but it was the other two walls—floor to ceiling—that caused his jaw to drop.

"Books?" Elveth said, her lips twitching in disdain. "By the way you went on, dear, I thought you were talking *jewels*."

"More than jewels," Simon said in low voice full of awe and desire. "These are treasures beyond compare."

"Mother, you and I may crave gold, but you must not know Daddy if you don't know how much he hoards books," Golden said as she waved them inside.

"Well, I always knew he was a little strange," Elveth allowed, "but I don't recall all that many books—"

"That, dear, is because books burn," Simon said absently, completely oblivious to Elveth's shocked snort. He left her behind as he strolled to the first row of books, his hands outstretched longingly but touching none. He paused to move one misplaced red book onto a shelf and then continued, very *much* like a gold-struck dragon, from one end to the other, eyes scanning up and down. His stride broke briefly as he caught sight of the rolling ladder that was braced into a metal railing that allowed it to swing to any location on the two walls.

"My father was thinking of adding a set of shelves in the middle of the room, but …" Erayshin said, her voice breaking in a sniff. Golden's hand went to her, and the princess took it.

"Did Aleen like it here?" Simon asked.

"Oh, Father, he did! There is absolutely no doubt that he has your love of words," Golden told him.

Erayshin confirmed this with a watery-eyed nod of her own.

"Perhaps he'll turn out human," Elveth murmured in what she thought was a quiet voice—at least, until she found herself under the baleful watch of three pairs of eyes. She met them unflinchingly, adding, "Well, I never heard of a *dragon* who reads."

"There are not so many male dragons that one would know," Simon said mildly, his eyes going back to the books and then to Erayshin. "Would you, Princess, happen to know how extensive this collection is?"

Erayshin smiled. "I've read about half of the books here."

"I used to read her to sleep when she was pregnant with …" Golden's voice broke, and her lower lip trembled in recollection. She collected herself, and her eyes shone as she said to her father, "I thought maybe the baby would like them."

"I read to you when you were in your mother's womb," Simon recalled, giving his daughter a fond look.

"I thought that was to keep me from eating you!" Elveth complained. She glanced toward her daughter and then back to her husband. "Did you pervert my child with knowledge?"

"You, too, dear," Simon agreed calmly, reaching for her hand and grabbing it with both of his. "I started reading to you long before you were willing to get pregnant."

"And you're going to read to me again," Elveth declared, her eyes straying toward the bookshelves with a different expression.

"Gladly," Simon said. He turned toward Erayshin again. "Perhaps you would lend me some of these marvelous tomes?"

Erayshin glanced nervously between him and fire-breathing Elveth before sending an appealing glance toward her lover.

Simon snorted and nodded. "Don't worry, dear, I completely understand. Books are special places, some of them full of people we would never otherwise meet." He glanced one more time around the library and then pulled himself back to his task. "And, speaking of special people, perhaps we should return to Aleen's bedroom?"

Aleen's room was full of wooden toys, intricate metal men, a comfy, bouncy bed, a wardrobe, an attached commode, and a small shelf filled with books and half-jumbled toys.

"I thought it would be bigger," Elveth sniffed.

"He's only four," Simon guessed. "He doesn't need that much space."

A snort of disagreement came from the boy's two mothers. Simon and Elveth turned to look at them.

"He's a boy!" Golden cried. "He runs all over the place!"

"The other day he was in the market, all covered in dirt," Erayshin added with equal measures horror and pride. "He was playing dragon with the boys in the market."

"We need to find my grandson," Elveth reminded them pointedly.

"So, princess, you were under a great deal of pressure to acquire a prince and produce an heir, and …" Simon said, bringing himself back to the problem of the moment.

"And then the dragon came," Erayshin said, smiling at Golden.

"Ah," Simon said. "And then?"

"When we discovered that we—" Golden said, breaking off with a troubled glance at her partner.

"When you discovered that you were in love," Simon said for her, "what then?"

"Well …" Golden began.

"It was her idea," Erayshin said. She grabbed Golden's arm and turned her toward her parents, adding with pride, "Tell them."

"Well, when we decided that we were going to stay together," Golden began slowly, "we talked a *lot* about all the problems that created."

"A dragon with a human?" Simon guessed.

"A princess without a prince," Erayshin corrected. "Or an heir."

"Ah," Simon said, deflated. Her gestured for them to go on.

"Well, Golden figured it out," Erayshin said. "We were lying together one night—"

"I'm not sure I want to hear this," Elveth protested.

"We were in my lair, and I was a dragon," Golden said. A tear appeared in the corner of her eye. "I'd decided that I had to tell Erayshin everything."

"I'd met her first in human form, of course," Erayshin agreed.

"I had a migraine and was in a terrible mood," Golden admitted. "Nothing we could think of would work and, of course, with my gold lust, things were only worse."

"We have a very nice treasury," Erayshin informed them. "Lots of gold."

Elveth's eyes grew bigger.

"So, Daddy," Golden said, turning to her father, "I thought about how you taught me to break down a problem."

Simon smiled.

"And I said, 'We've got to convince them that you had a lover, get you with child, and somehow keep them from being worried about me,'" Golden recounted. "And that was that!"

"Pardon?" Elveth said.

"Well, Mother, it was simple," Golden said. "All I had to do was become a man."

"That's *all*?"

"After that, well … Erayshin and I could … you know … and then, once she was pregnant, we could introduce her prince and then have the dragon slay him," Golden said in a flow that halted and rushed as her face reddened with embarrassment.

"So you were a man twice?" Simon asked, brows knotted as he absorbed her words.

"More than twice," Golden admitted reluctantly. She glanced toward Erayshin. "She didn't catch the first time, so we had to try again."

"I much prefer you in your natural form, love," Erayshin told her.

"But how did the dragon slay you?" Elveth asked. "You couldn't be both."

"Oh, that was easy!" Golden said. "Erayshin and her prince went out to the countryside, and the dragon descended upon them there."

"So Erayshin came back with a tale … ?" Simon guessed.

"Erayshin came back with the two horses, chased by a flaming dragon, and told the tale of how her love, the prince, was devoured trying to save her," Golden corrected with a smug look.

"Ooh, nice!" Elveth crowed, glancing toward her husband as if to ask why he had never come up with such great deceptions.

"So after that, with the princess pregnant, what happened?" Simon gently prompted.

"Well, since I was known to be the late prince's sister, I stayed to console his bride, and we were *shocked* to discover that she had been blessed before his savage loss." Golden practically preened with pride. "She begged me, as her only contact with his memory, to stay at her side through her confinement."

"And since then, what with Aleen being such a handful, there was no question that I would need help raising him," Erayshin added in conclusion.

"I see," Simon said. "But are there those who would prefer a stronger throne?"

"Oh, no!" Erayshin said. "You see, they fear the dragon."

"Pardon?"

"Oh, that was Erayshin's idea," Golden said, beaming. "She gets to tell."

"Well, we knew that there would be a dragon seen from time to time—"

"There had to be; I had to get to my hoard," Golden quipped.

"—so we decided that I would consult my library to learn the best way to deal with the problem," Erayshin continued.

"And what was that?" Elveth demanded.

"I discovered a way to bind the dragon to me," Erayshin said with a sidelong look toward her lover. Golden snorted in agreement. "And so now, I have demonstrated that I have control of the dragon and that it guards our borders—"

"A lot of hard work, too," Golden put in with feeling.

"—in return for which, we leave it to its devices," Erayshin said.

Simon frowned in thought, then nodded. "That will work as long as no one discovers that dragons can take different forms."

"You have to be careful that no one sees you change," Elveth agreed.

"Most of the time, we tell people that I go to visit relatives in my homeland," Golden said. "Once, though, we had Erayshin ride me over the palace to show her control over me."

"Wise," Simon said. "So, who else is in your palace?"

"The servants," Erayshin allowed with a dismissive shrug. "Cleaners, cooks, chambermaids, the like."

"And the guard?"

"We have a small guard which reports directly to me," Erayshin said, drawing her small, lithe frame upwards in a noble stance. "The captain served my father and his father before him. His honor is impeccable. Besides," she added with a sad smile, "he loved Aleen like his own."

"Did everyone love Aleen?" Elveth asked.

"Yes!" Golden retorted hotly. Simon raised an eyebrow, and her fierce look cooled. "Oh, he could drive the staff to swearing with his antics, but he had the sweetest green eyes—"

"Green eyes?" Simon repeated.

"Very green and very mischievous."

"Green eyes are uncommon here, aren't they?" Simon said, pressing forward over his undiplomatic blunder. "Are there enough guards to search the town?"

"No," Erayshin said, her shoulders slumping. "Our guard is small to save on expenses. Mostly, my people are happy, cheerful, and well-fed. And they have a dragon guarding them." Erayshin smiled at her lover. "Golden's been a wonder in bringing pirates and brigands to bay."

"And my hoard's increased accordingly," Golden said with a larcenous smile.

"My people are not the sort to revolt," Erayshin continued, "and I work hard to keep it that way."

"Especially now," Golden agreed. "They've got a handsome prince with lively green eyes, his mother's dusky skin, and her dark, straight her. He's got a slim frame like his mother, but we're hoping he'll fill out to a handsome man."

"If we can find him," Elveth murmured, but only Simon heard her.

"And you're hoping that Aleen will inherit his *father's* abilities?" Simon asked. "A dragon prince?"

"We don't know," Golden admitted with a troubled look. "He might just be a normal human boy."

"But we're hoping," Erayshin chimed in loudly.

"A dragon prince," Simon repeated softly to himself. "It would be difficult," he said at last, "but, with the right upbringing, not impossible."

"Are we the right parents?" Golden said with a whimper. "Is that why he ran away?"

"He asked us about his father," Erayshin noted.

"What did you tell him?" Simon asked.

"He would hear it from the servants," Golden said, "so we told him the story of the dragon and the prince."

"What?" Elveth demanded hotly, eyes once again glowing with fire. "Whatever possessed you?"

"But—but—" Golden said, her troubled eyes turning in appeal toward her father.

"I'm afraid your mother is right," Simon said. "Any young boy—particularly a prince—would insist upon avenging his father, finding his killer and destroying him."

Princess and lover turned to each other and said, "Oh."

"So he ran out of the city?" Elveth said.

"Where would he go?" Golden shook her head. "We never told him where the battle took place."

"He could have learned in the market," Erayshin allowed in a miserable tone.

"But no one said that they'd seen him that day in the market!" Golden protested.

"Tell me where!" Elveth demanded.

"What?" Golden replied, confused.

"To the east, in the valley beyond the hills, just by the river," Erayshin said. "There's a tree and a shady spot."

"I'll go look," Elveth declared, moving swiftly toward the nearest door.

"You'll be seen!" Simon cried.

"Think of something," Elveth told him. "I'm going to find my grandson." As she sprinted away, she could be heard muttering, "Poor boy! Alone for days! And thinking that dragons …"

"Should I go after her?" Golden said, glancing toward the exit.

"Alone for days," Erayshin repeated miserably to herself. "He must be hungry—starving!"

"Little boys *do* eat," Simon agreed, trying to think of some way to sound comforting.

"He was always leaving food around," Golden said with a sniff. "The ants were everywhere."

"Ants?" Simon said. "There were ants in the library."

"Of course," Golden agreed. "He'd never clean up, so there were ants everywhere."

"Who fed him?"

"We did," Golden said. "And he was always getting treats from the cooks—or anyone else he could wheedle."

"Ants in the library," Simon said to himself. He turned his head in that direction. "Ants!" His tone changed and he raced out of the room.

"Father!" Golden cried, scurrying to catch up with him. "What is it?"

"The ants!" Simon said. "I saw some on the shelves when I put that book back!" He was racing now.

Golden could keep up with him, but Erayshin was smaller, her legs shorter, so Golden slowed to match her. "Drat the man!"

"Actually," Erayshin said in a thoughtful tone, "he might be on to something."

* * *

Simon was way ahead of them when they arrived, his eyes scanning the library in the dimming light of late afternoon.

"Father—?" Golden began just as Simon let out an exalted shout and pulled a red book off the shelf.

"Ants!" Simon said, scanning the shelf where the book had lain. "I knew it!"

"But Father," Golden began slowly, "I don't see—"

"Come here, both of you," Simon commanded. Golden's spine stiffened but she moved to his side, the result of years of parental influence. Simon gingerly turned toward them, the book cradled in his arms. He looked at Erayshin. "Princess, have you ever seen this book before?"

"It's beautiful," Erayshin said with a gasp, extending her arms in an invitation to take the red book.

Simon passed it to her with a slight bow and the under-voiced imprecation, "Careful."

"The eye!" Golden cried as she caught sight of the book, leaning over Erayshin's right shoulder. "Look at the eye!"

In the center of the red book was one wide green eye.

"Aleen?" Golden breathed in wonder. "Aleen, is that you?"

"Can he do that?" Erayshin said, glancing up to Simon and then over her shoulder to Golden. "Can *you* do that?"

"No," Golden said, shaking her head. "I couldn't change until I reached maturity."

"I know of no dragon in the second generation," Simon said slowly. He pursed his lips firmly. "It is not beyond possibility."

"So what do we do?" Golden demanded.

Simon shook his head.

Erayshin, with a sob, clasped the leather—soft leather with deep grooves as though of dragon scales, warm leather as though blood flowed through it to provide heat—tightly to her chest. "Baby, my baby!"

* * *

"*Do* something!" Elveth demanded of Simon when, hours later, she returned from her fruitless journey and met them at the entrance. "He's your grandson; *do* something!"

"He must be starving," Simon said to himself.

"He must have a terrible headache," Erayshin said. She saw Golden start and explained, "You always get them when you transform, and, worse, he's starving."

"And scared," Golden added in a small voice. "He must be very scared."

The green eye on the cover of the book was stuck open.

"We need to bring him to your hoard," Elveth said. "The gold will soothe him."

"Now?" Golden asked.

"Right now," Simon said. "And get something for him to eat."

"As a dragon?" Erayshin asked, her dusky skin going lighter.

"As a boy," Simon said.

"Um … my hoard?" Golden said, casting a worried glance toward her mother. Then, seeing the look on Erayshin's face, she said, swallowing her worry, "Okay."

* * *

They took off from the top of the palace in the dark of the night, two dragons—one gold and one copper—with two riders and one red book.

Golden's hoard was not far away. Simon brought a sack of fruit and nuts. Erayshin held the book tightly to her chest the whole way.

"I'll start a fire," Simon said as they entered the darkened cavern with its floor gleaming of dull, cold gold. Surprisingly, Elveth moved to help him.

"You must keep him warm," Elveth said as they left princess and daughter clutching the book.

Simon noted that her orders were superfluous; Erayshin would not let the book out of her grasp.

They found a nice dell in the mountains of gold, and Simon quickly got a small fire going, which they surrounded, hands outstretched for warmth.

"I feel better," Elveth said, leaning against her husband with a sigh. "Gold is so friendly."

"I didn't understand," Erayshin said, "until Golden showed me."

"The effects of gold on genus *draco* is understood more apocryphally than in reality," Simon agreed.

"Well," Golden said, moving closer to her lover, "we're here. My mother, who killed *her* mother for her gold, is here in my secret domain."

"I was here before," Elveth reminded her waspishly. "And you never met my mother."

"Elveth, Golden," Simon said in a warning tone, "we're here for Aleen."

"Yes," Golden agreed, her eyes flashing briefly toward her mother before dimming again as she looked toward Erayshin and the book. "Now what?"

"I think we need to understand a very confused little boy," Simon said slowly. "Aleen is only four. He was told that his father was killed by a dragon." Golden's eyebrow arched in warning. Simon ignored her and moved away from Elveth, closer to Erayshin. He beckoned for the book. Reluctantly, the princess relinquished it.

"Aleen, how did it feel to ride on a dragon?" Simon asked, addressing his words to the book. "Were you afraid? Your mother was holding you tightly, so I know you weren't cold."

"Daddy—" Golden started, but Simon silenced her with a raised hand.

"Would you like to be a dragon, Aleen?" Simon said. "I know that your mothers said that your father was killed by a dragon." He paused a moment. "That's a lie. You know it now because you saw your mother change into a dragon and back."

"Simon—" Elveth's tone was nearing anger, but Simon glared at her, and she subsided, muttering, "I hope you know what you're doing."

"No one knows what I'm doing," Simon said. He turned his attention back to the red book with the green eye. "My name is Simon, and I'm your grandfather. The copper dragon, Elveth, is mother to *your* mother, Golden. Your mother turns into a beautiful golden dragon with white flaming breath. Your mothers are very much in love with each other. So much so that your dragon mother, Golden, turned herself into a man so that they could have you.

"Think on that, Aleen," Simon continued. "Your dragon mother loves your human mother so much that she would change in any way to please her."

Golden sniffed.

"They want to be together for as long they live," Simon said. "But people fear dragons, and people think that a princess can only marry a prince." Simon's tone made it clear how silly he thought *both* of those notions were. "They love you very much. They want to be your parents for as long as they live too."

Simon felt a twitch in the lump he held.

"It's scary, being human," Simon said. "It's just as scary—in a different way—being a dragon."

The book twitched. In the dim light, Simon thought he saw the green eye go wider.

"Your mothers think that you decided to slay the dragon that killed your father," Simon continued. "They thought that you had run away to do that. So your dragon grandmother flew off to see if she could find you." Simon glanced toward Elveth with a smile. "She cared so much for you that she risked being found or even killed."

The book quivered. It definitely quivered.

Simon stroked it soothingly.

"But you are smarter than that, aren't you?" Simon said with a touch of pride in his voice. "You wanted to learn how to slay a dragon before you went after it, didn't you?"

The green eye twitched.

"So you went to the library," Simon continued, "and you looked at all the books and you ate and you got tired and you fell asleep."

Silence.

"You fell asleep and dreamed about killing dragons," Simon guessed. "Something scared you, and you dreamed about the books—about the book that would tell you what you wanted to know."

"He did?" Erayshin said in a small voice. "Oh, baby!"

"And when you woke, you found yourself in this book," Simon said, his voice growing warm with awe and sorrow. "You were the book that had all the answers to your questions."

The book quivered.

"But you're scared," Simon said. "You're scared because you can't read the words written on the pages. You can't learn how to slay dragons because you've learned that you really *are* a dragon."

"A red dragon?" Elveth cried. "He's a red dragon!"

"A red dragon with green eyes," Simon agreed, stroking the leather cover gently. "A hungry, scared red dragon with green eyes."

"But I couldn't change until I was twelve!" Golden protested.

"*That*," Simon said, "is because you are not your son." He smiled down into the green eye. "Because even though, my daughter, you are a most beautiful golden dragon and a sweet golden-haired girl, you were *never* nearly half as mischievous as your green-eyed son."

Simon leaned down and stroked the red book lightly. It quivered. Simon suddenly looked up at his daughter, and his eyes were gleaming.

"But you're just as ticklish!" Simon cried with joy. He ran his fingers all over the red book, and it was suddenly quivering and shivering and giggling and—

—then there was a little boy wriggling in his lap, his face contorted with laughter.

"Ah!" Simon said. "Aleen, I believe!"

"Am I really a dragon?" Aleen asked, trying to recover from his giggles.

"A very ticklish dragon," Simon assured him, leaning in to tickle the green-eyed boy into another uncontrollable bout of laughter.

"With two mothers?" Aleen said, gasping for breath. "I have *two* mothers?"

"Indeed, my prince, you do," Simon said. He handed the giggling boy over to his parents, adding, "And they love you very much."

Golden and Erayshin raced to him. Golden was the first, but she paused to let Erayshin grab him and then wrapped herself around the two of them.

"You know," Elveth said as she looked happily on the reunited family, "this is a rather nice place." Her eyes glinted as she glanced around the gold-filled cavern. "I could get used to it."

Golden turned her head toward her mother. "This is *my* gold, Mother."

"You can share," Erayshin told her firmly.

Golden turned back to her lover, eyes wide.

"I'm afraid—" Simon began, but Erayshin cut him off.

"They need the gold to shelter from the magic and help their headaches," Erayshin reminded him, glancing toward Elveth and then back to Golden. She said again, firmly, "They can share."

"You heard her, Golden," Elveth said, squatting down to grab a handful of coins and let them spill slowly through her fingers. "We share."

"Yes, Mother," Golden said, leaning across her son to kiss her lover on the lips. When they broke free, she added, "I learned long ago that Erayshin is always right."

"Which makes her *nothing* like your father," Elveth observed with her usual waspish tone.

Simon suppressed a smile, nodded in gratitude toward Erayshin, and—wisely—said nothing.

O O O

Todd J. McCaffrey is a U.S. Army veteran, a cross-continental pilot, a computer geek, and a *New York Times* bestselling author.

His latest work is the near-future AI thriller, *City of Angels*, published by WordFire Press.

Fifty words is too short to be informative, so visit his website at http://www.toddmccaffrey.org.

SWEETLY THE DRAGON DREAMS

David Farland

Life finds a way. We dropped planet-killers on Mursadoni, scorching all three continents, and when I returned forty-two years later, the land was covered with green ferns that provided food for clouds of lightning moths.

So I searched the heavens further. On Remiseas, nine hundred years after its immolation, I found forests and birds and lizards—all which should have been decimated—and I discovered new life-forms rising from the ashes of the old.

On Danai, the infestation was much worse. A few of the higher life forms were gone, but after six thousand years, I found wide variations in the flora and fauna. Included among the survivors is a thriving population of humans led by a hive of skraals. My supply of planet-killers and sunbusters has been exhausted. I will drop flash-heads into the hive with the hope that the resultant nuclear contamination will wipe out the skraals' queen. Further steps will be required to eradicate the biological contaminations.

—final transmission from the cycor drone ship *Death's Head*

In the dry days on Danai, the moons lure the damselfly nymphs from the slow-flowing waters. Soft of flesh they come, minute hunters from the marsh, climbing ashen stalks of cattails or perchance some slender green reed.

At the rising of the sun, they settle at the base of a frond, letting the light take them and transform them, until their old bones crack and their new form breaks free.

For a moment they will hesitate, poised, their new wings still wet, waxen and thrumming, as they examine their own glory.

Soft new carapaces shine in the sunlight—glimmering like cinnabar or rubies, or the green of dappled leaves.

That is how young Tallori found them that summer morning as she waded along the shores of the marsh. The rising sun hung like a golden shield upon the shoulders of the world, and the young damselflies just seemed to be waiting for her to pluck them from their perches.

She had caught nearly a hundred in a dozen different hues, placing them in a reed basket. She felt happy to be catching them. Tallori would be paid one silver penny for every five damselflies. She could make a small fortune in a few weeks.

Tallori was a bright child, but not bright enough. She had not been found worthy of schooling. She was a mere human, and thus far inferior to skraals that ruled Danai.

The damselflies were to be food for the Holy Maiden Seramasia, and Tallori felt grateful to be of service. Not only would she make more than she had ever dreamed, she would also be assisting a goddess.

Tallori was large for an eight-year-old girl. Her hair was yellow sunlight, and her eyes, set deep beneath her brow, were greener than the sea. She sang a rhyme as she picked the damselflies from the stalks:

A blue one to ease my lady's cares,
A red one to make her grow.
A white one to match her skin so fair,
A gold one to make her glow!"

That is when she found the monster.

Tallori tiptoed over a break in the cattails, a space less than ten yards across, when she noticed how rough the ground felt beneath her feet. The dark water was as brown as her father's beer, and she could not see through it, yet at times she could feel clams in the mud with her toes, or find small freshwater crabs to eat. The rough surface made her wonder.

She stopped to pick a scab from her knee and eat it. That's when she looked down. A vast eye stared up at her. She screamed.

* * *

"Over here!" Tallori shouted, dragging her father, Angar, to the edge of the wide river. At the child's insistence, he'd brought a huge ax. He stopped, unwilling to muddy his sandals.

He suspected this was all some plot on his wife's part to get him to do some work. When Tallori had come with her story about a monster in the bog, Angar's wife had said in a businesslike tone, "Bring back some reeds, and I'll weave some baskets."

So he was skeptical of Tallori's motives in bringing him. He was a fat man with fondness for strong drink. Rather than wade off into the mud, he squatted in some reeds and rubbed his temple, wishing the sunlight did not aggravate his hangover so much.

"Come quick!" Tallori shouted. "The monster is over here. You can see its big teeth!"

Only when Tallori tugged his arm and became frantic did Angar pull off his sandals of woven reeds and bother to step into the mud.

Twenty feet from shore, he saw it there, beneath four inches of tawny water: an eye as large as a platter, reflecting the golden sun. It was set in a serpentine head that looked to be some nine feet long and four feet tall. The whole of it lay in the water, staring out.

Mankind had been living on Danai for over a hundred thousand years. From time to time, something odd turned up in the bog—petrified men or ancient tools.

But this was too good to be true. "I know what this is," Angar said, trying to convince himself of his fortune. "It's a dragon!"

A *dragon* was a flying reptile, one of the first biologically advanced beings that mankind met when they had first ventured to the stars. In some ways, the dragons were even superior to the godlike skraals, and had been friends and counselors to the skraals back in the days of Bliss—before the cycor began their great war and turned the heart of the galaxy into a great void.

The last dragon had been expunged more than six thousand years ago in an attack that had left Danai a wasteland.

Angar inspected the remains. Last winter's flood must have stripped mud from the banks of the river, uncovering the creature.

"My, look at those teeth," Angar said. The beast had great teeth as long as his hand. Each was stained yellow from millennia in the mud, and the cutting edges were serrated.

"I'll bet folks would pay nicely for one of those," he mused. Maybe even the holy maiden. He seemed to remember hearing that even now, the goddesses took a peculiar interest in the remains of dragons.

Yet he had to wonder. Three months earlier, a cycor scout ship had come to Danai and rained flash-heads upon the capitol. The supreme mother had been killed, the holy maiden wounded, and though the scout ship was destroyed, it was only a matter of time before the enemy returned with greater weapons. Now Holy Maiden Seramasia had gone into hiding, preparing to meet the cycor threat.

Yet Angar suspected he could find her. All he had to do was send a message through the boy who was buying the damselflies.

* * *

That night, deep in a forest called Shadowfest, a twelve-year-old boy named Anduval inched along the limb of a boa tree covered in white spirit fungus. The tree was large so close to the ground, perhaps four feet in diameter. Boa saplings tended to snake along the forest floor, rising and dipping at random, until they sensed a hole in the canopy high above. Then the trunk would twist upward, seeking the heavens. Thus, for long stretches, the trees sometimes formed a path above the forest floor.

Twenty feet below, a sounder of wild pigs lay asleep, half-hidden, having rooted beneath patches of wild fungus and plates of spongy lichens. The colossal boars weighed as much as three tons each and stood eight feet at the shoulder. A full-grown boar had a mouth large enough to swallow a man whole; their enormous tusks were as sharp as sabers. The boars were savage hunters, fiercely protective of both their young and the patches of mushrooms in their territory.

An old sow grunted curiously and opened her eyes. Anduval halted, heart pounding. He dared not move. With each step, spirit fungus dislodged from the log and rained down on the wild boars.

He couldn't see exactly how the tree twisted ahead. He was guided only by the light of a jar filled with tiny glow beetles whose green luminescence carried only a few feet. But Anduval had memorized the trail over the years. The glass mushrooms were about ninety feet ahead, where the boa tree dipped down and touched the forest floor.

Anduval wrapped his hand around his jar, obscuring the light, and waited for the sow to return to sleep.

One slip, and he would fall to the forest floor. The ground was spongy, covered with layers of leaves and old lichens that had rotted here for forty thousand years. He'd probably survive a fall, but not an attack by the boars.

So he held tight. The boles of the boa trees twisted crazily in a tangle, and their foliage in the canopy blocked out the stars, so the forest floor lay in perpetual gloom.

The only sound was the dripping from above—sap falling in an ever-present mist, spiders dropping lifeless from old age. A huge growler swept overhead, uttering a soft rumble as it sought for flying insects. The air smelled of ten thousand varieties of mold.

After long minutes, the even breathing and occasional grunts of pigs assured Anduval that they were dreaming contentedly. Morning was coming, and the pigs would soon waken. Time was short. Anduval would have to sprint back to the palace when he got his prize.

Breathlessly, he inched along in the dark, feeling his way across the log until bones cracked beneath his feet. He pulled out his light. A small, lizard-like creature lay dead on the log, having fallen from the canopy, its wings akimbo. Fungus grew over the body in colored patches, reclaiming the moisture and minerals.

Ahead, water tinkled down the boles of several trees, forming a pool. At the water's edge, ghostly mushrooms rose up like spears, some to a height of three feet. Anduval raised his light, inched forward, and spotted a mushroom dripping with its own sugary dew. It looked to be newly sprouted, for it was still the color of tinted glass. He pushed his way past older mushrooms, those that had been trampled by pigs or had dried out, and examined the new one closely. He reached into a pocket, drew a harvesting scythe, and slashed through the mushroom's stalk. Using a wet cloth to lift the mushroom so that it would never have been touched by human hands, he placed the mushroom into a pouch woven from twisted leaves, and smiled. It was a good harvest. He suspected the mushroom weighed seven pounds.

Anduval glanced up, searching for a second mushroom, when he heard a startled grunt at his back. A boar scrambled up from the detritus and let out an angry squeal.

He had been found.

He whirled and raced back toward the bole of his boa. A huge black boar rushed from the darkness. Anduval leaped aside. The boar barreled past and went splashing into the shallow pool.

He lifted his light. The boar squealed in outrage, whirled, and gave chase.

Anduval sprinted where the bole angled up gently. The boar charged, but it could not see in the dark, and it had to take care not to slip.

He realized it had to be following his light. The bole veered left, then right. Below him, wild pigs squealed in anticipation. Seldom did they get fresh meat beyond the occasional insect or worm.

The huge boar grunted and redoubled its speed. Anduval could feel its breath at his back. He reached out and held his light far to his right.

The boar veered toward it—and slid from the damp bole of the tree, just as Anduval had hoped.

The pigs squealed in delight at the fresh meat that thudded down around them.

* * *

In a subterranean palace deep beneath the mountainous trees, Anduval arranged his fungi on a platter.

He had three spears of yellowcap, firm and meaty, set beside a clump of ruffled young brain fungus, all in shades of gray with blue fringes. A dozen "black buttons" took up the center of the platter, while his single clear glass mushroom—as long as a baby's arm—curved around the platter's rim. Sprinkled over the glass mushroom were tiny "blue dot" mushrooms no larger than grains of sand.

When he felt certain the arrangement would be pleasing, he carried it through the arched alcove and into the dining hall of the Holy Maiden Seramasia.

Other attendants had arrived earlier and placed their offerings upon the table. The offerings included a wide variety of fungi, but

Anduval felt certain that they would not please his mistress. The pile of dark green swamp lettuce looked too stale to be appetizing. A single white sweet globe was overly large, and thus its dark center would be flavorless. Others looked slightly more palatable.

He thought to shove the central platter aside, but he knew it contained the offering of the kitchen steward, and he did not want to get a beating.

Anduval's offering was last to the table, as he had hoped. His would be the freshest of the fare. But he had to take care to leave soon, for ancient custom dictated that he could never occupy the same room as the maiden or pass within two hundred feet of her.

He set his platter upon the outer edge of the table, hoping that if the holy maiden chanced to circle once, she would be tempted by his offering. The other attendants had all put their platters near the door to the maiden's meditation chamber, hoping to be first to be seen. But there on the far side of the table, his platter stood alone.

He took one last second to turn his platter, just so, to better display his rare and succulent glass mushroom as he prepared to flee.

Footsteps issued from the maiden's entrance, and he glanced up.

Terror took him. The holy maiden stood beneath a white marble arch, glorious and resplendent, not twenty feet away. Skraal guards flanked her.

The guards were taller than men. At eight feet, their height was imposing enough, but it was the guards' reputation that most frightened him: in their zealousness to protect the maiden, they sometimes got rough. The guards were far more powerful than humans. The least touch of a skraal could leave a bruise. Should one of the creatures grasp him, their slender fingers would rip through his flesh as easily as rice paper and would shatter his bones as if they were made from straw.

Trembling, heart pounding, Anduval dropped to his hands and knees and prostrated himself. "Have pity on me," he cried, "for I am but a foolish child."

He closed his eyes. He had seen the holy maiden up close, which was forbidden, and he relished that instant. She was naked, for skraal nymphs rarely wore clothes.

She had been beautiful. Though she stood upon two legs, her similarity to humans ended there.

She had no breasts or hair.

Her face had been as white as the petal of a swamp lily, as white as the lining of a cloud, and fleshy around her silver eyes. Her legs and arms were slender. Her abdomen, shaped like an inverted pear, was full and fat.

She had a gracefulness to her, like the elegance of a crane or a roe deer. In the way of skraal nymphs, her oral-dactyls, the fingerlike appendages that shoved food into the vertical slit of her mouth, were clearer than crystal.

He could see little evidence of the wounds she'd received in the cycor attack. She had nearly been killed when the drone ship had dropped its flash-heads and then smashed into the capitol so hard that debris flew up from the far side of the world. Seramasia had been a hundred miles from ground zero, yet the radiation burns had left part of her exoskeleton pitted.

Anduval's heart pounded, but not from fear. He had seen the holy maiden up close, and he hoped to savor the image.

Then she spoke, her mouth-fingers playing rapidly, her voice deep and mellow like a woodwind. "Have no fear, frail one," she said. "Your presence here pleases me. And though you may be young, I believe that you are wise beyond your years—perhaps wise beyond all understanding."

Anduval braced himself, not trusting his ears. Humans were never allowed near skraal nymphs. In all of his life, he had never heard that the maiden had spoken to any human except Magus Veritarnus, a mysterious man who strode through the palace in black robes with his head hunched in thought.

"Now," she said, "stand before me, and do not avert your eyes. I have questions for you; choose your words well, for I will permit you to continue in my presence only if you speak perfect truth."

Perhaps at no time in his life had Anduval felt more frightened. Tears flooded his eyes, and his stomach clenched alarmingly. Though he had not eaten since yesterday, he felt that he might vomit on the floor. When he managed to stand, his legs quivered, and it was only with great effort that he stilled them.

He looked up and peered steadily upon the holy maiden. She strode toward him, and her guards stiffened in alarm. Their instinct demanded they protect her. And, like dogs, they wished to lead the way, to stand between her and Anduval, but she brushed them aside.

"My lady, please," a guard begged. "The danger—"

"There is no danger from this one," Holy Maiden Seramasia declared. "I sense only … devotion."

As a skraal nymph, Seramasia had powers of the mind that no human could match. She was not mature, and had not therefore transcended, but she could still see into a man's mind as easily as a child might gawp at tadpoles at the bottom of a clear pool.

Anduval gazed into her eyes. She had four of them, two large ones that peered forward, and two small ones upon her temples. The large ones did not have whites. Instead, they were silver, like the eyes of a fish, and deep in the center was a dollop of light blue, as if from summer skies. The eyes upon the side of her head were dark, like bits of onyx.

He saw now that her skin was not really white. It was gelatinous, almost, and only looked white from a distance, though he could see that it was beginning to harden. Beneath the clear skin, he could make out tiny blue veins. Her muscles, in fact, were opalescent, and her fine bones were as clear as glass.

She smelled sweet and earthy, like vanilla poured over moss.

Anduval had never seen anyone with such breathtaking beauty.

There was movement in the fine musculature of her face, a skraal smile as her lips tightened. "How old are you," the holy maiden asked, "in human years?"

"I am twelve years and three months," Anduval answered softly, filled with awe.

"You are young, even for a human. Do you know how old I am?"

"Two hundred seven years, nine months, three days, and almost nine hours," Anduval answered.

The holy maiden laughed, a clear melodic sound like an oboe. "So perfectly honest. You please me. Your offering pleases me. Did you know that for nearly three months now, I have not eaten from any other platter but yours?"

Anduval fought back the urge to gasp. He'd never known what had become of his offerings. Each morning and evening he delivered his platter, but at the end of her meal, all of the offerings were thrown away. "I am honored," is all he could manage to say.

"Three months," she said. "Since the attack, your offerings have revived me and healed me."

She gestured at his platter. As a nymph in the early stages of her life, she could not eat anything but fungus. "Your yellowcaps, so bright and crisp. These ones sprouted in the night. You had to have harvested them well before dawn, before any sunlight could beat down through the swamps and touch them. And this glass mushroom—you had to travel miles into the forest to find it, for the steward tells me that the nearest ones grow only at the base of Mount Dimlock."

Now she peered into his eyes. "You know my tastes—my needs—better than I know them myself. How did you guess that I craved glass mushrooms?"

For a moment, Anduval stood frozen as he tried to choose his words.

The libraries of Magus Veritarnus were filled with ancient tomes that detailed the feeding habits of nymphs. It was a vital subject. Some nymphs developed vast powers. Most did not. So scribes had recorded the feeding habits of past nymphs, trying to unravel the secrets as to which would succeed.

Anduval had studied the texts tirelessly, and had gone much further—charting Seramasia's growth against that of other maidens, studying texts that plumbed the secrets of various fungi—the content of their vitamins, minerals, phytogens, and hormones.

A truly great skraal mother had not risen in more than six thousand years. The world needed one; it needed a mother right out of legend.

Anduval suspected—as did the skraals—that there were inadequacies in the nymphs' diets. Many species of fungi had been lost in the ancient cycor attacks.

Of course, Seramasia knew all of this. So Anduval tried to explain his choices.

"The air is dry this morning," he said. "I thought you would relish the glass mushroom's moisture. I know there is some variation, but skraal maidens crave certain foods, according to their age, their closeness to ascension, the heat and humidity. The injury you sustained in the attack, this too amends your needs. As I studied the records, I began to see patterns."

"All of my other attendants are skraals, and they are supposed to be intellectually superior to humans. Why could *they* not see these patterns?"

Anduval did not want to admit it, but sometimes he thought he was smarter than most skraals, even though tradition held that it was impossible.

"As I pondered what you might want, I felt the answer in my bones."

"Then tell me," she asked, "what I will want to eat tomorrow."

"Your ascension is almost upon you," Anduval said. "Your skin is hardening. Tomorrow, or sometime soon, you will begin to crave insects with your fungus. You will need the protein to build your chrysalis. Tomorrow I will bring mallow mold, and I have hired children to collect young damselflies."

The holy maiden considered his words. "You traveled by foot into the dimmest part of the forest this morning, beneath boa trees so vast that the ground never sees light. Were you not afraid of being eaten by a colossal boar?"

Anduval almost decided to lie, to boast at his courage, but the holy maiden had demanded the truth. "I was."

"Then why did you do it?"

"I wanted to please you," Anduval said.

"More than you cared for your own life?" the holy maiden asked.

He was afraid she might laugh at him or mock him.

"Yes."

"Do you *love* me?"

At her back, a guard hissed. Cessari was her personal attendant and the most dangerous skraal on Danai. Indeed, he held the title of Consort, and in the fullness of time he would become the holy maiden's mate.

It was dangerous for Anduval to confess his feelings for the maiden. He was only a boy, and he had been told he was not old enough to love. But he knew what he felt.

"I do love you," Anduval answered, afraid that the consort might crush him for his boldness. "I have loved you from the first time that I saw you at a distance, two years ago."

The holy maiden peered into his eyes and smiled in satisfaction. "I know what you want from me," she said. "You hope that in time I will learn to love you, too."

Among the skraals, she was but a child, like him.

He did not have to confess his feelings. She could divine them.

"You understand," Seramasia said, "that human emotions are but a shadow compared to what I feel. If I were to love you, you would never understand the depth of my passion. If I were to love you, our minds would meld into one, and my love would destroy your ability to reason. There is a purpose behind the law that keeps you at a distance."

"I understand," he said.

She grew thoughtful. "You please me," she said. "It is my hope that in time you will find a human woman to love. I will go into transcendence soon, and when I do, I will be gone for a number of years. Seek for a human woman to love.

"I fear the cycor will return soon. I do not know if we have four years or four hundred, but we must prepare to defend ourselves. Yet I fear that our preparations will be in vain.

"Therefore, we make the best of the time we have left.

"As for now, your devotion must be rewarded. You will continue to bring my morning meals until I go dormant, but in the afternoon you will begin an apprenticeship under the magus. You, too, shall become a magus."

Anduval considered. There were technologies that were undreamt of by men, and it was the duty of a magus to master them. It would greatly add to his duties. But he was only a human and did not have the strength or endurance of a skraal. He did not know how he might manage it.

More importantly, he would arouse the jealousy of the maiden's skraal servants, and that was a dangerous thing to do.

Suddenly Anduval recalled something, a message that he had hoped to deliver to the magus, a message for the holy maiden. Compared to the dangers posed by the cycor, it seemed rather inconsequential.

"Milady," Anduval said with a bow. "I have heard a rumor that might interest you: in the bogs outside the forest, the skull and body of a dragon have been found."

The holy maiden drew a breath in surprise, and her guards leaped forward eagerly.

"Is the skull intact? Has it been opened?"

Anduval shrugged. "As far as I know, it has not been taken from the bog."

"We must go look upon it," she said, glancing toward Cessari. "This is a great treasure."

"Beware, milady," Cessari said. "This may be a trap to lure you from the safety of the forest!"

But the holy maiden whirled and peered to the east, as if her mind sought out beyond the miles. "No, I can feel it now. There, at the limit of my powers. How sweetly the dragon dreams …"

They would have to go under the cover of darkness, Anduval realized, when the creatures of the forest ventured out to forage. She would want to go in secret and hide her heat signature from cycor ships.

The holy maiden riveted Anduval with a look and said, "Go and tell the magus what you have heard."

* * *

Angar was drunk by midday. He went to the pub and told the town about his dragon, and as the tale spread, many an oaf just like himself came and offered to pay for rounds.

By early afternoon, the size of the dragon had grown enormous in the telling, and many a man gaped in disbelief at stories of a talon a yard long and a wingspan of a hundred feet.

There were offers to buy teeth. "I'm the best scrimshaw artist in Moonravis," one fisherman boasted. "Lend me the ivory, and I shall double its value!"

But Angar did not like the man's work. It was true that he was the best in town, but with a find like this, the ivory should go to the best carvers on Danai.

"I'll bet I could make fine boots and belts from its skin," the cobbler suggested in a wheedling voice, his hands making little groping gestures.

The innkeeper offered, "Five gold rings for a tooth—and all the beer you can drink for a year!"

"Two years!" Angar demanded.

"Sold!" the innkeeper shouted instantly, and Angar rued the bargain.

"I should have demanded more," he grumbled.

But the innkeeper forced a mug of his finest into Angar's hand, and in moments Angar was so happy that he was dancing on the bar while the other guests serenaded him with drinking songs.

"You know," a blacksmith called out in the midst of the song, "that it is not the teeth or hide that is the greatest treasure of a dragon. It is found in the dragon's skull!"

The blacksmith pointed to his own skull and nodded wisely.

Angar's head was reeling by then, but somehow the blacksmith's image, his message, kept whirling about in Angar's mind. It was like a piece of oat straw caught in a dust devil. It spun around and around.

Suddenly Angar fell from the table, and several peasants leaped to be the first to help him up.

"Leave me, leave me alone," he said. "I've got to go get that dragon out of the bog."

With superhuman effort, he hauled his massive belly off the floor and began to weave in the general direction of his home. But the patrons of the bar all shouted, "We'll come and help!" and Angar was still sober enough to realize that he would be grateful for twenty strong hands.

So the townsmen went to the edge of the bog and, with picks and shovels and pry bars, they dug into the mud and freed the dragon, pulling its half-petrified corpse into the sunlight on the riverbank. Flies buzzed around it curiously for a while, then rejected its ancient flesh as an unworthy home even for maggots.

The townsfolk gaped in amazement at the dragon's size. Surely it would have had an eighty-foot wingspan. And its talons really were over two feet long.

But the leather did not look to be worth much. Most of it had been devoured by worms and discolored by the tannins in the peat, it seemed.

Meanwhile, the ivory in its teeth was discolored and had gone soft with age. Angar feared the innkeeper would rescind his offer of two years' free beer.

One of the townsfolk even laughed at Angar, saying, "I would not like to have to bury that thing!"

As Angar fell into despair, a skraal warrior came to the bog and ordered the people not to disturb the dragon's remains.

"The holy maiden will pay well for a skull that is still intact," the warrior offered.

So Angar shooed the townsfolk off his property and stood guard over the rotting corpse. He settled in the shade of a hazelnut tree and lay in the tall grass for a long while, trying to figure out how to make the most money from his smelly prize, when he fell asleep.

Two full moons were up when he finally roused himself.

The greatest treasure *is found in the dragon's skull!*" he recalled, the thought whirling about him like dry autumn leaves.

He wondered at that. Angar was not an educated man. Education was for skraals; farming and petty labors were for humans. But Angar knew a bit of folk wisdom.

Sometimes, when a large bird died, it would leave piles of small stones as its craw decomposed. There was an old wives' tale he had heard about a farmer who discovered diamonds amid such remains, and a further search revealed that a nearby hillside was covered with them.

Perhaps dragons did the same. Maybe dragons swallowed rubies or emeralds, or maybe such gems just formed naturally in a dragon's skull!

Why should the skraals get all of the treasure? They got the best that men had to offer, and what did the hardworking people get in return?

With that in mind, he staggered home to find his ax.

* * *

"Magus Veritarnus, my name is Anduval. I am to be your apprentice."

The magus shot Anduval a dark look, hesitated for an instant, and said, "I can't waste time on such nonsense." He turned his back on the boy.

Anduval had found the magus in his operations center. The magus was a tall man with a lean physique and a haggard look. His skin was as midnight-black as Anduval's. He had his long hair braided in cornrows and slung over his neck onto his chest. The magus peered up at a glass wall where squiggly chains made from green, red, yellow, and blue were wrapped into cords. The magus had a crystal wand, and when he pointed at one of the rods, he would speak, and the chains would break. The colored blocks would then rearrange according to his command.

"Let's have a look at chromosome twelve, gene one hundred eleven, marker four, shall we?"

The image on the wall shifted, rushing down the coiled chains, until it stopped. The magus squinted at the image on the wall, ignoring Anduval.

Anduval prompted, "It is the wish of the holy maiden that I be your apprentice."

"Go and tell her to mind her own business," Magus Veritarnus shot back. "We are in a state of emergency."

"The holy maiden seems to think that I can help."

The magus turned, looked down. "Time that I spend with you is time taken from more important duties. Do you understand?"

Anduval understood far more than most adults thought he should. For weeks now he had been gathering bits of information overheard in palace halls and in the markets outside of town.

"You are preparing for the cycor attack," Anduval said. "You only have a few years to do it. You're gathering seeds and spores and hiding them here, beneath the fortress. I know because I know of the children that you've hired to begin the work.

"You hope to weather the attack, as our ancestors did. But you are afraid that it won't work. Six thousand years ago, the cycor hit us with planet killers. But that didn't work, so you're worried that they'll be more thorough this time.

"You're trying to save what you can, the seeds of humanity. But you are doomed to fail, for there are hundreds of millions of people who will die. There isn't room to protect them all, down here in the depths of the palace."

The magus straightened his back, sighed, and peered down at Anduval as if in defeat.

"You're damned smart for a twelve-year-old." Anduval hadn't told the magus his age, but then, the magus was rumored to have phenomenal powers of observation. "I wasn't that smart at your age.

"This isn't a palace, you know. It is a bunker, designed to withstand cycor attacks. That is what it was built for."

He studied Anduval as if weighing him; Anduval realized that the magus needed time to make up his own mind.

"I was told to inform you that the body of a dragon has been found."

"Frozen?" the magus asked hopefully. "Preserved in ice?"

"No, it was found in a peat bog. I hear that it has not decomposed. The holy maiden has asked that I lead you and her to it."

The magus stopped for a moment, breathless, riveted by the news. He nodded slightly, eagerly, black pupils shining.

Then a look of defeat entered his eyes once again, and he said softly, "Let us hope that it is whole."

* * *

Anduval had to sprint that night to keep pace with the quicker skraals.

Their entourage was small—the holy maiden, a pair of guards, Anduval. Magus Veritarnus ran at the tail of the group, his black cape flowing behind.

Anduval led the way. The light of two small full moons, the angry twins, shone red and glaring on the fields of dry grass, bathing the night in blood. He ran, and in doing so he tried to hide his humanity. He dared not slow or stop. He could not beg for rest. Anduval wanted to prove that he could move as swiftly and effortlessly as a skraal.

So he sprinted through the fields, his heart pounding, lungs heaving like bellows, until he was dizzy with fatigue. His feet winnowed the dry grasses, knocking ripe grain from stalks of wheat.

The scent of grass and stinkweeds carried on the warm night air.

The others raced behind him. They did not have far to go outside the great forest, but the stars overhead seemed threatening to Anduval. At any moment, one of them could turn and dive—a cycor warship that would explode like the sun, washing the planet in fire.

It is only a matter of time, he told himself. *They will come, and the world will become void in a flash.*

A wind came from the deserts in the east, blowing a thin veil of red dust high into the air. Lightning flickered in the empty heavens, and the skraals, agitated, ran faster.

The skraals moved swiftly and effortlessly, and Anduval knew that they wished his small legs would go faster. But Holy Maiden Seramasia did not condemn him. She jogged at his back, sometimes whispering words of gratitude and encouragement.

Thus they reached the cottage where the farmer Angar lived. The house was made from squares of sod, with poles angled up at the top. Bundles of cattail reeds served as a roof.

The girl Tallori answered Anduval's call at a door made from scraped sheep's hide, her mother being too weary to rise, and the child led the way to the dragon's corpse, racing through the tall cattails.

There, beside the slow-flowing river, they found Angar under the starlight, standing upon the dragon's skull, his ax raised overhead.

Magus Veritarnus saw what he was about to do, and let out a cry of shock.

Putting all of his bulk and might into it, Angar let his ax fall.

The dragon's skull split easily, the rotting bone breaking with a sound like a melon.

What happened next, Anduval could never clearly describe.

Shimmering lights rose from the dragon's skull, as soft as fog, as bright and sparkling as opals. They gave off no sound, no smell. Instead, they only glittered, rising up like thistledown.

"Catch them!" Magus Veritarnus shouted, and the holy maiden leaped magnificently, bounding perhaps twenty feet in the air and seventy feet in distance, so that she seemed to fly over Anduval's head.

He raced forward, seeking to catch a light in his cupped hands, but the lights did not move on currents of wind. They seemed to be alive, darting about of their own volition.

Angar the drunkard stood, eyes wide with amazement, and Anduval saw lights pass right through him, then circle back around his head, as if seeking entrance and finding none.

One of the coruscating lights drew near, and Anduval reached out and caught it in both hands. Strange currents passed through him. He felt his hair stand on end, and the light rose up. It was as long as a small serpent, but its body was flat and eyeless, much like ribbon, yet it waggled a tail to propel itself through the air.

Opening his mouth in amazement, Anduval was about to shout a question when the light burst upward and into his brain.

In the way that sometimes happened with Anduval, he dreamt two dreams simultaneously. It was a gift he had, a gift that he had only recently discovered.

* * *

Anduval was a dragon, hunting beside the river. His scaly hide was the tan of dying reeds, with stripes of dark green and silver. With such camouflage, he could easily hide among the rushes and ambush the hippo-like creatures that waded near.

He looked up and spotted wings in the sky. Another dragon with a soft-blue underbelly soared above the clouds.

A thought struck him, an argument so lengthy and complex that a human could take months to unravel and comprehend it; yet Anduval recognized that it was an argument over territorial boundaries and disputes.

The dragon vocalized, sending loud clicks in the air so swiftly that no human could have decoded their meaning.

* * *

A second dream struck simultaneously, in which the dragon piloted a starship. The creature was hanging upside down in a cockpit, sending his mind out among the stars, feeling ahead for meteors and bits of space debris, then weaving a safe path through the void.

The cycor were following his ship doggedly, and he glanced back in anger. He so desired to turn the ship and face the enemy …

* * *

Anduval found himself lying flat on his back, blinking up at the stars, while the girl Tallori knelt at his side. Magus Veritarnus hunched over him, two fingers pressed against Anduval's neck, checking for a pulse.

"You will be well, child," the magus said. Those were the first words the man had spoken to him all night.

Tallori was weeping. Anduval could not be sure if she wept from fear for him or in awe of the holy maiden or simply because the combination of events left her overwrought. Humans that lived outside the palace were simple creatures.

The magus turned aside, as if listening for some inner voice, and then whispered, "It is not for humans like us to touch a dragon's dream. Doing so was unwise. The dragon's memories, its hopes and lore, all are stored in a brain that is nothing like ours.

"The dragons came from a far world, you know. Humans cannot even pronounce the name of their species—much less speak their tongue. So our ancestors called them *dragons*, after creatures from legend.

"We cannot even begin to comprehend the math they understood, their mastery of flight. Perhaps if we had a floccular lobe to our brain, as birds do, we might understand some of the things that are innately known to dragons.

"The skraals can sometimes unravel it." The magus jutted his chin, and Anduval peered a few yards away. The holy maiden stood atop the dragon's body, and the lights were circling her, as if greeting an ancient friend, their opalescent hues sometimes bursting into colored sparks.

"The creatures that you see are called *piezoelectric life-forms*. They're symbiotes. They grow and reproduce in the minds of dragons. Our thoughts and memories are stored in twisted strands of DNA—which is so much less efficient than the crystalline structure of a skraal's brain."

Holy Maiden Seramasia stood for long minutes, and one by one the dragon dreams entered her. As they did, her eyes filled with tears, and her thorax trembled as if she might shatter.

Anduval worried. "Should we stop her? It looks as if it hurts."

But the magus shook his head. "She does not hurt. Those are tears of joy, tears of revelation. The dragon dreams must find a home quickly, or they will die. So they are lodging within her skull. Like hermit crabs, they need a place where they can survive. A skraal's brain is not like a dragon's either—the dreams will not survive there for long, a few years at the most—but our holy maiden is learning things that none of her kind have been able to comprehend on this planet for more than six thousand years."

The magus turned to Anduval, looked into his eyes. "You're right about my fears. The cycor will make sure that nothing on this planet survives the next attack. They'll hit us with a sunbuster, send a missile to the planet's core, and let it explode so that we are shattered into fragments."

Anduval was horrified. He knew of border disputes that sometimes happened among human tribes, but that was all that he knew of war. "Why would they do that? I mean, if they wanted to take over, that I could understand. But killing everything—that seems like such a waste!"

"The cycor don't need plants and animals to feed upon," the magus said. "Biological life forms evolve, and highly evolved creatures are a danger to them—so all life represents a threat.

"For millennia, we have hoped that a dragon would come to our world. We're trapped here. Oh, we could build little ships that float through space like rafts upon a lake and try to escape, but the cycor would only find us that much sooner. The dragons alone have the knowledge necessary to build the fast starships that we so desperately need if we are ever to escape.

"But I fear that the last of the dragons have been hunted to extinction. Indeed, this world may be home to the last vestiges of humanity. The center of the galaxy is nothing but a void. The stars have all gone dark, and the planets that whirl around them are destroyed. The home world of the dragons is gone, along with the ancient home of mankind. Perhaps some of our brethren have fled the galaxy, but if so, we may never reunite with them again."

Magus Veritarnus glanced down, the whites of his eyes reflecting the lights of the piezoelectric creatures.

For long hours, they waited in silence as the moons slid inexorably down to the horizon and beyond the shadowed hills. The stars had begun to fade, though the sun was not yet up, when the last of the opalescent creatures entered Seramasia.

Anduval could see them there still, deep within her crystal skull, their lights sparking from time to time.

He could not understand completely what was happening. Perhaps such things were beyond the comprehension of mere humans. But Anduval peered up at Magus Veritarnus and saw a change in the man. He had always walked about with hunched shoulders and a careworn look.

Now he had hope in his eyes.

When the last of the creatures had burrowed into her skull, the holy maiden looked around at her small crowd of followers.

"It is done," she said. "I know how to escape, but time is short if we are to build a worldship."

* * *

The weight of the whole planet fell upon Anduval's shoulders that night, and as he trudged back through fields misted with morning dew, he understood why the magus always walked with his head bowed.

The palace became a madhouse as the holy maiden began to issue orders to her skraal attendants, demanding that they begin to gather vast amounts of rare metals from across the world.

Over the coming days, the skraal nymph closeted with Magus Veritarnus for unending hours, discussing her plan to create a worldship. Sketches were drawn and sent to far cities, where modules for the great ship were to be produced.

Amid this bustle, Magus Veritarnus seemed to forget that he had been assigned to be a mentor, and Anduval felt as if he had been cast aside.

It was not a feeling that he could live with. Anduval had no mother or father that he knew of. He had been raised in a crèche in the palace beneath Shadowfest, one of nine human children.

All of his life, he'd craved to belong, to find some sort of companionship. He'd hoped that by working hard, he could prove himself and win acceptance from others.

Somehow, as a child, he'd proven himself well enough to become the holy maiden's attendant. But the skraals were not humans. They showed nothing in the way of affection, and the other workers never offered any praise.

Yet Anduval hoped.

So he continued his duties as an attendant, bringing fungus and damselflies for the holy maiden each morning, hoping to prepare her for transcendence.

But with each passing day, he grew more concerned. In his brief vision, he had seen into the mind of a dragon, and the threat of the cycor was a shadow that flooded his mind. The cycor were not human. Properly speaking, they were not even alive. They had no compassion, no emotion, no hope or love in them.

There could be no swaying such creatures from their wanton destruction.

And the end would come swiftly, he knew.

Cycor ships were fast. When a spaceship accelerated, the force of acceleration exerted pressure upon its occupants. Thus, a ship that was constantly accelerating created its own artificial gravity. But it also had certain limits. Accelerate too quickly, and the gravity field would crush its occupants. The safe speed for acceleration over an extended period of time was only a little more than one gravity.

But a cycor ship carried no living creatures within; it could safely accelerate at a speed of one hundred gravities.

Human ships were infinitely slower.

Our only real hope is to hide from the cycor, Anduval reasoned.

But hiding was no longer possible. They had been found.

The holy maiden wished to build a worldship, but it could be destroyed as easily as a planet.

What shall the holy maiden do? Anduval wondered. *What* can *she do?*

After two weeks, Anduval was finally able to corner his master. He found the magus bleary-eyed and swaying from fatigue as he left the holy maiden's meditation chambers. Anduval had just returned from his nightly run to gather fungus.

"I want to help build the worldship," Anduval begged. "We are in a race against the cycor, and every moment is precious."

"I agree," the magus said, "and someday you shall help to build our ship. But the holy maiden's personal needs are more immediate."

"She has twenty other attendants," Anduval said. "Surely they can bring her food. I can even tell them what to collect."

The magus studied the boy for a long moment, weighing his argument. "You, too, have been touched by the dragon's dream," he said, "if only for a moment. How much do you understand?"

Anduval bit his lip, struggling to explain. The dragon's dream hadn't come to him in his native tongue. It was like pure intelligence that had flowed through him, only for an instant, and much of what he knew was just stray impressions.

"The scout ship that found us could not have been a long-range vessel," Anduval said. "It had to have come from a mother ship. That means there is a warship nearby, or possibly a fleet of them."

"Agreed," the magus said. "If a vessel had been stationed in this solar system, the cycor would have destroyed us by now. Our nearest stellar neighbor is nearly two light-years away. Let us hope that there is not a warship so close."

Anduval bent his head in thought. It would take two years for a message transmission to reach the nearest star, and if a warship was there, it would take a few months more than two years for the enemy to reach Danai. "The cycor will be near a planet, won't they?"

"Mining," the magus agreed. "They do not need food, but they may be mining asteroids for minerals or mining the gravity fields of a nearby sun for fuel."

Even the dragons had not understood how the cycor could mine and store gravity.

"Can we build a ship in four years?" Anduval asked.

The magus shrugged. He was not reassuring. "We must try."

Even if we can build a ship, Anduval wondered, *will it be fast enough to outrun the cycor? How far beyond the edge of the galaxy must we go to escape them?*

The magus rested a hand on Anduval's shoulder. "Let us hope that the cycor are farther away than that. I will consider your request, but until further notice, you are the head steward. There is nothing more important than the feeding of Seramasia. Even in ancient times, only one in a thousand holy maidens truly transcended. I can find no genetic reason for this, and so it must have to do with nurture.

"The holy maiden has begun to talk to me about the requirements of our ship. We will build it in modules—engines, the hull, life-support. It must be a large ship, large enough to carry every man, woman, and child in the world.

"It will be a complex task …" A look of defeat passed across the magus's face. "I confess, I do not understand how it all works. We can only hope that the holy maiden will guide us."

* * *

Four days later, Anduval was summoned into the holy maiden's meditation chamber. The deep gray room itself was vast, with a sixty-foot ceiling, and perfectly round. Within this space, white silk sheets tangled on the floor, creating something that was not quite a bed, not quite a chair.

Holy Maiden Seramasia lay cradled in silk. Candles in glass cups provided footlights around the room, but brighter than the candles was the holy maiden's womb.

Her abdomen, that perfect inverted pear, glowed brightly from inside. Anduval could see her ripening eggs through her skin, like clear marbles.

Along the backs of her arms and legs, and all down her spine, mucilage had begun to ooze out—a clear gel that would harden within a few hours into a chrysalis.

Her courtesans crowded near, like bucks in musth, and from time to time, they would stoop and nuzzle her abdomen, pushing against it, trying to arouse her.

The sexual tension in the room was electric.

Anduval felt grateful to see the holy maiden, but not like this. There was a soft glow all about her, and she was more beautiful and sensual than ever. He had no desire to watch the skraal males fight over her.

Even being here was dangerous, lest one of the males inadvertently strike out.

"Come near, little one," the holy maiden urged.

Anduval trembled and drew close, until the big male, Cessari, snorted and charged.

Anduval leaped backward, and Cessari lashed out with one long arm. Anduval ducked beneath the blow. The holy maiden reached out and grabbed Cessari, restraining him.

"Stay back, little one," Cessari growled. "This one is not for you!"

The holy maiden calmed her consort, patting his head. Cessari crouched beside her and placed a hand over her womb, as if claiming it for his own. He glared at Anduval but dared not resist the will of the maiden.

"You have served me well," the holy maiden told Anduval. "As you can see, I will be going into my long sleep soon. I will eat no more until I wake."

"But it's not time yet!" Anduval objected.

"Many factors help determine the time when a skraal nymph goes into transcendence. I have been under a great deal of stress these past few weeks, and that has tipped the scales.

"I hereby release you from my service," she said. "I will no longer need you to attend me."

She would be gone for years—somewhere between three and twenty—sleeping in her chrysalis, lost to the world.

This was bad. An ancient adage came to mind. *Early to the cocoon; late to bloom.* Chances were good that she would sleep for many, many years. The ancient tomes suggested that the long sleep was a coping mechanism, a way for the nymphs to deal with hard times.

Anduval had read tome after tome about the holy maidens. He knew that a maiden who went into chrysalis phase early would come out stunted—both physically and mentally. Seramasia would not come out with the great powers that Anduval had hoped for.

Panic took him. "But milady, you're the only one who understands how to build the worldship!"

Seramasia nodded sadly. "I have left what instructions I can with the magus. Much of the work can proceed without me. While I am gone, you will grow, and you will help build our ship. I wish you well. I hope that when I waken, it will be to a better world for us all.

"Young man, find love with one of your own kind, if you can. The girl with the damselflies, do you still see her?"

Anduval nodded.

"Bring her to the palace. She wishes to fight the cycor. She will need someone to teach her, to watch over her. I want you to care for her as you have for me.

"Reward her parents. I will prepare a payment for them, to ease their loss."

Anduval recognized what she was doing. She hoped to deflect his affection. She hoped he would fall in love with some human girl.

But Tallori was only a child, and he had no interest in her.

"Go now," the holy maiden said, "and get her. By bringing her to the palace, you may save her life."

Anduval stood for an instant, wondering. The holy maiden could sense things about people. She could read their thoughts and emotions. Was it possible she knew something he didn't, that Tallori might someday grow to be someone that he could love?

Perhaps, he thought. But the holy maiden was not an adult yet. She had not transcended and gained all of her powers, and nothing guaranteed that she would. Not all maidens broke free of their chrysalis. Many died in the attempt. Even those who broke free did not always develop great powers. Years of meditation and good food might help ensure that a maiden became a powerful adult. Yet most of the time, maidens awoke with little more psychic power than they'd held before.

So if the holy maiden suspected that Anduval might find love with this girl, it might still be nothing more than a hunch.

Ever so gently, Cessari reached down and positioned the maiden's womb so he could gain entrance, rolling her onto her stomach, and then leaning above her.

The holy maiden let out a little piping call of desire, and Anduval felt the touch of her mind.

It was like being dragged into a whirlwind of desire. The longing for her came upon him so strongly that it drove all other thoughts from his mind. He was only twelve, but at that moment he felt a man's desires and found himself staggering forward.

She wants me, Anduval thought. *She wants me as much as I want her.*

But then the maiden caught herself, and her desires withdrew, leaving him empty and embarrassed.

"Go," she pleaded. "Get out of here before it is too late."

She was almost mindless with the need to mate. Anduval turned and ran.

* * *

That night, the stars were blazing overhead when Anduval walked to Tallori's sod house.

He breathed in the rich scents of the night air as he walked. It was late autumn, and the farmhouses along the path boasted trees ripe with fruit—tart peaches, sweet pears, and fat plums.

In the night, the deer had come from the shadows of the forest. They huddled under the apple trees, sometimes rising up on their back legs as they picked fruit with their mouths.

Anduval saw a herd of four deer under Angar's apple tree. The small buck that led them showed no fear of Anduval but simply held his ground, as if claiming the tree for his own.

At the sod house, the rich smell of peat and earth mingled. The hide flap that served as a door allowed easy entry, but Anduval stood outside and clapped until, at last, Angar came to the door.

The huge man was drunk and wavering on his feet.

"What do you want?" Angar demanded.

"I've come to pay you for your service to the holy maiden," Anduval said. He produced a pouch and handed it to the drunkard. "The price of a dragon's head."

Angar shook the pouch and frowned when he did not hear the clinking of coins. "Wha's this?"

"Rubies, emeralds, and diamonds," Anduval said. "Enough so that you can swim in a lake of beer, if you like."

A maniacal grin spread across the man's face. Excited shouts issued from inside the house. His wife had heard the news.

The young girl, Tallori, appeared at her father's back, peeking out from the shadows.

She isn't really pretty, Anduval thought. Her face was plain and freckled, her hair too bleached by the sun. She was not a promising child.

Does the holy maiden really know something about her? Anduval wondered.

"The Great Lady wishes to bless you, too, Tallori. Your damselflies served her well. What boon would you ask of her?"

The girl looked down at the ground as if studying the dirt on her bare feet, then glanced back toward her mother. She was obviously poor. Her dress was little more than a sack made of the crudest brown cloth. It looked as if the only comb that had ever gone through her pale hair was her fingers. Anduval waited for her to ask for money. Peasants were such simple creatures that wealth was the only reward they could imagine.

"I want to fight the cycor with you," she declared. "I want to come live in the palace and help build the worldship. If the holy maiden has any power at all, then she knows this."

If all children spoke with such ferocity, Anduval thought, *even lions would fear us.*

Immediately, Tallori glanced back into the room where her mother hid. Regret was stamped upon the child's face, as if she had betrayed the family.

"The lady bids you welcome to the palace," Anduval said.

Tallori stared at her mother in the darkened room and asked, "Can I go?"

There were sobs from the mother then, and the peasant woman came and gave her daughter a hug. Angar made a huge show of hugging his daughter, and Anduval had to wait at the door while her mother got Tallori's things and kissed her good-bye time and time again.

Anduval had never had anyone treat him so, and he stood for a long moment out in the shadows, watching the stars twinkle overhead. As he watched, one of them flared for an instant and then winked out.

Somewhere, he knew, a distant star had exploded. The cycor had struck again.

He heard a gasp and saw Tallori standing outside the doorway with a small bundle of belongings tied together with a rag. Her face was tilted upward. She had seen it too.

So they took off, running through the warm night, Tallori struggling to negotiate the path in the darkness with her bare feet.

Once again, Anduval felt the weight of the world falling upon his shoulders. He was no skraal nymph, but he could sense the cycor out there in the heavens, hunting him.

Tallori surely felt it too. She looked small and frightened as she hurried under the starlight.

Somewhere along the path, she reached out and grasped his hand for comfort.

* * *

Anduval became the big brother that Tallori had never had. He began that night as her mentor and tutor, but she had been raised in a world where the most complex tasks included weaving wool on her mother's loom and churning butter.

In theory, Anduval was an apprentice to the magus. But after only two weeks of instruction, the boy's understanding of physics soon dwarfed that of the magus. It was widely rumored that he had been blessed of the dragon, had accepted its dreams, and Anduval went to work as head of construction for the most complex system of the worldship—its navigation system.

Anduval tried to make Tallori his assistant, but she often became frustrated and wept when Anduval tried to teach her. She grasped basic math well enough—simple things like trigonometry and calculus—but Anduval's mind was far more powerful than her own.

His memory was flawless. He recalled everything that he both saw and heard, but his mental prowess went far beyond that. He could multiply or divide any pair of numbers in his head, or calculate pi to a thousand decimal places.

More importantly, when confronted with a mystery, he could often consider it for a moment and intuitively recognize the answer.

She tried to keep up with him, but one day as she tried to multiply two six-digit numbers in her head, she began to sob uncontrollably.

Anduval put his arm around her, patted her on the back, and said, "Don't cry, little sister. Don't cry."

They were in Anduval's room where he was studying a sketch of the celestial navigation system for the worldship. He had been making notes about gravitonic sensors, red-shift resolution equations, and skraal brainwave-computer interfaces.

Even with all of his understanding, he struggled to make sense of the holy maiden's often-crude schematics.

"I can't keep up with you!" Tallori blurted, wiping her nose.

"It's not your fault," he said. "The skraals can't keep up with me, either. Even Magus Veritarnus has been humbled. But all of us must learn as fast as we are able.

"It's not your fault that you were raised in a stone-age existence," he explained. "The skraals willed it to be so for many reasons. Technology carries inherent dangers. If we had used ancient telecommunications equipment, it would have unleashed radio waves that would have alerted the cycor to our presence. Power plants would have left energy signatures that cycor scouts could easily pick up. And even the simplest of electric machines can emit energy fields that adversely affect a skraal.

"Danai is a world in hiding. Now we must come out of hiding and escape before the cycor attack.

"We must master a hundred thousand years of technological advancement in the next four years. Everyone must do all that they can, or we shall all die in the attempt.

"We can't lean upon the skraals for help. We can't hope that some great leader will save us. The time has come for each of us to be great."

Anduval stood for a moment, looking sober and hopeful.

"I don't know if I can be great," Tallori said. "But I know I can do more than other people believe a child can do."

Thus, as Tallori began to understand the dangers, she often longed to return to blissful ignorance. Just as she wept for her ignorance, she soon learned to weep for her enlightenment. She began to understand why Anduval was such a brooding and driven young man.

He worked for twenty hours a day, napping for a few minutes in the afternoon, sleeping two hours a night, taking only moments to cram a bit of food into his mouth. Then he would get back to work.

He became a shell of a young man, and Tallori became more than just his pupil. She began to feed him, care for him.

She soon found that the entire world was in turmoil. Their world was called upon to evolve, but the going was extremely slow.

Before a ship could be built, Magus Veritarnus had to design and manufacture its various components.

Before the components could be constructed, factories had to be erected, tools had to be created, and workers had to be trained how to do their jobs.

The factories in most cases required nuclear power systems to run the various smelting and metalworking tools.

Of course, before the power systems could run, the fissionable metals had to be mined.

So the skraal consorts ventured across the land, urging potato farmers to dig for uranium here, begging that sailors manufacture selenium crystals there.

At every step, the lack of technology and training became a stumbling block. It seemed that for every day of progress that was made, Magus Veritarnus discovered three more days of work to be done.

For instance, to build the basic hull of the ship—the easiest component to fabricate—the people needed to create selenium crystal beams and plates capable of resisting impact with space debris while traveling near light speed.

The selenium first had to be mined from rock, ground up, and dissolved in an acid bath.

The selenium solution was then placed in tanks and an electric current passed through it. The charged selenium particles would bind to a titanium plate and begin to form crystals. In this way, beams and plates could be "grown."

But once they were grown, the selenium crystals were so tough that even diamond could not cut through them. So in order for them to be shaped and fastened together, laser cutting torches were needed.

Thus a single rod for the hull could not be finished until the titanium was also mined, the acids and their containers created, the electrical systems installed in the baths, the laser cutting torches made, and so on.

Confusion reigned, and the people of Danai hit setbacks at every turn. Much of the planning for the construction took nine months to complete. Too many questions had to be answered. What facilities needed to be built, when, and how? Who would do the work, and who would manage the workers? How could you train a stone-age woodcutter to build a gamma converter or a crystal AI?

Some work was done in fits and starts while other projects were planned, but farmers who had to dig for ore with picks and shovels proved too slow, missing deadlines. The factories were not completed on time.

After a year, the work had hardly begun, and some of the skraals began to worry about human saboteurs. Cessari called the magus and Anduval to task, insisting they launch a search for the imaginary saboteurs.

But good work did get completed. Anduval helped devise an early warning system in case of a cycor attack. Graviton-detecting telescopes were built and aimed toward the heavens. The gravity drive on a cycor ship would register as a massive planetoid or black hole racing toward Danai. Simple farmers were trained to man the scopes.

Listening stations were constructed to eavesdrop on cycor ships.

Meanwhile, the magus provided holographic interfaces for himself, Anduval, and dozens of project leaders around the world. The devices were simple silver bands that went over the forehead and wired straight into the optic and aural nerves. Thus, they could relay sights and sounds from one leader to another, so that the magus and Anduval could personally monitor situations and take care of training from afar.

But in the third year, a hurricane hit the hull's manufacturing facilities, and the factory was swept into the sea. A week later, at a separate construction site, a small nuclear power plant went into meltdown, and four hundred square miles of land had to be evacuated—along with a newly completed rebreather for the life-support systems.

Upon learning the news, Cessari himself burst into Anduval's laboratory.

"Now will you search for the saboteurs?" he demanded.

Anduval had only learned the news of the meltdown the day before; he'd spent a sleepless night trying to figure out how to get the work back on schedule.

"No, I will not," Anduval said. "There are no saboteurs. None of our people caused the hurricane, and the meltdown was an accident. The fuel rods are cooled by water from a nearby river, but the floodgates that control the water flow broke. They froze shut and could not be reopened."

"Where is the man responsible for opening them?" Cessari asked. "I want to question him myself."

"He died this morning from radiation poisoning," Anduval said. "He stayed far too long at the site, struggling to cool the reactor's core even after it had gone into meltdown."

Cessari raged in the way of his kind, striding back and forth, striking the air with his empty fists. Finally, he turned back to Anduval.

"The deadline for completion of the project is coming quickly. You must meet the deadline."

"We all are doing the best that we can," Anduval said.

Tallori knew that even their best was not good enough. "But we will not meet the deadline. Our only hope is that all cycor ships are far, far away."

At this, Cessari rushed up to Anduval. He did not dare strike the young man, but he warned, "You cannot fail our queen. If the cycor attack before we are ready, I shall make sure that you are the first to die."

Anduval bowed his head in acquiescence. "I assure you, under such circumstances, I would have no wish to live. Yet I must also warn you, even skraal law prohibits murder. I will be within my rights to protect myself."

Cessari blurted an obscenity and stalked away.

"What are you going to do?" Tallori asked Anduval when the skraal was gone. "You have to protect yourself. The skraals are faster and stronger than us."

Anduval merely shrugged. "But I am smarter than they are."

* * *

Tallori grew from a child to a young woman. She found that she could not comprehend the math that Anduval was mastering, but she found her niche. She planned Anduval's meals, freeing time for him and making sure he did not fall ill due to fatigue.

When a plant manager looked as if he would miss a deadline, Tallori ran interference for Anduval, bolstering men's spirits with praise and honors, offering bribes when it was prudent, and, when necessary, reminding them that failure meant death.

Time and time again, she marveled at what her people had accomplished. There were little farmers, working their crops by day and mining by night, breaking their hearts in order to meet a deadline that they did not understand so that their ore could be turned into something that they could not comprehend.

Old women and children worked in factories from dawn to dusk.

The world was full of heroes, she discovered.

In another age, no one would have given her the time of day. But as Anduval's assistant, it was rumored that she had the ear of the magus, and all men gave her high regard.

Thus, she became the mother that Anduval had never had. But as she neared her teens and her body began to morph from that of a child into a woman, she wanted more.

Anduval loved a skraal nymph, and Tallori began to realize that she was in love with him.

She wondered if Anduval would ever even notice.

So the day came when, at the age of twelve, she sought out Magus Veritarnus at his laboratory. He'd spent long years collecting seeds, spores, and animal embryos, and then freezing them for storage. As she had anticipated, he was busy when she found him. He was always busy.

The world on Danai had been divided into ecological zones, and the plants and animals from each zone represented species selected from various worlds. The deep forest at Shadowfest was comprised of plants and animals from the skraals' home world. It was an impenetrable jungle where boa trees rose up in vast tangles for thousands of feet. The ground beneath them was a silent tomb, filled with fungi that digested the fallen leaves and dead animals.

Most of the alien proteins in the creatures and plants within Shadowfest were inedible to humans, though some terrestrial animals—like the wild pigs—had begun to evolve the ability to eat them.

Around the skraal forests, humans lived in the plains and wooded hills.

So the magus had to store specimens from both zones. Even a few plants and animals from the dragon's home world still thrived here. Women still planted dragon's breath vines beside their homes. The vines were prized for the mildly narcotic smell that their flowers emitted in high summer. Old folks, bowed by arthritis, loved to take their ease beneath an arbor of dragon's breath.

Tallori had little interest in the magus's efforts to save the specimens from this world. Whether the people of Danai fled on a worldship or simply tried to weather another cycor attack, the magus's work was vital. But everyone's work was vital, from the farmwife who simply tried to feed her husband, to the husband who mined a little each day, to the factory worker, to folks like Anduval—each was essential to the effort.

But Tallori was too focused upon Anduval's efforts to build a prototype of the celestial navigation system. So she dared to interrupt the magus, hoping for a moment of his time.

"How comes the prototype?" Magus Veritarnus asked as she neared. He stood squinting up at his monitor, repairing the damaged DNA of some embryo before he sent it to the freezers.

"Well," Tallori said, managing only a mildly sarcastic tone. "We are only fourteen months behind schedule. Anduval hopes to have it finished in three months."

"A full-sized starship can be piloted even with a simple prototype. If he gets it working, we will be able to make do."

The magus did not bother to mention that everything else was behind schedule, too. The prototype ship would be small, only able to carry a few hundred people.

But it was vital to the efforts. So many of the holy maiden's sketches were ... mysterious. Knowing what a starship's drive system was supposed to do was one thing, building it so that the nuclear-powered lifters, ion propulsion units, gamma-wave converters, and so on all worked in unison was another.

"You know we will not make our deadline of four years," Tallori said.

The magus nodded. "Some of the skraals hope that it will be done in five years. Anduval imagines that if all goes right, it will take eight. Personally, I do not believe that we can get it done in twenty."

He said it casually, in the way of one who has accepted that he will die in a vain struggle.

"Anduval is not like other people," she said. "He's smarter. He sleeps very little, in the way that the greatest of geniuses do."

"Anduval is not like other people," the magus agreed.

"The thing is," Tallori said, "I love him. But I feel that I'm too stupid for him. I can't talk to him about math or physics."

The magus had been staring up at his monitor, switching out little blocks of ATGC. Now he peered at her.

"A man can love a woman for something other than her native intelligence. He can love her for her goodness, her kindness. I know that Anduval is fond of you."

"But I can never be his equal," Tallori said.

"Intellectually, no," the magus admitted. "Anduval is a special boy. Evolution does not always take place in tiny steps. Sometimes it comes in giant leaps. Anduval is the next leap."

The magus fell silent for a moment, and Tallori stood her ground, waiting for him to explain. Reluctantly, he said, "Two million years ago, a manlike creature roamed the earth, a creature called Homo habilis. It had a small brain that could comprehend little. It could make a leaf-shaped house and use a few simple tools—a stone knife, an awl to poke holes in furs, a needle.

"But one day, one of the creatures evolved. The gene that told the brain how large it should be simply formed a double string, and suddenly a new specimen was born, one with twice the brainpower. It was called Homo erectus.

"It created a few more tools, better weapons, and over time its genetic superiority was confirmed. The old species died out, and those with the new, larger brains took their place.

"Eventually, a second mutation occurred, and mankind was born—a creature with dual brains that were connected by a bundle of nerves, so that the two halves of the brain could talk to one another. Each half of a brain was dubbed a 'lobe,' and that is where you come in. You can feel the evidence of those two brains. Often you will feel them arguing, struggling for control. When faced with a moral dilemma, one of your lobes may argue one course of action, while the other lobe demands another.

"But always, it was suspected that evolution would take its next bound forward. As had happened time and again before, a new form of human would be born, one with doubled cranial capacity."

Tallori could not understand everything the magus said, but she understood there were genetic reasons why Anduval was smarter than she was. "So, Anduval has a larger brain?"

The magus shook his head. "He has four brains—two frontal lobes and two posterior lobes. Each pair of lobes is connected by its own corpus callosum, its own bundle of nerves.

"When you hear two voices arguing in your mind, Anduval hears four in his."

The magus now turned and looked her full in the eye. "There are those who would argue—rightly, I think—that true intelligence is not merely the ability to recall correctly, but to make intuitive leaps, to use the stored information to unforeseen advantage. That is Anduval's gift."

Tallori was thinking furiously. She was wondering what that might mean for her future.

"Anduval cannot have children with you," the magus said gently. "You are from common human stock, and he has been greatly modified. Even if you were to try to have children, they would not be viable."

The words hit her like a punch to the gut, taking the air from her lungs.

But the magus said softly, "Yet he needs someone to love, and his line must be preserved. If you marry him, I can take your eggs and a few cells from his heart, and create a child, one that will express the best traits in both of you."

Tallori looked up at the magus, and for the first time she understood the significance of his oversized head, the bumps on his temple. "Anduval is your son, isn't he?"

The magus appeared to be at a loss for words. "Close. His full name is Anduval Nine. My birth name was Anduval Eight."

* * *

The memory of Seramasia haunted Anduval throughout the years. At night he dreamt of her, sprawled out on her silk sheets, her womb glowing with urgency.

At such times, he was filled with longing, and he rededicated himself to his work.

But a thousand days after Holy Maiden Seramasia entered her long sleep, Anduval had a special dream.

In it, he was preparing his celestial navigation system for testing on the prototype, and he worried over the artifact, a glowing ball of crystal with engravings upon it, shot through with colored wires and bound in platinum.

The navigation system was meant to be used by a skraal navigator. But would a skraal be talented enough to pilot the ship?

Originally, all navigators were dragons, whose minds were uniquely adapted to flight.

Anduval had boosted the ship's long-range detection capacities in an effort to make it easier on the skraals. Beyond that, he had eliminated the need for physical manipulation of the controls. The skraals' crystal brain structure created a powerful electric field, a psycho-electric cloud that could easily interface with the control mechanisms without need for physical contact.

All he needed to do was tune the interface to the proper frequency so that it did not damage the delicate neurons and axons in the skraal's brain.

A holographic display would appear in the pilot's mind, showing the space ahead and revealing obstacles that could include anything from clouds of dust or plasma to small planetoids.

As the ship neared such obstacles, lasers would pulverize smaller debris, and the ion shields would route the particles into the fusion drives for use as fuel.

But the pilot would have to weave a path through the larger obstacles. At slow speeds, that would not be hard.

Yet he worried still. A skraal would be able to pilot the ship, but would the pilot be talented enough to outrun a cycor vessel?

Anduval had no way to know. His limited information on cycor vessels was six thousand years out of date.

So in his dream that night, he was pondering how to speed up the system when Holy Maiden Seramasia suddenly appeared at his side.

She was a holy maiden no more. In the dream, she was filled with glorious light. Gone was the fat and fragile flesh. Now she was all hard lines. Her skin had turned to blue crystal, and the brilliance radiated from her abdomen, her thorax, even her head.

Tiny baby skraals were crawling on her back, like large scorpions made of glass. Even as he watched, the newly hatched were exiting her womb.

Anduval hardly dared look at her, for it hurt his eyes so. A feeling of rapture overwhelmed him as the holy mother addressed him, her thoughts a storm that beat upon him, her love a gale that blew through him.

"It is beautiful," Seramasia said of his navigation system. "Have no fear, my friend. It will work, and it will save us all."

"Do you know this," Anduval begged, "or is it merely a hope?" He was no longer sure if he dreamed or if Seramasia had indeed transcended and now communed with him through a mind-touch.

"I see the future, frail one. I see all things. I see your love for me, and it is not nearly as great as my love for you." Her voice trailed off. She glanced to the side and down, and Holy Mother Seramasia suddenly disappeared.

Anduval woke in his room. It had not been an hour since he had gone to sleep. His eyes still felt gritty and were probably bloodshot.

Every bone in his body ached from fatigue.

For years he had been afraid of failure, but the dream had comforted him. Yet he worried that it was false comfort.

Was it a dream, he wondered, *or did Seramasia really appear to me?*

It was possible for a powerful holy mother to send dreams to her subjects, to communicate from a thousand miles away.

He raced down from his bedchambers, past the crèches in the human quarters, and took the grand corridor to the royal chambers. He entered through the old dining hall and reached the closed door to the meditation chambers.

There, a trio of skraal courtiers guarded the chrysalis. Twisted ropes of bone, yellowing with age, still bound the holy maiden. The chrysalis only vaguely hinted at the shape of the woman sleeping within.

The skraals leaped to readiness.

"Halt!" one warned. All three held disruptor rods—pale white rods that emitted a killing jolt.

Anduval stood for a moment, panting, staring at the egg-shaped chrysalis in disbelief. He'd expected to see it cracked open, the new Holy Mother standing resplendent and glorious.

But it had only been a dream, and now he felt the fool.

"Any movement?" Anduval begged. It was not uncommon for the queen to grow restless inside her chrysalis, to stir for months before it opened, even to cry out to her courtesans or speak briefly.

"She sleeps deeply," a courtesan answered, "and moves not at all."

Of course it was just a dream, Anduval thought.

It was too early for her to emerge from her chrysalis. She would still be deep asleep, comatose.

Even when she does awaken, he thought, *Seramasia will not be a vessel of light. She will not be glorious and powerful. She will come out of her chrysalis with a hardened skin, nothing more.*

* * *

Two days later, an emergency meeting was called in Magus Veritarnus's laboratory. The skraal lords in charge of palace security were there, along with dozens of guards. Tallori stood at Anduval's side.

"The cycor are coming," the magus said. He flipped on the screen of his workstation, which took up one vast wall. It showed an area of space—a bright star like a glowing world, with tens of thousands of lesser stars beyond.

Static played, and suddenly there was a loud squeal that seemed to emit from the star.

"That squeal is a signal burst," the magus said. "A cycor warship sent a message to its command center. They are coming to Danai."

One of the city guards asked, "How long will it take to get here? It looks as if they are far away."

"The drone scout that discovered our world relayed our whereabouts," Anduval explained. "It sent a message burst, similar to the one that you heard. That message traveled at light speed to the star that you see. The warship received the message and then sent out a report of its own before moving out. That ship will be racing toward us now at near the speed of light. It will take only a day or two to reach maximum speed."

"So you're saying that we have four years?" the guard asked hopefully.

"I'm saying," Anduval corrected, "that the cycor learned of our position two years ago and set out immediately. Depending upon their speed of acceleration, they will attack shortly—within days."

Suddenly, up on the screen, there was a distortion in the star field. A dark blur erupted, as if a planet had formed, and immediately began to enlarge.

A cycor ship was approaching quickly.

"Well," the magus said in resignation, "here they come."

The world was about to end, and he had given up. After all of their preparations. Yet Tallori could not give up hope so easily.

She thought frantically. It would take years still to build a worldship. Most of the components for the prototype had been completed, but the hull was a thousand miles away, being towed across the ocean by sailing ships, while the drive system was scattered over the southern half of the continent. It would take weeks to gather the parts, assemble the prototype. And even when it was completed, it would only be able to carry the elite of the planet, three or four hundred people.

But we'll never finish it, she realized.

Heart pounding, she looked to Anduval and realized that everyone was staring at him, waiting for an answer. But Anduval had none.

"We must hide," Magus Veritarnus said. "Tell the people everywhere to seek out their assigned shelter—deep in caves or bunkers, wherever they can! They will need food to last a year, at least."

Anduval studied the approaching doom and then turned and strode away. Tallori followed him back to his personal quarters, her mind racing.

The palace was about to become a madhouse. The simple farmers at the edge of Shadowfest would rush here for safety, hoping to gain entrance. The smarter ones would bring animals and food to eat, whatever they could carry.

But the palace wouldn't be able to hold them all. It might be able to protect a few thousand, but it couldn't hold the *hundreds* of thousands who would come.

The skraals would be forced to drop the shield walls and block all entrances.

Tallori's heart pounded, and she imagined that it sounded like the drumming of closed fists upon the shield wall doors. She imagined her mother and father, trying to break into the palace, crying out for help.

She found Anduval kneeling on the floor in his spartan quarters, staring at the wall. There were storage containers built into the wall for his personal effects, a toilet, a sink, and a bed low to the floor. Nothing else. The baths and commissary were down the hall.

She knelt beside him. "What can we do?"

He shook his head slowly, staring at the wall as if at some private horror. "Nothing," he said. "We can hide, but the gravity field emitted by that ship is too large. If they even draw close, they could siphon off our atmosphere or rip the crust of the planet apart. They won't even need to use weapons."

"Can we fight them?" Tallori asked.

Anduval shook his head.

He turned, and there was infinite pain in his eyes. "I've failed you, Tallori."

A shock of fear pierced her, more powerful than anything she'd ever felt. The skin on her forehead tightened, and the hair rose on the back of her neck.

"I love you, Anduval," Tallori said.

He nodded slightly, as if to say that he knew.

"Will you kiss me?" she asked in a small voice.

Tallori was only twelve and a half, far too young to marry. But she had been in love with him for nearly four years, and she did not want to die without having felt the touch of lips against hers.

If I'm going to die, she thought, *I want to die in his embrace.*

Hesitantly, Anduval reached out and stroked her face.

He was not the kind to lie to her. If he kissed her, she knew, it would be an admission of what he felt.

He leaned close. Their lips met, and she wrapped her fingers in his long hair. She leaned into him, so that she felt his heart thrilling, and just enjoyed the taste of him.

Anduval pulled back and said, "You deserve better than I can give you. You deserve a full lifetime of love."

Tallori shook her head. "This will have to be enough," she whispered, when the door to his room burst open.

Cessari stood in the doorway, a disruptor in hand. "You have failed," he said coldly. "You shall be the first to die."

With superhuman speed he attacked, aiming the disruptor rod. Anduval shoved Tallori aside, out of harm's way.

A burst of electricity arced across the room, a bolt of violet lightning. It struck Anduval's silver headband. Sparks flew; Tallori smelled a rush of ozone.

Cessari let out a trumpeting call, a skraal cry of pain, and collapsed to the floor.

The skraal lay convulsing.

Tallori gaped at Anduval in wonder.

He stepped closer to Cessari, and the skraal's muscles all clenched simultaneously. His mouth flew open, his oral-dactyls spasming, and his eyes jiggled. His head turned up and to the side, while his legs and arms curled in. He gasped, struggling with every fiber of his body to breathe.

"I told you I would protect myself," Anduval said. He removed the silver headband, pulled free the platinum leads that hooked into his nerves, and threw the device down upon the skraal.

Cessari went completely rigid and quit moving, a gray-green effluvia exuded from his pores.

He stopped breathing, stopped moving.

Tallori was confused. She stood, staring down at the skraal. "What … what did you do?"

"I built a skraal brain-wave interface into my headband," Anduval admitted. "It had no power source, but it was designed to accept the electrical impulse given off by a disruptor. When Cessari shot me, the electric charge overpowered the interface, which shattered his brain."

The skraal consort was dead, his life fleeing as smoothly as a candle going out.

"He could have hit you," Tallori said. "How did you know he would use a disruptor? All he had to do was crush you like a bug."

"He brought a disruptor when he threatened me earlier," Anduval said reasonably.

He stood for a long moment, peering down at Cessari.

The skraals would be angry. Tallori had never heard of a human killing a skraal. They were faster, stronger, smarter than humans. They were biologically superior.

Anduval had only acted in self-defense.

She wondered what his punishment might be.

Suddenly the floor began to rumble, and in the halls, a warning horn sounded. Tallori looked around, wondering if there was an earthquake or if this signaled the beginning of an attack.

"They're closing the blast doors," Anduval said, "sealing the palace."

It had not been fifteen minutes since the warning had gone out. The people who lived in the nearby forests hadn't had time to reach the palace. Tallori's mother and father probably hadn't even learned of the danger yet.

Suddenly Anduval's eyes lit up, and he shouted, "There is one thing that we can do!"

He turned and raced down a hallway toward his laboratory, and Tallori struggled to catch up. She found him at his console, where he grabbed the navigation system—a ball of crystal shot through with wires of gold and silver and veins of turquoise and crimson.

* * *

Anduval sprinted to the holy maiden's meditation chamber and found that the doors had been thrown wide open.

The skraal courtesans knelt before her chrysalis, that great mass of yellowing bone.

One of the skraals was pounding upon the chrysalis as if to break it with his fists, while the courtesans all chanted in reedy voices like woodwinds, supplicating in their musical tongue, "Waken, O Holy Mother! Waken, O Bearer of Light!"

But all of their pounding, all of their prayers, would not waken Seramasia, he knew. It was too early for her to waken, perhaps months or years too early.

He strode to the base of the chrysalis and held up the orb, as if to show it to Seramasia. But in fact, he only needed to get it near her skull.

"Back away," he shouted to the skraal supplicants. "Get back, all of you!"

Confused, the skraals began to retreat. Anduval pressed the power switch on his navigation unit and pleaded, "Wake up, great lady. Behold the danger. Our enemy approaches."

He held the device near. He knew what it should do. Active sensors down in his laboratory were constantly mapping space for a light year in every direction.

Sun, planets, moons, and meteors—all would be thrown up against the backdrop of space.

And the image would pierce the holy maiden's mind, show her the advancing threat. Even in her deepest sleep, even in her comatose state, Anduval hoped to reach her.

Whether Seramasia could do anything to stop the cycor, he did not know. Most probably, if she became aware of the danger at all, she would only be able to shrink away in horror and despair.

* * *

Magus Veritarnus stood at his console. He peered up at the star field and struggled to come to grips with his imminent death.

The cycor ship had grown large. It was less than a tenth of a light year distant, according to the sensors. He could see it clearly, a large dark orb rushing toward them.

Inside that orb was a black hole, sucking all light and matter into it—all but the cycor warship, a silver needle that floated ahead of the great pearl.

The cycor ship defied the laws of physics as the magus understood them. It should have been sucked into the black hole.

Ah, he thought, *but there you have it. Death is a mystery. Should it not come in a mysterious fashion?*

He watched the field growing steadily. The warship was slowing, decelerating at fifty Gs. Yet still it seemed to be rushing upon them.

In a heartbeat, the whole ball shifted, as if making a course correction, and a puff of blue smoke issued from the silver needle as if something had exploded.

Instantly, the ship disappeared.

For a long moment, the magus merely stood, heart pounding, unable to accept his good fortune.

A malfunction, he thought. *That is the only explanation—a mechanical failure aboard the cycor ship.*

The black hole had turned and was veering away. It would bypass Danai entirely and exit the solar system in a matter of hours.

In the hallways, warning horns were still blaring.

But suddenly a new sound arose, a clarion call like a thousand flutes and oboes, a song sung by skraals only upon transcendence of a holy maiden.

She has left behind her pharate form and ascended to imago, the magus realized.

Magus Veritarnus whirled and rushed to worship at the feet of the new holy mother.

* * *

Seramasia broke from her chrysalis. She did not do so with a pounding of fists, with kicks or shouts. Rather, a fierce light sprang up, playing through the corded ropes of bone, sparking in hues of gold and green.

After a tenth of a second, the chrysalis burst outward. Seramasia crouched within the effluvium, blazing with a light so fierce that Anduval was forced to cover his eyes with his arm. Tallori shouted in awe.

Every bit of Seramasia was as clear as crystal. Every bit of her was filled with light whiter than the sun. Not in ten thousand years had such an imago taken form.

"Holy Mother!" Tallori cried out, breaking into tears.

The skraals raised their voices in triumph, singing to the goddess in a symphony of praise.

"Fear not," Holy Mother Seramasia called out. "The cycor threat has been overcome!"

From all through the palace, people came running—skraal teachers and physicians, the old human women who mopped the floors, the chefs and servants.

The people broke into song, their hearts breaking with relief and joy.

Last of all came the magus, striding through the halls, his black robes flowing out behind him. Amid the shouts of praise and wonder, he clapped Anduval upon the back, and whispered in his ear, "Should we thank the god who saved us, or should we thank *you*—the man who made the god?"

Anduval glanced at his mentor and smiled in satisfaction. "Our world is full of enough heroes," he said. "Let Seramasia take the praise."

* * *

That day, the parts to the prototype of the worldship came together.

The hull that was floating out at sea, towed by a great-masted sailing vessel, broke free of the cords and rose slowly into the air. Two thousand miles away, the propulsion systems cracked through the roofs of their warehouses. From all across the world, pieces rose into the sky and raced through the heavens until, at last, they rested in the blue skies above Shadowfest.

When the pieces had all fitted themselves together, the ship hovered in the sky. At sunset, Anduval found himself rising up through the dense foliage as easily as dandelion down borne on a summer wind.

A blast of wind greeted his upturned face.

Seramasia floated above him, a great light in the sky, while Tallori and the magus and dozens of technicians and scientists from the palace rose up to meet her.

Stores of food floated up as well: great casks of water, sacks of grain, all of the fruits and vegetables of the field, and all things that might appeal to a skraal.

At the edge of the world, a sliver of red sun straddled the horizon, an ember among darkening ash.

Down below, the sounds of the jungle rose up from Shadowfest—the squeals of colossal boars, the rumbling call of a growler, the shrieks of flying reptiles.

Anduval reached the hovering ship and entered the threshold, wondering what to do.

He felt a touch in his mind and heard Seramasia's voice. "Be at peace, my truest friend, and rest, for we have far to go."

Anduval took Tallori's hand when she arrived, and he felt content. Together they walked through the ship's corridors and up to the navigator's console.

Holy Mother Seramasia was at her seat, resting easily. As the ship smoothly accelerated out of orbit, she peered up into the field of stars displayed on the console above.

The ship veered and set a course—not for the far dark reaches beyond the borders of the galaxy, but toward the void at the galactic center.

"Of course we cannot run," Anduval whispered aloud, for he too had been touched by a dragon's dream, and the dragon dreamt of vengeance.

* * *

On the dry days on Danai, the damselflies take their maiden flights, rising into the summer morn in all their glory.

Lightning bolts of blue, bright sparks of molten fire, the small creatures from the marsh take leave of the earth and climb the sky on trembling wings, tiny hunters on the wind at last.

O O O

David Farland is an award-winning, *New York Times* bestselling author in both science fiction and fantasy with dozens of novels and short story anthologies to his credit. He has helped train dozens of other authors who are also *New York Times* bestsellers, including folks like Brandon Sanderson (Wheel of Time), James Dashner (the Maze Runner series), and Stephenie Meyer (Twilight). Currently, Dave lives in Saint George, Utah, where he is working on the final book in his Runelords series.

About the Editor

Lisa Mangum has worked in publishing since 1997. She is currently the Managing Editor for Shadow Mountain Publishing. She is also the author of four national best-selling YA novels (The Hourglass Door trilogy and *After Hello*) as well as several short stories and novellas. She edited *One Horn to Rule Them All: A Purple Unicorn Anthology* and *A Game of Horns: A Red Unicorn Anthology,* also published by WordFire Press.

She graduated with honors from the University of Utah and currently lives in Taylorsville, Utah, with her husband, Tracy.

Additional Copyright Information

If You Liked ...

If you liked *Dragon Writers*, you might also enjoy:

A Game of Horns

Decision Points

One Horn to Rule Them All

Our list of other WordFire Press authors and titles is always growing.
To find out more and to see our selection of titles, visit us at:

wordfirepress.com

Made in the USA
Lexington, KY
11 December 2016